the hidden hours

Also by Sara Foster

Come Back to Me
Beneath the Shadows
Shallow Breath
All That Is Lost between Us
You Don't Know Me

the hidden hours
SARA FOSTER

BLACK STONE

PUBLISHING

Printed in the United States of America

ISBN 978-1-09-409402-1
Fiction / Thrillers / Psychological

1 3 5 7 9 10 8 6 4 2

CIP data for this book is available
from the Library of Congress

Blackstone Publishing
31 Mistletoe Rd.
Ashland, OR 97520

www.BlackstonePublishing.com

the hidden hours
hours
SARA FOSTER

BLACK STONE
PUBLISHING

Printed in the United States of America

ISBN 978-1-09-409402-1
Fiction / Thrillers / Psychological

1 3 5 7 9 10 8 6 4 2

CIP data for this book is available
from the Library of Congress

Blackstone Publishing
31 Mistletoe Rd.
Ashland, OR 97520

www.BlackstonePublishing.com

For Kaz—
Thank you
for lifelong friendship,
for your steadfast belief in me,
and for always knowing how to make me laugh

prologue

April 2010

Tim Willis collects the manila folder and sees his last client of the day is Eleanor Brennan. Fifteen years old, with two overdoses and some self-harm under her belt already. His notes convey the weeks he's spent sitting patiently with her, getting nowhere. Her determination to shut the conversation down had proved a match for anything he could offer. She'd told him, more than once, that she was only here because her mother had begged her to come.

Until last week. They had been going through the same motions when he had pressed her for a happy memory. To his surprise, she'd suddenly started to talk. She'd told him a sweet story about her family, how her father had a party trick he'd learned as a kid. A Japanese friend had taught him how to make paper cranes, and he often used to fold them while Eleanor slept, leaving them on her pillow. She had vague memories of them in her cot; clearer recollections of them appearing next to her in her first big bed.

However, her father had stopped doing this when he lost his job, she'd explained quietly. Although by then her older brother Aiden had learned to copy him. For a while, scruffier cranes would sometimes land next to her while she slept, the white paper blotched with thumb prints. Then Aiden had stopped too, when they moved.

"Did you ever feel that these birds were their way of telling you they loved you?" Tim had asked gently.

Eleanor had gone rigid at the question. Her face paled; her hazel eyes widened. She had stared at him wordlessly for a moment, before letting out a guttural groan as she folded into herself and sobbed with her forehead on her knees. *Hallelujah,* Tim had thought as he watched her fragile body quivering, *finally we're getting somewhere.*

His step is light today, as he clutches the folder and heads toward the waiting room. He rounds the doorway and sees Eleanor and her mother sitting next to one another. "Hello," he says in his friendliest tone.

Gillian Brennan responds, but her smile is forced. Eleanor ignores him. As soon as Tim sees her stiff posture and averted gaze, he knows they have somehow gone backward.

"Ready, Eleanor?" he asks brightly.

She still won't meet his eye as she gets up to follow him. *Damn,* he thinks, as he closes his office door and they take their seats. He tries not to show his disappointment, readjusting his focus toward this traumatized girl in front of him, who still desperately needs his help.

"All right then," he says, his mind busily searching for new ways to reach her. "It's good to see you, Eleanor. How are you today?"

1

an announcement

December 2016

The body bobs lightly against the gray stone wall, ensnared by something unseen, resisting the current. A police diver slowly untangles it, and gently pushes it toward the waiting boat. People watch from the footbridge, transfixed. Some cover their mouths with gloved hands, pointing, gasping, retching. Others clutch their phones in a choke hold. One woman takes furtive pictures. They are all relieved it hangs facedown in the cold, murky river. No one wants to see the person to whom that long blond hair once belonged.

The body floats toward waiting hands. A tiny crab scuttles down the slim line of one of those ghostly white legs and disappears into the gloom.

Three hours later

Eleanor joins the back of the crowd and waits. She is shivering, desperate to sit down; her head pounds and her legs ache. The air is rife with murmurs and confusion. No one wants to be here. Only a handful of people are already aware of the chain of events that began at dawn.

The message had pinged up on-screen five minutes ago, summoning the entire workforce to the courtyard *immediately*. Eleanor had grabbed her bag then followed the group from her office, eavesdropping, with no one to talk to. She had prayed this wouldn't take long, because she couldn't shake the nausea that had been there since she woke up.

The last of the morning's frost still glitters on the ledges of doors and windows. Bulging gray clouds obscure the sky, and the cobblestones are slippery from overnight rain. Eleanor hugs herself, wrapping her cardigan tightly around her, in part to keep her warm but also to hide her wrinkled cheap white blouse, as she shifts apprehensively from foot to foot. She is still getting used to the eviscerating coldness of London in December.

The courtyard is surrounded by red-brick office blocks, hidden from the street, connected to the main road by one narrow, high-walled passageway with security gates at either end. The open space is lined with huge trees set in man-size pots, silver tinsel winding down each trunk, and on the northern side, a wide flight of stairs marks the entrance to Parker & Lane, one of the book industry's darlings, already crowned Children's Publisher of the Year for the third year running.

There must be well over a hundred people now, and more keep arriving as the minutes tick by. They are a jittery bunch, huddling together, waiting for someone to tell them what is going on. It's a far cry from the pictures of this courtyard that line the foyer walls just inside the entrance to Parker & Lane—famous authors holding wine glasses, a blur of smiling faces just out of focus, and the backdrop of tall trees festooned with multicolored lights.

Eleanor's gaze drifts over the crowd, but she doesn't recognize anyone. She's only been working here for three weeks, there has not been much time to form friendships, but from what she can gather, this company-wide summons is unheard of. Snippets of speculation swirl through the air. An emergency drill? A company collapse? A takeover, maybe? Immediate redundancies just weeks before Christmas? Surely not.

Each conversation begins to float away, one after another, until the only sound is of someone clearing their throat. Eleanor follows the collective gaze and looks upward. The black-and-white sign for Parker &

Lane stands proudly above the revolving doors, and just above that, on a small balcony, is Caroline Cressman from HR, wringing her hands as though she has forgotten her lines. Eleanor has a horrible urge to shout, *Deny thy father and refuse thy name!* as she had once needed prompting herself in high school. She stays quiet, but her heart is restless—every few seconds she feels it stall and tense, willing the next beat. Everybody is hushed, waiting.

"I will only keep you a moment—this is the one place we could gather you all together at once." There's a discernible tremor to Caroline's voice. She takes a deep, shaky breath. "I am so very sorry to tell you all . . ."

Eleanor's thoughts tip, beginning to gain speed. Something big is coming.

". . . that Arabella Lane has passed away."

Shock steals the air from Eleanor's lungs. The scene before her disintegrates; she is powerless to stop it. *This cannot be true*, she thinks. *It cannot be true.*

She waits for the collective gasp, but there is nothing, absolutely nothing. Perhaps it doesn't seem real to anyone else. Perhaps they are thinking, as she is, that only a few hours ago their director of marketing and publicity had been very much alive at the Christmas party—drinking and dancing, working the crowd, her face animated, her body in constant, seamless motion.

A few images strobe through Eleanor's mind. Arabella is dead, and Eleanor knows what a dead body looks like. Parched in places and purple in others. A waxen effigy of a real person. Nothing like Arabella.

A distant memory rises swiftly, like a vulture startled from carrion. It draws closer and closer, until Eleanor can feel its black wings beating against her neck and she ducks away, terrified, her legs buckling under her. Coins tumble from her pocket as she hits the cobblestones.

For a moment she is no longer twenty-one. Instead she is nine years old again, standing in a small room in the middle of the Australian outback. A body swings in front of her, his face obscured by flies, and the tips of his toes brush the floor, as though he were almost through a jump when that rope twisted and caught him, slicing across the bulge of his neck.

Without realizing, she flings her arms over her head, trying to protect herself from the memory, before the vision can fully claim her. Nevertheless, she begins to dry heave.

"Eleanor," someone is close by, talking to her. "You okay, Eleanor?"

She remembers where she is.

Arabella is dead.

Elegant, graceful Arabella, who plays with her hair while she talks, whose bangles jangle when she moves, whose laugh can make you smile even when you haven't heard the conversation.

Arabella is dead.

She opens her eyes. It's Will Clayton, the art director, leaning over her. His thick eyebrows frame his concerned expression. She's gotten to know him a little over the past few weeks, has enjoyed their flirtatious banter, particularly in contrast to the disinterested glances of others. However, now his face is grim and pale as he offers her a hand and sets her on her feet. He picks up the loose change and hands it to her, his fingers cold but his touch a reassuring link to reality.

She's alert enough to nod, although she's not okay at all. She feels for her bag, pats the strap looped over her shoulder, and clutches it close. Those in the vicinity have all turned to watch them. She wants them to stop looking at her—she wants to go back to being invisible.

Luckily, Caroline helps out. "There will be an investigation," she wails above them, hiccuping her words, seemingly ignorant of what's happening below. "Her body was found near Waterloo Bridge at dawn."

There are sobs. Someone cries out. It's real now.

"The police will be here shortly to take statements about Arabella's last few hours, and we ask you all to cooperate fully. There will be rooms made available for the process, and we will also have places set aside for those who need somewhere to take a breather." She takes a big breath herself. "Or if you would like to pray. Please come and see us, or talk to your manager and tell them what you need." She pauses. "Our hearts go out to Nathan . . ." Her voice breaks. "And to all of Arabella's family and friends. There will be further announcements shortly as to how we might best support them in the terrible days ahead."

Nathan. Eleanor feels a stab of horror at the mention of Arabella's husband. It's been hard enough temping for him these past few weeks, but she has no idea what the duties of a PA might involve for a grieving man. She tries to soften the antipathy she has felt for him, reminding herself of what he must be going through, but all she feels is numb.

Will hovers beside her, until a colleague leans forward and whispers in his ear. He nods, gives Eleanor a brief pat on the arm. "Are you all right now?" As soon as she nods, he turns to leave.

Quickly, Eleanor turns her focus to the day that looms ahead of her and is overcome with dread. Instinctively, she searches the melee for Susan. She will help, won't she? But Eleanor can't see her anywhere among the crowd, or on the balcony. Surely, as the company CEO, Susan Mortimer should be here?

Caroline has gone as suddenly as she appeared, and people begin to disperse. Most walk in stunned silence, a few have their arms around one another, holding on tight. Some go toward the main entrance, while others head around the side of the building for the fire exit that leads to an internal set of stairs. Eleanor decides to follow the latter group. She needs to drag out every second she can while she tries to wrap her thoughts around what this means. She feels feverish, gripping the banister tightly as she makes her way to the second floor. Her bag bangs against her side with its new weight of guilt, as though she were concealing a murder weapon.

She attempts to recall the previous evening from start to finish, but there are hot knives in her brain, pressing against half-formed memories that fail to trigger. She knows she talked to Arabella for a while, but her last recollections of the party are hazy, recalled through a blur of dry ice and spinning faces.

In a daze, she interrupts a small group that has congregated in the stairwell, two women leaning together, crying heavily, while another woman clasps a tissue in a shaky hand and pats one of her pals on the back. "She was planning her thirtieth birthday just last night," one sobs. "She said she wanted to go to Paris." Eleanor almost apologizes for the intrusion, then realizes they are absorbed in their grief. She passes by them unnoticed, a will-o'-the-wisp lost in daylight.

As she makes her way through the office, some people are already back at their desks, frowning at their screens, looking for answers or just an escape. Or perhaps they have no choice but to carry on. In the brief time she's been here, Eleanor has come to understand that daily deadlines and crazy hours are part of most people's work ethic.

She passes the closed doors of management, aware of stricken voices and low murmurs. She glances past the hanging Christmas decorations—oversized baubles gently twirling as the heat from the radiators rises—and instead keeps her gaze fixed on Nathan's door at the far end of the office. Just to the left of it, behind a partition, is her own desk. She hurries past giant cardboard cutouts of *Smoky the Cat* and *The Pig That Could Fly*, two of Parker & Lane's recent acquisitions. Their strong lines, clear colors, and gaping smiles don't seem to belong here anymore. Her legs feel weightless and hardly under her control as she staggers toward refuge. She needs to hide awhile and try to compose herself.

Relief washes over her as she reaches the partition. Until she sees the CEO of Parker & Lane sitting in her chair.

Susan's right elbow rests on the files that Eleanor was meant to stow back in the cabinet yesterday, while her left hand has crept across to open Eleanor's sketchbook, and she is flicking through the pictures, her head down.

Eleanor is furious at this breach of privacy. "That's private," she says, before she can help herself.

Susan looks up, her eyes red and weary. She stands up, fingertips smoothing the sides of her sleek black hair, which is pulled tight into a bun. She closes the book without a word, straightening her Chanel suit jacket, while Eleanor's throat burns with the abruptness of her words. She swallows, trying to absorb her anger into something more palatable. She knows that Susan holds virtually all the cards to her life right now. She's not only her boss, but also her landlord. And her aunt.

They have had an uneasy relationship from day one. When Eleanor's uncle had invited her to stay in their Notting Hill home when she arrived in London, she hadn't expected such a frosty reception from his wife. They had known of one another for over ten years, but had never met until three weeks ago, and Susan was not at all what Eleanor had expected. She suspects the feeling might be mutual.

Susan is scrutinizing her, making no attempt to smile. Eleanor can't think of the right thing to say, but she tries. "I'm so sorry about Arabella."

Susan sighs and looks away for a brief moment. Then she fixes Eleanor with a stare. "You look dreadful. Do you want to go home? I can get Priscilla to take over here today, there will no doubt be phone calls from the press and from authors. I don't expect you to have to deal with all that. We'll figure out something else for you to do on Monday."

She doesn't know, Eleanor thinks. *She doesn't know I spoke to Arabella last night, or she'd tell me to talk to the police.*

And yet, unintentionally or not, Susan is throwing her a lifeline. This is her chance to escape, to gain time, to think over what to do before she has to tell anybody what she's concealing. Instinctively, she pats the cloth of her bag, wondering if she has made this up. Can it really be happening?

"Thank you, Susan." She reaches over and grabs her sketchbook, slipping it into her bag. She's about to turn to go when Susan says, "Oh, and Eleanor . . ."

Before she can reply she hears heels clacking quickly down the corridor. She turns at the noise and finds Caroline hurrying toward them, faint streaks of mascara on her cheeks.

"Susan, Sky News is setting up outside the building," Caroline says breathlessly, eyes shining like a startled animal. Whatever Susan was going to say to Eleanor is forgotten. She smooths her hands over her knitted jacket, then says softly, "And here we go."

Eleanor watches them leave, before collecting up the paperwork on her desk and pushing it back into her in-tray. Then she grabs her coat and hurries toward the stairwell, anxious to be gone before any more news crews arrive. Her temporary status requires her to sign in and out at reception, and once downstairs she heads quickly across to the logbook, which is left permanently open at the front desk. Two of the receptionists are deep in discussion.

"I just cannot believe she would jump off a bridge," one of them is saying.

"Me either," the other replies. "She was always such a happy person."

For a moment, Eleanor cannot move the pen in her hand. *Not last night, she wasn't.*

Before they can engage her in the gossip, she turns toward the doors. She sees a cameraman screwing something on to the front of his camera. The reporter clutches his microphone to his chest like he has just caught a bridal bouquet. Two lackeys have been tasked with holding umbrellas over the men, to protect them from the persistent rain.

They all look at Eleanor as she exits the building, but before they can decide if she is important enough to accost, she has hurried down the passageway, waved her key card at the exit gate and continued toward the main road beyond. She pauses a moment, her head spinning in this shining world where the shops twinkle with Christmas lights, and an accordionist plays "Jingle Bells," and the cars are adorned with reindeer antlers and all is merry and bright. She takes a few gulps of air to steady herself, and then she sets off for the Tube, for Uncle Ian, for some semblance of safety.

2

the christmas party

*I*n these times of high security, Theodora Hannas, London Underground ticket inspector, has been trained to watch people closely. Therefore, the nervous young girl fumbling for her ticket immediately catches her eye. Theodora observes the whitened lines of the girl's knuckles as she grips the strap slung across her shoulder. The small movements of her jaw, as though she's involuntarily clenching or grinding her teeth. She looks so frightened that Theodora is still debating whether to raise the alarm or ask if she's okay, when the girl races off toward the platform. Immediately, Theodora is distracted by a family whose suitcase has become stuck in one of the barriers, and as she pads across the tiles the girl is almost instantly forgotten.

Eleanor cannot catch her breath as she hurtles down the steps of the station. A train is just leaving the platform, its engine in crescendo as it picks up speed. She's almost at a run—as if haste will lessen the dizziness or the fear that the police will want to talk to her before long. She needs to rehearse the story of the previous night and try to fix the details in her mind before they can blur at the edges. Only twelve hours ago she had spoken to Arabella, and while she knows she cannot go back in time, it still feels so recent, so fresh, that if she squeezes her eyes tightly shut and clicks her heels together, surely she might just make it.

The Christmas party had been on the *Atlantic*, the latest project of celebrity chef Preston Harlen, an old steel barge given the five-star treatment and converted into London's trendiest floating restaurant. Parker & Lane had secured the exclusive booking because of Preston's wife, Mia, the author of a succession of mediocre children's books about a talking dog, which had fortuitously found their way to the shelves of every Tesco and Asda in the country. Ahead of the party, Susan had come home briefly before setting off to central London in a limo. Eleanor had watched from the first floor as Susan got into the car on her own, and wondered whether her aunt had any inkling that there was enough space for one more.

The half-hour walk to the Tube had been more painful than usual, the winter frost nipping into Eleanor's peep-toe shoes and settling in the gaps between the waterproof lining of her long coat and her bare arms and legs. She had spent most of her first week's earnings on a short, red velvet dress that now felt too tight, while the lace edging that had looked good in the changing room kept snagging on her bag. There was no glamour on the Tube either, with the seats bristling against her and the person opposite rocking like a lunatic as they nodded in sleep. When she got to Embankment she had snuck into a back-alley bar first and had a double shot of vodka to warm her up a bit. It made the prospect of an evening trapped on a boat, trying to get to know people, a little bit easier.

At the pier, she was wary of the doorman as she climbed onto the softly swaying vessel—she'd heard how exclusive Preston Harlen's venues were—but the surly fellow redirected her to a hostess in a cocktail gown. One swift tick on her sheet, and Eleanor was checking in her coat and heading through the small foyer toward another set of double doors that led to the main arena.

The huge bar in the middle was shaped as a super yacht, while tables floated on the blue carpet like dainty, subservient little life rafts. To one side was a dance floor so polished that Eleanor feared for her safety in three-inch heels. It was busy already, and she had a feeling that the little cliques dotted around the place were exactly the same as those she would find at work. Keen not to stand alone, she had let herself fall into conversation with Calvin from the post room, who was eager to ply her with the free beverages and acted oblivious when she moved away from his roving hands. By the time Laura from accounts saved Eleanor from Calvin's attempts to drag her onto the dance floor, the boat was well into its cruise along the river. Eleanor had complimented Laura's hairstyle—an intricate winding braid that made her look like a European princess—while Laura had noticed Eleanor's accent. It turned out Laura had visited Australia two years ago and could describe her road trip, to places Eleanor had never been, in enthusiastic and impressive detail. Once Laura had had two tequilas, she admitted to looking out for Philip from the international sales department who had recently split from his girlfriend. When Philip arrived, Laura disappeared in an instant, knowing no more about Eleanor than she had when their exchange had started.

As Eleanor searched for someone else to talk to, she caught sight of her boss. Nathan was wearing the suit she'd seen him in earlier at work, charcoal gray with a silver tie, and he was leaning forward, explaining something to his companion, his face serious, his hand occasionally banging on the table, punctuating his argument. As Eleanor watched, Arabella slipped onto the seat next to him, and whispered in his ear. He had carried on talking without acknowledging his wife, who waited, and waited, and then got up and left them to it.

Around Eleanor, everyone was talking, laughing, dancing, and drinking, buoyed by their deeper camaraderie. She could feel herself slowly sinking away from them, invisible, despite every inch of her straining to fit in. She ate every canapé that was offered just to give her something to do, until she began to feel nauseous. The bartender cast her sympathetic glances, his pity palpable. She itched to move somewhere less humiliating, but the corner booths were all occupied, and she couldn't bring herself to intrude. She had held out such hopes that this would be the night she got to know people—everyone was always so busy at work. She kept telling herself someone would talk to her eventually, but after a while she went out onto the deck and gazed alone at the sights of London, until she saw they were arriving back at the pier. Once it had docked, Eleanor went inside again and tried to join in the revelry. After a few short-lived pleasantries, she'd taken off to the restroom as soon as she noticed Calvin hip-wiggling his way toward her again. She sat in the stall, head in her hands, feeling the gentle drop and lift of the boat, trying to decide whether to go back into the party, or stay put. She'd thought that perhaps Susan would take pity on her for the return leg, but since her first drink she hadn't been able to spot her aunt in the crowd.

Raucous groups of tipsy women came and went, while she sat there, undecided about what to do next. Eventually, boredom propelled her out to wash her hands in the marble basin. She was marveling at the pink orchids and decadent assortment of hand creams and perfumes set out for use, when a cubicle door opened behind her and Arabella emerged, wiping her nose across the back of her hand.

Their eyes caught in the mirror. "What a shit party, hey," Arabella said, coming over to the sink. "Which idiot booked a boat?"

Eleanor took in Arabella's shimmering silver dress, a similar shape to her own but obviously a superior cut and fabric. She watched Arabella's slim hands under the running water, their jerky movements highlighting the glinting stone on Arabella's ring finger, an exquisite sapphire nestled within a circle of smaller diamonds. The platinum band shone beneath her beautifully manicured French-tipped nails, and Eleanor quickly withdrew her own hands and turned away to dry them.

Should she leave or try to talk to Arabella? She wasn't sure, but when she glanced back Arabella was watching her. She frowned. "Hang on, you're my husband's new PA, aren't you?"

"Yes."

Arabella moved forward. "And how are you finding it, working for the wonderful Nathan Lane?" she shouted over the noise as she took her turn at the hand dryer.

Eleanor paused, unsure how best to respond. The truth? She'd already decided that Nathan Lane was an obnoxious idiot—that he had only one way of speaking and that was to issue commands, whether to her or anyone else on their floor. That while honing his managerial talents he seemed to have forgotten how to be a civilized human being. He was nice looking, sure, with little wavy kinks in his golden hair and those pale, piercing eyes, but Eleanor suspected the majority of his charisma came from an arrogance and belief that, should he so choose, he had the absolute right to be the center of attention in any room he walked into.

However, the reality was that his wife was asking the question. And even though Arabella didn't sound very pleased with her spouse right now, Eleanor couldn't afford to be careless and lose her job in the next five seconds. So, she had shrugged noncommittally. "Fine."

Arabella gave a loud, humorless cackle as she turned back to the mirror to preen her hair. "Now, we both know *that's* not true. I should imagine it's about as horrid as being married to him."

When Arabella looked up and saw Eleanor's mortified expression, she laughed again—a gentler, sadder laugh. It was then that Eleanor noticed how glassy her eyes were.

"I'm making you uncomfortable. Come and have a drink with me, you look like you need cheering up. Let's see if we can liven this party up a little."

Arabella had grabbed her hand without waiting for an answer, leading Eleanor out as though they were best friends. She ordered them double shots at the bar, pushing one at Eleanor and gesturing for her to down it. Eleanor watched as Arabella picked up her own glass and tipped the liquid down her throat, shaking her head and crying, "Whoa, that's better," then immediately ordering cocktails.

To begin with, Eleanor could feel eyes on them from all sides of the room, but Arabella's determination to enjoy herself was infectious, and soon Eleanor forgot anyone might be watching. She laughed as Arabella mocked various people on the dance floor, and when the cocktails were delivered, she saw Arabella sprinkle a little something into both glasses. "This will make things sizzle," Arabella had said with a wink, downing her cocktail as though it were another shot.

It's at this point the memories become hazy. As Eleanor comes back to the present, a sudden rush of air blows her long hair away from her face as a tube train approaches. That mojito last night had been one drink too far, tipping Eleanor into the next few swirling, disorientated hours. All she can recall beyond Arabella pulling her over to dance are blurred faces spinning in strobe lighting. It feels more like a series of hallucinations than true memories. But in those flashing images she is sure she remembers Arabella leaving her and walking over to Nathan. Eleanor's body had still been shimmying to the frenetic beat as Arabella lifted a hand and, in plain sight of everyone, slapped Nathan hard across the face.

3

the train home

Superintendent Louise Thornton picks up the phone. "Yes?"

"We've heard from the Coroner's Delegate," Detective Inspector Priya Prashad tells her. "The first indications are that Arabella was alive when she hit the water, and there are also signs of a struggle. We're calling in the Murder Investigation Team."

Thornton finishes the call and sits back in her chair. She's glad Priya Prashad is such an experienced detective, because this one is going to be big.

The train Eleanor catches is half empty. The somnolent shake of the carriage would usually encourage her mind to drift, but today it's too much like floating toward oblivion and she keeps jolting back to high alert. She can't stop thinking of Arabella.

I wasn't singled out, Eleanor keeps telling herself. *Our meeting in the bathroom was pure chance. One thing led to another.*

But it is not that simple. Eleanor had woken half dressed, her singlet and underwear wet, every muscle throbbing, her vision blurry. She had vomited twice in her small en suite and recoiled at the vision of herself in the mirror—the blanched face and scraggly, long dark hair—before she noticed that the soles of her feet were black with grime, and the pristine white bed sheets were smeared with dirt. She had taken two strong painkillers and laid down again for half an hour, running through all the excuses she could find to stay in bed. She had tried to recall the previous evening and found that a lot of it was missing. Eleanor had never tried recreational drugs beyond marijuana. She didn't even know what she'd taken, and that scared her. She desperately hoped she hadn't made a total fool of herself. She had not been at work for long; she still needed to make a good impression.

She had struggled up, but collapsed again with trembling legs, heart racing, her mouth dry. It was no good. She had opened her small handbag to find her phone and call in sick, and that was when she had found the polished sapphire and diamond ring snuggled innocently between her lipstick and mascara.

It had taken her a few moments to realize it was the ring she had seen on Arabella's finger the previous night.

And she still has no idea how it had come to be in her possession.

It had, however, been the catalyst she needed to drag herself into work. She had brought it with her, intending to give it back, convinced there must have been a mix-up, one that Arabella would be able to explain. Perhaps Eleanor had tried it on and forgotten to return it. But now what should she do? What will happen if Eleanor confesses she has a valuable piece of a dead woman's jewelry in her bag? How is she going to decide whether to admit it, hide it, or lose it?

The receptionists had mentioned something about a bridge, and Eleanor can picture it so clearly, it's as though she were there. She pulls her pad from her bag and starts to sketch the scene: the long bridge, a small figure straddling the railings, clinging on, her dress whipping around her as though desperate to pull her back from fate, her hair lifted like kite tails in the breeze. She becomes aware of her neighbor peering over her shoulder and snaps the pad closed, pushes it deep into her bag. She hopes that's the end of it, but he nods at her empty lap. "You're good." She gives him a tight smile and twists away, setting her back to him.

She clutches her bag. She doesn't want to dwell on the contents and what they might mean, but how can she think of anything else? She daren't look around in case she catches someone's eye, because in that moment of connection, when their eyes lock, it is as though she cannot shutter the window to her soul, and they might peer in and see everything she most wants to hide. She has long felt her sins reproach her. Is this the moment when fate comes full circle, and the consequences for her childhood crimes are finally meted out?

She leans over, elbows on her knees as she massages her temples, trying to think. What happened last night? Why are there so many gaps? Why can she picture Arabella so clearly now, when before she'd heard the receptionists speaking about her, she'd had no recollection at all?

It's not a memory, it's just your imagination, she tells herself. But the scene is too vivid, too distinct, for her to be sure.

Her body aches and her head throbs. Why had she let Arabella put something in her drink? She has never wanted to try drugs—she has seen the damage they do. And besides, she's too scared of the hallucinations, of who she might summon into being. She is unnerved by last night's haziness, the glimpsed snatches of euphoria amid blank hours that cannot be reclaimed, and this deplorable comedown.

As her thoughts unravel, she shudders. The drugs. The ring. She doesn't know what has happened, but it feels like she's being set up. But why? She looks around wildly as though she might be being followed, but everyone on the train has turned away from her—eyes closed, noses in books, mouths humming along softly to unheard tunes piped straight into ears. Nevertheless, the scene seems surreal, like she might get up and find they are all made of wax. She stares at the passenger opposite until the woman senses the intrusion and looks up.

Eleanor quickly turns away in relief. Her face is burning. *Get a grip*, she tells herself. *Think this through.*

It's hard to stop the panic closing in. With no paper bag nearby, she has to breathe into her cupped fingers as she tries to think. She runs through the people who might help her. Her mother? She's too far away, and the old wounds are always there, just beneath the surface. She tries to think of other names but the blankness is terrifying.

"The next station is Notting Hill Gate."

The voice jolts Eleanor back to her surroundings. She's nearly back to Uncle Ian. He'll be at home now, working. They might not have had time to form a close bond, but they are still family. Surely he will help her.

The question is, can she trust him?

Can she trust anyone? Can she trust herself?

The train slows. Rush hour is over and the crowds have thinned, but there are still a few people standing, edging closer to her seat as they sense she's about to move. She sees it: the attempts at courtesy covering the edge of competition. She desperately wants to believe the best of people, but it's hard when she knows that humans are rivals for anything—even five minutes on a germ-ridden seat.

She chooses the person she wants to win—a woman with a sparkly bag who smiled at her a few stops ago when they caught one another's eye. She gets up and blocks the suited man on her other side so the woman can slip into her seat. The loser turns away, carries on reading his newspaper as though he was never in the running. She'd wanted a reaction. She wants someone else to feel as desperate as she does. Perhaps she should ask him if he's ever watched a woman's body fall from a height, spinning into black water, in the middle of the night.

4

ian

Carlos Lucias, mortuary attendant at Hammersmith & Fulham, slowly and reverently pulls open the long drawer that holds Arabella Lane's naked body. An ashen-faced Dickon Blythe waits behind a glass panel, with a policewoman at his shoulder. It has been three hours since Arabella was formally identified by her husband, but her father had insisted on seeing her too. In other circumstances Carlos might have given him a moment alone, but he cannot do that with a suspicious death. He has to make sure he follows the police request to keep the red markings on one wrist hidden under the pristine white sheet.

It is nearly four weeks since Eleanor moved in to Harborne Grove, and she is a keen observer of the lives that surround her. Her cousins, who until a few weeks ago were just names appended to cards in strange handwriting, are now the most vibrant points of her day, whirling in and out of her life. She suspects that seven-year-old Savannah, as delightful as she is right now, is most in danger of becoming a clone of her mother, bossy and wilful and sharp as a tack. Naeve, however, is six years older and a visionary. Her room is peppered with drawings that remind Eleanor of the worlds of Shaun Tan, even though the after-school classes she takes are the same ones as her sister: hockey and piano and Latin—*Latin*!

Eleanor watches as they wolf down their breakfast in the morning and brush their teeth, and she comes home just as they begin a strict evening schedule of homework, food, bath, and bed. She seeks them out to remind herself what it's like to see the world as exciting and extraordinary, and they look for her too—probably because she lets them bounce on her bed or watch TV in her room, things that are strictly forbidden on the lower floors. All the light, pure energy in the house comes from these two girls. Without them, Eleanor doubts she would have stayed.

As Eleanor exits the Tube station and begins the short walk to her uncle's house, she wonders how she is going to explain the events of the past twenty-four hours. Perhaps she shouldn't tell him. It's not that she doesn't like her uncle, but in the past few weeks it has become obvious that the tag of *family* cannot hide the fact they are strangers, and it has been much harder than she'd hoped to get to know him.

Until a few months ago, she had hardly been aware of the existence of her mother's brother and the extended London family. One evening, as she had been discussing her travel plans with her mother, Gillian had suddenly said, "I suppose you should have Ian's number, in case of emergency."

At that point Eleanor hadn't known much more about Ian than he was seven years younger than her mother, and that the siblings had never been particularly close. "I was a geeky girl and he was a rough-and-tumble boy," Gillian had explained. "When our parents split up, I went with Mum and he stayed with Dad. It seemed natural at the time, but I'm sorry now that I didn't know him more as he grew up. By the time he'd reached his twenties, your father and I had moved here." She'd shrugged. "But at least we've stayed in touch. He's done well for himself too, I gather. His wife Susan is a few years older than him. She runs a publishing house, and he's a freelance architect. They both sound very successful, don't they?" There and then she had produced an address book, and by the end of the evening they had googled her uncle and aunt and viewed the impressive Harborne Grove town house via street view.

Still, Eleanor hadn't expected to end up living there, but then her mum had taken matters into her own hands and made a phone call. To both Eleanor and Gillian's surprise, Ian had been so enthusiastic about the prospect of Eleanor's visit that she'd found herself taking him up on the offer to stay "until she finds her feet." A few weeks later he picked her up from Heathrow and drove her to her temporary new home.

It suited Eleanor, because while she longed for adventure, she was nervous too, not that she would admit that to her mother. She had expected Gillian to be pleased with this arrangement, since she could sense her mother fretting every time she mentioned hostels and bar work. However, Gillian had been quiet on the subject, until the night before Eleanor left, when she had suddenly said, "I don't know Ian and his family all that well, so don't feel obliged to stay there any longer than you want to."

Which left Eleanor feeling both curious and concerned, but as it turned out Ian had been great to begin with. He was a youthful looking thirty-seven, with thick, dark hair and glasses, just a smattering of gray hair visible around his temples. He dressed in casual trousers and open-necked shirts, and his friendly manner made him easy to warm to. He had immediately guessed that Eleanor needed a job, and organized an interview with Caroline. Before she knew it, Eleanor had a temporary PA position at Parker & Lane because Nathan Lane's assistant was suffering from horrific morning sickness. This was better paid than the kind of work she'd been anticipating, but now that all the practical matters have been attended to, her relationship with Uncle Ian seems to have stalled, closing down into courtesies. Either that or she is asked to watch the children while her uncle heads out for a while. This has happened so often that she now has a sneaking suspicion he has co-opted her as a live-in babysitter without her consent. Yes, Ian asks her now and again how she is doing, but it is always a distracted inquiry while he is busy with the girls or on his way out the door. He asks at times when the only thing that will suffice is a simple, "Fine, thank you." She understands that he is busy—aside from his family commitments he is a sought-after freelance architect—but still, she can't help but hope for more.

And then there is Susan.

Eleanor has been wary of her aunt ever since her first night in Harborne Grove, when she had trailed downstairs after Ian in her pajamas to meet Susan, and realized from his silent, stiff walk that something was wrong. When they had reached the kitchen, they found Susan sitting on a high stool at the long island bench, reading the *Financial Times*, a cup of tea next to her. Ian had stepped aside so Eleanor was in view. "Susan," he'd said. "I'd like you to meet Eleanor, my niece."

Despite having seen photos online, Eleanor was still unprepared for the formidable presence of her aunt. Susan's black hair was swept back into a perfect bun, her nails gleamed with a deep red polish, and she wore a thick, woolen designer suit. Eleanor did a quick mental comparison. Her own hair was only a few shades lighter, and sat well past her shoulder blades, but she only ever tucked it behind her ears. She thought her nails looked good if they weren't bitten, and felt overdressed in anything other than jeans and T-shirts. She felt instantly inferior beneath her aunt's assessing gaze.

As she'd walked forward to shake Susan's proffered hand, she had glanced back at her uncle. She wasn't prepared for the barely concealed antipathy in his eyes, or the challenge returned in Susan's stare. They were all stuck in the moment, with Eleanor looking between them, until she tried to release the tension with a smile and an upbeat hello. Susan had given her a tight smile in return then leaned on the counter sipping her tea and openly appraising Eleanor without another word, while Eleanor sat miserably on the stool opposite, longing to escape back to the lovely little loft room. She had considered numerous threads of conversation, but they'd all knotted on her tongue before she could get them out. "You have a lovely house," she'd begun eventually. Hesitantly, she had looked at her uncle for support, but he just watched them both, standing by the window, saying nothing.

"Thank you," Susan had replied, her lips twitching again as though attempting appreciation. "Ian," she'd added without turning, "remember it's housekeeping tomorrow, won't you." Then she'd risen, newspaper in hand. "I'm exhausted, it's been a long day. Enjoy your stay with us,

Eleanor," she'd said, and then she was gone with a swish of fabric, her heels loud on the polished floor.

Eleanor had hoped that once Susan was out of the room her uncle would explain what was going on, but when he spoke it was to say, "You've arrived at rather a difficult time for us, Eleanor, but you are very welcome." He gazed at a point beyond her, and she saw him sigh. "Do you mind if I go to bed? I hope you don't think I'm being rude."

"Of course," she had smiled. "I'll see you in the morning."

Once back under her warm, weighty covers, Eleanor had been unable to sleep. It was obvious she had entered some kind of war zone, but nothing was clear enough to make sense of yet. It seemed that if she wanted to stay, she would have to find out where the land mines in this household were laid, and how she might negotiate them. If, as she suspected, there was a battle going on between her aunt and uncle, then she was firmly on Ian's side.

However, in the time that has passed since, there has not been a need to draw battle lines. Susan has so many evening commitments she is hardly home, and Eleanor rarely sees her at work. Her uncle bears the responsibility of getting the girls to and from school and all their activities, otherwise he's locked away in his study, or dashing out too. Eleanor has gleaned from her cousins that there used to be a nanny, but she left a few months ago and hasn't been replaced. Neither girl knows why.

On Eleanor's walk from the Tube station to the house, she has been lost in these reflections. As she opens the door, she immediately notices how quiet the house appears. Her uncle's office door is closed, and she tiptoes toward the stairs, not wanting to disturb him.

"Eleanor? Is that you?"

His voice sounds gravelly and rough. Moments later he appears at the kitchen door. His eyes are bloodshot and all color has leached from his face.

He stops speaking, seeming to take in her disheveled appearance, studying her expression as he comes closer. "Have you heard?" he asks, a catch in his voice. "About Arabella Lane?"

"Yes."

Ian staggers over to the stairs and sits down. "Susan just called me. I can't believe it. We have known her for years—we've spent so much time together, and the girls adore her. I . . . I just . . . I just . . ." He interlinks his fingers over the back of his neck, dipping his head toward his knees. He stays like that for a few moments, breathing deeply, and then jumps up and rushes toward the kitchen. Eleanor can hear him vomiting in the sink.

She wants to be anywhere but here. It's unbearable. She's itching and burning like maggots are burrowing into her skin. Should she go and comfort him? Their relationship isn't ready for this. How could it be? But just standing here seems awkward and cold.

She has dealt with too much for one morning. She has almost forgotten that she had so little sleep last night, but now her eyes are fizzing and her head is starting to swim. She takes one last look toward the kitchen and then bolts up the stairs. She needs to lie down; she has to try to sleep, to find some respite. Her world is beginning to unravel, pulling at the threads that bind the husk of her nine-year-old self, exposing the cruel edges of all that the years have failed to smother.

5

the dream

Susan has left the press waiting. She needs the all clear from the family before she can comment, and she also needs to gather her strength. Meanwhile, Caroline is still sobbing, and her PA Priscilla is busy organizing a room for the police officers who will be here within the hour to interview everyone. In this lull before the storm, Susan has fled to her private bathroom and locked the door. Priscilla knows she's there but is wisely leaving her alone for a little longer to grieve. Inside the cubicle, Susan burns with rage.

Eleanor is barely aware of her uncle on the phone downstairs, his voice full of fury and emotion. Nor does she hear the two light pairs of footsteps running through the house, ignoring their father's room as soon as they see Eleanor's coat on the stand by the front door. Her mind is elsewhere, busy searching through her memories for the key that might help her unlock whatever it is she has forgotten. She is back on the *Atlantic*, sitting opposite Arabella, and this time Arabella is leaning forward, so close that Eleanor can smell the alcohol on her warm breath, and her hair and skin are dripping wet as her eyes widen and she whispers, "Help me, Eleanor. You have to help me."

Eleanor sits up with a start, gulping air, trying to reorient herself into the starkness of her designer white guest room and not the dimly lit interior of the *Atlantic*.

What *was* that? The dream image liquifies, swirling with memories of the night before—they are coalescing as she desperately tries to separate them before they merge and distort.

That wasn't a memory, was it? She wouldn't have forgotten that. She has just imagined it. But why are her thoughts pricking at her, urging her to reexamine her recollections, to flesh out the detail? She tries to think back again, but now it's impossible. The last thing she remembers is Arabella slapping Nathan. The second half of the night is either blurry or missing, and that in itself is terrifying. What might have happened to her in those gaps? What might she have done?

She lies down again, pushing away her fears. The day is growing dark already. She checks the clock. It's not even four in the afternoon yet—she doesn't think she'll ever get used to these short days with their dull light. She feels the lightest of pressures on the back of her hand, as though something is urging her to return to the moment, and she jumps again, snatching her arm away, holding it close to her and rubbing her fingers, reassuring herself that all is well.

She used to feel these strange sensations all the time. Hypersensitivity, the doctor had called it, compounded by the anxiety that had plagued her teenage years. She had simply taken the meds he gave her, accepted the treatments they offered, and spoken as little as possible. She never told him she thought it might be a familiar ghost, reminding her he was there, that he hadn't forgotten her, that he never would.

However, this presence had felt so much quieter in the past few years. She had begun to hope things were changing. But is he back now? Or is this a new sensation—a new ghost? Will she be haunted by Arabella's death too?

This thought is so confronting that she tries to refuse it admittance, but it performs a trick of osmosis, permeating every part of her before she can block its way. She shivers, hating being alone, hardly daring to look around the room in case there are shadows being cast by something other than the furniture. She squeezes her eyes shut and replays the evening again. She tries to fill in more of the night, but the harder she chases the memories, the faster they run, until everything is dark and empty. The void is terrifying.

For fuck's sake, Eleanor, she tells herself, *whatever happened last night, it's not your fault.*

And yet.

She sits up and reaches for her bag. Perhaps this morning has all been an unreal nightmare. Perhaps there is no sapphire and diamond ring in her bag, and she has just woken up and the day is yet to start. Perhaps Arabella is walking into the lobby of Parker & Lane holding her coffee right now and giving Alfred a friendly wave.

Eleanor unzips her purse. The ring nestles inside, its brilliance dulled in that tiny cavern. She touches the cold metal, feels the rebuke.

You have to help me.

If Arabella had really said that, then it looks like Eleanor has failed already.

The door bursts open and Savannah runs into the room, her silky black ponytail bouncing as her little elfin face lights up. "You're home!" she says, crawling onto the bed and cuddling in to Eleanor. Eleanor quickly pushes her bag underneath her pillow, grateful that the intrusion sweeps all the specters back to the shadows. She tries to relax as she holds onto Savannah. How she loves this unselfconscious seven-year-old who will fling open a shut door without a thought, so assured is she of a warm greeting. Where has she gotten such spontaneity, with a mother like Susan?

Eleanor looks across to the door and sees that Naeve is skulking there, her black-rimmed glasses disproportionately large for her petite face. What happens to kids between the ages of seven and thirteen that they lose all spontaneity and replace it with edginess? Is it inevitable—or do they meet one too many accusing glances, harsh words, looks behind the back, or exasperated sighs during this time, and begin to register that the adult world is a big crock of two-faced shit? All those adolescents who walk around looking grumpy and disappointed while everyone makes fun of their mood swings. It was a hard thing to realize life wasn't really tooth fairies and Santa Claus, but tax returns and piles of washing. Even harder, Eleanor thinks with a pang of sorrow as she shifts to make space for her cousin, when life explodes before your eyes and you realize some things can never be restored.

"Come on in, Naeve," Eleanor says, "there's always a space for you." She holds out her other arm, but Naeve rejects that and perches on the edge of the bed instead, pulling the clips out of her wavy brown hair and flattening the frizz with her fingers.

"What have you two been up to today?" Eleanor asks, trying to tune into their responses, even though Arabella's wide eyes are never far from the forefront of her mind. *Help me.* "Where's your dad?" Eleanor adds, as the girls settle themselves next to her and Naeve flicks on the TV and hunts through channels.

"His office door was closed," Savannah says.

As Eleanor watches Savannah, she becomes aware of the television getting louder and louder, a reporter's voice intruding into the room. Next to her, Naeve is holding the remote up high, working the volume control.

". . . No one from the publishing house has so far commented on today's events, but we do know that a body—believed to be that of Arabella Lane, the marketing director here at Parker & Lane, and daughter of popular conservative MP Dickon Blythe—was found in the River Thames this morning . . ."

Eleanor looks sharply across, to see that Naeve has gone white. No one moves.

"Oh no, Naeve, I didn't realize . . . Did you know Arabella?"

Savannah is staring between the two of them. "Did they just say that Arabella is dead?" Her bottom lip quivers.

It's as though Savannah's voice brings Naeve back to her surroundings. "Dad!" she yells, rushing out the room, her voice trailing her as she hurries through the house. "*Dad!*"

"Shit." Eleanor jumps off the bed and races after her, aware that Savannah is snuffling at her heels. They all gallop down two flights of stairs, and as Naeve reaches the bottom, Ian opens the door to his study. He looks as ashen as his daughter, and puffy eyed. Naeve stops when she sees him—this ghostly apparition of her father must all but confirm her fears. "The TV reporter just said that Arabella is dead."

Ian looks at Eleanor as though she had murdered Arabella herself. "How could you let them find out like that?" he hisses.

"I didn't know," Eleanor shoots back. "It was on the news as soon as Naeve turned the television on."

Naeve scowls at her, as Eleanor struggles to stay composed.

Savannah is behind them, her noisy sobs shaking the whole of her little body. Eleanor turns to cuddle her, but Ian races up the stairs and grabs her. "Naeve, Savvie, come in here with me," he says, and they all disappear into his study, the door slamming behind them, shutting Eleanor out.

She stares at the door that divides them. Injustice and anger join forces inside her, rampaging through her veins until she feels she is dissolving. She stands unsteadily on the stairs, willing herself not to tumble, while also wondering if she should throw herself down them, anything to make that door open and gain admittance. In a crisis, why is she always left alone?

It's the first time she's seen Ian really angry and she doesn't know what she can do to set this right. Now she can hear Naeve sobbing as well as Savannah. She pictures them sitting on his lap as he tries to comfort them. She hopes he isn't lying to them, telling them it's all going to be all right. She hopes he has more sense than that.

She imagines his fury and wonders if she has spent her last night in this house. Her mind is a jumble of fear and accusation. This was meant to be her new start, miles away from anything. How can all her demons still find her?

When her thoughts run their course, she finds she is still standing on this wide carpeted staircase, watching the closed door. She doesn't want to be here when that door opens—she doesn't want them to know she waited, or to catch her face unguarded. Perhaps she should go and pack, just in case. She tiptoes quietly back upstairs, reaches her room, sits on her bed and puts her hands over her ears, just as she had done as a child, when she hadn't yet realized that the voices were coming from within.

6

the argument

Dickon Blythe knows that a small crowd of journalists are waiting at the door of his town house, each hoping to be the first to get a statement about his drowned daughter. He can picture the printing presses whirring across London. His two living children, Arabella's older sisters, are already on international flights heading for London. He doesn't care about any of it. He lies with his arms wrapped tightly around his wife, both of them lost between sobbing and sleep.

In the middle of the night, Eleanor wakes suddenly—there is someone in her room. She can make out a shape bobbing about in the darkness, a shadow right beside her bed. She scrambles up and backward before her eyes adjust enough to realize that it is Savannah, but it doesn't stop the series of haunted faces that flash through her brain. Nor does it stop the pounding in her throat, the sensation that any second something cataclysmic will overtake her.

Savannah climbs up next to her. "Mum and Dad are fighting," she says matter-of-factly, pushing her face into the hollow of the pillow, where Eleanor's head lay a few moments ago. "They're noisy." Other than this, Savannah doesn't seem perturbed, and soon she has drifted back to sleep.

Eleanor does not settle so easily. She can hear the drumbeats of voices downstairs, angry, repetitive, banging against one another, the duel breaking the silence of the night. She is too far away to make out the words. She gets out of bed gently, tiptoeing to the door to open it a crack so she can try to listen better.

Once her door is open their voices are not so muffled. She's two flights up but in this cavernous house, sound doesn't have walls to contain it. It glides easily across landings and up open staircases.

"Get away from me. How *could* you!" Her aunt's voice is enraged, wrung through with venom. Eleanor pictures Susan's furious face, her hair pulled tightly into its bun, her eyes gleaming. Eleanor shudders for her uncle and takes another couple of steps down, trying to hear more.

As the staircase curves, she spots Naeve on the landing ahead of her. Her back is to Eleanor as she peers over the railing, her feet bare and her nightdress so flimsy that Eleanor can see the neat silhouette of her lithe body inside it. Before Eleanor can halt, her next step makes the tiniest creak on the stair and Naeve swings around in panic. Their eyes lock, but Naeve's gaze travels straight through her, then she scurries quickly to her room and closes the door.

Eleanor glances back at her own open doorway. She should take refuge in the safety of the loft room. If she's caught eavesdropping it will surely be the end of her stay. But she can't help herself. She takes another three steps down, testing her weight before planting it firmly, praying there are no more telltale sounds of her feet on the wood, and wishing this staircase was carpeted like the main staircase below.

"Please just listen to me." She has never heard her uncle sound so pleading, so strained. "I'm so sorry. I will do everything I can to make things right."

"After everything we've been through, Ian . . . What are you trying to do to me?"

There's a long pause where no one speaks, and then Ian starts again, his voice a little lower, and more resolute. "We can work this out, Susan, please." The pleading in his tone is clear. He is asking his wife for mercy.

Eleanor waits. In the silence she can hear every noise of the house, the tiny hum of the radiator, the distant thrum of a car engine. And yet, it still takes her longer than it should to realize that footsteps are heading up the stairs.

"You know what—fuck you, Ian. *Fuck you*. I'm going to bed."

Eleanor's panic overcomes her urge to be quiet. She bolts up the stairs, making herself pause at the last moment to close the door gently. She leans against it, trying to recover her composure, looking at Savannah's inert form on the bed.

Then someone taps on the wood right behind her head, sending a small vibration through her skull. She jumps, every nerve ending on fire, tensing as she hears her uncle's voice say softly, "Eleanor?"

She doesn't dare answer, but she feels terrible. They know she was snooping, and now they are going to tell her to go.

She waits. Even breathing seems loud and dangerous. When nothing else happens, she starts to relax, ever so slightly, although she doesn't dare move from her place leaning against the door.

Then Aunt Susan's voice reaches her. "You know this is the worst time for a house guest, Ian. Especially one who comes home paralytic in the early hours of the morning."

"*Sssh*. Don't you think I know that?" His voice is trailing away as he speaks. "I thought it would be good for all of us to have her here. What do you want me to do?"

Eleanor presses her ear hard to the wood, but whatever Susan says next is lost within distance and footsteps. Eleanor steps away from the door, staring at it, trying to calm herself. They know she was in a state last night, yet neither of them has discussed it with her. Now she has no choice but to wait and see what they do in the morning.

Ian doesn't feel so much like an ally anymore.

The cream walls seem to press in around her, urging her to fling open her suitcase and pack her things before she has to suffer the indignity of being asked to leave. She turns and looks at the snug little body asleep under her duvet, and wonders what her aunt and uncle would make of their youngest child seeking refuge from them with the niece they are about to evict. Why does she feel so responsible for these two young girls in the house? Why does the sight of them wandering around in the night, sleepy and vulnerable, make her want to curl up and cry?

Eleanor is tense as she climbs back into bed. Savannah is still sound asleep. It occurs to her that if her aunt and uncle were to check on Savvie there might be pandemonium if she's not in her bed. But after half an hour of silence, Eleanor relaxes enough to close her eyes. In the morning she will have to talk to Ian and ask him if he wants her to leave. She tries to tell herself that it will be a relief. There are more cracks in her uncle and aunt's marriage than in a Grecian urn, and she doesn't need to add their complications to hers. And yet, however hostile the atmosphere is here, right now it feels safer than being on her own.

She snuggles down into the bedclothes for a while, but no matter how she tries, sleep has gone and she can't convince it to return for her. She wants to switch the light on, but she's worried about waking Savvie. She reaches for her phone instead, intending to browse online, but stops as she sees three messages from her mom.

> Eleanor, please answer me. I just want to check you're okay.

> Eleanor?

> Eleanor, I'm getting worried. If you don't answer me soon, I'm going to ring Ian before I go to bed.

Eleanor can't type fast enough.

> Mum, I'm fine. PLEASE don't stress if you don't hear from me straightaway. Had a tough day at work—someone died unexpectedly. Everyone is upset.

She rereads the message then deletes the last two sentences, letting it finish at *straightaway*. There's no reason this information should upset her mother, on the other side of the world and not involved, and yet she knows it will make her worry all the more. When Eleanor thinks of her mother, she feels guilty for coming here in the first place. They have spent the past ten years with only each other to lean on, and it had been her mother doing most of the supporting, while Eleanor went through various medications and therapy so she could try to blot out the nightmares and function somewhere near normal. So, instead, she finishes the message:

> How are you?

She has only just laid the phone down on her bedside table when it buzzes with a reply. She picks it up again.

> I'm fine. I miss you.

Eleanor lies very still, staring at those words for so long that the phone gives up waiting for her to type anything and its light fades away. It seems that her mother is able to reach halfway across the world to wrap an ethereal hand around Eleanor's heart, squeezing it over and over.

Eventually she types:

> Miss you too. Going to sleep now.

Then she switches the phone off before her mother can ask her what she's doing up at this hour, or anything else she might try to keep the conversation going.

She lies down and pulls the duvet around her, tugging it across from Savvie, who shifts in her sleep and lets out a sigh. She stays there for a long time, but she can't get her arms or her feet to warm up properly, not even when Savvie rolls over and snuggles close enough to lend her some warmth. She's unused to having a person pressed against her, their flesh soft and vulnerable.

Eventually, her head drifts, but she keeps waking with a start, feeling the darkness press against her. Her ghosts whisper, telling her that some-day she will be laid out cold too, just like Arabella is tonight.

7

saturday

etective Inspector Priya Prashad wakes before dawn, thinking of Arabella Lane, that fragile body on the slab. Adrenaline courses through her so swiftly that she chooses to forgo her usual stop for a double espresso and heads straight to work. On cases like this, trails can go cold fast. They need to get on top of the CCTV, the evidence, the suspects. Chances are, if there was foul play, it will have been committed by someone Arabella knew.

When Eleanor wakes up, for a brief moment she has forgotten everything. Facts lag five seconds behind consciousness, but the most important one returns to her quickly: Arabella Lane is dead.

Savannah is no longer snuggled next to her, and the bedclothes have turned cool and uninviting. She gets up and goes to the window, hoping for distraction, but it's the same view she has found herself looking at every morning since arriving. So far, winter in London is not living up to Eleanor's expectations. Since the beginning of December, she has been rushing to the window in her loft room each morning, hoping the urban scene will have transformed and she'll find herself in the midst of a Dickensian snow globe. It has been four weeks and the closest she's got has been a couple of rounds of hail, but she has witnessed more rain than she has ever seen in her life. Half a world away, during her childhood they had spent the late summer months willing the heavens to open. Here, everyone has been praying for a break from it since September. How clever can nature be, really, if it can't figure out how to share its basic spoils equally across the planet?

Eleanor has come to know other things about a northern hemisphere winter. The English rain is unforgiving, injecting cold, merciless water through the linings of coats and shoes and gloves; deluges collect in puddles where the road meets the curb so that car wheels can spray unlucky pedestrians with only a slight adjustment of steering. This city is wet and dark and cold, yet Eleanor is mesmerized by the rainbows of color, the swirling symphony of light and sound, the ceaseless movement—so many people packed together, managing to negotiate their way around each another on the roads, the Tube, the buses, the lanes, and the skyscrapers. She daydreams of flying over the city and following a few people here and there—the hidden army of cleaners out while it's dark, removing and repainting and repolishing the city structures, back in their beds by the time the second, suited army marches through, the drones behind computers and the slick city types with their deals and double-dealing. It's only a few Tube stops between mansions and ghettos, a few hundred feet between parliament and the homeless asleep on benches in Westminster Square, a few footsteps between the hottest clubs and the dingy back alleys. It's hard to be confined to one place at a time. She wants to witness it all, absorb every facet of life into herself, see if it can help shape her ambitions into something more than the best routes of escape.

She takes a quick shower in the en suite and dresses in jeans and a sweater. As she heads downstairs, she recalls the argument last night and her tread on the stairs is tentative. She hasn't yet encountered Susan alone in the house, and she doesn't want this to be the moment.

There are noises from the kitchen—a drawer rattling, the microwave pinging. When Eleanor peeks around the door, she sees Naeve busy making her breakfast. "Where is everyone?" Eleanor asks, relieved, coming in and taking a mug down from the frosted glass cabinet.

"Mummy and Savvie are still asleep, I think," Naeve says. "Though Mummy might be working on her laptop in bed. Daddy has gone."

Eleanor stiffens. "What do you mean, gone?"

"He came in this morning to see me before he left. He has some business to do across town today."

Eleanor sits down at the table. Her brain is humming with scenarios and possibilities. Could this be to do with the argument last night? What is Ian trying to fix?

Then it hits her: there is no one here to protect her from Susan. A nervous prickle works its way through her body. Why does she feel she needs protection? Is she really frightened of her aunt?

"When will he be back?"

Naeve shrugs. "I don't know."

Eleanor's thoughts tumble over themselves in a rush. She feels giddy as she stands up and pushes her chair back. It makes a harsh noise, and she grabs for it. She doesn't want to do anything to alert Susan to the fact she is awake.

"Are you okay?" Naeve is frowning at her.

"Yes, yes," Eleanor mumbles, despite the tingling in her fingers, her lips, her toes. She has to get out of this house until she has had a chance to compose herself. She stands up in a rush, but as she turns for the door, Susan is there, blocking her way.

Even at this early hour, Susan is dressed as though she's going out for lunch. Her black silk blouse is perfectly ironed; her pencil skirt hugs her slim thighs, and her hair is up in that elegant bun. Eleanor tugs self-consciously at her casual clothing, remembering she hasn't even brushed her teeth. She fears she looks slovenly, and the way Susan is regarding her does nothing to dispel her worries.

"Eleanor, I have to go out for a little while this morning," Susan announces. "Would you mind looking after the girls?"

There is barely a question in the way she asks. Susan knows Eleanor will say yes, of course she will, because Susan controls everything. It doesn't matter, thank goodness, because Eleanor loves Naeve and Savannah, but she feels for them too. It's clear Susan's priorities lie elsewhere for much of the time.

"No problem. Do you have any instructions for us?"

Susan smiles thinly. "I know Savannah would love to go ice-skating in the park. Would you like that too, Naeve?"

Naeve doesn't even look at her mother, she just shrugs. Susan doesn't respond, as though this is normal. She opens her wallet and pulls out some money. "This should cover it."

Eleanor reaches across to take it. "Thank you."

Is it her imagination, or does Susan hold on to the money a fraction longer than she should? Eleanor looks up sharply and meets her aunt's eyes. Susan's gaze is so cold that it is hard not to flinch, but a surge of courage helps Eleanor stand her ground. She stares back, silently saying, *I know you have secrets. And I know what it's like to try to hide them. The question is, can they stay hidden forever?*

The moment is gone so fast that when the crisp bills is in her hand, Eleanor is unsure whether anything really just happened. Susan turns to go, then pauses. "Oh, and Eleanor, please don't let Savannah sleep in your bed again."

Moments later the front door closes and Eleanor and the girls are alone.

8

ice skating

"*T*oxicology is just in," *Detective Sergeant Steve Kirby tells Priya as she meets him by the back entrance to the station.* "*Alcohol, painkillers, cocaine, and Rohypnol were all in Arabella's system the night she died.*

"*She was really intoxicated,*" *he adds as they get into their unmarked car.* "*Perhaps she jumped in while she was high and no one saw her.*"

"*Maybe,*" *Priya murmurs, her mind running through possibilities. But she already has a hunch that this case won't be quite as simple as that.*

An hour later, Eleanor and the girls are hurrying through Hyde Park, along the Broad Walk, and past the Round Pond. Savannah is a few paces ahead, striding quickly along, while Naeve trudges by Eleanor's side with her hands in her pockets.

The huge Winter Wonderland funfair is set up in a corner of the park. The booths are already steaming with fried food, while the skyline is dominated by a Ferris wheel and a giant glistening Christmas tree. Savannah flits between the throngs of people, agog at everything she sees, while Eleanor tries desperately to keep sight of her amid bulky parka jackets and winter boots, also making sure she doesn't lose Naeve.

Despite Savannah's pleas to try out some of the rides, Eleanor hurries them toward the ice rink, determined to follow Susan's instructions and not give her aunt any more reason to dislike her. When her phone rings in her pocket she pulls it out and sees an unknown number. She hesitates, then answers, "Hello?"

"Hi Eleanor, it's Will."

It takes her a few moments to realize it's Will from work, and he must sense her uncertainty, because he quickly adds, "Will Clayton."

His unfamiliar deep voice causes butterflies in her stomach. "Oh, hi."

"I just wanted to check you were all right—you left the office so quickly yesterday."

"How did you get my number?" She doesn't mean to sound so suspicious, but the words are out before she can stop them.

"Priscilla gave it to me. Look, is there any way I can meet you today? I'd like to talk to you."

His tone is intensifying her unease. She looks around. "I'm at the ice-skating rink in Hyde Park."

"Oh, the Winter Wonderland one?"

"Yes."

"Can you wait there? It'll take me about half an hour to get to you."

"Okay."

"Thanks, Eleanor. See you then."

When the conversation is over, Eleanor cannot focus on her surroundings. She tries to bring herself back to the moment, saying an over-the-top "Wow!" as they reach the bandstand and see the skaters, everyone wrapped up warmly in thick coats and scarves and hats. She sniffs and rubs her nose, already red and cold.

"Come on!" Savannah waves them forward to the small tent where they can rent skates. Ten minutes later, they all walk awkwardly toward the ice. Eleanor's fears of falling on the hard surface are at least a temporary diversion from Will's impending appearance. Savannah holds her arm while they step on to the rink, but to her surprise Naeve glides away as though she has done this many times before. Eleanor can't catch sight of her expression until she's coming back toward them, but when she does, she sees her cousin is stone-faced, as though this endless skating in circles is some kind of mission she's determined to complete.

Eleanor hasn't skated since she was a child. She steps gingerly forward, holding on to the rail at the rink's perimeter. Behind her, Savannah lets go, studying her feet as she works on her balance, then calling out, "Naeve!" and holding out a hand. On her next circuit, Naeve slows down and grabs Savannah's hand, pulling her along. Savannah turns around and beams at Eleanor, and Eleanor wonders if it's the skating she enjoys or being looked after, rather than ignored, by her big sister.

As Eleanor moves slowly around the rink, she glances side to side, studying faces, her nerves buzzing. What on earth can Will have to say that he needs to come and find her like this? Is it connected to Arabella? Does he know something that might relieve her fears? Or could he be coming to confront her?

"You are not responsible," she says to herself, under her breath. "You couldn't be." But in her mind's eye, a body spins slowly on a rope, turning to face her.

She clutches the rail harder, watching her exhalations vanish in the air, willing the image away with each one. She hasn't felt this unsteady for a long time. She's learned from bitter experience that the memories get stronger if she fights them; she has to feign nonchalance as her thoughts taunt her with horrors, and just breathe until they quiet.

Suddenly a tall figure is beside her and then in front of her, his skates grinding against the ice as he comes to a halt.

"Hey, Eleanor." Will catches her expression, "Are you okay?"

"I'm fine," she says shyly. He is wearing dark jeans, a padded red jacket, and a gray beanie that highlights his angled cheekbones and sharp, shadowed jawline. His nose is red from the cold, but out here in the stark daylight she can't avoid noticing how penetrating his deep brown eyes are. He doesn't look much older than her—he can't be much more than midtwenties. How can he already be the art director for a major company, when she is still figuring out her path in life?

"It's a good day for skating," he says, gesturing toward the clear skies, each of the breaths between his words momentarily visible in the cold air. "I'm glad you're here. I needed to do something to clear my head."

Eleanor nods. "Me too. Did you know Arabella well?"

He looks away and she can see him struggling to compose himself. "Yes, I did. She was a good friend of mine—we've worked together for five years." He stares at a spot somewhere over her shoulder. His eyes grow moist and there's a nerve twitching in his jaw. "I still can't believe it. It's unreal, isn't it? I keep waiting to wake up."

Will is about to say more when Savannah shouts, "Eleanor!" and waves as they fly past her.

Will watches them go. "Are they Susan's girls?" he asks.

"Yes."

Will stares after them, while Eleanor begins to fidget, feeling the cold engulf her now she has stopped moving.

"So what is it you wanted to talk to me about?"

Will turns to her and hesitates, biting his lip. His gaze is a spotlight, but she's not sure what he's searching for. "Thursday night, of course. I don't quite know where to start. Do you remember anything of what happened?"

He looks so solemn. What does he know? And what has she done? "I . . . I'm not sure. Why do you ask?" she stammers.

"Well, there's no easy way to say this, Eleanor. We had to pull you off the bridge. You were climbing over it. You were—well, I don't mean to be blunt, but you were rambling, completely incoherent. I really thought you were going to jump."

Eleanor forgets she has the skates on and takes an automatic step backward, losing her balance. She flails and Will is there quickly, his hand on her elbow, steadying her.

"The bridge? I don't understand."

He studies her for a moment. "You really don't remember anything?"

"No, no. I don't remember being outside. The last thing I can recall is seeing Arabella slap Nathan, at the party. Unless I've made that up?"

"No, that was real, all right—I saw it myself." Will grimaces. "And then she ran out and you and I followed. Arabella was crying and you were frantic. I chased you both down to the bridge, to make sure you were all right, but Arabella stopped and yelled at us and then took off, sprinting farther ahead. I went after her and had just caught up when she spotted you and began shouting again. I had no idea you'd stopped, but you were twenty feet behind us, climbing over the railing in the pouring rain. A woman passing by was already trying to grab onto your legs. We ran to you and managed to wrestle you back with a couple of other people helping out. And then you just collapsed to the ground and sobbed." He puts a hand on her arm, staring so intently that she cannot help but blush. "You scared the crap out of me, Eleanor."

"Oh god, oh god." Eleanor turns away to hide her face. Why on earth had she done that? It must have been the drugs, but the flashback to her teenage years is immediate and painful. "I don't remember anything. And what about Arabella? What happened next? There's such a horrible gap in my memories . . . Please tell me what you know."

Will holds onto her arm as they move over to the side, then leans on the railing next to her. "Arabella was fine at that point. When she was helping to pull you off the bridge, I realized she was either drunk or high, because—because she couldn't stop laughing. I was furious with her and I told her to come with us, but she wouldn't. She said she needed to make a phone call, so she stayed behind."

Eleanor stares at the glittering white ice, not wanting to catch Will's eye. "And was that the last time you saw her?" she asks softly.

"No. She came back to the *Atlantic* a little while later. The party was beginning to break up, and I'd laid you on a sofa in the reception area. You seemed to be falling asleep, so I'd gone to see if I could find someone to help get you home."

Eleanor sags back against the railing. "Oh, thank god. I was worried I'd been wandering around London on my own, completely out of it."

"Hang on," Will looks solemn. "That's not all of it. When I came back to find you, Arabella was with you. She was crying and holding your hand, talking to you, even though you still looked half asleep. Then Judith Lyle spotted Arabella, said Nathan was looking for her. Judith seemed really worried, she said Nathan was livid about being slapped like that in front of everyone. She suggested Arabella go somewhere else, and Arabella didn't need telling twice, she just ran out again. I went after her, followed her down to the Embankment. I tried to tell her I would make sure she got home safely, stay with her if she wanted, but she shook me off. She was in a really weird mood—half euphoric, half agitated, but I couldn't persuade her to come with me, so eventually I just left her there, by the Embankment." He pauses and his eyes fill with tears. "If I hadn't given up, perhaps she would still be alive." He takes a slow, deep breath and Eleanor sees his jaw tighten. "I don't mean to burden you with that on top of everything else. I just needed to check on you today because I'm still trying to piece together what happened."

"So did you go home after that?"

Will looks dejected. "Yes, I did—but first I went back for you, only to find out you'd disappeared. The staff were really unhelpful. I'm so sorry, I didn't mean to abandon you. I can't tell you how relieved I was to see you at work. I was planning to talk to you about it yesterday, but you'd gone again before I could."

Eleanor is staring at him, trying to absorb what he is saying. "How did I get home after the party?"

"I have no idea."

Eleanor turns away from him and stares across the park, trying to process this. A few yards away, a toddler is running to keep up with his parents and drops his cotton candy, immediately letting out a howl of anguish. His mother hurries back and kneels down next to him, plucking bits of grass from the spun sugar while talking to her son, giving him back the white cloud on a stick and kissing him on the cheek, making him giggle.

Eleanor finds she is crying. She pushes the tears away angrily.

"Eleanor? I feel terrible upsetting you like this. Can I do anything to help?"

Reluctantly, she turns around to see Will still watching her.

"No, I don't think so. I'm embarrassed that I caused you so much stress. I don't remember anything. I'd taken something—some sort of drug."

"What do you mean 'some sort of drug'?"

Eleanor catches his eye and sends a silent plea for understanding. "Arabella put something in my drink and I have no idea what it was. I don't think she meant any harm, she just wanted us both to enjoy the party. She put the same thing in her drink too."

Will looks up at the sky for a moment, and it's clear his focus is far away from the ice rink. Then he shakes his head and comes back to her. "That doesn't surprise me. There's plenty of gossip in the office about Arabella's social habits, and I've seen her high before. It might have been roofies. I have friends who think they go well with cocaine, not that I've experienced it."

Eleanor gasps. "You mean Rohypnol?"

"That would explain why you can't remember much. Perhaps you were hallucinating on the bridge. You kept saying the same thing over and over. 'Forgive me. Forgive me.' But you weren't looking at me—it was like you were looking over my shoulder."

Despite the cold, every inch of Eleanor's body is burning, but she forces herself to stand straighter, unflinching. If she had been hallucinating, she knows who she saw. It might be the first time she'd been drugged, but it's not the first time she's tried to harm herself to escape visions of him.

If her mother found out about any of this, she would take the twenty-hour flight to London immediately, and she wouldn't leave until Eleanor was with her. But Eleanor couldn't go back to that stultifying house, to the person who had witnessed the worst of her. This was to be her fresh start, yet it is already going horribly wrong.

An awful thought occurs to her. "Oh no, did my aunt see what I was like at the party?" If Susan had witnessed any of this behavior, maybe her mother already knew.

"No, Susan never stays at a party for the whole evening. I'm sure as soon as the boat docked, she disappeared. It's not normal for the CEO to dance the night away with her minions."

The image of her aunt letting loose on the dance floor comes unbidden, distracting Eleanor for a moment, and she even lets a small smile slip.

But then Will adds, "She may have heard something by now, though. A few people saw you chase Arabella outside, and for some of them, it may have been the last time they ever saw her."

Eleanor nods. Her legs feel too wobbly to take the whole weight of her, and she clutches the railing. Will is beside her instantly.

"It'll be okay, Eleanor," he says, his expression kind. "The police are talking to everyone—just tell them what you know. That's all you can do."

He smiles reassuringly at her, and she relaxes just a little. She hadn't realized how lonely she had felt since arriving in London, but it's so good to have a friendly face to talk to outside of the family. She really wants to trust him. Her heart begins to thud. The ring is still in her bag and the revelation is on the tip of her tongue. But she hesitates. Will is the only person showing her any sympathy right now, and she doesn't know if she can bear the suspicion in his eyes if she tells him.

Before she can say anything, Will speaks again. "I'm not sure what's going to happen at work now, but don't trust Nathan. He's despicable— he's treated Arabella so badly for so long. If she did jump into the Thames, no one would be surprised. And remember that Nathan and Susan have a long history—if she's forced to make a choice, she may take his side."

"Really? What do you mean?"

"Ernie Lane, Nathan's dad, is Susan's mentor. Ernie owns the company. He founded it and gave Susan the reins. Nathan always fawns over Susan—there's a rumor he tried to persuade her to date him before she married your uncle, but the story goes that she wasn't interested. Ernie obviously realized Nathan could be difficult and didn't want him in charge of the company he built, so Susan is there to keep him in check. It's a tough job, and while she might not be completely loyal to Nathan, she's fiercely loyal to Ernie. Arabella didn't make Susan's life easy either. She seemed quite jealous of Susan, she often sniped about her, and I'm sure Susan felt the friction."

Eleanor tries to take in all this information. Would her aunt really stay loyal to Nathan if she were aware of his behavior? In the few weeks Eleanor has been at Parker & Lane she has already seen flashes of Nathan's volatility. He had once raged at her for giving him the wrong files for a meeting, shouting so the whole office could hear, leaving her stunned. He had no qualms about yelling at people on the phone either, although he usually closed his office door, which at least dulled the noise. She had witnessed the way people approached his room, tense and wary, and the way their shoulders sagged in relief as they left. She had quickly begun to feel that way herself, grateful that he spent so much of his day in meetings.

And since Nathan was so disagreeable at work, she couldn't imagine what it would be like to be married to him.

"I feel like I'm in so deep, but there's so much I don't know or understand," she tells Will.

Will is watching her with concern. "Here, let go of the railing and just come with me for a minute," he says, holding out his gloved hands.

Gingerly, she lets go and grasps his fingers, allowing him to pull her into the middle. He holds both her hands, skating backward easily, occasionally looking over his shoulder to check the way is clear.

"Just bend your knees a little bit and relax. I'll pull you. Close your eyes for a second and try to let everything else go."

Eleanor does as he bids and as she tries to tune everything out, she grows ever more aware of the physical connection between them. It feels too much right now, she wants to pull her hands away but if she does, she'll be on her bottom within seconds.

Then she hears a little voice next to her. She opens her eyes to see Savannah skating alongside them, hands on her hips, staring at Will. "Why are you holding hands with our cousin?" she demands.

Eleanor blushes, but Will smiles at them then raises his eyebrows at Eleanor once the girls have skated ahead. "Cousins! It's bizarre that you are related to Susan. You two couldn't be more different."

"We're only related by marriage, but I'll take that as a compliment."

The words are out before she realizes, and she reddens, relieved when Will lets out a snort of laughter.

"She's not just hard to talk to at work then?"

"No." Again she has an urge to tell him more—all about what it's like to live in a mansion with an ice queen for an aunt, about the argument she heard last night, but her eyes are drawn to her young cousins skating along. Savannah is looking up at Naeve, chatting away, while Naeve stares ahead, her expression determined. To say more right now would feel like a betrayal. And she doesn't really know Will—yet it's easy to be in his company, holding his hands, letting him pull her along. While she'd like to trust him, she's learned from experience that once she confides in someone, and they begin to drag down the walls around her, she is liable to crumble.

Will is speaking again. "Do you want to go back to the side?"

"Yes," she says, allowing a wave of disappointment to wash over her.

As he pulls her toward the edge of the rink, her phone begins to ring in her jacket pocket. Once she has one hand back on the barrier, she grabs it and sees Susan's name.

"Eleanor," Susan says as she answers it, without even waiting for her hello. "You need to come home right away. The police are here and they want to talk to you."

She hears the click of disconnection, as Susan hangs up without preamble. Eleanor's face begins to burn. She almost drops the phone over the barrier, and Will grabs it too, clasping her hand briefly as he does so. He is watching intently, but she can't hold his gaze.

"Are you okay?" he asks. "You've gone white."

She cannot reply. Why is this happening to her? Why does she feel so guilty when she has no memory of doing anything wrong?

"The police want to talk to me," she says to Will.

Will gazes over her shoulder and takes a long, slow breath before turning back to her. "It was always going to happen. I'm sure they'll talk to me too. Better you get it over with sooner rather than later."

She wants him to say something more reassuring, but he looks worried. She searches for Savannah and Naeve, and when Savannah glances across she gestures for them to come over. Savannah must see something in her expression, because she stops smiling and pulls on Naeve's arm.

"Your mum wants us to get home right away," Eleanor tells them when they get close enough.

Naeve just stares at them, then nods. "Oh!" cries Savvie. "I wanted to skate until it snowed."

Eleanor tries to smile. "I think we might be waiting a long time for that." She turns to Will. "I've never seen real snow before. For some reason, I thought it would have snowed by now."

"London weather is never predictable," Will says as they make their way to the exit. "But everyone gets excited about the possibility of a white Christmas. People place bets on it. Even if it doesn't snow on Christmas Day, I'm sure you won't have to wait all that long."

Their small talk drifts away once they are back at the tent, replaced by an ominous silence. Eleanor takes off her boots and helps Savvie with hers, then they hand them in and head out of the funfair.

Once they are back in Hyde Park, Will gestures to one of the paths. "I'm going this way. Good luck, Eleanor."

She doesn't want him to leave, but she nods. They share a long look before he turns around and walks away.

9

the police

Eveliina Virtanen, Finnish backpacker, is almost at the peak of the London Eye's rotation when she decides to take a picture of Cleopatra's Needle. While she frames the photo, she sees a distant male figure holding what looks to be a bunch of flowers. As she presses the button to capture the scene, the man suddenly leans over the squat wall and throws the flowers into the dismal gray water of the Thames, watching them drift away from him.

As Eleanor and the girls reach the bottom of the steps leading up to the house in Harborne Grove, the door opens and Susan is there, hands on her hips. She is in the same outfit as earlier, all black with chunky silver jewelry, and for the first time Eleanor realizes her aunt is dressed appropriately for grief, whereas underneath her coat Eleanor wears her long-sleeved Billabong shirt and jeans.

As Eleanor stops at the door, she thinks about Arabella's ring in the bag slung over her shoulder and feels the full force of her fear.

"Girls, could you go and wait in the kitchen, please," Susan says as they reach the top steps. She turns to Eleanor and adds quietly, "They are in the front room." As they catch one another's eyes, Susan frowns. The question could not be clearer. *What do they want with you?*

Eleanor hesitates. She could run, but of course she doesn't. Instead she wills her heavy legs to move toward the first door on the right. The front lounge is the most intimidating place in the house. She has never known such a formal sitting room before. She hasn't been in this one since her first morning, when she'd put her glass down on a table and the housekeeper came in ten minutes later, tut-tutted, and whipped it away, then spent the next hour in a red-faced panic because the ring mark wouldn't come out.

She expects to find people in uniform, but a man and a woman in dull-colored suits sit on a pair of high-backed chairs. The woman is small with curly black hair that sits just above her shoulders. The man has a crew cut and is tall, built like a rugby player. He looks too large for his seat as he leans forward with his hands clasped. There's a black briefcase on the table, and for a moment Eleanor imagines they could be a pair of traveling salespeople. It makes them less intimidating somehow, and she begins to relax—and then reminds herself that that's probably exactly what they are hoping for. Relaxed people are more easily caught off guard.

They both jump up when they see her and shake her hand one after the other. No one smiles.

"Detective Inspector Priya Prashad," the woman says.

"Detective Sergeant Steve Kirby," the man adds as they clasp hands.

Eleanor is conscious of her sweaty palms. Have they noticed? She pulls her gloves out of her pockets briefly, as though offering an explanation, and then stuffs them back in again.

"We're sorry to disturb you," Priya Prashad says, "but we could do with your help. We're trying to piece together Arabella Lane's final hours."

"Okay." Eleanor walks towards the sofa, intending to sit down, but to her surprise the two of them remain standing.

"Actually," Prashad says, "we were hoping you would come to the station with us and answer some questions there."

There's a long pause as Eleanor looks between the two of them, her heart thudding. "Are you arresting me?" she asks hesitantly.

She doesn't miss the glance that passes between them as they hear those words. She balks—has she just made herself sound guilty? She squeezes her fists tightly.

"No, not at all," Steve Kirby replies. "It's just much easier for us to get everything recorded. You are not under arrest. You'll be interviewed under caution and you are free to leave at any time. We can drop you home again afterward."

Eleanor stalls, trying desperately to hide her panic. The ring is still in her bag, and she cannot take it to the police station. She hunts around desperately for some reason to get away from them, and realizes her jeans are wet. Water has seeped up the bottom hems, and she has cold patches on her knees from when she fell on the ice.

"Would you mind if I changed my trousers? We've just been ice-skating . . ."

She is terrified they will say no, but Prashad says, "Of course," although she keeps her steady gaze trained on Eleanor as she agrees. Eleanor hesitates, almost expecting to be escorted up the stairs, but then Priya Prashad raises an eyebrow, as if to say, *What are you waiting for?*

"Right, I'll just be a second."

She rushes up the stairs and once the door is closed, she fumbles in her bag until the ring is in her hand. She looks desperately around the attic room for somewhere to hide it. If she had more time, she could pull out the chest of drawers and look for a weak spot, or even unscrew one of the plug sockets, but there is no chance with them waiting downstairs. She lifts up her mattress and pushes the ring as far as she can beneath it. It will have to do until she gets back.

There are feet on the stairs, coming closer. As she lets go of the mattress, it falls back onto the bed slats with a thud, and she hopes it didn't dislodge the ring. She roots through her drawers, grabbing a dry pair of jeans and pulling them on as fast as she can.

"Eleanor?"

It's Savannah. Eleanor relaxes, lets out a long breath.

"I'm getting changed, Savvie. What is it?"

"Do you know when Dad will be back?" she calls through the door.

"I don't, I'm afraid. Why don't you ask your mum?"

Savvie doesn't reply, but to Eleanor's relief she hears the footsteps move away.

She goes to the mirror and sees how wild her hair looks after an hour in the wind on the ice; her cheeks are red and her eyes are wide. She looks like a tormented version of herself. *Those who are innocent look neat and demure, not scruffy and frantic,* she goads herself. But even though she can brush her hair it's not so easy to stop her fingers from trembling.

There is no time left or someone will come up to find her. She pulls her boots back on and hurries down the stairs, to find the detectives waiting in the front hallway. As she follows them toward the front door, Susan appears from the kitchen.

"Eleanor has agreed to come down to the station for her interview," Priya Prashad says. "This is just a matter of procedure; she is not under arrest."

Susan doesn't even look at Eleanor. "Does she need a lawyer?"

"We will provide police counsel . . ." Prashad looks across at Eleanor.

Eleanor wishes she could disappear from underneath their piercing gazes. "That will be fine," she says. She doesn't dare look at Susan again as they head out and down the steps. The day has turned cloudy and the first spots of rain reach her face. It had rained last night too, she remembers, but not until much later on. For a moment she has a vision of herself lying on the front doorstep, soaked and shivering, crying as she comes to, flinching as the porch light goes on.

10

the interview

ickon Blythe is sick of the vultures outside the house; he's sent his lawyer out there with a hastily written press statement, hoping it will satisfy those ogling bastards for now. Meanwhile, he has just finished abusing his son-in-law on the phone for failing to protect his precious daughter. As Dickon hangs up, he clutches his chest, trying to breathe through the griping pain, aware that his thirty-year friendship with Ernie Lane is now over.

Detective Sergeant Steve Kirby opens the back-passenger door for Eleanor, while Prashad gets in the driver's seat. To Eleanor's relief, the car is an ordinary civilian one. As they drive away, she turns toward the house and thinks she sees Naeve's face watching them from the window, but they move out of sight too quickly for her to be sure.

The drive to the station seems to take forever. Perhaps because no one says anything, except for a few short inquiries from Kirby. "Are you warm enough, Eleanor?" "You okay back there, Eleanor?" She watches the crowded streets of London whiz past, people sprinting or hurrying along sidewalks. Many are opening umbrellas or huddling in doorways as the rain begins in earnest. It's rare to spot anyone ambling.

They park outside a tall redbrick building and walk together to the entrance. To her surprise, at reception Eleanor is asked to empty out her bag and pockets. The word *routine* is mentioned again, but this feels anything but procedural to her. What would have happened if she'd had the ring on her? Would she have been arrested on the spot? She shudders, picturing it under the mattress. What the hell is she going to do with it?

Eventually they lead her along a corridor and into a small room, where she is left on her own for almost half an hour before a middle-aged man with a bushy gray beard bustles in.

"My name is Howard Green," he explains. "I'm the defense lawyer here. Do you understand that you are here to answer questions only, you have not been arrested or charged with any offense? Nevertheless, I would urge you to assert your right to silence if any line of questioning makes you feel uncomfortable. Is there anything you wish to tell me before we begin?"

"I have nothing to hide," Eleanor says, her voice shaking.

Howard Green then proceeds to ignore her for ten minutes, opening his briefcase and rifling through papers.

When Detectives Prashad and Kirby enter, they each hold a mug in their hands. Neither offers Eleanor or the solicitor a drink. They don't look at Eleanor until they sit down, whereupon Kirby leans forward and fixes her with a glare.

"This interview will be videotaped, Eleanor. You do not have to say anything, but it may harm your defense if, when questioned, you do not mention something which you later rely on in court. Anything you do say may be given in evidence. Do you understand?"

This time Eleanor cannot bring herself to say she has nothing to hide. She just nods.

"As you already know, Eleanor, we're investigating the death of Arabella Lane," Prashad begins.

The words hit Eleanor almost as hard as the first time, when Caroline had made the announcement from the balcony. Eleanor can deal with this fact so much better on her own—push it away, pretend it's a bad dream. But other people keep intruding, making her confront the reality over and over.

"Can you tell us about working at Parker & Lane?"

This isn't the question Eleanor was expecting. She tries to turn her thoughts from last Thursday evening. Coughs to clear her dry throat. "It's fine . . . I mean, I haven't been there long."

"How long have you been there?"

"Only three weeks. I'm working as a temp for Nathan Lane."

"And what does your job entail?"

Eleanor can't see how this is relevant. "All his admin. He's the managing director; he oversees all the different departments, so it's pretty busy. Lots of letters to type, running around delivering things to people, making him coffee, making his guests coffee . . ."

"And how do you get on with Nathan Lane?"

"All right. He's not particularly friendly, but he's my boss."

"Did you see much of Arabella at work?"

"No, hardly at all. Just when she wanders around or pops in to see Nathan—but they are both busy, it doesn't happen often." She realizes she's begun by using the wrong tense, and bites her lip, but the detectives don't miss a beat.

"And you went to the party on the *Atlantic* last Thursday evening?"

"Yes."

"What time did you get there?"

"About eight o'clock."

"How did you travel there?"

"By Tube, then on foot. I stopped off for a quick drink first."

"On your own?"

"Yes, on my own. I needed Dutch courage—it's hard walking into a place where no one knows you very well."

"So, why did you decide to go?"

Eleanor hesitates. She'd never considered not going. "It was a night out. I thought it might help me get to know people a bit better, if they weren't rushing around at work." She says, "But," then stops herself.

Prashad is on it straightaway. "But?"

"It was pretty cliquey. Everyone hung out in the same groups as they do at work. I was disappointed."

"So what did you do?"

"I stayed at the bar for a little while, then I went outside and watched the world go by, chatted to a few people . . ."

"Did you talk to Nathan?"

"No."

"What about Arabella?"

Eleanor tenses at the mention of Arabella and hopes it doesn't show. "Yes. I met her in the bathroom, and she spoke to me. We had a drink together and a bit of a dance. Then I remember her walking over and slapping Nathan, but after that I can't recall much." She tries to hold eye contact with them but is unable to stop herself from glancing away now and again.

"What do you remember?"

They hadn't reacted to Nathan being slapped in public by his wife, she notices. Perhaps they already knew about it. Should she mention that Arabella put drugs in her drink? Is it wrong to accuse a dead woman of something like this? "Very little. I must have had too much to drink. And I wonder—I wonder if my drink was spiked."

"What makes you say that?" Priya asks sharply.

"My memory blank and the hideous hangover yesterday," Eleanor replies.

Priya nods. Pauses. Checks the papers in front of her and then looks up again. "Do you have any idea what time you first spoke to Arabella?"

"I went to the bathroom around ten thirty. I know that because I was thinking of heading home, and when I checked the time, I thought it was still pretty early. But I'm not sure after that."

"What did you talk about?"

"She asked me my name. Then she asked what it was like to work with Nathan."

"And what did you say?"

"I said it was okay, but she didn't seem to believe me."

Steve Kirby leans forward. "Why do you say that?"

"She was quite sarcastic about him. She was calling him wonderful and stuff like that, but it was obviously not genuine. And then she went and slapped his face, so it was clear she was pretty annoyed with him."

"How do you find Nathan Lane?"

Didn't they just ask her that? "Well, his manner is pretty gruff and he can seem a bit cold."

"You find him cold?"

"A bit, yes, but I haven't known him for long."

"And after Arabella slapped Nathan, what do you remember?"

"Not much. I spoke to a friend this morning; he told me I'd run out after Arabella and—and I'd been upset on the Hungerford footbridge. He'd brought me back to the party."

"And this friend's name is?"

"Will—" It takes Eleanor a moment to recall his surname. "Will Clayton. He works at Parker & Lane." It felt strange calling him a friend, but Will had acted like one today, hadn't he?

The detectives are watching her. Steve Kirby twirls his pen between his fingers. "Just think for a moment," he says, "see if you can remember anything else that might be relevant."

She pauses. "I've been trying, but nothing's coming back to me."

"When did you start remembering things again clearly?"

"Not until I woke up yesterday morning."

"You don't have any recollection of the evening after your conversation with Arabella?"

Why do they keep asking her the same questions? *She was crying*, Eleanor wants to say. *I know she was crying, outside, in the dark.* The thought makes her tremble. How does she know that?

And now she can see Arabella's eyes, wide and pleading. *Please help me.*

Don't say it, don't say it, because it didn't happen.

Did it?

Stop it.

Eleanor tries to calm her thoughts. She has already told them that her recollections are muddled. She doesn't want to insert her flights of imagination into a police investigation.

"You don't recall Arabella leaving the party?"

"No. Will told me I ran after her, and we were all on the bridge for a little while, then he brought me back to the party. He said Arabella came back to the *Atlantic* briefly and spoke to me while I was half passed out, but I don't remember any of that."

She doesn't miss the quick glance between Prashad and Kirby. She isn't sure what it means, but she still squirms.

"Who do you remember seeing Arabella talk to at the party?" Kirby continues.

Eleanor tries her best to refocus. "Only Nathan, really. I noticed her speaking to him once toward the beginning and he wasn't really paying attention to her, so she got up and left. Then I saw the slap a little while later but that's it."

"Who else did you see at the party?"

Eleanor rattles off a few names. "There were more people there, but I don't know everyone's name yet."

"So you don't know what time you left the party?" Priya says, almost before Eleanor has finished speaking.

"No, I'm not sure. I know Will took me back and I was lying down in the reception area for a while, but he told me that I disappeared again when he came to try to help me get home." She hesitates. "I don't know how I got home from there."

Prashad nods. Looks down at the briefcase. Then turns to look at Eleanor again, unblinking.

"Your aunt says you didn't get home till around two o'clock in the morning."

Eleanor frowns. Surely that can't be right. Why would Susan say that? Then she remembers overhearing Susan talking to Ian. How had she described Eleanor? As coming home paralytic, in the early hours of the morning. Eleanor dreads to think what Susan witnessed. No wonder she wasn't keen on Eleanor right now.

"Do you remember checking the clock at all during the night or when you got home?"

"No. Only at half past ten when I was at the party and then when the alarm went off yesterday."

"We have witnesses saying you and Arabella left the party between eleven and half past—the party finished at around twelve, and yet you weren't found on the doorstep until two. But you haven't any idea of what you were doing between those times?"

Eleanor's stomach lurches. They think she has something to hide. And does she? Why is all that time a blank? What was her aunt doing awake at two o'clock anyway? How could she know all this?

What the hell is going on?

She clutches the edge of the table, trying to calm herself. Priya Prashad is watching her intently. "Eleanor? Did you hear the question?"

Eleanor looks up at her and meets her eye. The woman in front of her looks kind and concerned, not hostile.

"I don't remember," she replies, her voice wavering. "I'm sorry," she says louder, striving for confidence. She knows she must hold their gaze—the first sign of guilt is looking away.

"We have some CCTV footage not far from the *Atlantic*." Steve Kirby produces a photo from a folder in front of him. "This is a photograph taken from it at half past eleven. Could you take a look at this, please, and tell me who you see there?"

Eleanor looks at the photo. "That's—that's me—and Arabella."

"In the video you are both hurrying, almost running. Then you put your hand out to Arabella, and she holds both of hers up and backs away from you, shaking her head. What do you think you were both doing?"

Eleanor stares hard at the photo, trying desperately to bring it to mind, but there is nothing. "I don't know." She doesn't mention how upset Arabella looks—she's sure they can see that for themselves.

"You have no idea what was going on there?"

They wait. No one says anything. Eleanor can feel the room slipping away from her. She thinks she's going to pass out and perhaps it would be a good thing, if it got her away from this interrogation.

"Eleanor, do you remember this?"

"No."

"You don't know why you were chasing her?"

Eleanor shakes her head no.

"Eleanor," Priya says gently, "don't wait to tell us what you know. It's much easier if you tell the truth now and avoid trouble later. Is there anything else you can tell us, Eleanor? Anything at all?"

Eleanor thinks of the ring. It could be critical evidence. This is the moment for her to confess she has it and hand it over to the police. Already she can see they don't quite believe her story. If she keeps things from them, then everything could get a lot worse.

She opens her mouth, but a surge of fear stills her tongue. What if they don't believe her? What if she's arrested? She cannot cope with their suspicion. She feels so guilty. She just needs to get away to try to figure this out on her own.

"No, there's nothing else," she tells them in a small voice.

No one speaks as they make their way out of the station, stopping to collect Eleanor's belongings. In the car on the way back to Harborne Grove, Prashad turns to look at her. "We may well want to talk to you again, Eleanor. Are you planning to travel anywhere outside London in the near future?"

"No."

"You are a witness in this investigation now, even though you don't remember all of the evening, so for the time being you need to notify us if you leave the city."

"I understand." Eleanor wraps her arms around herself and stares out of the window again, but this time she is too lost in her thoughts to notice anything.

At the house, she is escorted right up to the front door. Eleanor finds herself standing awkwardly beside her aunt, saying goodbye to the detectives. The space between them bristles with everything unspoken as the detectives head down the steps to their vehicle. Prashad swings around. And there it is. Suspicion as clear as day. But mingled with something else—kindness, sympathy? Eleanor regrets misleading this woman. She wants to run upstairs and hand over the ring before things get murkier and messier. But in the few moments that she thinks this, Prashad turns around again and is gone.

Once the door is closed, Eleanor rushes up the stairs without a word to her aunt and closes the door to her room. She puts her hand under the mattress, feeling around for the ring. Only when it's in her grasp again does she begin to calm down. Without thinking, she slips it on her finger, studying the way it reflects the light and trying to decide what to do next.

11

the bridge

Priya Prashad is aware of Steve watching her, trying to read her thoughts. She doesn't speak. She's replaying the interview, reviewing all the moments that had set alarm bells jangling, trying to decide whether they can trust Eleanor at all.

"So what do you reckon?" Steve asks eventually. "You chose not to mention a few things back there. You think this girl has something to do with it?"

"I don't know." Prashad watches the road as she drives. "But whatever is going on, Eleanor Brennan certainly has something to hide."

There is a curt knock, then the attic room door begins to open. Panicked, Eleanor pushes the ring back under her mattress just as Susan's head appears around the door.

"What did the police want with you?"

Susan has never visited her here before and the little attic room no longer feels like a refuge. Eleanor's heart is still pounding; she prays she pushed the ring in far enough and it doesn't drop out at her feet.

"I talked to Arabella briefly at the party," she says hesitantly. "They just wanted to know what she said."

When Susan doesn't reply, Eleanor meets her gaze. She's expecting to see that shrewd assessing look that Susan always seems to pin her with. The worried frown takes her by surprise.

"What did you tell them?"

Eleanor only pauses for a second. "Nothing much. I don't really remember—I was drunk."

Susan's mouth tightens. Eleanor hesitates longer this time. Can her aunt sense the lies that are building? How can she tell Susan about the ring, the memory loss, the CCTV images? They all point to Eleanor being reckless and impulsive at best, and at worst—what?

"When will my uncle be home?" she ventures, keen to change the subject. Although, once she's said it, the question seems bold, as though she is crossing some personal boundary, but she is desperate to know.

"I'm not sure." Susan sighs. "I've put the girls in the family room and said they can watch as much TV as they want today. They both seem very tired. Thank you for taking them out this morning."

This is the closest Eleanor has ever had to an amiable chat with her aunt. And that's not the only thing that's strange, because there's a schism in Susan's appearance today. Eleanor cannot miss the paleness to her face, the fact that her makeup doesn't sit quite right. Her eyeliner and mascara are too heavy; there are cracks in her foundation around her nose and hairline. Eleanor has wanted to see behind Susan's facade, but this frightens her. Her uncle is missing, her aunt is floundering, Eleanor feels unstable, and the girls are creeping around at night. This family is coming apart.

She is aware that she is trapped up at the top of the house with only one route of escape. "I think I might go out for a walk, then," she announces impulsively. "If you don't need me here."

"Fine. Just keep your phone on in case there's reason to call you," Susan says, turning back toward the stairs.

It's a fair request, but Eleanor doesn't want to think of the reasons she might get such a call. Once Susan has gone, Eleanor wonders where she might go. She needs to unscramble her thoughts, away from the emotions and questions that are beginning to pervade all familiar spaces. She changes her clothes again, and as she undresses, it is as though she's stripping off some of the weight of the day. She checks on the ring beneath the mattress, pushing it further into place. The cold touch of it makes her shiver. It isn't just a piece of jewelry—it's like she has brought a piece of Arabella into this house, an insidious connection with a dead woman that's slowly leaching fear into the atmosphere.

She grabs her scarf, gloves, and hat, heads downstairs and out the door. Immediately, a blast of cold air hits her. It's only four o'clock in the afternoon, but the light is already fading from the day, replaced by the insipid yellows from streetlamps and cars, along with the brighter flashes of overhead signs and mobile phones. She keeps her head down as she walks toward the Tube, navigating the uneven slabs of stone pavement, keeping an eye out for puddles.

Twenty minutes later she sits on the train, trying to look inconspicuous even though she is convinced everyone is casting covert glances at her. She hasn't even acknowledged to herself where she's going, until she hears the announcement for Embankment and shuffles to the exit. Once on the station concourse she slowly makes her way out, shaking her head at the *Big Issue* seller who catches her eye. Back in the cold air, she wraps her scarf tightly around her neck and pulls on her gloves, trying to ignore the huddled groups and their animated chatter, the Christmas merriment of everyone, it seems, except her.

On Victoria Embankment she stops opposite the pier. The *Atlantic* is moored today, and she gazes at the blue-and-white sign on top of the boat. She doesn't dare go closer, but she's desperately trying to recall herself leaving, to retrace those missing hours. Yet all she sees, over and over again, is Arabella standing opposite her in the bathroom, that monstrous ring glistening on her finger.

And then her heart misses a beat as two figures appear at the entrance to the pier. She turns away and looks around for somewhere to go, running toward a small accessories shop tucked away under the railway bridge. Once inside, she stands near the window, facing away, trying to calm herself before she dares to look again.

When she finally peeks through the glass, detectives Kirby and Prashad are at their car, which is parked on the street. Prashad climbs straight in the driver's side. Kirby, however, stops and turns around, looking back at the *Atlantic*, before his gaze sweeps across the road toward the little shop. Surely, he cannot see her glancing at him from one corner of the window, since the glass is half covered in fake snow spray and she has pulled her hat down and her scarf up over her nose.

It's only a few seconds until he turns away and climbs into the vehicle, but it feels like forever.

Just as she is beginning to breathe again, a voice behind her asks politely, "Can I help you?"

She jumps and swings around. A shop assistant, fake smile pinned in place, waits for a response. "I'm just browsing, thank you," she replies, noticing how hot it is in here, how bright the lights are on her, and how garish these scarves are in their rainbow colors and myriad fabrics. She is struggling for breath. She has to get out now.

She heads for the door quickly, opening it and feeling another furious surge of cold air. The contrast between the overheated indoor spaces and the relentless cold of outside is making her dizzy, and her nose is already beginning to run. As she turns around, she spots the assistant from the scarf shop openly watching her through the window. She quickens her pace, hurrying back toward Embankment Tube station, through throngs of shoppers and past a large group dressed in black and wearing Santa hats, singing Christmas carols, those at the front shaking collection tins in time to the music. There's a group of people waiting for the Tube and she changes her mind, unable to bear the claustrophobia. She walks out of the station and takes the stairs up to her right, which lead onto one of the Hungerford footbridges, the same bridge she and Arabella had been on just a few nights ago.

As she walks toward Waterloo, she is overcome by a wave of desperation. This was meant to be a new start for her, and yet here she is scurrying through these unfamiliar places alone, crippled by a grief she can't name, and burdened with a crushing weight of guilt. She has traveled halfway across the world hoping that everything would change, but nothing has. Instead, all these feelings have swollen, becoming more intense than ever.

You need to sleep, she tells herself and automatically glances back the way she's come, trying to decide whether to go home. But as she does so, a man in a dark jacket and jeans, wearing a thick woolen hat, stops abruptly and turns away from her.

In an instant, she is sure he is following her.

She turns away and rushes onward, wanting to wrestle out of her own skin, certain that the only way to achieve calm would be to step outside of herself. The wide bridge stretches away from her, across to South Bank. She stops and reaches out to the railing, not daring to look back until she has caught her breath. When she turns, the only people behind her are two women, walking together, deep in conversation, each with a scarf up around her mouth.

Did she imagine him? Just how crazy is she becoming? As she registers her hand's connection with the cold metal, something jars in her mind. Instinctively, she leans over, looking down into the dark water of the Thames. A few bits of rubbish float on the surface, nothing else. And yet for a fraction of a second, she was searching for something there. What was it? Why did she feel so desperate?

It's not even teatime and yet dusk is falling fast. Streetlights shine down onto the pavement, and she walks a little farther along and then glances both ways. A few groups wander toward and away from her, but there is no sign of the man.

She looks down again at the inky blackness of the river, hears the gentle noise of sloshing water. The sound seems to lure her toward it and she leans a bit farther over the rail, eyes straining, searching for an answer down there. This railing isn't too high, she could easily go over if she had a mind to. Why had she been so determined to on Thursday night? And how had Arabella ended up down there?

Her hand brushes against something papery. A small sticker is affixed to the railing. One typed sentence. Suicide is the Only Mistake You Can Never Correct.

The words hit her with such force that she only just catches the sob before it can escape. She looks along the railings and sees more messages. She hurries to the next one.

Everything Would Change if You Were Gone.

Heart heaving, she speeds up, reading them as she goes. Just these two sentences are written on all the stickers, which are spaced out evenly along this half of the bridge. Eleanor tries to imagine who put them here. The grief and desperation in those short pleas feel palpable. She wants them to be messages for her, to keep going, not to give up, to figure this thing out. But she's not sure she deserves them.

She looks up and sees the London Eye, its great struts leaning out toward the river, helping it to peer into the depths. Had people seen what happened on Thursday night from up there? She tries to imagine herself as she was, staggering to the edge, Will and Arabella and a group of strangers pulling her backward. But there is nothing in her head except what people have told her. She is going to have to search outside herself if she wants answers.

She thinks of the ring with a surge of regret. If she had brought it with her, she could have let it drop over the side right now. Then that part of her involvement would be over. Why had she left it at home?

She is almost at the south side of the river now, and she glances back along the bridge. There he is: the man in the dark jacket and jeans, back on the northern side, turned toward her, too far away for her to clearly see his face. He *is* following her. She sets off at a run, feet hammering the pavement, heart pounding to the same frenetic beat. She takes the steps down two at a time, pushing past a group of businessmen, hearing one of them shout, "Oi!" before she takes a right along the southern embankment, racing through the graffitied underpass before she comes out onto the grassed area behind the Eye.

She swings around, waiting for the man to reappear. She looks around for where she might hide, but she's scared of coming face to face with him around one of those shadowy corners. She finds herself running across to the ticket office, joining a short queue. Moments later she is purchasing a ticket for the Eye and hurrying to the barriers. As she waits in line, she nervously scans the grass and the walkways, but still he has not appeared. Five minutes later, she is ushered into one of the capsules with a group of excited twentysomethings with northern accents. The doors close and the wheel begins to move, and even though she is trapped, she feels calmer now she is confined, with the view spreading out before her. From her vantage point she surveys the bridge. Halfway along, a dark figure leans on the railings, looking out over the water, but from this distance she cannot tell if it is the same man. She follows his gaze toward the point where the Thames disappears into the enveloping night, beneath the glistening lights of London, and reminds herself that somewhere down there, on Thursday night, Arabella was swallowed in that maw of water. Without Will's intervention, would there have been two bodies found yesterday morning?

It was the drugs, she tells herself, over and over. *You would never have climbed those railings if you weren't intoxicated.* But when she looks down, she sees her hands are trembling. It seems that no matter how far or high she travels, there will be no escaping her fears.

12

nathan

Ernie has been waiting impatiently for his wife to finish her phone call. "Nathan is asking to come home," Emily says when she hangs up, her eyes wet and pleading.

Ernie grimaces. It's a terrible thing, what happened to Arabella, but in truth, all he can think about is making the fairway tomorrow. Three days without golf and he can feel the knots in his knees, his arms, his disposition.

"No—it'll only encourage the press. You go to him if you need to."

Emily walks off without a word. She'll be angry with him, even though she knows their son is a reprobate, a perpetual disappointment to the Lane name.

He can hear the chatter outside the window; they don't even bother to keep their voices down. He's been enjoying the anonymity of retirement, and now, thanks to Nathan, the press is at his door again. If they don't fuck off before long, he'll take one of those bloody clubs and tee off on the doorstep, straight at their ignorant heads.

For a long time on Saturday night, Eleanor cannot sleep, staring at the pristine white ceiling above her, willing the room to stay still, trying to breathe through the panic and telling herself that she is in an airy room far away from water, so there can be no rational reason for her lungs to insist that she is drowning.

She cannot move without asking herself questions she doesn't want to ask, telling herself things she doesn't want to know. *You are so lonely,* she says, even as she insists that no, it cannot be that—she'd spent so much time in her own company as a teenager that she'd thought she was immune to loneliness. Sure, she has come here to distance herself from the slow-burning fuse of anger and despair that crawls and crackles a little further along whenever she thinks of her childhood. She has come here because if ever there were a place with a pulse, with a beating heart of its own, it had to be London. So how could this place of her dreams have failed to reflect her desires and instead be mirroring her torments?

When she does sleep it is fitful, and she doesn't wake until almost nine. She puts off going downstairs until her stomach is rumbling, and as she makes her way quietly down, she can already hear people in the kitchen.

As she creeps closer, to her dismay she discerns Susan's solemn tone, although she sounds somewhat milder than usual. And there is a man's voice too, although she is at the doorway in her dressing gown before she realizes it is not her uncle.

Her aunt stands with her back to Eleanor, and, opposite her, sits Nathan Lane. He is wearing baggy jeans and a crumpled T-shirt. His face is blotchy and unshaven, his hair unbrushed. There is little to recognize from the Nathan Lane she has experienced at the office.

"I just didn't know where else to go," he is saying to Susan, rubbing his face.

Eleanor is about to back out of the room when he looks up and spots her. As their eyes lock, she sees his expression change to one of utter hostility. She has no chance to escape before he has sprung out of his chair, and in an instant he is shaking her, one of his hands locked tightly around her throat. "What the hell did you do to her?" he hisses, his face purple with rage. "I saw you together—I saw you go after her. Tell me what happened, *tell me right now.*"

Eleanor cannot speak. Instead she makes a horrible gurgling noise, clawing at him, trying to force air into her lungs.

"Nathan!" Susan is shouting. "Nathan, stop!"

"Hey!" someone yells behind her. Eleanor is suddenly free, jostled out of the way by her uncle, who has grabbed hold of Nathan, pushing him away. She collapses to the floor, holding her throat, tears streaming down her face. She looks up to see Ian, in his pajamas, his face livid, still holding onto Nathan's arms.

Susan watches the scene with a hand to her forehead, but she doesn't take a step toward any of them.

"There is no excuse for that, Nathan!" Ian shouts. "*No excuse*, do you hear? In *any* circumstances. We are deeply, *deeply* sorry for your loss, but I think you need to leave now." He pushes Nathan roughly away from him, toward the door.

"Ian, I'm sorry—" Nathan begins.

"Don't apologize to me," Ian cuts him off. "Apologize to her." He points at Eleanor.

Nathan looks back at Eleanor. A muscle twitches in his jaw. "If you know what happened, you had better tell someone," he growls.

"Nathan, you really should go now," Ian says firmly, going to help Eleanor up, putting an arm around her shoulder.

"Nathan," Susan says, moving across to him, "I'll meet you at the Aberdeen, give me fifteen minutes to get dressed, and we can keep talking."

Nathan glances between all of them as though trying to decide on his response. Then he looks back at Susan and nods. "All right." He turns around and moments later the door bangs shut.

Eleanor begins to sob, and Ian pulls her to him. "It's okay," he murmurs, stroking her hair. "He was completely out of line."

Susan snaps her head toward her husband. "Ian—"

"No, Susan, we cannot stand by and watch Eleanor be assaulted, not even to protect your job."

Eleanor sees Susan's mouth drop open for a moment. Ian and Susan glare at each other, and with every second that no one speaks, the room fills with such pressure that Eleanor is braced for an explosion.

Then Susan swings around to face her, eyes narrowed. "Why did he go for you like that, Eleanor?" she asks. "First the police, now Nathan. How the hell are you involved in all this?" She looks at Ian. "Or is there even more to this story than I know?" she spits.

"I'm not involved!" Eleanor cries, looking pleadingly at Ian. "I just talked to Arabella the night of the party, that's all. It was pure chance. I met her in the bathroom, and we had a drink together."

But Susan's attention has shifted. Eleanor follows her gaze to see Naeve and Savannah standing in the doorway, their little faces clearly shocked and frightened. Savannah clutches Naeve's arm with one hand and her toy unicorn with the other. "We heard shouting and the door slamming," she says in a small, shaky voice. "Who was that?"

Ian lets go of Eleanor and hurries over to them. "No one. It doesn't matter. Come on, let's go and turn the TV on—you can watch whatever you like."

He ushers them away, leaving Susan alone with Eleanor.

For a moment, no one speaks. All their unanswered questions hang in the air between them.

"I don't know what's going on here," Susan says finally, "but if you are involved, then I will make sure I find out about it." Susan fixes Eleanor with one of her death stares, not waiting for a response before she turns and leaves the kitchen.

As soon as everyone has gone, Eleanor bolts for her room. However, once she's there, she paces from one side to the other like a trapped animal, trying to decide what to do next. At the back of her mind, a little voice is muttering that Nathan should have pressed harder, it would have been a relief.

She doesn't want to be alone, listening to this voice—the one that scares her most of all. She is afraid she's spinning out of control. She needs to get out of this room, but where can she go? She can't bear to be alone, but she doesn't have anyone to turn to. Her uncle will be occupied with the girls now. When is she ever going to get the chance to talk to him? Unless . . .

She grabs her phone with trembling hands and searches for Will's number from yesterday. When it rings, she isn't sure whether she is doing the right thing, but before she can hang up his voice is saying, "Hello? Eleanor?"

"I'm sorry," she says, beginning to cry. "I didn't know who else to call."

"Eleanor, what's happened?"

"It's Nathan—he came to the house and attacked me."

"What?" Will's tone is incredulous.

"He thinks I did something to Arabella. Oh god, what if I did? What happened to me after I left the *Atlantic*? Why can't I remember anything?"

"Eleanor, you could hardly walk on Thursday night, let alone overpower anyone."

That calms her a little. "I suppose . . . it's just . . . just . . ." Her hand strays to the mattress, aware that the ring lies beneath it. She can't bear to divulge it over the phone, but she can't keep this to herself any longer. She has to tell someone. "Please, can I meet you?"

"Er . . . sure. I have to talk to an illustrator this morning, we're installing some of his artwork at the Museum of London for a big promotion we're doing. Can you make your way there, and we can grab some coffee while I'm on a break?"

"Yes, thank you."

"It's all right, Eleanor. Don't do anything st—I mean, you're doing the right thing, we'll talk it all through again, okay?"

As soon as she ends the call, she gets dressed and grabs her jacket—hesitates, then pulls the ring from underneath the mattress and slips it into her purse.

13

the museum of london

"*W*hy haven't you arrested Nathan?*" Tilly Blythe demands as soon as she is introduced to detectives Prashad and Kirby. "We've been waiting for this day ever since he married her. He drove her to drink first, then to drugs, and now he's finally, inevitably driven her to her death. I'm sorry, Mum," Tilly says, her voice softening as she puts an arm around her keening mother, "but we all know it's the truth, don't we?" And she watches her mother lift her head long enough to nod.*

No one notices Eleanor leave the house. She glances around as she heads to the Tube station, wondering if Nathan might be waiting for her somewhere in the shadows, debating if he could be the person who stalked her the previous night. Her nervousness doesn't dissipate on the train. She sits in the corner of the carriage and watches everyone carefully, unable to stop her foot from beating out a frantic rhythm.

As soon as she's at the museum, she calls Will, but he doesn't pick up. Moments later there's a text:

Still in meeting—might be a while, will let you know as soon as I'm finished.

With nothing else to do, she wanders aimlessly around the exhibits. After a while she goes back to the clay head of the Shepperton woman, reconstructed from a Neolithic skeleton found crouched in a ritual burial site. There is something particularly unnerving about the woman's masculine face, blankly staring across five-and-a-half thousand years of history. She sits down and pulls out her sketchbook, but as always, the features distort and her drawing ends up more male than female, and before she knows it, she has sketched a noose cutting into the disembodied neck.

She tears the picture out and crumples it into a ball. She should be used to the way her mind works by now, but she isn't. She stares at the Shepperton woman, trying to figure out what is so compelling about her. Perhaps it was because if you stared long enough, the living would avert their gazes sooner or later, but when you were caught in the stare of the dead, they never looked away.

She shivers, moving through the gallery quickly, wanting to find something less troubling to look at until Will is free. As she studies the map, her phone buzzes in her pocket with another message.

Heading for the café. See you in 5.

She follows the signs to the café, to find Will waiting for her. He jumps up as soon as he sees her. "Coffee or tea?"

"Just water, please."

"Right." He heads for the counter, and she watches him place their order, the confident way he jokes with the barista, who is wearing a Santa hat and a tinsel scarf. Will comes back smiling but when he catches her eye, he turns solemn again, and as soon as he sets their drinks down, he starts talking.

"So what happened with Nathan?"

"He was in our kitchen when I got up this morning. He—he just went for me." Her eyes begin to sting. "I thought he was going to strangle me right there."

Will brushes her hair back from her neck. "Jeez, you still have a red mark."

As his fingers lightly touch her neck, she catches his eye and starts to blush. Will's hand returns to his drink, but his eyes don't leave hers. He sits back. "You should go to the police. That's assault. Your aunt and uncle would back you up, surely."

She considers it. "I'm not sure. He's just lost his wife; he must be crazy with grief. Besides, I'm not sure Susan would back me up about anything, actually."

Will looks uncertain. "Really? I know she can be a cold fish, but I doubt she'd condone assault."

Eleanor grimaces. "I don't know, it's the way she looks at me. I don't think she likes me very much."

"I'm sure that's not true. Her manner can be a bit off, but you're her niece."

"We're not related—only by marriage," Eleanor reminds him. "She'd never even met me until a few weeks ago. She probably thinks I brought all this trouble to her door."

She stops.

Has she?

Will is watching her carefully. "Eleanor, you have to stop blaming yourself. Your involvement is just unfortunate, that's all. I don't for one second believe you could have harmed Arabella." He sits back and for a moment his face clouds with an anger that takes her by surprise. "However, Nathan is a different story. There have been rumors about him for a long time. Arabella once came to work with an awful bruise on her neck that she'd tried to hide under a scarf. Another time, she got drunk at a party and told me she was terrified of Nathan, but the next day she wouldn't admit she had said it. Even so, we've all seen how volatile he can be. As soon as Arabella slapped him at the party, I was frightened for her. That's why I went after her—because I knew Nathan wouldn't let that go, but she refused my help. I'm sure he killed her.

That's probably why he's so mad at you, he's just looking for somewhere to deflect his guilt."

"Do you really think so?"

"I do. He's an awful human being, Eleanor. I have no idea why Arabella stayed married to him. He always treated her like shit—and when he's that cruel in public, I can only imagine what he would have been like behind closed doors."

"Why would she stay with him then? She didn't seem afraid of him. She went and slapped his face in front of everyone."

"Yes, she did, didn't she?" Will leans forward. "Look, this is probably an awful thing to say, considering the circumstances, because I saw for myself how upset Arabella was at the party, and she was a friend, but there were plenty of times when Arabella was anything but the damsel in distress. She could be very cutting to people, she adored being the center of attention, and her love of cocaine was no secret around the office either. If she shone her light on you, you couldn't help but bask in the glow— yet the next day you might find her giving you the cold shoulder. When her back was turned, people would whisper, and it wasn't always kind. But when she was there, everyone fawned over her. Of course they did— for most of them, she was either their boss or the boss's wife. Who knows what happened in the end, but I can imagine Arabella would have built up quite a few frenemies during her time at Parker & Lane. Let's face it, half the time even her own husband seemed to despise her."

When Eleanor stays quiet, Will touches her hand. "None of this is making you feel better, is it?"

She shakes her head. "It's not that, it's . . ."

She hesitates. The tension hangs between them. She studies his face. Can she trust him? She has no choice; she cannot carry this burden alone any longer.

She reaches into her bag, unzips her purse, and pulls out the ring, laying it on the table between them.

"What's this?" Will seems bemused at first, picking up the ring and studying it closely. As Eleanor watches, he appears to realize who owns it—or owned it. He suddenly puts it down on the table and covers it with his hand, looking around them, ducking low as though someone might come over at any moment. His face has gone red. "What the fuck . . . I hope that isn't what I think it is. Bloody hell, Eleanor, please don't tell me this is Arabella's?"

Eleanor's face is burning too. She doesn't say anything. She doesn't need to.

Will leans closer. "Why have you got it?" he hisses.

Eleanor meets his gaze. "I don't know. It was in my purse when I woke up on Friday, but I can't remember how it got there."

"Seriously?" Will searches her face, as though trying to decide whether she can possibly be telling the truth. "Shit, Eleanor, this is . . . this is—" He pushes it toward her. "Put it back in your bag, it shouldn't be out on the table. And you shouldn't have shown it to me. What the hell were you thinking? Why haven't you given it to the police?" His face is still red, and he seems furious with her.

"I'm sorry," she pleads, returning it quickly to her purse. "I'm trying to figure out why I have it. Maybe Arabella gave it to me when she came back to the party. You said she was with me when I was out of it, but why would she do that? And if she didn't, what if someone is setting me up? I'm afraid, Will. I know I shouldn't have involved you. I just don't know who else to turn to."

Will seems to be making a conscious effort to regain composure. "Do you know the police have talked to me already?" he whispers, leaning forward. "I chased after her, remember, when she left the *Atlantic* for the final time. I caught up with her and she brushed me off. If there's any footage from CCTV or witnesses or whatever, it might have looked like an argument." He puts his head in his hands. "I was one of the last people to see her alive, and that makes me a prime suspect. Shit," he clenches his fists. "*Shit!*"

"I'm sorry, Will. I really am." Eleanor leans closer. "Are you going to tell the police?"

For a moment, even though she is terrified, she wants him to say yes, to take this whole nightmare out of her hands. She waits as Will blows out a long breath, then his gaze focuses on her. She tries not to shy away, to keep her eyes on his, to show him she's genuinely remorseful. "For god's sake, Eleanor, I don't know. You've just—you've completely thrown me." He gets up. "I've got to get back to the exhibition, and I need some time to think." He grips the back of the chair and looks at her as though he's seeing something unbearable, making her flinch. "I'll talk to you later, Eleanor," he says, and then he is gone.

14

parker & lane

"More flowers," *Tilly announces, her arms full of bouquets as she walks into the kitchen.*

June closes her eyes. She's coming to hate the sickly, pungent smell of them—the living scents that will forever represent the horrific, unendurable hours that followed the death of her youngest child. She vows she will never again buy flowers for anyone in mourning.

Eleanor wakes early on Monday morning and checks her phone straightaway, hoping for something from Will. She has sent him three texts, apologizing, but he hasn't responded to any of them.

But she does have one message:

> Come to my office this morning when you get to work. DO NOT go near Nathan's desk. - Susan.

Since her boss tried to strangle her less than twenty-four hours ago, she's not sure she can face work today. Eleanor debates disobeying and climbing back under the covers, but she doesn't want to push Susan any further. She checks the time on her phone: seven thirty. There are three messages from her mother asking for updates, and she sends a hasty reply.

I'm fine—late for work, more later.

Then she swings her legs out of bed and slowly gets dressed. Before leaving the room, she checks the ring is safely stowed under the mattress. When she goes downstairs the house is quiet. It looks like everyone has already gone for the day.

As Eleanor heads for the Tube, she can't stop thinking about Will's reaction to the ring. What will he do now that he knows? She keeps reliving the expression on his face, the shock and disgust. She takes every step as though in a trance, half expecting to find the police waiting for her when she gets to work.

The carriage is quiet, and every commuter except Eleanor seems to be reading the *Metro* this morning. The front-page headline shouts WHAT HAPPENED TO ARABELLA LANE? above a small headshot of a smiling Arabella in the summer sun, her hair blowing in the breeze. It seems to be everywhere Eleanor looks, and each time she sees it she experiences a new frisson of fear. After a while, she keeps her head down.

An hour later, she is walking through the double doors of Parker & Lane. No police are in sight, but she hastens past the mound of flowers by the front entrance, trying to make herself inconspicuous. After signing in she goes across to the elevator, stepping inside and pressing the button for the top floor.

She knows the layout of the first two floors well, because she has regularly run errands between the admin and editorial staff. However, Susan's office takes up a good portion of the third floor, alongside HR and Legal. When the elevator pings open, she sees the layout is quite different up here. On the lower floors, the management are arranged along the edges, soldiers guarding the battlements, secreted away from the open-plan melee in their offices of polished white and chrome. A few frosted-glass panels reveal small vignettes of the working day: a hand tossed in exasperation as figures are analyzed, a quick jump to the feet signaling the end of an awkward meeting, a pencil twirled between fingers as the artistic merits of book covers are debated. Eleanor has often glanced through these smoke screens on her way to the kitchen or the bathroom, and has learned a few things about people. She knows that Michael Alton, financial director, keeps a small transistor radio in his top drawer, and his computer is often logged on to one of the gamblers.com sites. Jenny Malone, senior editor, likes to pick her nose when she thinks no one is looking. Malcolm O'Halloran, publisher for young adult fiction, is usually staring out of his window, his door shut. Apparently, he recently split up with his wife.

On the top floor, the boardroom runs all the way along one side of the square building, and adjacent to that, a set of grand, white double doors mark the entrance to Susan's office. Eleanor walks across to them and knocks. When there is no answer, she slowly opens one of the doors, and pokes her head around.

The enormous outer office belongs to Susan's personal assistant, Priscilla. Her workstation is on one side, while on the other are two huge sofas set against a backdrop of bookshelves, on which Parker & Lane's current titles are proudly displayed. Priscilla is sitting at her desk, opposite a woman Eleanor doesn't recognize until she turns around.

"Eleanor, come in," Priscilla says when she sees her. "You know Marisa?"

Of course, Arabella's PA. When Marisa turns around, Eleanor expects to see the grief writ large on her face, but Marisa looks remarkably composed and unaffected.

"Sit down, Eleanor," Priscilla says.

Eleanor obeys.

"We are in uncharted waters here," Priscilla begins. Her face is plastered in makeup today, and a garish necklace of large multicolored stones draws the eye away from her black blouse. "Susan thinks it is best if I look after Nathan's admin for the next few days. She would like you both to help her. Okay?" She plows on without waiting for an answer. "Eleanor.

You're to answer the phone and take messages, and do whatever else she asks. If journalists call, you just say Susan is unavailable and ask them to leave their contact details. You don't comment on anything else. Marisa, you'll do Susan's dictation, meeting minutes, and suchlike."

Eleanor sees Marisa grimace. Priscilla notices too, and frowns at her. "It's important we all pull together until things calm down a bit. Susan won't be in until this afternoon, so we're to hold the fort until then."

Eleanor relaxes. All she has to do is answer the phone. Susan won't be in until later. This day isn't going to be as bad as she thought.

"The police have cordoned off Arabella's office for now, so you will both have to sit up here. Marisa, I'll get you an extra seat. Susan has asked that you go through Arabella's online journal and cancel everything you need to. I realize it will mean some difficult conversations. Are you up to it?"

"Yes." Marisa nods. "It's got to be done."

"Right then," Priscilla says. "Oh, Eleanor," she turns to Eleanor and frowns, and Eleanor immediately feels uncomfortable. "Susan has asked that you do not leave this floor for the time being. Until she has had a chance to talk to you. All right?"

Eleanor sees the curiosity in Priscilla's glance. "Fine." She's actually grateful for the instruction—she doesn't want to run into people today, knowing how she behaved on Thursday night. She doesn't want to feel the force of the gossip that must be swirling.

Once Priscilla leaves, Eleanor sits behind the desk. Answering the phone doesn't seem like much of a task, and she wonders if the time is going to drag, but once the day gets going there are a stream of calls to Susan, mostly about Arabella. Eleanor scribbles messages for most, but the journalists are harder. They are reluctant to leave details, but keen to press for information.

"When will Susan be available?"

"Did you know Arabella Lane?"

"Tell me about what happened on Thursday night."

Eleanor replies "No comment" time and time again, but after a while the questions ring in her ears even in the gaps between calls. They are pushing too close to everything that frightens her. When the next one calls, Eleanor shouts "No comment!" down the phone, and finds she is shaking. Marisa takes the receiver from her and puts it back on the handle without even checking if the caller is still there.

"Would you like me to take over for a while?" she asks.

Eleanor balks, immediately embarrassed—she has been given one task, and she can't even do that. But Marisa doesn't wait for her reply and moves the phone over to the middle of the desk. On the next ring, she picks it up and transcribes a message for Susan.

"It's okay," she says, turning back to Eleanor once she's finished. "It's a lot to take in."

"You seem to be dealing with it well."

"Hmm, I don't know about that. I'm just not shocked, if that's what you mean."

Eleanor stills. "Why do you say that?"

Marisa leans closer. "Arabella was always a law unto herself." Her voice is low, the word *always* comes out as a quick sigh of frustration. "Unfortunately, she had tremendous mood swings, never knew quite what she wanted. Some days she was brilliant to work for, and we had a good laugh. Other days she would make my life hell. When I came in every morning, I never knew which Arabella I would get. It was exhausting." Marisa turns to Eleanor, and Eleanor sees the guilt in her eyes. "I *am* shocked, but I feel numb too, because I was already emotionally drained. I've got two young kids who go to day care five days a week, and I was constantly late or calling to apologize because Arabella would drop things on me at the last minute. But we need the money—my husband has been laid off twice in the past two years. So what could I do? I'm just exhausted, to be honest."

"I'm sorry," Eleanor says, not knowing what else to offer.

"Me too," Marisa replies. "I'm sorry about all of it." She turns back to the computer. "I think I've canceled most things," she says. "I'm being a chicken and doing what I can by email. However, Arabella had a meeting with the IT department every Thursday afternoon, where she'd update blogs and websites and all that, but I can't find the person she was dealing with. I would have thought it would have been Jenna Dixon, but she doesn't know anything about it."

As Marisa stares at the screen, the phone rings again. Her hand shoots out but Eleanor is faster.

"Don't worry," she says, "I can do it." She's feeling bad for Marisa, and instinctively wants to lighten her load.

"Parker & Lane," she answers.

"Priscilla, it's Nathan," comes the voice on the other end.

Eleanor freezes, but Nathan doesn't even pause for breath.

"Tell Susan the memorial service will be on Wednesday, and I want her to do the eulogy," he says, his tone leaving no space for discussion. "Two o'clock in the afternoon. I'll call back later with the details. Oh, and Priscilla?"

"Yes?" Eleanor whispers.

"Tell her that I expect her to fire her fucking niece!" he shouts down the phone, and then there's a click.

Shocked, Eleanor fumbles with the handset, dropping it onto the receiver with a clatter. Marisa looks up sharply. "What's wrong?"

"I'm not feeling well," Eleanor says, getting quickly to her feet. "I think I should go." She grabs her coat and hurries for the door before Marisa has a chance to reply.

As she leaves the office, she is rubbing her neck at the place Nathan had grabbed it. The sound of his voice had brought back memories of him lunging at her, his unyielding grip on her throat. He'd sounded so angry on the phone. She remembers Will's words, his fears for Arabella. What if Nathan is coming after her next?

Her thoughts become wild as she sprints along the corridor. When she reaches the elevator, her fingers hammer the call button. She doesn't realize there are people in the glass-walled boardroom, all watching her, until she hears a voice.

"Eleanor?"

Will is hurrying along the balcony toward her. As she sees him, she experiences another huge pang of guilt at the impossible situation she's put him in.

"Eleanor?" he says as he gets closer. "What's happened?"

"I just answered the phone to Nathan," she replies, looking around to make sure no one else is in earshot. "He thought I was Priscilla, and he told her he wants Susan to fire me. The way he spoke—it's like he despises me."

To her surprise, Will grabs her hand and pulls her through a door, into a nearby stairwell.

"Are you going to tell the police about . . . about—" she stammers.

"Not yet," he says. "I've had time to think about it now, and I don't get it. I cannot figure out how you could have ended up with that ring when you were so wasted you could barely stand up."

"What if someone planted it on me?" Eleanor asks miserably. "What if they're trying to frame me?"

Will looks thoughtful. "It's possible, but why choose you? No one here knows you very well yet, do they?"

Eleanor shrugs. "Exactly. I'm expendable. I don't matter." She feels the force of her words and gulps.

"Look." Will covers her hands with his briefly and gives them a squeeze. "Let's think about this rationally. What are the options? Number one: Arabella gave it to you. If so, why would she take her engagement ring off, unless she was really mad at Nathan? And we all saw her slap him. Which makes Nathan a prime suspect in whatever happened to her.

"Or you forcibly took it from Arabella. Now, that's an unlikely possibility. Why would you want to rob her, and how would you overpower her? She's a good bit taller than you, and she was pretty fit. Would you really take her ring and then stick around—if you wanted to pawn it you'd be gone already, surely?

"So, option three: someone else put it in your bag. If so, then whoever it is has some knowledge of what happened to Arabella and they are willing to involve you. That's not good. But if you tell the police, surely these are their lines of inquiry too. You'll have some support, and you can let them investigate which one is the answer. Take it to the police, Eleanor. You might get into trouble, but it will look a lot better if you come clean yourself and don't wait for someone or something to catch you out."

His words make Eleanor think. His perspective is so logical, and it is exactly what she needs. She has been so caught up in thinking about what it means to have the ring that she has forgotten to consider it as an objective piece of evidence. Thank god she hadn't thrown it in the river—she might have been tossing away a crucial link to the crime. What if having the ring wasn't just a curse after all? Might it help them figure out exactly what had happened?

Will is watching her. "What are you thinking?"

"I'm thinking you're making a lot of sense."

Will smiles. "Well, I have to get back to work," he says. When he releases her, he doesn't step back. His face is still close to hers as he looks into her eyes. "You need to go to the police, Eleanor." He strokes her hair away from her forehead. "Promise me you'll think about it."

His voice is soft, and his touch is so unexpectedly intimate that as she holds his gaze, she hopes he doesn't notice her shiver. "I promise."

He opens the door for her. "I'll call you later. Stay strong," he says, heading away.

She presses the elevator button and the door opens immediately. She scurries inside, grateful it's empty, and once she's downstairs, she signs out and leaves the building as fast as she can.

She is finding it hard to picture herself walking up the steps to the police station and presenting Arabella's ring to the detectives. She is finding it even harder to imagine what might come afterward, and that's the really scary part. But as she sits on the train, her upset begins to turn to fury. They have manipulated her, one after the other: first Arabella giving her drugs without asking; then Susan bossing her around; and now Nathan taking it all out on her without a scrap of evidence. She will take the ring to the police this afternoon. She will tell them everything she knows. She doesn't care if they believe her or not; she hardly even cares if she ends up in jail. It will just be a relief to end the struggle, to no longer deal with all this alone.

The house is still quiet as she races back in. But in the hall, a monstrous Christmas tree has appeared from nowhere, its tip almost touching the high ceiling. It looks like it came straight out of the Laura Ashley catalogue, decorated with pure white and silver crystal ornaments, although there is already a thin scattering of pine needles on the tiled floor.

She runs up the stairs and stops abruptly.

The door to her room is wide open.

Clothes have been picked up and her bed is freshly made with new linen.

Monday is housekeeping day. How could she have forgotten that?

Heart thudding, she walks slowly and pulls up her mattress.

The ring is not there.

Keep calm, she tells herself, wrenching all the bedclothes off and piling them on the floor, shaking them out and dropping them down, trying to encourage the ring to fall out. She lifts the whole mattress off the bed and searches between the slats. She goes through her drawers and pulls out clothes, at first keeping them folded, later flinging them behind her in a frenzy. She tips out the contents of her bag, just in case, but it's not there. She takes her room apart, and then puts it back together, piece by piece. And only when she has finished does she sit on her bed with trembling hands.

The ring has gone.

15

home

November 2004

The wide-open space is a perfect square, its edges delineated by untidy lines of bushland—stumpy grass trees and bent-backed eucalyptus rising amid plants whose tangled tendrils smother the dry ground, thirsty twigs jostling for scraps of water.

"What do you think?" Eleanor's dad's sweater hangs loose, his jeans sag from his hips. He puts an arm around her mother, pulls her toward him, and kisses her forehead. She smiles, her eyes closed.

Aiden has gone ahead, walking the perimeter, kicking at divots, hands in his pockets. He hasn't spoken to any of them for a week, except for a few gruff responses when asked a direct question. Eleanor's mom has told them to go easy on him. He's missing his friends, in particular, the girl who lived close by, Brianna, who has been by his side since preschool. They've been dating for nearly a year, and Brianna had waved them off earlier with tears streaming down her face.

"Well?" Martin stands close by, waiting for an answer.

Eleanor shrugs. "It's okay." But all she can think about is Tippington Road, the only home she had ever known, the place she had loved with all her heart for the last nine years. Now it seemed like a distant, safe harbor to which they would surely one day return, once they had finished floating around the dried-up waterholes of the outback. Last night she had woken up in a bland motel room, gasping at the thought they might never go back.

But her dad is chuckling. "This had better be okay because it's ours." He walks forward, lifting his hands, framing the scene with his fingers. "We'll put the house right there. It's gonna be great."

It's the most excited they've seen him since he lost his job. The lines on his face, built up over a year of whispered worries about money, have softened. Eleanor had believed him when he'd sold it to her as an adventure, but now, standing here, all she sees is nothing to do and no one to play with.

Her father is watching her, waiting for her to say something.

"How long is it going to take?"

"Well, that depends on how good your mum is at building."

Eleanor glances at her mother, who laughs, although she looks exhausted already. Eleanor isn't sure if it's a joke. Her mom gets flustered when faced with an Ikea flat pack—how is she going to help construct a house?

Martin comes over and this time his arm goes around his daughter. "Seriously, I don't know when we'll finish. But does it matter? This isn't just about completion; this is about the joy of building something of our very own with our bare hands."

"What's that?"

His gaze follows Eleanor's pointed finger. To one side of the field stands a khaki-colored building made of corrugated iron. It has a roller door that's big enough for a car to drive through, and a smaller wooden door to the right.

Aiden comes up behind them, and her father beckons them all forward with expansive arm movements, unable to contain his excitement. They follow him across to the building. The grass in front of it has worn away. Millions of bulldog ants run across the parched red dust on the urgent business of their queen.

It's dark inside. As they crowd around the doorway, Eleanor's dad leans in and flicks a switch. Her eyes follow the power cable upward, to where a bare bulb dangles from a hook, its feeble light struggling to illuminate the space. Spiderwebs decorate the low ceiling, their handiwork forming the ghostly outline of a filigree stage curtain drawn up high. Something scuttles in one of the shadowy far corners, then falls silent. The floor is a concrete slab. There is one tiny window, no other natural light. The air is dense and almost too hot to breathe.

"This," Eleanor's father says, walking into the center of the room, a manic edge to the way he flings his arms out wide, "is home."

16

zombie

eorge Mellor, doorman at the Chancellor Hotel in Soho, picks up the bound stack of newspapers just delivered, a copy to be slipped under the door of each paying guest before they wake. As he does so, he notices something familiar about the front-page picture. His tired eyes peer closer and he realizes it's her, the one who used to visit every Thursday afternoon; the one he had joked about with the reception staff, while wishing it were him being led up the stairs in her wake. He thinks hard. He can't remember what name they knew her by, but he's pretty sure it wasn't Arabella Lane.

"Eleanor, Eleanor!"

Someone is shaking her. Eleanor begins to scream and a hand clamps over her mouth. *"Eleanor, stop it, stop it now."*

She bites the hand and hears a loud, "Fuck!" It brings her back into the room, where her uncle and aunt are both staring at her, Ian in pajamas and Susan wearing her dressing gown.

"For god's sake, she's drawn blood," Ian says, hopping from foot to foot, holding his injured hand under his armpit.

Eleanor staggers backward, until the island bench jars against her vertebra. She is dimly aware of her surroundings, the black-and-white tiled floor, the stainless steel appliances. But she can see flames too, through stinging eyes. The heat of them is all over her, she smells burning wood and vegetation.

"Eleanor," Susan comes over and grabs both her shoulders. "Do you know where you are? You're in London, with me and Ian." She turns back to Ian. "She was sleepwalking," she hisses. "You're not meant to wake them."

"I'm calling Gillian," Ian mutters, striding out of the room.

That is the last thing Eleanor wants. The mention of her mother's name jolts Eleanor from her stupor. She opens her mouth to call after Ian, tell him to stop, that she'll talk to her mother later. But he has already gone.

Susan helps her onto one of the high kitchen chairs. "Sit down," she says, and steps across the room, returning moments later to hand over a glass of water. They say nothing as Eleanor drinks the cool, clear liquid, grateful for its soothing coldness.

Susan perches on the seat next to her before she speaks. "Marisa says you ran out of the office this morning." Her tone has lost its usual sharp edge, but she still sounds more matter-of-fact than kind. "What happened?"

Eleanor remembers the angry voice on the phone so clearly. "You had a call from Nathan. He said he wants you to do Arabella's eulogy at the memorial on Wednesday. And—and he wants you to fire me."

Susan looks away, staring at a spot in the corner of the ceiling. "I spoke to him this afternoon, and he repeated both things." She sighs. "Look, it's best if you don't come into work for the time being. I have lots of contacts in different places. I'll sort something else out for you after Christmas. It's a shame, but I can't see another way around it."

Eleanor frowns. *It's a shame?* Susan has never intimated that she enjoyed having her niece at Parker & Lane in the slightest.

Susan goes across to the fridge, opens it, and collects a bottle of water. "I used to sleepwalk now and again when I was younger," she says as she pulls another glass from a cupboard. "And most times it was because I was under some kind of stress." She pours herself a drink, takes a long gulp, then turns to face Eleanor. "Is this something you do often, Eleanor? We need to know—I don't want you scaring the girls."

At the mention of stress, Eleanor remembers the ring. Immediately she recoils from her aunt's gaze.

Where could it have gone? Her prime suspect was the housekeeper but surely she wouldn't have kept it? When the girls had got home from school, she had asked them, as nicely as she could, if they had been in her bedroom while she was out. Both of them had denied it, which left Susan, who may have seen Eleanor sneaking it back into its hiding place when she'd burst in on her the other day. Or her uncle, whose reasons she couldn't imagine, but who was still a suspect simply because she couldn't rule him out.

But whoever had the ring had chosen not to talk to her about it. Which meant what? How much more was going on than she knew?

She has forgotten that Susan is waiting for an answer, until she realizes her aunt is staring at her. "Eleanor?" she prompts.

Eleanor studies her water glass. "I used to sleepwalk as a child," she admits. "But I haven't done so for a long time. The last thing I want to do is scare the girls, but it's not something I can always control."

Ian comes back into the room. "Your mum wants to talk to you," he says, holding out his cell phone.

Reluctantly, Eleanor takes it. "Hello, Mum."

"Eleanor," her mother's voice is tremulous, "what's going on?"

"I'm fine."

"Really? Sleepwalking in the night doesn't sound fine. Biting Ian's hand doesn't sound fine."

Eleanor sighs. "I know, but it's all a big mix-up. I didn't mean either of those things to happen."

"Perhaps it would be better if . . ."

Eleanor is sure that the next words will be *come home*. She is too exhausted to stand up for herself, and the tears begin to overwhelm her. "Mum, I promise I'm fine. Please, just give me a chance—" Her voice cracks.

Without asking, Ian takes the phone back from Eleanor. "Gillian, this isn't doing anyone any good. Don't fret, I shouldn't have called. We've all been under a lot of pressure lately, we haven't been helping Eleanor to settle in. I'll fix it, okay? I'll talk to you in the morning. Please."

Eleanor can only guess at her mother's response, but Ian hangs up moments later without saying anything more.

"Eleanor," he begins, sitting down at the table, laying his palms together as he speaks, as though to reinforce his point. "Your mum says you only sleepwalk when you're highly stressed. Can you please tell us what is going on?"

"I—" She hesitates, looking between them. *Which one of you has the ring? Why are you not mentioning it?*

"This is to do with Arabella, isn't it?" Susan asks. "What did the police say to you?"

Eleanor looks from one to the other. Neither face gives anything away—they both look as exhausted as she feels.

"They just want to know what happened," she begins. "But—but I can't remember anything, because Arabella put something in my drink, some sort of drug."

Ian puts his head in his hands, while Susan's jaw tightens. Eleanor waits, unsure how to read their responses. "Arabella drugged you?" Susan asks eventually, her voice low.

Eleanor nods.

"Are you sure?"

"I watched her do it. She acted like it was going to be fun. I didn't know . . ."

Ian looks up again. "Why are you only just telling us this?"

"I . . . I was scared." She speaks slowly, picking her words with caution. "When she slapped Nathan and ran out, I went after her. Will Clayton followed us both and—and he saw I was very upset and brought me back to the party. Arabella came back too, a while later, looking for Nathan, and spoke to me before she disappeared again. But I don't remember anything about that. I can't even remember getting home."

"We found you outside at two in the morning, soaked and freezing," Susan says. "Ian had to carry you upstairs to bed."

"It looked like you'd collapsed on the doorstep," Ian adds. "You kept mumbling that you couldn't find your keys."

Eleanor gapes at them, recalling the brief vision she'd had of herself lying there. It had really happened. No wonder she had felt so awful the next day. She pictures herself shivering on the cold concrete, surrounded by darkness, oblivious to the shadows. "Why didn't you tell me?"

"We were going to talk to you about it straight after it happened, last Friday," Ian says. "Once you'd had time to recover. I spoke to Gillian, and she assured us it was out of character for you. But then, with Arabella—" To Eleanor's surprise, Ian's voice cracks as he says her name. "Events overtook us."

Eleanor stares at her uncle, hunched over, one hand covering his eyes. He seems so . . . so broken. Her thoughts begin to shift, her mind pouncing on possibilities that seem outrageous. She frowns.

"Oh, for god's sake, Ian." Susan is watching her closely. "And I thought you were so good at deceit."

Ian's head snaps up. His mouth opens but no words come out. He looks at Susan, but she closes her eyes for a moment in apparent disgust, then gets up and walks out of the room.

Once Susan has gone, Eleanor turns to Ian. "What's going on?" she asks. But she suspects she may already know.

Ian's face is white. "Oh god, Eleanor, I . . . I was having an affair with Arabella," he says. He covers his eyes again with the palms of his hands, and takes a few long, ragged breaths.

Eleanor's mouth falls open. In the midst of this revelation, she tries to picture her uncle with Arabella. To her surprise she can see them together. In fact, she realizes, it's easier to think of him with Arabella than it is with Susan. There's an old-world charm about her uncle that would have complemented the gregarious Arabella she remembers at the party.

Ian is still talking. "Susan and I, we have had a few problems—not that I'm blaming her for this," he adds quickly. "It is all my fault. I kept trying to end it, but Arabella wouldn't accept it was over, and I couldn't completely turn my back on her. She wanted me to help her get away from Nathan—she was frightened of him. He seemed to have a hold on her that

I never understood, although after seeing what he did to you on Sunday, I dread to think what she suffered from him behind closed doors."

Ian falls silent, and Eleanor waits. She can see he is struggling. Instinctively, she puts a hand on his, and he jumps.

He looks back up at her. "I didn't know what to do. Susan and the girls—they didn't deserve any of it," he says, his eyes seeming to plead for leniency. "When I first explained my position to Arabella, she seemed to understand. But she would often call me when she was upset, and sometimes she'd insinuate how easy it would be to tell Susan everything. A short time ago I was an idiot and gave her quite a large loan. Of course we're not going to get it back now, and I've had to confess everything to Susan—the money, the affair. She may have had her suspicions, but it's quite another thing to have them confirmed."

"But . . . but she seems so calm."

"Susan keeps her emotions very well hidden, but believe you me they are all there," Ian says. "I suspect she's not calm right now. I think she's glacial with rage."

Eleanor shudders. Ian reaches for her hand. "Eleanor, you cannot say anything to anyone. I have already been to talk to the police, and I've told them everything. Now I'm desperately trying to keep this from getting out because if it does, it will make Susan's job untenable, and she's worked harder than you'd ever imagine to achieve all that she has. But if Ernie or Nathan find out about this, they'll be livid. And Susan will have to make a choice. We're just hoping these investigations reach a quick conclusion. It's a terrible time, but the fact Arabella latched onto you the night she died has just made it worse. I can't help but wonder if she singled you out because of me."

Eleanor considers this. Had Arabella known that she was talking to her lover's niece? Did that put yet another shade of complexity on the events that followed? She's exhausted by all the questions and the worry. She can't deal with all this alone.

"I had her ring," Eleanor blurts out. "I . . . I thought you might have it."

Ian stares at her. "*What?* What are you talking about?"

"Arabella's engagement ring. I don't know how I got it. It was in my bag when I woke up on Friday morning. I didn't tell the police because I was afraid of what it might mean when I couldn't remember anything. So I hid it under the bed. But I forgot about housekeeping yesterday, so my bedclothes got changed, and now it's gone." She pauses. "Do you know what happened to it?"

"No." Ian has gone pale. He looks horrified. "I don't. Eleanor, are you sure it was Arabella's?"

"Pretty sure. I've never seen anyone else with a ring like that—it's the huge sapphire, surrounded by diamonds."

"Oh fuck, *fuck*, that sounds like it," he breathes. "I remember the day she first showed us. They stood in our lounge, and she was beaming while Nathan informed us it was worth over forty thousand dollars—he seemed prouder of that fact than of his new fiancée." He leans closer to Eleanor. "Why didn't you tell us straightaway? *Fuck*." He bangs a hand on the table and Eleanor jumps.

"I was scared," Eleanor replies quickly, her voice moving up a pitch as she tries to assuage him. "I thought I might be in trouble."

"You *are* in trouble, Eleanor." Her uncle's face is gray now. "Have you heard of 'perverting the course of justice'? You've withheld information from the police. If they find out about it, they will wonder what else you are hiding."

Panic fills Eleanor's chest. "But . . . I was terrified. I thought someone might have been setting me up. Won't they understand that?"

"I don't know, Eleanor, but even if they did, what are you going to do now, if you've lost it?"

"I don't think I've lost it," she objects. "I think it's been taken. If you don't have it," she continues, "then could the housekeeper have taken it?"

Ian is still staring at her. "We've known Lilian for years. I really can't see her making off with a ring that doesn't belong to her. I'm sure she'd come to me."

"What if she went to Susan instead? It's a woman's ring, after all."

Ian thinks for a moment. "But Susan was at work yesterday, and Lilian hardly ever sees her since she always works during the day. And if Susan knew you were hiding Arabella's ring in your room, I'm pretty sure she would confront you. Unless—unless—oh, I don't know, she's not herself at the moment, but what reason would she have for keeping this to herself?"

"Has she told you that Nathan asked her to do the eulogy at the memorial on Wednesday?"

"No—oh god, *no*," Ian slams his fist onto the table again, "she hasn't told me." He leans forward, and Eleanor automatically recoils from his wide, hollow, red-rimmed eyes. "I'm so scared for her, Eleanor, I'm scared for all of us. I'm not sure how close she is to the edge." He gets up. "I'll talk to her. Don't tell her anything about the ring. Don't go to work tomorrow—hang tight here, and I'll see what I can do."

As Eleanor watches him leave, it's hard for her to believe that just a few weeks ago she didn't know this family at all. She'd come here with such high hopes—not entirely sure what to expect, but something better than this. Something that might prove the fissures within her own family were an anomaly; that people were capable of doing more—of being more—for one another. But now, embroiled in circumstances that seem to have come out of nowhere, it seems she has been wrong again. And it occurs to Eleanor for the first time that Susan and Ian may need her help as much as she needs theirs.

17

the shed

On their first night in the shed, Eleanor pretends to go to sleep straightaway, but really she is squeezing her eyes shut, trying to ignore the smell of damp earth and her brother's farts, desperate to remember the details of her old home. Her real home: the place where she had emerged "ridiculously fast" from her mother's womb in October 1995, caught in the bathroom by her father's shaking hands before she could slither onto the rumpled, towel-sodden floor.

At Tippington Road, she had conducted meticulous daily inspections since the time she could crawl. As a result, she knew the place with an intimacy she couldn't possibly forget.

On the bathroom shelf, there was often a dancing spider smaller than her thumbnail, whose back looked like an obsidian eye.

Cicadas serenaded each another in the bushes next to her bedroom window.

If she got on her belly and felt around underneath the couch, she would find a rip in the covering, where she could push small trinkets into the foam for as long as she needed to keep them secret.

The space below the bottom shelf of the pantry would gladly harbor a small body wishing to hide.

The kitchen cupboards had springs that liked to eat fingers if they weren't quickly withdrawn.

The hot tap of the bath had lost its splotch of red paint but could still produce scalding water well before you were ready for it. Eleanor knew the sting of burned fingers; she knew where the salve was kept.

There were a few floorboards to avoid stepping on in order to safely explore the detritus of Aiden's room. She would take a CD carefully from its box and steal away to listen to it on her brother's old Discman. She was already acquainted with Pearl Jam, Good Charlotte, and the Red Hot Chili Peppers, music she suspects will never be played in the shed.

Her brother sleeps above her on one bunk, her mother and father on another within arm's reach. Until now, she has never truly appreciated her own room in Tippington Road, with its purple wall and stenciled fairies, its soft gray carpet, and four shelves of books that have now been sold or put in storage. In Tippington Road she would rush into her parents' bedroom at the front of the house as soon as she woke, pulling the blinds up to let in the light from their quiet suburban street. Always, her mother and father pretended to sleep until she crawled along the narrow trough between their bodies and woke them with kisses that were instantly, gratifyingly returned. She liked to lay her head between theirs and look from left to right. Her parents' pillows had different smells: a musky cinnamon for her father; a sea-scented soap for her mother. Their morning breath wasn't so pleasant, but she endured it to stay close to them. At night she would hang out in Aiden's room, begging him to play Uno with her or to read her a story. Either that or she would drift toward sleep as he practiced his guitar, until her mother scooped her up and transferred her to her own bed.

But now another family with toddler twins have purchased the house, and she can see all too clearly those careless boys marauding through her hiding places with their toy cars and planes, squashing the spider as it dances, crushing the cicadas as they sing. They will not value the treasures of Tippington Road as she does. How dare these strangers snatch her beloved house for themselves and call it "home." And how dare her parents hand it over without a care and bring them all to this tin box to live among spiders and reptiles. To this place where there is nothing good or beautiful at all.

18

missing

*E*oin McDowell, Chief Pathologist, leads detectives Prashad and Kirby into his office and waits for them to take a seat. "We've undertaken an MDCT—a virtual autopsy," he explains. "It has confirmed drowning, due to a number of factors: frothy fluid and congestion in the lungs, as well as fluid and sediment in the stomach. And there is also this on her upper right arm." He puts a photo in front of the detectives.

"Jeez, is that . . ." Kirby leans in.

"Yes, it could be a handprint bruise," McDowell agrees. "The thumbprint is on one side and fingers on the other, see, as though she was held hard. It's old, nearly a week and fading out. However, whoever grabbed Arabella Lane a week ago and made this mark did so with a brute and painful force. And don't forget those red marks on her wrist too, which could also be consistent with being held against her will, even though they didn't have time to bruise." He pauses as he studies the picture in front of him. "If you're considering murder, then this may be your man," he states, tapping repeatedly on the photo.

On Tuesday, Eleanor wakes and realizes she doesn't have to get up for work. Instead, she lies in bed, with everything going around and around in her head.

She hasn't sleepwalked for years, and it still has such strong associations with trauma that, even hours later, she is uneasy. She had been comforted by the assumption she had grown out of it; that it was a childhood habit. Her mother told her she'd first sleepwalked when she was very small, surprising her parents by marching into the lounge room and collecting the remote controls for the TV and DVD player, taking them back to bed and putting them under her pillow. That was in their first house—Teppington Road—or was it Tippington? Those memories have faded and warped, since there's so much of her now that never belonged there. Besides, to even think of the place means allowing her thoughts to wander back through all the nightmares that came later. She feels like an intruder into her own memories nowadays, unsure whether she is embellishing anything. She wishes she could just leave them alone, pristine and untouched, rather than revisiting to sully them.

When she checks her phone there are two texts from her mom, different phrases asking how she's feeling, telling her it's okay if she wants to come home. There's one from Will too:

> Have you told anyone yet?

She doesn't reply to any of the texts. How on earth is she going to tell Will she's lost the ring? She wishes she'd never involved him in the first place. She can't tell her uncle that Will knows about the ring either; she doesn't want to induce more panic.

Hunger eventually drives her out from between the covers. As she pads down the stairs from the attic room, she hears noises farther along the corridor, rustling and banging. She stops. Everyone should be at work or school right now.

It's coming from Ian and Susan's room, and she's never been in there. She heads for the next set of stairs, but more strange sounds continue from the room down the corridor. There's no way she'll be able to relax without investigating.

She turns back and edges forward until she is close to the door frame. She peers around the corner.

Her uncle stands in the middle of the room—drawers on the floor next to his feet, the bed a mess of clothes and belongings. His chest rises and falls rapidly, one hand pressed against his temple, as though he's deciding what he might trash next.

Eleanor tries to creep away, but she stands on something hard and her hand bangs against the wall as she reaches to steady herself. She looks down to see a tiny Barbie stiletto hidden within the thick carpet. She reaches to pick it up.

"Eleanor?"

She turns to find her uncle standing in the doorway, watching her. "I didn't want to disturb you," she says. "I just heard a noise and was worried. I thought you were at work."

He throws his arms up in the air. "I should be, but I can't think straight. I'm going crazy about this ring. I was having a look through Susan's things," he says. "You are sure Arabella was wearing it at the party?"

"That's when I first noticed it."

He pales. "Show me where you hid it."

She trudges back up the stairs, her stomach growling in protest. She flings open the door to her room and points to the mattress. "It was just under there."

Ian heaves the mattress up, propping it against the window and looking between every slat, then getting down on his hands and knees to scour the floor.

"I'm sorry," Eleanor says, for lack of anything else to offer.

He doesn't answer her.

"What shall we do with it, if we find it?"

Ian sits back on his knees, staring towards the window. "Good question. I don't know." He looks at Eleanor. "Are you sure you can't remember how you came by it?"

She shakes her head. "Believe me, I've been trying everything, but I'm drawing a blank. I'm not going to remember anything now, I don't think, because of the drugs. I keep asking myself why she would do that to me."

He grimaces. "She liked company when she was indulging herself. She used to encourage me to drink too. It made her feel better about her own vices, I think." He stares toward the window. "The drink and drugs sometimes turned her into somebody else, but without them she was . . . she was . . ." He stops, shakes his head and gets up slowly. "I'm going to have to ask Susan directly about the ring, but perhaps I'll leave it until after the memorial. I don't want to put any more stress on her. What a fucking nightmare." He maneuvers the mattress back into place and sits heavily on the bed. Eleanor stands by the door and waits, unsure.

Ian is watching her. "I'm going crazy, Eleanor. I have this horrible feeling of being followed all the time. And now—with the ring—it's like someone's trying to set me up."

I feel exactly the same, Eleanor wants to say. But before she can, she hears a door bang downstairs.

She jumps. "Who's that?"

"Don't worry, it's just Naeve. She said she didn't want to go to school today. All her friends are on a high this close to Christmas, and she's struggling—she came home in tears yesterday, and she looked so pale this morning I let her stay home. She isn't talking to me much, and I know she's deeply affected by Arabella's death, but I'm not sure how to reach her."

"Do you think she knows about you and Arabella?"

He grimaces. "No, I don't think so. We were careful."

"What if Susan—"

Ian swings to face her. "She wouldn't," he snaps. Then he stops. "Oh, I don't know—maybe she would . . . We haven't shared a room since she found out. I hardly get to see her alone anyway, and I'm not even sure if she's speaking to me." He hesitates. "Perhaps you could you chat to Naeve," he suggests, his tone softening, "see if you can discover what's troubling her? I want her to have support from somewhere, and she and Susan have always tended to clash." He gets up. "I have to get some work done. I'll see you later."

Eleanor trails him downstairs and sees him close the door to his office. She heads to the kitchen to fix a quick breakfast of fruit and yogurt, then goes to find Naeve. She suspects this may be a doomed mission, because

Naeve hasn't spoken to her much since Friday; she's not sure she has been forgiven for letting the girls switch on the news.

She eventually finds her cousin in the conservatory at the back of the house, sitting in one of the upright chairs, staring out at the garden, hugging her knees to her chest. Eleanor takes a seat close to her and trains her eyes toward the window too, imagining how lovely this view would be in summer. For now, it's spoiled by the rain spatters on the glass, and the gray pall that descends from a bitter sky to hang over the perennials.

To Eleanor's surprise, almost as soon as she arrives, Naeve gets up to leave. Eleanor puts her mug and plate down quickly. "Naeve, wait!" Without thinking she reaches for the girl's arm, and as she pulls slightly Naeve turns, and Eleanor sees such a look of terror on her face that she flinches and pulls away.

Immediately, Naeve flees, with Eleanor chasing her. "Wait, Naeve, what's wrong?" As they pass through the hallway, her uncle emerges from his study, drawn by the commotion, to see his daughter scurrying up the stairs. On the first floor, Naeve runs into her room with both of them in pursuit. Eleanor expects the door to be slammed on them, but instead Naeve scurries over to her bedside table, pulls open a drawer, and turns to face them.

Arabella's ring glints in the daylight, pinched between Naeve's fingers. "Is this what you want?" she yells.

Ian holds his hands up, drawing closer to her. "Where did you find that, Naeve?" he asks, his tone low.

"Lilian gave it to me for safekeeping." Her voice is half screech, half sob. "I recognized it straightaway." She turns to Eleanor. "Did you kill her?" she demands, her voice cracking, her strength visibly wavering. "Did you kill Arabella?"

Ian steps forward quickly and takes her in his arms. "Of course she didn't, Naeve," he says, but Naeve pushes him angrily away.

"The newspapers say her death is suspicious. And when you carried Eleanor to bed, she was all wet and dirty. Are you telling lies for her too?"

"Naeve!" Ian leans back from her and holds both her shoulders, forcing her to look at him. "Eleanor did *not* kill Arabella! You saw the state of her—did she look like she could have harmed anyone? Somebody drugged her at the party. None of this is her fault. Now, give me the ring, you shouldn't have that."

Naeve hands it over, and Eleanor watches him slip it into his pocket. He pulls his daughter close and lets her sob against his chest. Then, to Eleanor's surprise, he holds out his arm to motion for her to come too.

Initially she welcomes the embrace, but quickly she finds herself stiffening in Ian's arms. She thinks of the confident way he denied Eleanor's involvement. His affair with Arabella. The way he has just swiftly pocketed the ring without asking, even though it was surely—technically—still Eleanor's decision to make.

"I'm scared, Daddy," Naeve snuffles against his shirt. "Please tell me that we're all going to be okay."

Does Eleanor imagine it or does she feel Ian tense as he holds them, as he whispers reassuring words into his daughter's hair, keeping Eleanor close, so she cannot see his face.

19

christmas

December 2004

The sand sneaking into Eleanor's pockets and shoes is not white but a dirty red. It's a week until Christmas, and they are about to spend it in a shed. A year ago, they went to the beach on Christmas Day—the Santa hats they tip out of boxes this evening are still encrusted with dried saltwater. Eleanor pushes one against her face and breathes, inhaling memories, feeling them float and settle within her, a promise that there are still worlds beyond this one.

The shed has metamorphosed. No cobwebs anymore. The concrete floor now appears as a series of stepping stones around boxes and badly wrapped furniture, portable cooking equipment, open suitcases doubling as closets and a series of color-coded tubs pressed into operation as sinks, storage, and bins. In one corner are two dilapidated pine bunk beds. Everything is flat and depressed, from the mattresses and pillows to her mother's hair and her brother's eyes.

Outside, nothing has changed. The land still belongs to the kangaroos that come through at dusk, the possums that sometimes land with a clatter on the shed's roof, the cockatoos and galahs that roost in every available tree and greet the dawn with frenetic screeches, ensuring no one ever gets to sleep.

Eleanor's father is relentlessly positive. He assures them that once the slab is laid, they will be able to get building. He celebrates the triumph of installing electricity in the shed, two plug sockets in perpetual demand. He attends multiple bricklaying courses. He takes advice from everyone they meet. Today he insisted they open the Christmas box and hang decorations on nails—he's put tinsel around the dartboard they haven't yet used, and there's a fake wilting holly wreath fixed to the front of the shed door. He has somehow sourced a lopped-off tip of a pine tree, stuck it in a pot, and brought it inside, knowing they don't have enough room for much of a tree but determined to find space for something. For the past few hours since dinner, Eleanor has been tasked with decorating the puny thing. She begins with tenderness, determined to add some cheer to the place, but the tinsel overwhelms the tree. It sags, smothered, as though begging for respite. She winds ornaments around weak, spindly branches, and they immediately shed their needles from the shock of assault. She pricks her fingers on these cast-offs; they catch in her socks and poke their sharp, unforgiving tips into her soles. Eventually, she gives up and leaves the tree stooped and disheveled in the corner, an awkward house guest trying and failing to fit in.

She can't decide whether to draw attention to her creative catastrophe or not. Her mother is organizing a bag of clothes for the launderette, and her brother is outside somewhere. Aiden disappears regularly and no one asks what he does. He can't go far, surely, even with a flashlight—it's pitch black out there. "Fifteen-year-old boys need some space," her mother had replied when Eleanor asked about it.

Her dad is reading one of his DIY manuals, but he stops when he notices her step away from the tree. In the shed, you cannot move without all eyes turning toward you.

"It looks great," he says.

You're such a liar, she replies in her head. Since they started living in such close quarters, she has realized just how much her parents lie about everything, big and small. It's disturbing.

"What do you want to do now?"

"I haven't written my Santa letter yet."

"I think Santa is on a tight budget this year," Martin laughs, "so don't ask for too much." She catches her mother glaring at the back of his head as he leafs through his book. His words sink in. That look sinks in.

A horrible thought pops up. She can't shoo it away.

They lie about everything.

No, she tells herself. *You can trust your own family to tell you the truth, of course you can.*

Eleanor sits at the small portable table they use for dining. "Mum, can I have some cake?"

"I thought you wanted to write that letter."

Her elbows are on the tabletop, fists pushed hard against her cheeks. Her eyes, glistening, squint at nothing. "Perhaps I'll just have a surprise this year."

Is it her imagination or does she see her mother's shoulders loosen as she hears these words? "All right. And yes, of course you can have some cake."

Moments later, a bowl is set down in front of her, a neat triangular slice of chocolate cake inside it. She picks up her spoon, toys with it, finds she doesn't want to eat it now.

Her mom sits next to her on a folding chair and puts a hand on her arm. "You okay?"

She nods, not trusting herself to speak. Since they moved here, Eleanor has felt an unspoken need to be gentle with her mother, not to blame her for things that are beyond her control. Perhaps it's because Aiden seems to give her such a hard time, huffing and snarling through each day, scowling as she speaks, growling in reply. Can't he see that their mother is already as weary of this life as they are? It's their father Eleanor is furious with, for pushing his dreams onto all of them.

Her father closes his book with a snap, jumping her from her thoughts. "I'll go and find Aiden," he says. "It's getting late." She hears the familiar grinding squeak of the deadbolt, and then she is alone with her mother.

"Come here, love." Gillian pulls Eleanor onto her lap. Eleanor rests her head on her mother's shoulder, her worries unwinding as Gillian strokes her hair. *Ask her,* a voice insists. *Ask her. She'll tell you he's fat and funny and lives in the North Pole. She'll promise he's real.*

Neither of them speaks. The shed door bangs softly on its hinges. The portable fan whirls in a fury, unable to cool the room.

20

carols

"**J**ez, come here for a sec."

Philip Bevan is dressed, ready for work, scanning through the morning news as he reads the iPad. Jez pads through in his dressing gown and kisses Philip's head. "What is it?"

"Isn't that the woman we saw by the river last Thursday? The one freezing her tits off in the rain."

Jez peers closer. "Yeah, I think you're right."

Philip turns to his boyfriend with wide eyes. "She's Arabella Lane. She's that woman who was found floating in the Thames near work."

Jez picks up Philip's cell phone and holds it out. "Then we'd better call the police."

In Naeve's bedroom, Ian, Naeve, and Eleanor regard one another warily. "Eleanor had a bit too much to drink at the party last week," Ian explains to Naeve as he moves to lean against the dresser. "It happens. I was disturbed too, when I saw the state of her, and I'm relieved she managed to get herself home safely."

"I'm sorry, Naeve," Eleanor adds quickly, wondering where Ian is leading this conversation. "The last thing I would ever want to do is scare you."

Naeve looks from one to the other. Eleanor opens her mouth to add more, but then stops. She sees that Ian is trying to shield Naeve from the scarier truth, that Eleanor might have been drugged against her will. And yet it makes her want to scream. She has witnessed too much of this sort of deception in her life, and she can see already from the suspicion in Naeve's eyes that they haven't really protected her from anything. Naeve knows there's more to the story; and now she understands she's not allowed inside it. Her father has just made her feel more alone and uncertain than ever. It's all Eleanor can do not to put her hand out to clasp Naeve's, but she stops herself, knowing her reasons might be misread.

"I don't remember much," Eleanor says gently instead. "I found the ring in my purse in the morning, and I took it to work because I had no idea then that Arabella had died. I thought I was going to hand it back and find out how it came to be there in the first place. I was hoping that by the end of the day it would just be a stupid anecdote. But when they announced she was dead, I was shocked because I couldn't remember anything. I came straight back here, but I didn't tell anyone for a little while because I was too scared. That's why I hid it. I just didn't know what to do."

Naeve's eyes are wide. "But . . . but," Naeve says, glancing between them, "if you don't remember some of the night, how do you . . . how do you know you weren't involved?"

"Because she's barely taller than you and she could hardly stand up," Ian says, with a sharpness that makes them both tense. "And Arabella is around five foot ten and goes to the gym all the time—she's had kickboxing lessons, for god's sake. There is no way Eleanor could overpower her, especially while she was under the influence."

He sounds so certain, so commanding. As Eleanor and Naeve stare at him, trying to take in this fact and weigh it against all they know, Eleanor can already think of the counterarguments. She certainly doesn't have a water-tight alibi. However, Naeve nods, even though her eyes brim with tears.

Instinctively, Eleanor reaches out and puts a hand on Naeve's arm, ignoring the way she flinches. "Naeve, look at me."

Naeve turns slowly.

"I'm just as scared as you are about all this, and I promise I would never put you in danger." She holds Naeve's gaze to implore her cousin to trust her.

Eventually, Naeve nods. "It's just that when I saw Daddy carrying you inside you looked like a mess, I didn't know what to think."

"That's completely understandable," Ian interjects, "but we have to consider the repercussions before we go to the police. Your mother is caught up in all this too—she could lose her job for something that's nothing to do with her."

Naeve looks down. "Who cares," she mumbles. It's not subtle enough for either of them to miss, and Eleanor watches her uncle's face darken.

"Really, Naeve? Really? You don't want to live in this house anymore? You don't want to go to your beautiful and very pricey school anymore? You don't want all your clothes or all those gizmos you've got in your bedroom anymore? You don't want to go to your super expensive art classes anymore? Do you know how much your mother's job provides for you?"

Eleanor silently digests her uncle's list of valuable assets in Naeve's life. She wonders if her cousin attributes the same worth to them, or if there are other things she might prize more.

Naeve's expression has hardened at her father's words, but she doesn't object. She stares defiantly, and father and daughter face off for a protracted moment.

"I know you understand me, Naeve," Ian says, his tone noticeably colder than a few minutes ago. "In an ideal world, of course we would go to the police, because they would believe we were innocent until proven guilty. But we live in the real world, and things don't work that way. And that is why you will not say a word of this to anyone until we have figured it out. Our family is too important to be dragged through the mud—because that's what it will be,

Naeve—walking down school corridors with people whispering and pointing; and who knows how long it will last, and what will come of it."

Eleanor watches Naeve's tough stance falter as her face pales, even though she is obviously trying hard to stay composed. Cold winter light has dulled the whole room. Could she be reading this wrong, or is she really watching her uncle blackmail his child into silence, when they all know that the ring should go straight to the police, whatever it means for them? She stares at Ian. Is he just trying to protect them, or does he have more to cover up? Because despite his profession of openness, Naeve is still in the dark about Ian's relationship with Arabella—and that is bound to cloud his motives. Is he trying to protect the family, or is he just looking after himself?

Ian turns back to his daughter, and when he speaks his voice is a thousand times softer than it was only seconds before. "You must be exhausted from all this worry. Come and sit in the family room with me, we'll put the TV on—don't tell your mother—and you can try to get some rest."

Naeve lets him lead her away, but Eleanor cannot summon up the energy to move. Her mind has flown over the tower blocks and spires of London, back through the wormholes of time, to sit once again at the bar opposite Arabella, watching her hand move, the powder being sprinkled into her drink, imploring herself not to reach for it, not to be so stupid, but of course she does, and she is.

And then . . . is there anything stored in her brain between the moment Arabella slapped Nathan and the next morning? Dark blurry shapes, the rain on her face—perhaps—and that vague memory of lying on the front steps to the house as the porch light goes on. However, now she's been shown the CCTV footage, and Will has told her what he saw, her imagination is filling in other blanks: the pure white of a lifeless body in cold water, the scream of a woman falling. She is already uncertain as to what counts as memory and what is being sketched in by witnesses and theories other than her own. These new nightmares are beginning to taunt her, and she knows this feeling all too well. She understands that if she allows such provocation to linger in her mind for long enough it becomes its own reality, one that's far more terrifying than anything truly real. She also knows that if she fights it, then it will take that dark energy and use it to become more vivid and more powerful. So, what is left? How can she ever truly escape?

"Eleanor!"

She jumps as she realizes her uncle is standing opposite her once more.

"You're very pale," he says as she makes an effort to focus on him. "Are you going to be sick?"

"No, no," she waves her hand, "I'll be okay."

His gaze narrows. "Have you remembered anything?"

She closes her eyes for a moment and says softly, "I wish I could." Then she focuses on him again. "Tell me what happened when you found me on the front step."

Ian moves closer. "Your clothes and hair were wet, and your feet were dirty, but it was raining outside, and goodness knows how long you'd been there before I found you."

"So why did you come downstairs?"

He hesitates. "I heard a noise."

"From me? What kind of noise?"

Ian doesn't speak for a moment, studying her solemnly. "I don't know if it was you or not," he says finally. "I just heard something downstairs, so I got up to check, and that's when I found you."

Eleanor thinks through his words. There is more she wants to ask about this, but there are also other pressing questions.

"What are you going to do with the ring?" she says. *Because I found it, so surely it should be my choice,* she adds silently. *Mine.*

Ian stares over her head as though thinking hard. "I promise you, in ordinary circumstances we would take it straight to the police. But we have to think through the consequences. You still don't remember anything, and the ring could get you into serious trouble now. You saw what Nathan was like the other day—he's dangerous when he chooses to be, and he doesn't need any more ammunition. I need some time to think about all this. You can see how affected the girls are, I can't bear the thought of frightening them any further. Don't do anything for now, Eleanor, please."

His words make sense, and she finds herself nodding, wanting to protect the girls too. Yet Eleanor fears she has set them all on a terrible path. Suddenly, she is nine years old again, sobbing on a bed in a moldy motel room, her mother's arms around her. The pressure builds in her head, but before the memories can sharpen, Ian's phone begins to ring.

Quickly, he pulls it out of his pocket and looks at it. "It's Susan. Just give me a second."

He connects the call. "Yep," he says tersely. He listens for a moment, his face getting redder and redder. His voice, when he finds it, is loud. "Oh no . . . okay. I know . . . *I know*. There's been a lot going on here, poor Naeve is in a state . . . Yes, *I know* that, for fuck's sake, Susan, I'm going right now."

By the time he ends the call, he is gripping the phone as though trying to throttle it. He lets out a long sigh as he gets up.

"We forgot Savvie's carol concert," he says. "Susan is furious. Savvie is crying at school, apparently, because we weren't there. I've got to go and get her."

He pushes his chair in and pats his pocket, catching Eleanor's eye briefly. "I'd totally forgotten it was Christmas, to be honest," he says, before he hurries from the room.

Minutes later, the house is silent. Eleanor remains sitting at the bench in the kitchen for some time, thinking through everything she has witnessed. Something is definitely off here, but she's feeling less and less certain of how to interpret it. She had never thought to cast doubt on her uncle's character, but now she is growing increasingly nervous. He's had an affair with Arabella. He's lent her money. He's told Naeve to keep quiet. And now he also has the ring, and no plans to divulge it to the police. Just what the hell is going on?

21

new year's eve

December 2004

They are getting ready for the countdown. It's their first New Year's Eve party in the country, and they have decided to splurge. Pub dinner and dessert. In this backwater there's no fuss about minors staying until midnight, like there would have been in many city places. There are a few other children here, and the landlord brings out a giant game of Connect 4 to keep them busy. Eleanor likes the girl with the purple T-shirt who lets her take a turn; she isn't so keen on the boy who keeps slamming the pieces into the slots before she can get her hands out.

Eleanor's parents are chatting to locals at the bar. There is only one pub in town, so if they want to be accepted, they have to be friendly. Gillian casts regular concerned glances toward the doorway—Aiden has been gone for a while now. As soon as they'd arrived, he'd mumbled something about phoning Brianna in private, then disappeared.

Eventually, Eleanor sees her brother slouch back into the room, his head down and his shoulders so stooped that she hardly recognizes him. But then, so much has changed in the past few weeks. Not even Santa can be trusted any more—no longer an uncomplicated hero, but rather a man of ultimate mystery and, quite possibly, catastrophe. Eleanor refuses to articulate her thoughts to anyone, afraid that if she does, he might be cross at being doubted, and therefore vanish and never return. To her relief, her worries hadn't stopped her stocking from being full on Christmas morning, with books and games and sweets and on the very top a beautiful, soft black-and-white toy dalmatian she'd seen in a city shop before they left town for the back of beyond. This rallied her spirits because at the time her mother had said she thought Eleanor was getting too old for stuffed toys, so it was unlikely she would have purchased this herself. She's brought it tonight, hidden in her bag in case the locals agree with her mother.

Toward midnight, families begin to stick closer together. After a rousing countdown come hugs and kisses and a spontaneous rendition of "Auld Lang Syne," the pub full of awkwardly crossed arms and sweaty clasped hands. "This time next year we'll have built a house," Eleanor's father says during the height of the arm pumping, his stare overly bright and his face shining. Standing across from Aiden, Eleanor notices how red and swollen his eyes are. When he sees her watching him, he scowls.

In the car on the way back to the shed, Eleanor's head lolls against the window as she drifts in and out of sleep. Her mother drives slowly, determined not to begin the new year by killing a roo. Her dad is quiet in the passenger seat save for the occasional beer-sodden snore. Aiden sits next to Eleanor, his long legs invading her side of the car, forcing her knees toward the door. He might be asleep too—every now and again he sighs.

There's nothing to do but watch the dim outlines of small, neat clouds drifting beneath a scattering of diamond dust. The night sky of the outback is beyond anything she's seen in the suburbs, but she'll never give voice to her awe, because it might sound like a tick mark for living in the shed. Her gaze traces the cloudy stripe of the Milky Way, a cataract streak in the eye of the universe, and she feels so small and so lost. So impermanent. As she dozes, she flies to the clouds and sits atop them to watch their tiny matchbox car with its headlights straining in the dark, their lights illuminating such a short distance, and beyond that just one big black void. She wonders what this year will hold for her, for all of them. Right now, she has no idea; only a dragging sense of dread that refuses to leave the pit of her stomach.

22

messages

"**I**'m here investigating a suspicious death," the woman tells Sunaad Shyam, manager of the Chancellor Hotel, as she takes a seat. "We have traced credit cards back to the hotel, and I would like to know if any of your staff recognize either of these two people." She places photographs on the table.

Sunaad isn't entirely surprised by the visit. He picks up his phone and calls in Travis, one of the receptionists. When Travis arrives, smoothing his tie nervously, Sunaad repeats the question.

Travis stares at the photo. "Of course—that's Arabella Lane, we've all read the papers this week." He turns to the woman. "She didn't use that name on the booking, though."

"And was this the man who accompanied her?"

Travis reddens. "Yes." He hesitates, gulps. "But there was more than one," he says quietly.

"How many?"

"A few over time. Three, maybe."

The woman leans forward. "Can you describe them?"

"Well, apart from this guy," he taps the photograph, "there was a blond *man, probably in his thirties. I think he had short wavy hair and olive skin, but there wasn't much else remarkable about him. There used to be another man with longer dark hair who would come in casual clothes, but we haven't seen him around for some time."*

The woman collects up the photographs. "Thank you. I may well be back with more questions, but that will do for now."

Sunaad and Travis stare at one another once she's left. Only then does Sunaad realize that while the woman had spoken exactly like a policewoman, she hadn't offered her credentials, nor had he asked for them.

Once Ian has gone to collect Savannah from her carol concert, Eleanor heads quickly to her bedroom. Her cell phone is still plugged in to the charger, and as she picks it up she sees she has four new messages.

Three are from her mother.

> So how are you this morning?

> Please let me know that everything is okay.

> Eleanor? Please text me back when you see this. I'm worried about you.

They had been sent at half-hour intervals. Eleanor imagines her mother pacing at home, trying to restrain herself from checking her phone every five seconds as she waits for a response. She considers her reply carefully, because Ian is Gillian's brother, and she doesn't know where to begin. She recalls the way her uncle's voice had changed from soft to hard and back again as he talked to Naeve, and decides not to burden her mother unless it becomes absolutely necessary. Her fingers nimbly tap out her response.

> All fine this morning. Hope we didn't scare you last night. Ian isn't used to sleepwalkers!

She hesitates before she presses send, wondering if this sounds a bit too merry, but then she taps the button anyway, knowing she'll be here for hours if she tries to get the tone just right. And besides, she wants to think about the other text. The one from Will.

> What's happening?

Again, she stalls, but then she remembers the way Will consoled her in the stairwell. She can only hope that he will stay on her side.

She dials his number, and as soon as he answers she blurts out, "My uncle found out about the ring, but he's reluctant to tell the police."

There's a pause. "Really? Why?"

"I think he's worried that I might get into a lot of trouble. He's asked for some time to think about it."

"Well, I suppose I understand that," Will says. "I feel the same, or perhaps I'd have gone to the police by now too. I've thought about it some more, and I can't see how you could have got hold of the ring yourself. No offense, but last Thursday I remember thinking I'd never seen someone so out of it and still conscious."

Eleanor takes in his words. The description of her disheveled state is strikingly similar to the one drawn by her uncle for Naeve only an hour ago. While it might be a horrible image, it's comforting too. Although, if all those around her are utterly convinced she was incapable of harming anyone that night, why does she still feel culpable?

"I'm scared," she tells him. "What if the police don't believe me? What if you're right, and someone else is involved? Perhaps I'm being set up. I haven't even got the ring as proof anymore. The police will think I'm either devious or insane."

"You don't strike me as either of those things," Will replies. "What about Susan—could you confide in her? Perhaps she could help."

"I don't know." Eleanor thinks of her aunt's pale, pinched face. "Susan's always at work and I'm not coming in today. She's told me not to come back at all. She thinks Nathan won't be able to handle it. She says she'll help me find work elsewhere after Christmas. What's it like there?"

"Not a lot of fun," Will tells her. "I can't wait to get to the Christmas break. And you never know, perhaps it will be different in the new year," he suggests. There's another pause, then he continues, "You know, I was thinking about Nathan attacking you the other day. In some ways it doesn't surprise me, but the manner of it does. Why would he do it so recklessly, in front of your aunt like that?"

Eleanor thinks this over. "He looked completely out of control at the time. I'm not sure he thought it through. It just happened."

"Maybe," Will says. "Maybe he was just mad with grief. But what if he was mad because of something else? I just keep going back to the way Arabella slapped him at the party—and then the next day she turns up dead. We all know that when someone is murdered, the suspicion often falls on those closest to home—and that's without everyone witnessing a spat beforehand. Nathan must be feeling the heat. I know through work gossip that he's already been questioned multiple times by the police. Perhaps he's trying to find someone else to take the blame."

His words make Eleanor uneasy, but she can see the sense in them. "And perhaps he's hoping that it will be me. Do you think Nathan could be the one trying to set me up?"

"I wouldn't put anything past Nathan," Will replies gruffly.

There's a long silence. "So," Will says eventually, "what do you plan to do now?"

It is the crucial question. The one Eleanor needs to find an answer to, fast. She has come halfway around the world to escape her demons, and yet they seem to have followed her. Fleeing hasn't worked.

So, what does that leave? A fight?

The answer arrives unexpectedly, but as soon as she thinks of it everything seems clear. "I'm going to do everything I can to find out what happened to Arabella," she announces. "I have to. I feel like the ring is some kind of message, urging me to do something. What *happened* that night? I'm not going to sit and wait for the police to come back again. I'm jumping at every little thing already; I constantly have this sense of being watched or followed."

She can't tell him the rest of it, the sleepwalking, the paranoia. She wants his support, not his suspicion.

"That sounds like a plan," Will says softly. "The more information you have to protect yourself, the better. Good on you, Eleanor. And I'll help you, if you like."

"Why?" she asks. "Why do you want to help me?"

"Because Arabella was my friend," he says. "And also, because I want to take you ice-skating properly after all this is over, so I can hold your hand again."

Eleanor is glad Will can't see her surprise. Perhaps he's trying to cheer her up and make her smile, but this suggestion leaves her nervous. *Slow down*, she thinks, but she doesn't want to put him off, and she does like him. When all this is over, she might feel differently.

"The police obviously still have their suspicions too," Will continues. "That's why it's a memorial tomorrow and not a funeral, I reckon. They're holding onto her body for now, while they try to figure it out." His voice drifts away and Eleanor can hear him talking to someone in the background. "I've got to get to a meeting in a minute, so go be a detective, Eleanor," he urges her as he comes back on the line. "Don't give up. You're right. At the worst, you'll be in the same place you are now, but at best you might just find something that will set you free from all this."

As Eleanor hangs up, she hopes he is right.

23

building

February 2005

Things begin to go wrong a month into the New Year, when the slab for the house has been down for two weeks. Her father is a man possessed, leaping up in the morning as soon as it's light, and getting straight to work. He doesn't stop until well after dusk, and brings things into the shed so he can keep slaving away in the evenings. Her mother is focused in a steadier way, churning through a never-ending list of mundane tasks to keep their lives functioning smoothly. Her newest job is as building assistant, and when she is needed, she's expected to drop everything.

Today, Eleanor has come inside for lunch. She is hunting around the shed for a hair tie—it's so hot outside that the back of her neck is damp with sweat. No one wants to spend much time in the shed in the heat of the day. The metal walls absorb the heat, sending it pulsing into the room in headachy bursts.

She had hoped to help with the house construction, but her parents don't have enough time to teach her how to do anything. The days have run into one long, aimless season of throbbing heat, and the only light on the horizon is that school starts in seven days. Eleanor is counting down the hours. The bus will stop on the corner, especially for them. She is nervous, but it will be fine, because Aiden will be there.

Her brother has been very quiet these past few weeks. Gillian had pulled Eleanor aside on New Year's Day and told her not to ask Aiden about Brianna anymore. Meanwhile, Martin had given Aiden two options over the long school vacations: help with the building work, or keep an eye on his sister. To Eleanor's delight, Aiden chose her, and although he's seemed lost in his thoughts at times, she's enjoyed the extra time with him. He's taught her how to make paper cranes, gently mocking her misshapen efforts. Together they have investigated bird's nests and ant hills, caught crickets in jam jars with traps of sugar and newspaper. Aiden has shown her the old bathtub that has been dumped on the property next door, full of murky water and tadpoles. And they agree that they hate the shed. In rebellion, they have collected all the large sticks on the property and built their own cubby house down on the far corner of their block of land, a protest project, hidden away from the noisy building progress, beyond the ridge of the hill and their dad's cursing. Their mother has brought them an old piece of carpet to put inside, and Eleanor goes down there for a while every day with one of her sketchpads or something to read. They have come to an understanding: it is her place in daylight, and Aiden's after dark. Whenever she asks to go with him at night, the answer is the same. "No, Shrimp, stay with the oldies. I need some time to myself."

Sometimes, after dark, when she takes the bags of smelly trash out for her mother, she stands on the lip of the hill and watches the flashlight flicker inside the cubby. She wishes she knew what he was doing in there, but there is no way of finding out. He often takes his guitar with him, but she never hears it being played. Mind you, the length of their block of land is over one thousand feet, she's probably too far away to hear anything, and she's not prepared to creep through the invisible nighttime grass, which might be full of snakes, without at least a flashlight to help her.

She has spent the past week watching her brother carefully. Besides the guitar, he doesn't seem to take anything with him. Their parents seem happy enough to let him go.

But last night, after dinner, she noticed his hand stray under his mattress as he got ready to leave. He quickly put something in his jeans pocket. And now, alone in the shed in the daylight, with Aiden busy shifting bricks for their father, she is determined to find out what it is.

She feels about under his mattress. Pulls out some cigarette papers and a chunk of what looks like dried brown mud. It gives off a pungent, exotic smell. She puts it to her nose and sniffs a few times, sits on the bed, turning it over in her palm.

The door clangs, making her jump. Her mother has returned unexpectedly with an empty washing basket.

"What you got there?" she asks.

"Nothing." Eleanor's hand goes instinctively behind her back.

"Eleanor, show me!" Her mother comes across, and Eleanor reluctantly hands over the little package, trying not to picture Aiden's face if he could see this exchange.

"What is it?" she asks her mother.

Her mother just sighs.

That night Aiden doesn't go to the cubby. The next day, as Eleanor is sitting beneath a sprawling gum tree, she sees him stomping down to the edge of the field. She jumps up and follows him, shading her eyes with her hand to try to see what he is doing, then realizes he's dismantling the cubby, stick by stick, hurling each one into the bushes as he goes. She begins to run—"Aiden, don't!"—but her foot hits an unseen dip and she is sent sprawling to her knees. Alfie the toy dalmatian flies from under her arm and lands hard on the ocher earth. A small cloud of dust rises, and when Eleanor picks him up, the fur is stained red in patches. It is the end of Eleanor's love for the dog—because the stain will never come out, but also because whenever she looks at it, she gets a horrible guilty feeling in her gut.

It takes Eleanor a few days to forgive Aiden for destroying their safe haven, but she's not sure he even notices. For the last week of the school vacation, he keeps away from them all. He won't even talk to her while they wait for the bus on the first day of school, and when her mother kisses her and she gets on first, she sits in a spare double seat at the front, expecting her brother to plonk himself next to her, but he acts like he can't see her, and heads straight for the back.

24

the office

Malcolm O'Halloran dials his wife, but Lucy doesn't answer. He sighs as he hangs up, resisting the temptation to leave her an irate message. She'll have to forgive him soon, won't she? He doesn't want to spend Christmas in a hotel. How many times can he say he's sorry? He'd never have gone near Arabella if he'd known she'd turn vindictive and start leaving messages for him at home. He's thankful she's dead, if he's honest, and it might sound callous but when he thinks of his two boys, pining for their dad, it was a wonder he hadn't throttled her himself for all the trouble she's caused.

Eleanor's phone call with Will has filled her with a renewed sense of purpose. She turns her thoughts to the memorial tomorrow because it will be an opportunity to observe everyone closely. Perhaps when emotions are running high, it might be easier to see who knows more than they are telling.

Lost in thought, she heads downstairs, skulking along the hallways, wondering if Ian and Susan are back yet. As she passes the doorway of the family room, she looks in to see Naeve settled there, watching some kind of animal show on television.

"Can I join you?" Eleanor asks, hoping to engage Naeve in conversation, find out what else she might know, and learn more about her aunt and uncle.

Naeve just shrugs, which Eleanor chooses to read as a yes, so she takes a seat on one of the sumptuous cinema chairs in the dimly lit room, trying to tune in to the strange scene on television, where an anesthetized tiger is laid out on a vet's operating table, having its teeth cleaned. The vet has to keep pulling the tiger's large sagging lip, working away at that giant incisor. A nurse absentmindedly strokes the tiger's fur, as though trying to soothe it, but seeing as the creature is unconscious and obviously unaware of the movement, Eleanor suspects that it is more about the thrill of touching what is normally forbidden. There's a rush of power that comes with making contact with something dangerous and surviving without a scratch.

She is absorbed in the show without realizing it, and when she looks across at Naeve again she sees her cousin has fallen asleep, her glasses on her lap and the chenille blanket held close to her chin, reducing the years in her face toward pure innocence. On her lap is a small sketchpad that Eleanor hadn't noticed when she came in. She gets up quietly to leave, and when Naeve doesn't stir, she can't resist taking a peek at Naeve's pad.

She sees a series of unusual shapes, romantic drawings of leaves and flowers and doorways and candle flames, each item given eyes that are either lost in sleep or occasionally staring, wide open, right at Eleanor; knowing eyes that make her skin crawl. And Naeve has also drawn a quick sketch of Eleanor sitting on the couch watching TV, her hands resting on her lap, and a huge diamond-and-sapphire ring planted firmly on her finger.

As soon as she sees it, Eleanor steps backward, her heartbeat quickening. Is this an attempt to bait her? She waits, but when Naeve doesn't stir she stops and moves closer again. Naeve's breathing is noisy and even; she's obviously resting. Perhaps she doodles in the same way that Eleanor does, and draws rings instead of nooses.

Nevertheless, Eleanor is aware of every nerve ending as she heads out of the room toward the stairs. She's about to go up, but then she looks back over her shoulder at Ian's office.

Should she?

She creeps across and tries the door, which gives without a creak. To begin with, she peers inside without crossing the threshold. She knows she shouldn't go in, of course she shouldn't—yet Will's words ring in her ears: *be a detective.* Heart racing, she tiptoes into the room and begins to scan from floor to ceiling, with no idea of what she is looking for, convinced only that she needs to find anything her uncle might be hiding.

With every passing second, she grows edgier. There is nothing to see. Just piles of paperwork, leaflets, boring brochures. Her conscience is screaming at her to get out—*What are you doing? You'll be thrown out of this house in seconds if someone comes in!*—but she cannot help herself. It's as though she might find a hidden reel of film that will match the missing portion of her memories, but she knows it's just a sign of how desperate she feels that she would even entertain such outlandish thoughts.

Once she has checked over the main desk, she turns to the big architect's drawing table on one side of the room. It is a mistake. Those outsize sheets of papers with their detailed plans provoke painful memories. As she pauses there, it is as though her dad comes to stand to one side of her, wearing his baggy, patched, unraveling sweater, those jeans of his hanging loose against his scrawny backside. "Let's have another look at these," he says, and in her mind's eye she sees him picking them up and heading past her—no, through her—like the ghost she is nowadays, even though once upon a time she was a flesh-and-blood girl stepping aside for him, unnoticed.

Eleanor is well aware that it's always a mistake to let in the shadows of the past. Her conviction wavers and her thoughts blur, twisted by the rage she feels whenever she thinks of her father. Her body becomes unsteady, and she clutches the back of the enormous office chair, praying she doesn't pass out, to be found on the floor in here. Once the swirling sensation is over, she turns, and in one last panicked rush she goes over to the filing cabinet and pulls it open. She flicks through the top, finding file inserts for passports, banking, investments, all the private aspects of her uncle's life, all things she really shouldn't see. She goes faster and faster through each drawer, sure she is about to hear the door open or a voice cry out in horror. She can barely breathe as she pushes the bottom drawer closed and turns for the door, finally conceding defeat.

She exits the room, carefully pulling the door closed, forcing herself to slow down to bring it quietly onto the latch.

When she turns, ready to flee up the stairs, Naeve is standing barely two steps away from her.

"What are you doing, Eleanor?"

Eleanor is lost for words. She tries to read the expression on her young cousin's face, because although she was expecting disgust, what she sees is more like intrigue—she might almost say respect.

25

heatwave

Shool is spiky grass and jostling for rusting play equipment and kids who already have friends and don't need any more. Eleanor is quiet in class and on the bus and in the shed. No one notices. Everyone is too busy.

Week after week, the temperature in the shed keeps rising. A quartet of fans now whir through the night. Nevertheless, the nape of Eleanor's neck is clammy each morning and the back of her head soaked in a cooling, sticky sweat. By the end of February, there is also a padlock on the inside of the shed door. Her father's last act each night is to click the shackle into place.

Everyone goes to bed at the same time—Dad and Aiden on the top bunks, Eleanor and her mother at the bottom. Occasionally, Eleanor feels her bunk shake, as though Aiden is nervously tapping the wood, but for the most part he is a sound sleeper. Her mother straps on a headlamp and reads for a long time each night. Eleanor is always grateful for that little light, its beacon of comfort breaking through the unremitting darkness. Her father sometimes mumbles things in his sleep, grunting and shifting around, disturbing them all. In a way, she is glad they are so close together in this strange environment, which doesn't feel any more like home than the first time she set eyes on it. At least it staves off the physical dimension of her loneliness. Yet, at other times she has never felt further apart from them all. It's like they are lost in transit, as though they've been sleeping in an airport or train station for a few months, waiting for their transport to arrive and whisk them away, back to their real lives.

One Saturday morning early in March, Eleanor wakes up last. The rest of the family sit at the camp table. Aiden and her father are shoveling scrambled eggs into their mouths, while her mother pushes her food around her plate, lost in thought. Eleanor sits up slowly, aware of the tight stretch of her bladder, trying to put off the moment she has to go outside to use the hot, stinking portable toilet. Her mother looks over. "How did you sleep?"

Everyone stops eating. The energy in the room swells, pressing against Eleanor. "Fine."

"You don't remember?" Aiden looks suspicious.

"Remember what?"

"You're a good faker, I'll give you that." He laughs.

Eleanor hates the sneer in his tone. She wants to cry. "What?"

Her mother comes over, sits on the bed and puts an arm around her. "It's nothing, you gave us a scare, that's all. You got up in the night and found the padlock key in Dad's pants pocket. Managed to unlock the door and were on your way out—thank god the door makes a noise when it opens."

Eleanor frowns. "I don't remember that. Are you sure?"

Her father leans back in his chair. "You went sleepwalking a few times when you were little, back in Tippington Road. We didn't think of it happening here. It's been a while. Don't worry, honey, I'll hide the key somewhere different each night, you won't be able to get out so easily then."

"You were like a zombie, Shrimp!" Aiden jumps up and holds his arms out and staggers elaborately over to Eleanor. When he gets close, his hands go around her neck and he pretends to strangle her. She knows he's only joking, but he does it too hard, and she grabs his fingers roughly and throws him off.

"Don't, Aiden, it's not funny."

"Sorry, Shrimp." He ruffles her hair in a way that makes her instantly love him again. Aiden as her protector is the side of him she craves the most, yet she so rarely sees it any more. He squats down so their faces are level. "Are you sure you're not faking?" He winks.

She pushes him, but she's laughing now. Her mother pulls her close, kisses her head. When she comes back from the toilet, everyone seems a bit happier as they eat their breakfast.

It's strange to have other people tell her what she has been up to, and not being able to remember. But she's glad of the sleepwalking now, because it has brought some lightness back into her family at last. As she scoffs her eggs, she tries to think what she can do to hold on to this moment.

"Dad?" she asks tentatively.

"Yep." He is looking down at the architectural drawings on the table, making little marks with a stubby pencil.

"Can you have a day off? We could go to the national park or something—there's meant to be a waterfall you can swim in. Pleeeeaaaase."

He catches her eye and shakes his head. "We can't, I have to go and get some more bricks today. I've got the plasterer coming on Monday, so I need to finish the front outer walls this weekend."

She turns in her seat. "Mum, can you take us? Please?"

"No can do," her dad interrupts. "I need all hands on deck, Eleanor."

Aiden gets up and grabs his T-shirt, heading out without a word, letting the shed door clang closed behind him.

"Well, can I help you both, then?" she asks.

"Not with this bit, honey," her dad says, reaching across to put his hand on hers. His fingers feel as dry as wood bark. She stares at them. There are little cuts all over his hands and his nails are black and grimy. "It's a bit complex, and we're under so much pressure right now," he says. "It's a race against time to get as much done as we can before the full mortgage kicks in."

Eleanor can barely hear these words through her rage, let alone absorb them. "Fine." She pushes her hands against the table, meaning to move her chair back, but the force upends the wobbly structure, and her father's papers slide to the floor.

"For god's sake, Eleanor," he cries, scrabbling to pick them up again, "what the hell—"

Eleanor is heading for the door.

"Hey!" her dad shouts angrily, making her jump. "Get back here."

"Leave her," she hears her mother hiss at him, and she takes that as permission to keep going. Behind her their voices continue to rise over the top of one another. *She's only asking for one day.* / *You know what we're up against with the bank.* / *So how long do we have to ignore our kids for?* / *We're building them a fucking house, for Christ's sake!*

Outside, there's nowhere to go. Eleanor does the best she can to get away from them, running down the gentle hill toward the remains of the cubby. Her head is a mass of confusion, her face a mess of snot and tears. How long until she gets her family back? Her parents don't have time for her anymore; while Aiden's teasing this morning has only made her realize how rarely he talks to her nowadays, and how much she misses him.

In her distress, she runs beyond the dismantled cubby until she gets to the fence line, which is set into a small valley between the two properties. Beyond is a field that trails away uphill. In the distance she can see rusting farming equipment, a burned-out car, a shed with a broken window. She stalks along the fence until she finds a weak point and scales it, then sets off slowly toward these strange obstacles, her heart racing in rebellion, heading toward the line of trees at the top of the hill.

As she reaches the top, she comes to an abrupt halt. Beyond the trees, not far in front of her, is a small weatherboard house. It had been hidden by the incline, so she suddenly finds herself standing much closer to it than is comfortable. And the sight of it—the little terrace of flowers at the front, the truck parked alongside, a cat lazily licking its paw as it lies stretched on the windowsill—is so homely and unexpected that all she can do is stare. For a moment she wonders if she is lost in another waking dream.

Then there's a bark. And another. The noise jolts her into action; she shouldn't be here, whoever lives here will think she is spying. She barely has time to see the curtain twitch at the window before she takes off at a run, haring back down the hill, half expecting to hear a panting mutt at her heels or, worse, feel razor-sharp teeth sink into her flesh. But she doesn't dare turn around to look. Jagged edges of fencing wire scrape the insides of her legs as she climbs it quickly and races back up the hill toward her family, not slowing until the shed is back in sight.

26

the visitor

*G*illian hasn't slept properly for days. There's no point putting this off *any longer. She puts on her reading glasses and sits down in front of the computer. It doesn't take long to find articles about Arabella online. Her horror begins to mount as she reads one after another, trying to clarify the events in her mind. Oh Eleanor, she thinks, one hand clapped over her mouth, unable to tear her eyes from the screen, to stop herself from clicking on the next link. Eleanor, sweetheart, what have you got yourself caught up in now?*

Eleanor lies on her bed, watching the night nudging out the daylight, unable to sleep, not wanting to go downstairs. Her first foray into investigating her uncle had resulted in a mumbled apology to Naeve. She had stammered out a few words before running away from her cousin like a coward, without explaining why she'd been trespassing. She can't imagine why Naeve would keep this transgression to herself, and she keeps jumping up and pacing her room, half expecting her uncle to knock at her door and ask what the hell she was doing in his office. She is trying but failing to think of a reasonable explanation. However, as the hours drift away, and no one appears, she begins to rethink her fears. She remembers the shrewd expression on Naeve's face, and wonders if her cousin might have her own reasons for keeping this a secret.

During the evening, the rest of the household are too far away for her to make out what they are doing. Unwilling to join them, she snacks on chocolate and nuts, and drinks water from the en-suite tap. No one comes to find her when she doesn't come down for dinner. From her turreted position at the top of the house, snatches of conversation drift toward her, fading away again as soon as she strains to hear them. Gradually, the house settles into its nocturnal tempo. No more voices, just one or two short sounds as doors are closed, and a few muffled footsteps falling on the first floor landing. She tries to rest, drawing the curtains against the black night, but although she is bone tired, her thoughts take a long time to slow down. Eventually, Eleanor drifts off to sleep.

When she wakes, she is standing in the darkness, in a room too large to be her own. Disoriented and unsteady, she grabs at the wall, just visible thanks to the soft glow of streetlights coming through the curtains. She tries to subdue the panic, to set her tumbling mind back in order.

There is someone in bed in front of her, unmoving. When she trusts herself to stand properly, she tiptoes a few steps forward to peer at the sleeping face.

It's Naeve.

Why Eleanor is here she has no idea. There are no rules or logic to sleepwalking. Slowly, carefully, she backs toward the door, checking her footing before taking each step, desperate not to wake her cousin by making a sudden noise.

Thankfully, the door is ajar, and she doesn't touch it once she's in the corridor, just pads as fast as she can back to her room. Too nervous to even attempt sleep again, she sits on her bed, shaking out the numbness that is crawling up her fingers. Twice in forty-eight hours—this hasn't happened since she was a teenager. Why would her subconscious want to pull her back into the past, when it knows how hard she has tried to escape?

Because you don't want to admit why you're so angry with yourself, a little voice says, trespassing through the traps in her mind. *You vowed you would never, ever take drugs. And yet when someone cajoled you, you didn't even hesitate. You could have given that drink back. You didn't have to down it.*

I had no idea what it was, she reminds herself. *I was just trying to relax and fit in. I didn't know what was going to happen.*

You didn't think about the consequences, the snide voice persists. *That's why you're in this mess. Should you really be here on your own? Perhaps you should seriously consider booking your flight home.*

She throws herself down, face against the pillows, and gives a muffled cry. No matter how much her fears taunt her, she will not go home. She will stay, not because the police have instructed her to stick around, but because if she runs now, she will never dare to strike for independence again. She is twenty-one years old; she cannot hide for the rest of her life.

She props herself up on her elbows, staring at the wall. So what now? She has to sleep at some point. Perhaps she will have to barricade herself in her room to be sure she doesn't disturb the rest of the family. Last time she had bitten her uncle, so thank god Naeve had stayed asleep. Does she really have to protect them all from herself?

As she sits up, she remembers what she said to Will. *I'm going to do everything I can to find out what happened to Arabella.* She picks up her phone, knowing that sleep is unlikely to come now.

An hour or so later, her eyes are blurry from staring at her phone, and her wrist is sore from taking notes. She doesn't have access to a larger screen or a printer, so this old-fashioned scribing will have to do, but it turns out there is quite a lot of information on the internet about Arabella and Nathan Lane—and about Susan and Ian Mortimer too. She has found business deals and new job announcements for them all. She has perused pictures of a younger Arabella supporting her father on parliamentary campaigns and on election night. Arabella is also mentioned on various socialite blog sites, and on a few occasions, there are photographs of her with Nathan's arm around her, eyes shining brightly for the camera—too brightly, it seems now, but that could just be the advantage of hindsight. Eleanor stares at Nathan. He looks proud and confident, but is this also the face of a man who could kill his wife?

Next, she searches for online news and carefully reads what has been reported so far on Arabella's death. Most of the journalists make it sound suspicious rather than an accident. A few mention witnesses near the river. One piece features a grainy shot of Arabella from above, walking by the low wall of Victoria Embankment, the camera too high up to capture her expression, her hair already flattened by the rain. She is the only person in the picture who doesn't have an umbrella, and so she stands out, jacketless in the middle of winter, her arms wrapped across her chest as though trying to warm—or protect—herself.

Eleanor stares at the photo as she tries to piece together what little information she has. The picture was taken twenty-five minutes past midnight. The party had been officially over by then, so this must have been the second time Arabella left the *Atlantic*. But *why* was she back down on the Embankment? Why hadn't she headed home? In the picture Arabella looks a lot steadier on her feet than Eleanor had been, considering they had the same drug in their system. Perhaps that's because Arabella was a regular user; she could handle it better. Still, how could no one have seen what happened to her in the end?

In the early hours, she begins to drift in and out of a doze, occasionally waking up sweating, her body on fire, only her face attuned to the London winter. Thankfully each time it's to find herself still in her own bed.

By morning she is exhausted. She listens to the others getting up, doors opening and closing again, footsteps heading downstairs, Ian calling to the girls that they are "leaving in five, or we'll be late." She goes to her narrow window. She can't watch the garage from here but she does see the car head off down the road.

No one has been to check on her or say good morning. She's like an unwanted ghost, banished to the top of the house. No one has asked if she is going to the memorial or offered to take her with them. But perhaps that's a good thing—she'll be able to sit at the back, unnoticed.

The gnawing pain in her stomach tells her she really needs to eat. She goes down to the kitchen and makes herself a strong cup of coffee, then sits at the bench, sipping it, thinking of all she discovered overnight. She gazes absentmindedly at the beautiful stained glass mural that frames the large bay window, and marvels again at the pure lines of chrome in the kitchen, the gleaming equipment, wondering if Susan has ever put an apron on in here and settled in to bake. She almost chokes on her coffee at the thought of it—but there must be another side to Susan, surely she cannot always treat her home like a hotel and her family like her work colleagues.

Just as she is beginning to relax, the doorbell rings loudly into the silence. Eleanor pauses, unsure what to do, then decides to pretend there is no one in. Her hands grip her mug tightly as she waits, hoping whoever it is goes away.

After a moment, when silence has returned, she creeps toward the kitchen entrance, from where she can see the front door across the expansive hallway.

A shadow loiters beyond the frosted panes of glass. And then the letterbox opens, and a woman's voice says, "Hello? Is anyone home? Susan? Ian? Is that you?"

Eleanor stops still, but there's no doubt she's been spotted. She doesn't recognize the voice. There's a lilt in the accent—Welsh, possibly, although she's not great at distinguishing these things. At least it isn't Nathan. "Hang on," Eleanor calls, and goes over to the door. When she pulls it open, there is a woman with long, dark hair waiting on the doorstep, wearing a tan trench coat, watching the slow-falling rain.

"Hello," she says. "You're not Susan or Ian. Who are you?"

"I'm Eleanor. I'm Ian's niece."

"Oh, well I'm Aisha, pleased to meet you. Are Susan and Ian home?"

"Not right now, no."

"Okay then, will you tell them I came by? Actually, would you mind if I just waited for a moment with you until this rain stops. I don't want to get soaked on the way back to the Tube."

Eleanor hopes her lack of enthusiasm doesn't show on her face. She's not keen to invite this woman into the house, but it seems impolite to send her back into the rain. "All right then," she steps back, "I'll make you a drink, if you like. How do you know my aunt and uncle?"

Aisha smiles, then steps in ahead of Eleanor. "I'm an old friend. I just wanted to see how they were doing after the awful events of last week. I thought perhaps they would be taking some time off work, but I guess I should have known better—work never stops for some, does it?" She heads to the kitchen and begins to take off her coat.

"Ian might be back soon," Eleanor says over her shoulder. "He's taken the girls to school."

Aisha looks at her watch. "I don't have long, but I might just catch him," she says, sitting down in the kitchen at the long bench. She seems to be waiting for something and Eleanor can't think what. Then she realizes. "Would you like tea or coffee?"

"Water will be fine. Thank you," Aisha replies with a warm grin. "So, how are you all holding up? I'm just devastated for Dickon and June. And Nathan, of course."

Eleanor is caught off guard. At first she bristles—she really can't bear to talk about this again. But as Aisha sits there, smiling sympathetically, she tries to relax. "It's been awful," she says. "Everyone is upset—the kids too."

"And no one knows what happened?"

Eleanor recoils from the blank spot in her memory. "Nothing. No one can believe it's happened. I don't know anyone all that well—I've only been here for a few weeks, and I only met Arabella once or twice while I was temping, but she seemed very nice."

"Yes, but did she seem happy, that's the question, isn't it?"

"What do you mean?"

"Oh, I've heard through the grapevine that her husband, Nathan Lane, is a piece of work. Lots of affairs. A conviction for brawling and an arrest for domestic violence a few years back, though it was never taken further. Can't imagine it would be easy being married to a man like that."

"Really? Domestic violence?" Eleanor is shocked but not surprised, remembering the way Nathan had grabbed her throat just a few days ago. Involuntarily, she shivers.

Aisha leans forward and puts a cool hand on Eleanor's arm. "Is something wrong, Eleanor?"

The gentle touch makes Eleanor pause. How much dare she say? "Nathan was here over the weekend," she begins tentatively.

"Oh." Aisha keeps her hand on Eleanor's arm. "How was he?"

Eleanor shakes her head. "Not good at all. Suspicious of me too, because I chatted to Arabella at the party."

"Well, he won't be thinking straight," Aisha says, withdrawing her hand. "Not while he's lost in grief."

"Yes . . . it's very awkward because I was temping for him. Susan has told me to stay away from the office this week, probably for good."

"Hmm, that is a shame." Aisha runs a finger around the rim of her water glass, deep in thought. "What will you do now?"

"Find another job after Christmas, I guess. Know of any vacancies?" she jokes half-heartedly, immediately embarrassed at how inappropriate it sounds.

Aisha smiles, but her eyes are ablaze with something Eleanor cannot fathom. "Oh, I don't think you'd like it where I work. Listen, I didn't mean to take up so much of your time this morning. I'll just go and use the bathroom and I'll be on my way."

She is up and out the door before Eleanor has a chance to reply. And as soon as she's gone, Eleanor realizes how hungry she is. She roots around for some cereal, hearing footsteps on the stairs, waiting for Aisha to return. As she prepares her food at the counter, it occurs to her that Aisha is taking a remarkably long time to come back.

Finally, those footsteps register. Why did Aisha go upstairs when there's a downstairs bathroom? She jumps up and runs up the stairs two at a time, checking the landing bathroom, which is empty, rushing to look in the other rooms.

Aisha is in the master bedroom, hurriedly opening and closing drawers. "What the hell are you doing?" Eleanor gasps. "Who are you?"

"I'm sorry, Eleanor," Aisha says, her smile twisted, "but when there's been a suspicious death, it is in the public interest to know who might be responsible." She brushes past Eleanor and heads down the stairs. "I wish you and your family only the best," she trills as she goes. "Thank you for inviting me in for a drink." Then she opens the front door and walks straight into the sheeting rain.

Eleanor runs into the front bedroom, from where she can see beyond the low wall at the front of the house. She watches Aisha climb into a sleek black car.

Eleanor sinks onto the bed in dismay, trying to make sense of what just happened. There must be some kind of law against coming into the house under false pretenses like that. Should she call Susan or Ian? She can't, not yet, not while they are both under such strain, with the funeral so close. It surely won't help to know a stranger has been searching through their house, and it will diminish their trust in Eleanor even further.

Eleanor's mind races as she thinks over everything she just said, afraid she may have unwittingly committed some monstrous indiscretion. *Who the hell was she? A journalist? An undercover detective?* She wants to chase after that car and find out exactly what Aisha wanted, but it has already gone.

Your thoughts are running away with themselves.

She breathes deeply, trying to calm down.

Will's words are loud in her ears. *The more information you have to protect yourself, the better.*

She has to keep hunting for answers. She goes downstairs and checks the front door is locked. Back in the kitchen, she tries to eat the stodgy cereal, even though it sticks in her throat, while she uses her phone to flick through the different articles over and over again, looking for anything new that might give her some kind of lead.

Eventually, Eleanor returns to one of the CCTV photos of Arabella walking along the Embankment, alone and drenched, her head down as she approaches the stone steps that lead up to Cleopatra's Needle.

Eleanor skims the article again. *Police are appealing for witnesses.* As she scans down there are more stills, showing different groups walking. In one of them, in the upper right corner, another slight figure without an umbrella leans over the stone wall as though looking into the murky waters of the Thames. Only the top half of the person is visible, the bottom half obscured by a cast-iron bench.

Eleanor's eye is drawn to the small items dangling from the woman's hand. Heart pounding, she tries to zoom in, but as she does, the picture grows ever more pixelated. However, could it be that the small figure is holding a pair of three-inch, peep-toe heels? Eleanor balks, her throat burning, remembering her dirty feet on Friday morning. Could it be that she is looking at a picture of herself?

27

solomon

The truck first rumbles toward them one Sunday morning in late March. The tires crunch on the loose graveled track, and Eleanor's parents both stop working to look up and shade their eyes as the truck draws a dusty circle in the dirt and comes to a halt.

Eleanor is inside the shed, trying to do her homework. She hears the vehicle first and watches its arrival through the window. An old man climbs out and ambles across the short distance toward her mom and dad, while a large black Labrador waits on the flatbed, still tied on but his paws up on the side, enthusiastically wagging his tail. She sees her dad hastily wipe his hands on his dirty jeans and reach out to shake the old man's. Curious, Eleanor heads out to join them, walking shyly down to where they stand. The stranger wears an Akubra hat and a plaid shirt tucked into trousers that are held up high on his thick waist by a large brown belt. Her father sees her coming, and says, "Eleanor, this is Solomon. He lives just over there," and indicates the distant block beyond their house.

When Solomon turns, it's with his whole body, as though he has stiffened up so much that his neck doesn't work independently anymore. He squints at Eleanor and she waves quickly, arm and elbow tight against her chest as she blushes. She glances toward the dog, who is leaning toward them and licking his lips in anticipation of a stroke.

"Go on, give him a pat, he's friendly . . ."

Eleanor walks over, reaches up and pets the dog, who begins to lick her hand eagerly.

"Charlie's just a big softie," Solomon continues. "Wouldn't even bite a trespasser."

Does she imagine it, or is he sizing her up when he says this? She remembers sprinting away from that little weatherboard house, and instantly her whole body burns with embarrassment. Has Solomon come here to discuss her intrusion onto his land?

But he doesn't say more. Instead, he holds out a hand. She has no choice but to shake it, and as their palms touch, she is repelled by his calloused, clammy grip. He is older than Eleanor had thought any living person could be. His face is a mass of veins and lines. It is impossible to think he had once been a child or a young man. His skin looks like it's slowly folding and firming into tree bark, as though one day he will stop where he stands and plant permanent roots in the earth.

He keeps his gaze on her for a moment, as though he's trying to decide something. She averts her eyes and waits.

Then Solomon turns away. "Came to see how you're going," he drawls to her father, pointing at the house.

"Hope we're not making too much noise," Eleanor's mother says politely.

"Nah. I'm too far away and half deaf." He makes a sound that could be a laugh or a cough, then stares up at the house, hands on hips, and Eleanor notices that although his body is still, his mouth is continually chewing on something. They all follow his gaze, but no one says anything and the silence grows awkward.

"Would you like a cup of tea?" Eleanor's mother asks eventually.

"One sugar," is all he says in reply. Eleanor's mother nods and starts walking to the shed. Eleanor follows.

"He's got to be the oldest person I've ever seen," she whispers to her mother, and gets a sharp *shh* in reply.

Once they are inside, her mother says, "I'm just grateful he's giving me a break. Your father is a complete slave driver."

"He just wants to get the roof on before winter, doesn't he?" Eleanor replies, unsure why she is defending him. "Maybe he'll relax a bit after that."

"Hmm." Eleanor's mother seems far from convinced. She takes her time brewing the tea and carefully adds one sugar, then flops down in a chair. "Here, you take it out to him."

"Mum, I don't want—" but then Eleanor sees her mother's expression tighten and relents. "Okay, okay."

She walks carefully across the yard, holding the mug as steady as she can. Even before she's halfway there, the boiling water has heated through the ceramic cup and is beginning to burn her knuckles. She quickens her step, desperate to hand it over, and finally reaches the men.

"Here," she says, and gratefully passes the tea over, but she hasn't taken notice of the tremors in Solomon's hands, and she lets go too soon. The mug full of hot tea clatters to the floor, its fall broken by Solomon's feet.

"Eleanor!" Her dad bellows, kneeling down and picking up the mug. "Can't you be more careful?" He grabs a rag and kneels in front of Solomon, dabbing at the mess on the old man's boots.

"Can't feel a thing," Solomon says, watching him. "Solid shoes."

Eleanor's father's face is bright red as he thrusts the cup back at Eleanor. "What are you standing here for? Go get another one."

She can feel tears already tipping over, running down her face. Who took her gentle, lovable bear of a father and replaced him with this horrible man? She runs to the shed, pushing the door hard and letting it swing back on its hinges with a great bang. Her mother, still sitting where Eleanor left her, looks up in surprise.

Eleanor slams the mug on the table. "I spilled it," she cries, and stomps across to her bunk, throwing herself on it. "You take it next time."

She listens as her mother prepares more tea and takes it out, hears more polite voices outside. It seems as though she lies there for hours, and even when she hears the truck rev up and begin to move, she doesn't get up. She hopes her father might come in with some gentler words for her, but nothing happens, and eventually she picks up her sketchpad and settles down to draw.

28

the memorial

milia Tate has decided on a striking pink dress for the memorial. She briefly considered black, but screw that, she's damn sure it's not what Arabella would have wanted. Besides, she's never been one for convention. There's a slight jangle of nerves as she puts on a pair of oversized, shimmering gold earrings, because she's heard Arabella was high on the night she died. But Arabella had sworn she wouldn't tell anyone who supplied her with blow. They had shared the highs and lows of having a father in parliament, the accompanying pressures to be good girls, and how bloody awesome it was to break free of the constraints. She sniffs and wipes away a tear. She's going to miss that stuck-up bitch like crazy.

Eleanor is on her way to the Queen's Head pub, where Will is waiting for her. His call had come as a surprise, and his voice had registered low and urgent as he asked her to meet him. Ever since she agreed, her nerves have been buzzing.

The pub isn't far from the church where the memorial service will take place in just over an hour. Eleanor is wearing a plain, black long-sleeved top and her gray work trousers, the most appropriate items in her limited wardrobe. She imagines all the mourners scattered around London, getting ready, their clothes somber, black neckties cutting into Adam's apples. Is Arabella's killer among them? Will there be someone in the crowd whose stricken face belies secret knowledge of just what took place after Arabella left the *Atlantic*? Whenever Eleanor tries to picture the memorial, she can't see beyond Nathan's livid expression and Susan's contemptuous stare.

The warm air from the pub fireplace hits Eleanor as soon as she walks in. Will is waiting at a small table in the corner. As she sits down opposite him, he leans forward and brushes his fingers lightly across her cheek. "You look really tired, Eleanor."

His touch makes her tense. "I didn't sleep much last night," she admits.

"Neither did I. This is taking its toll on all of us, I think. I'm dreading this afternoon." He hesitates. "So what's happening about the ring?"

She feels herself stiffen. "My uncle still has it," she says reluctantly.

"And you don't know what he's done with it?"

"No."

"Look," Will leans forward. "The police came to see me again yesterday evening. They know I was talking to Arabella outside, after the party finished. At the moment, as far as I know, I was the last person to see her." He runs his hands through his hair. "Shit." He leans forward, his eyes wide, and there's a vein bulging on his forehead as his face reddens. Eleanor sits back automatically. "They think I know something, I'm sure of it. Eleanor, you have to try to remember, why did you have that ring? Please."

"Are you going to tell them?" Eleanor asks quietly.

"How can I now?" he says desperately. "It might only make me look more guilty if I've known about concealed evidence. But if you could remember, if you could try to think how you came by it, it might really help."

"I wish I could," she replies miserably. She thinks about the CCTV footage she's stared at all morning, but she's not about to make Will privy to that as well. The bright edge to his gaze is unsettling. Could he be so eager to get himself off the hook that he would let more suspicion fall on her?

As she stares at him, he seems to finally sense her nervousness. "I'm sorry," he says, sitting back, "I'm just shaken up by it all. I've seen Nathan get away with so much, and he has friends in high places—I could easily become the fall guy." He checks his watch. "Anyway, we'll have to continue this later. Come on, we'd better go or we'll be late." He grabs his jacket from the back of his chair and pulls it on. Once outside, Will knows the way, so Eleanor tags along, shivering and hugging herself, her thick coat, scarf, and hat failing to keep out the cold. To begin with, they are still in the main shopping district, and an endless snake of Christmas shoppers push past and around them, people seamlessly navigating their way so that they hardly ever do more than brush against one another, despite the throngs. That so many people can live in one place without it being total anarchy still amazes Eleanor.

But today, as she and Will head toward the church, the dead seem to be everywhere too, hidden in the footsteps and shadows of the living. Eleanor glances at the strangers around her, wondering if any of them carry their own ghosts with them. *How neatly packaged these others are*, she thinks. When Eleanor looks at them, she sees complete beings, skin that loops them into a neat start and finish. So why does Eleanor always feel as though bits of her are escaping, running into the gutter with the rain, melted by sunshine or eroded by the wind?

As she follows Will down a side street, the people disappear almost instantly. Only a huddle of somber, terraced houses are present now, to witness them pass. With every step closer to the church, Eleanor regrets her decision to come. It's as though she's stretching, unwinding, pulling more and more taut toward the snap. With every step she tells herself she could still turn around and go back to Harborne Grove.

"Perhaps I've made a mistake," she murmurs.

"What do you mean?"

"People are going to wonder what I'm doing, like you did. I didn't really know her, did I?"

"Don't give them any reason to doubt you. Just hold your head high and act normal."

"I'll try," she says quietly. *Do I ever act normal?* she asks herself. *I don't feel normal.*

They cross a quiet park with rusting play equipment at its center, waiting forlornly for some children to bring it to life. When Eleanor sees the spire in the distance, she tugs at the scarf around her neck, sure it is too tight, on the verge of choking her.

Will checks his phone and quickens his pace. "Come on, we'd better not be late, or our quiet entrance will go out the window. And afterward, Eleanor, please think carefully about whether to go to the police. I know you're scared but other people are getting drawn into this now. You have to do the right thing."

As she takes in his words, she is nine years old again, hurrying along a dusty track with her father, trying to keep up. "You cannot tell *anyone*," he reminds her fiercely, as he's been doing for days now. "You have to do the right thing for all our sakes." She knows he has timed this conversation to take place while they are walking so he doesn't have to look at her. "Don't tell anyone, especially not your mother. Just try to forget that night, because this family has suffered enough. If you tell anyone, we will lose our whole future, do you understand?"

She had run away from him then, stumbling over divots, hearing him call out her name over and over. She cannot think of this now, but she can still hear his voice—"Eleanor, *Eleanor!*"—and she clamps her hands to her ears. "Go away, go *away!*" she shouts, doubling over, as though she might protect herself from a blow, even though that blow delivered its force a decade ago.

"Eleanor!" It is not her father's voice but Will's, and he has his arm around her as she folds over and into herself in this damp, gray park. "Just breathe. Are you going to be sick? What just happened?"

"It's . . . it's . . . ." She heaves herself to stand up, hands on hips, gulping lungfuls of the cold fresh air. "I don't think. . . . I can't . . . ." She gestures toward the distant church spire with her gloved hand.

"Just take a moment. You're bound to be nervous. I'm dreading it too."

His understanding is a comfort. A tear trickles down her cheek and she quickly wipes it away. She shifts her weight from one foot to the other, tries to regain strength in her legs.

Will keeps his arm around her, and his cold hand reaches up to stroke the side of her face, making her skin tingle. "Are you all right now?"

She looks at the spire in the distance and straightens. "Yes, I think so."

"Then let's hurry." Will holds out his hand.

She takes it, and they both quicken their pace. Will doesn't let go, and she is distracted by this new sensation of their bodies tentatively joined like this.

Soon they come around the corner and into view of the church. A row of black cars line the road by the entrance. Will immediately drops her hand and she feels a small jolt of disappointment as they separate, wondering if he is embarrassed to be seen with her in front of his work colleagues. Then he gestures to the small church gate so she can go first, and his hand presses briefly against her back as he guides her forward.

A few journalists lean against the stone wall, watching the mourners file in. Some stare, while others make notes or chat to one another. *Presumably*, Eleanor thinks, *they are looking out for the main players in this drama—Arabella's parents, and Nathan and Ernie Lane.* Most of them don't give Eleanor a second glance, but a woman turns her head away quickly and steps back.

As Eleanor stares at that shiny brown hair, a large black car draws up in front of the church, and all the journalists pivot to see who is arriving. The woman's profile comes into view again. It could be Aisha, but from this distance it's hard to see her features clearly.

"Looks like the family are here," Will murmurs. "We should go in."

Eleanor follows Will into the church. Inside he turns to her. "See you after, okay? I'd better go and sit with the rest of the team."

Before Eleanor can reply, he strides away without looking back. Discomforted, she takes a seat near the door, grimacing as the mournful organ music presses on her nerves. She wants to believe she is only here for the right reasons, to pay her respects to this woman whose death has wrapped itself insidiously around Eleanor's life. She wants to hold her head high and show the world she is blameless. Why, then, does it feel like she might be playing a dangerous game, rubbernecking at the grief of people she barely knows? Why does it feel like she is only pretending?

29

the accident

March 2005

After Solomon's first appearance, he begins to visit regularly, always arriving in his old truck with Charlie on the flatbed. He often says he is on his way back from the shops, but then he doesn't leave for hours. Instead he holds up the building progress, his chewing, saggy-lipped mouth in perpetual motion as he leans on his vehicle, leaving Charlie to sleep or watch longingly from the back of the truck. Sometimes he shouts advice to Eleanor's parents, while they sweat up ladders, passing each other bricks or tiles or equipment.

On other occasions he accosts them on tea breaks and regales them with stories of the past—what things were like when he and his wife worked the land out here. It turns out that the land Eleanor's family is building on used to be Solomon's, but he doesn't have a pension, so the sale was to make ends meet. Some of his tales capture Eleanor's interest, as she tries to imagine the horses and the crops in the fields, the smoke from the bushfires, the huge lightning storm that struck a tree, which then fell onto the barn and killed a family of goats. She tries to picture Solomon with a wife and child, but it's hard to believe he could ever have been that young.

It is almost Easter now, and the roof is taking shape. Eleanor's mother wants to hire someone to finish it, but her father remains confident that they are capable of pulling up and affixing the large corrugated panels. Eleanor has grown used to watching the intensity of their labor, and she's given up asking if they need help. Her parents are a well-oiled machine now; they complete the necessary tasks without much of a word between them. Meanwhile, Aiden uses any excuse he can think of to disappear.

In the last week of term, a girl called Katie Slater finally notices Eleanor. Eleanor is invited for tea after school, and follows Katie around feeding and petting an assortment of animals. Katie's mother is friendly until eight o'clock, an hour after Eleanor was due to be collected. There is no mobile reception this far out, and the woman grumbles about courtesy as she packs the kids in the car and drives out to Eleanor's place.

Eleanor is nervous. A year ago she would have been frightened, but right now it wouldn't surprise her if her parents are so busy, they have just forgotten.

As they slow down on the unmarked dirt lane, Eleanor sees the shell of the main house standing in darkness. She can't see her parents' car, but there is a light coming from underneath the door of the shed.

"You're living in there?" Katie's mother asks in astonishment as they come to a halt.

Eleanor is embarrassed. "Yes, but it's just temporary."

"It looks fun," Katie says.

Eleanor turns to her. "It's not."

She gets out the car, hoping Katie's mother will come with her, but the others stay put. "We'll just see you safely inside," Katie's mother calls through the window.

Eleanor pushes against the door of the shed, but it is locked. She hears footsteps coming closer on the other side, and then the rattle of the padlock being opened.

Aiden stands there, his face pale. Behind Eleanor, Katie's mother guns the engine and begins to reverse. Eleanor doubts she'll get another invitation any time soon. She looks past Aiden, trying to see their parents. "Where are Mum and Dad?"

"There's been an accident. Dad had to take Mum to the hospital."

As he says it, there comes the noise of a chair scraping behind him.

"What?" Eleanor's insides lurch. "Is she okay?" she asks, trying to peer into the room to see who just made that sound.

"I don't know. She fell off the roof. Hit her head and broke her arm. It looked bad."

Eleanor begins to cry, a snuffle at first, but it soon gives way to a sob. Aiden steps forward and puts his arms around her. Over his shoulder, she finally sees who is there.

Solomon is sitting at the picnic table, watching them. His mouth in perpetual motion, chewing as usual.

"Why is he here?" she whispers.

"He said he'd stay with us," Aiden hisses back. "I said there was no need, but I can't get him to leave."

Reluctantly, she moves inside, staying close to her brother. Every inch of the room is swollen with the absence of their mother. It seems darker than usual, but perhaps it's always been this way and her mother had added some of the light. It also looks like a storeroom tonight, not at all like a home.

These thoughts surprise her. When had the shed ever provided some semblance of a home?

"Hello, Eleanor," Solomon says without getting up. "I said I'd stay with you while your parents are at the hospital. I'm sorry about your mother. It looked like a nasty fall."

His words terrify Eleanor. She is trying not to picture the scene, but it keeps playing for her anyway—her mum losing her balance, a horrible thud as she hits the ground.

"You kids need to get into bed," Solomon says, "if yer got school tomorrow."

"I'm gonna stay up and wait for Mum and Dad," Aiden says immediately.

"Me too," Eleanor agrees. She goes across to one of the containers of water and uses the little tap to pour herself a drink. She wants to go outside to the toilet, but it is too scary in the dark without her parents nearby. She doesn't want to sit at the table either, so she goes to her bed and perches awkwardly on it.

"Where's Charlie?" she asks.

"Left him at home," Solomon replies. "Past his bedtime too," he adds, without a smile. He takes out a small silver box and begins to roll a cigarette. Eleanor takes furtive glances at the way his fingers shake as they press down the tobacco; sees that it takes him a couple of goes to pull the cigarette paper from its box. He doesn't look directly at her as he works, but she feels as though he is always aware of exactly where she is.

After a while, however hard she tries, she cannot help her thoughts from drifting, cannot stop her eyes from closing. She desperately wants her parents to be back. Her whole body is silently screaming for her mother to tuck her in.

The next thing she knows she is waking up again, her bladder bursting. She heaves herself up to see that Solomon is still sitting at the table, reading one of her mother's books. Above her, she hears her brother's snores.

She grabs her flashlight. "I'm going to the bathroom," she tells Solomon, and he just looks up and nods, doesn't say a word.

She's so uncomfortable as she staggers outside that she can't get the door open properly and she's begun to relieve herself before she makes the toilet. She sits down as fast as she can and finishes, but her knickers and jeans now have a large wet spot on them. She starts to cry, but then a rush of fear makes her stop. She can hear rustling outside. *It's kangaroos*, she tells herself, but she is panicked now. She has to get back to the others. She pulls her clothes up, the cold, wet patch sticking to her skin, and hurries back to the shed. It's so dark outside that a dozen eyes could be tracking her movements, and she wouldn't know.

Solomon sits exactly where she left him. There is no way she can change her clothes while he is here, and she doesn't dare go back to the portable toilet. She lies on the bed, trying not to press against the wet patch. She turns her face so that Solomon can't see her and lets the tears fall down her cheeks. When she is finished, she expects to be tired, but instead finds herself wide awake with fury. How could her parents have done this to her, to all of them? How could they have turned their lives into such a nightmare?

Solomon hasn't moved an inch. Every now and again there's the noise of the occasional drumming of his fingers against the table in the darkness. If she listens carefully, she's sure she can hear the soft, sticky sound of his chewing in the dark.

30

revelation

*A*isha McNally scoots out of view until she's sure Eleanor has gone inside. She doesn't want a run-in right now. She waits among the group of journalists, listening to the gossip. She's smiling to herself, thinking of all the juicy details they don't know. Wondering if there will be fireworks today.

Inside the church, the dirge of organ music is much louder. Eleanor looks over the rows of heads and sees Susan at the front, talking earnestly to an older man, her hands clasped around his. Ian stands just behind her. Ninety-nine percent of the time Susan has her game face on, but now Eleanor has seen the other one percent, she knows that there is chaos, confusion, and fear in Susan too. She thinks she can spot it now, in the way Susan's back arches and her shoulders stiffen every time Ian puts a guiding hand against her waist.

People from Parker & Lane have been arriving in dribs and drabs. When they see Eleanor, some stare curiously, while others look quickly away. At the front, facing them all on a giant easel, is a photo of Arabella—a professional bridal shot, close-up, her hair in perfect waves around her tanned face, her beatific smile setting off her gleaming white teeth. *There is no denying how beautiful she was*, thinks Eleanor. No wonder Ian had succumbed to her charms when he was married to such an ice maiden. The photo is a direct contrast to Susan's pale, pinched visage bobbing in front of it, her black hair pulled severely from her forehead into its usual tight bun.

Eleanor is still transfixed by that photo when the music changes slightly, and Nathan comes in, with a woman who must be his mother holding his arm, and his father behind them. Before they reach the front, Ernie Lane has paused to shake the hands of a few people, nodding at their condolences. He is a small man, much smaller than his son and not even as tall as his wife, yet with his presence, the tension in the church increases noticeably. They are followed soon after by Dickon Blythe and his wife. June has a tissue pressed to her nose, her arm linked with her husband's. He is patting her hand as they walk, and it is this gesture that causes Eleanor's eyes to cloud with tears as she watches them take their place. They don't even glance at Nathan and Ernie on the other side. Two young women follow them along the aisle, their heads leaning on each other, bent over like old women despite their smart suits and stilettos. They look like Arabella; Eleanor suspects they are her sisters.

Nathan remains hunched over throughout the service and doesn't move, even when everyone else stands up. Arabella's sisters speak first, telling stories of their childhood that Eleanor cannot reconcile with the Arabella she met. Arabella's mother is next, her soft, broken voice outlining all the things that made them so proud of their youngest daughter—her thoughtful gifts, her caring phone calls, her many achievements at school and work, her skill as a ski instructor while on gap year, and her love for her two nephews. Not one of them mentions Nathan.

And then it's Susan's turn.

Susan walks slowly to the lectern, perfectly composed, and takes a moment to put on a pair of black-framed glasses while she glances at her notes. Then she looks up.

"My husband Ian and I have known Arabella for many years," she begins, her tone crisp and businesslike, as though she might be presenting slides in a meeting. "We were there to witness her engagement, her marriage, and many happy times." She looks down at her notes, then glances briefly at Nathan, and Eleanor wonders if this is why he'd pressed Susan to speak. She might at least acknowledge his role in his wife's life.

Then she realizes that Susan hasn't said anything more, and turns her attention back to her aunt. It's hard to see from this distance, but it looks as though she may be composing herself. *How much of this speech is real,* Eleanor wonders, *and how much is a show?*

"Arabella was an astute businesswoman and masterminded many successful campaigns for Parker & Lane. In all these different facets of life, she will be greatly missed."

Susan's eyes stray from the paper at this point, and she turns slightly so she is looking at the left aisle of people. She might be addressing Dickon and his wife. She could as easily be staring at Ian.

"Arabella also had a very special ability to become a close part of people's lives. She was loved and adored by many, and although she is not with us anymore, the legacy she leaves will be deeply felt and long lasting. I know I for one will always remember the impact she had on the lives of me and my family."

Her voice remains steady. As she gathers her notes, there are no outward signs of distress. If it is a performance—and surely it must be—it is masterful.

Does anyone else have an inkling of this? Eleanor looks around her, and it's at this moment she spots Detectives Kirby and Prashad in one of the back rows of the adjacent aisle. Priya Prashad leans across and says something to her colleague, and Steve Kirby nods. Then, as though she senses she's being watched, Prashad turns and stares straight at Eleanor.

Eleanor flinches and looks down. Why did she not just nod and hold her gaze? Why is she reacting like this—like a guilty person? She's giving Priya Prashad every reason to suspect her of something.

The vicar is speaking now; calm, gentle words designed to assuage distress. Yet after hearing all the other speeches, his sentiment is obviously hollow. It's clear he didn't really know Arabella, that he is merely offering platitudes. Eleanor finds it depressing that this is the final word on such a vibrant life, a stranger intoning your virtues to the silent faces of everyone who knew you. She tries to listen and be drawn into his words of consolation, but all she feels is the numbness that's been in the marrow of her bones for so long, the coldness that crept in, uninvited. She can't help but think about the other funeral eleven years ago, the one she didn't go to.

Just as her heart clenches with memories, the organ strikes up so suddenly that she jumps. People keep their heads bowed as the families slowly file out first. She hears sobs but doesn't want to look up. After the family has left, everyone begins to follow.

Out of nowhere, her uncle appears by her side. "Thank god that's over," Ian says under his breath. "Let's get out of here. I'll give you a lift home if you like. Susan is heading straight back to work."

Eleanor nods as she steps out of the pew. They wait for the crowd to move, but Ian is glancing ahead of them and murmurs, "Oh no, no, no."

"What?" She looks up at him.

"There's a bloody receiving line," he mutters, eyes hunting around desperately for some other exit from the church. Eleanor follows his gaze. The only other door within sight presumably leads to the vestry. There is only one way out.

They edge forward with the rest. Eleanor can feel the stress emanating from her uncle. When they get outside, they see Nathan is the last of the line. Eleanor shakes hands with Ernie and Dickon and their wives, and they all thank her for coming, their eyes glazed or searching over her shoulder, obviously with no idea who she is. Ahead of her, she sees Ian reach Nathan and hold out a hand, and after the longest pause, Nathan takes it.

She watches them shake. And shake. Nathan doesn't let go. His grip gets tighter. As Eleanor moves closer, Nathan pulls Ian to him, as though they are about to hug, and says in a loud hiss, "My private detective has uncovered some *very* interesting stuff over the last few days. So let me tell you, Ian, you might have been the last, but you certainly weren't the first."

Ian recoils, pulling his hand out of Nathan's grasp. He staggers back and Nathan goes with him, pushing him to the ground. As Ian lands, his glasses fall off, and he sits on the wet grass, looking dazed. Nathan's demons have taken hold of him now. He's broken the line, and he squares up to the whole churchyard, chest out, arms half raised as though ready to swing a punch. "Who else was screwing my wife, hey? You?" He points to a red-faced man in a pinstriped suit, who shakes his head rapidly and almost runs down to the gate. "What about you?" Another victim makes a hasty retreat.

Ian watches in horror, frozen to the ground. Nathan looks like he is about to charge, but before he can, Steve Kirby intercepts, pushing Nathan back and talking to him quietly. Meanwhile, Priya Prashad helps Ian get to his feet, while a furious Dickon and Ernie look on. Arabella's sisters have their arms around their mother, who is hunched over, her face hidden against their shoulders, her body heaving with sobs.

"Ian," Priya says, her voice soft but firm. "Perhaps it would be a good idea if you came down to the station and answered a few more questions for us."

31

the dinner guest

April 2005

Eleanor's mother has suffered a mild concussion from her fall and comes back with her arm in a sling. It will take six weeks to heal, and Eleanor's father gets busy redrafting his plans, trying to figure out how to get the rest of the roof on. "Hire someone," Eleanor's mother says through gritted teeth, but only when she threatens to walk out altogether does a roofing company get involved, and finishes the roof in less than two days.

With her mother out of action, Eleanor is kept busy taking on more of the household duties and helping with meals. She doesn't mind this so much, at least it provides a purpose to her days over the Easter vacation. Katie's mother hasn't invited her back.

Solomon brings around a few bags of fruit and vegetables for the family. He offers to help Eleanor's dad and ends up driving to town a few times for parts and equipment that are needed. Eventually, Eleanor's mother informs them that Solomon will be coming for dinner that evening, and catches the way Aiden's nose wrinkles at the prospect.

"He's our neighbor," she chides, "and it pays to be friendly. Besides, I want to thank him for helping us out so much."

"He's weird," Aiden says, playing with the pull tab on a can of coke, working at it until the whole thing comes off in his fingers, then dropping it into the can. He gets up, leaving the empty can on the table. "Anyway, I'm meeting Coby and Timmo soon. Timmo's brother is driving over to pick me up from the end of the road."

Their mother stops from her slow process of pouring herself a cup of tea in a cramped space with only one good arm. "Well, you can put that can in the trash for starters. And I'd rather you asked me than told me about your plans, if you don't mind."

"Mum," Aiden pushes his chair back harshly, heading for the door, "I'm fifteen."

And he's gone. Leaving the can on the table.

Eleanor goes across to pick it up, hearing her mother mutter, "Exactly" under her breath, but she says nothing else, just carries on dipping her tea bag up and down, up and down in the cup.

Dinner that night is three packets of noodles mixed with frozen vegetables and fried up in a premixed sweet-and-sour sauce, but afterward Solomon pats his pot belly and declares it the "best meal I've had in years," while Eleanor struggles to finish what's on her plate. She has been seated opposite him at their embarrassingly small and intimate table, trying not to look up so she doesn't have to watch his mouth collapsing and expanding like an old accordion as he works on his meal. His gums are so wrinkled and concave, she suspects there may not be many teeth left in his mouth, imagines them worn down by years of enthusiastic chewing. She'd hoped he would bring Charlie, but he had turned up without the dog. "He likes to steal food," he explained to Eleanor when she asked.

Eleanor's father dominates the evening, droning on about building technicalities that go completely over Eleanor's head. He's like a machine nowadays, unable to think outside the scope of his own project. She wonders if he'll ever come back to them. When Martin finally pauses to eat, Solomon looks across at Eleanor. "And how do you like to spend your spare time, then?" he asks. "Not much to do around here."

"Oh, Eleanor is a budding artist, aren't you, Eleanor," her dad cuts in before she can reply. "She's pretty good, actually. Have you got your sketchbook handy, Els? Show Solomon your stuff."

Eleanor reddens. She balances her knife and fork on the lip of her plate, and goes across to the bed, collects the sketchbook, and shyly opens it to show Solomon one of her recent pencil drawings.

"Well, I never," Solomon says, taking the pad and holding it up to see it more clearly. "It's Charlie boy." And he lets out a rasping chuckle that makes everyone else smile too.

He hands the pad back to Eleanor, who studies her own drawing of the dog waiting on the back of the pickup, pride swelling inside her.

"Your father is right. You are very good," Solomon says, and she smiles back at him.

"My wife was a bit of a painter too," he tells them all. "My Lily, god rest her soul. We were together for forty-six years, emigrated in 1959 when Philippa was three. I tell you," he leans forward and his crumpled, rheumy gaze is fixed on Eleanor's father, "I loved that woman but I didn't tell her often enough. Hardly told her at all, truth be told. Too easy to take for granted, all she did at the time—I hoped she just knew, you know, without me getting all mushy and that. But when you end up like me, the one left behind, then—then you see things a little differently. And sometimes you wish you hadn't left so much unsaid."

Eleanor glances between the two men. Her father's eyes are wide. For once, it looks like he doesn't know what to say.

Solomon sits back and catches Eleanor's eye. "It's just nice to eat in company nowadays—Charlie's great, but he's not such a talker." And he gives that rasping laugh again.

Eleanor finds herself smiling and realizes that she is actually warming to this peculiar old man. She looks across to her mother, wondering what she's making of all this, only to realize that she isn't really with them. Her food is half finished, she's just pushing it around her plate with the fork clasped tightly in the palm of her good hand. Eventually, it's as though she can stand it no longer. "I thought Aiden would be back by now," she says softly to her husband in the brief lull in conversation.

"Where is yer boy tonight?" Solomon asks.

"He's made some new friends, but we don't really know them yet," Eleanor's mother admits.

"Not too many friends to make out here," Solomon says. "You know their names?"

Eleanor's mother hesitates.

"I think he said Coby and Timmo, didn't he, Mum?" Eleanor asks.

Solomon exhales slowly and purses his lips in a way that makes both Eleanor and her mom shift uneasily.

"You know them?" Eleanor's mother's voice is faint.

"Unfortunately, I do," Solomon says. "Coby ain't a bad lad, but he's easily led. That Timmo, though, you gotta watch him. Likes to pilfer stuff—been brought up that way, I'm afraid. His dad's the same and his mother's a rough old bird." He seems to remember Eleanor is listening. "Excuse me," he adds, nodding at her, "but it's true. The kids are different nowadays," he continues, gesturing at Eleanor but looking at her parents. "Lot of unhealthy stuff going on, too much access to all sorts of things, don't give a damn about their parents. Not like it was when our Philippa was a girl, but that was a long time ago."

Eleanor can't fail to notice the icy glance her mother shoots at her father. It's a look that says, *What have you brought us to?* To her surprise, for a moment even her father loses his usual zeal and appears perturbed.

"Well, thanks for the warning. We'll keep a closer eye on him. I'm afraid the building has been occupying me a bit too much of late." Eleanor's mother snorts loudly and they all pretend not to notice, although Martin glares in her direction. "But it shouldn't be too much longer now, at least not until the main structure is finished. Like I was saying," he continues, bringing the plans over and laying them out on the table, pushing the dirty plates toward his wife, "we just have to adjust the angle here . . ."

And he's off again, and it was as though they'd never had him back.

Eleanor catches her mother's eye and sees the glint of a tear reflected in the low, yellow light. She jumps up and quickly collects the plates from in front of her mother, who sits there with one arm resting in its sling, biting her lip, not speaking or looking at any of them.

Eleanor glances across at her father. His head is bent over his drawings. *How can he not notice this?* She wants to shake him.

Then she realizes Solomon is staring at her. He doesn't look away and there is some kind of meaning, some intent of transmission in his eyes, but she becomes too uncomfortable too quickly in that wrinkled gaze and breaks the eye contact before she has time to figure out what it means.

As she moves to the kitchen area, she finds herself unsettled by that look. Perhaps it's his ancientness—she can't help but feel repelled by the rough, uneven redness of his face, the way the skin beneath his eyebrows collapses into his eyes, the mole on his cheek sprouting thick gray hair, and his brown, uneven teeth. Yet when she'd caught his gaze, it felt like he saw something in her that the others didn't. And, whatever it was, she isn't sure she likes it.

32

aftermath

*C*hris Lennon, contracts manager at Parker & Lane, is heading fast down the lane away from the church, half expecting to feel a hand on his shoulder any moment. He is sure Nathan caught his eye as he roared at them all; sure he saw the guilt emanating from Chris, even though he bitterly regrets that one-night stand, and it was two years ago, for heaven's sake, and he's since lived in terror at the thought of it coming to light. He'll have to lie low for a while, he thinks, sweat pouring off him as he finally reaches his car.

In the churchyard, most of the congregation have turned to statues. A wind whips up as Eleanor watches Ian walk between the detectives, through the gate toward their unmarked car. A few late-fallen leaves skitter between the gravestones, and some of the mourners grab on to hats or tighten scarves. Nathan stares after Ian, chest heaving, his face aglow. No one seems to know what to do next.

The vicar breaks the impasse, his white robes billowing behind him as he moves to clasp the hands of Dickon and June and then walks between people, his steady touch releasing them from uncertainty. As soon as he has spoken to them, groups begin to drift away toward the gate.

Throughout this Eleanor has been aware of a distant noise, like the zaps of mosquito lamps. Now she realizes that a dozen cameras with long lenses are resting on the churchyard wall, clicking away.

She is still close to Arabella's family. June's head comes up from her daughter's shoulder, and she reaches in her bag for a fresh bunch of tissues, clutching them to her mouth. The sisters confer over their mother and begin to lead her toward the gate.

Once they have gone, Dickon turns to Nathan. "You couldn't control yourself for one day?" he growls. "Do you think this is what Arabella would have wanted? *Do you?* Oh, but I forgot, you have never cared one jot what Arabella might have wanted."

Still caught in the remnants of the receiving line, Eleanor is uncomfortably close to all this, but she doesn't dare move lest she draw attention to herself. She can only watch as Ernie comes toward Dickon, and Dickon holds his hands up, backing away. "Don't, Ernie—just don't."

Ernie gives Dickon a curt nod, then his gaze falls on his son. "Nathan, let's go." Ernie takes Nathan's arm and leads him away, but there's no escaping the small scrum of journalists that converge on the gate as they get closer. They remind Eleanor of seagulls, jostling one another, cawing for scraps.

It has all happened so fast that Eleanor has forgotten about Susan, but as it dawns on her that her aunt may have witnessed all this, she looks around. The churchyard is clearing surprisingly quickly, as though the air is tainted now. There is no sign of Susan, but Will stands a few feet away, and hurries over as he catches her eye.

"What the hell just happened?" he exclaims, clutching the neck of his coat tighter, hopping from foot to foot in the cold. "Was there any truth in that, or has Nathan gone completely insane?"

"No, he's not insane—well, not in this instance. My uncle was having an affair with Arabella."

Will's mouth falls open and his face reddens. "Are you serious?"

Eleanor is taken aback by his expression. She isn't sure if he's appalled or angry, or something else. She is trying to gauge how much to tell him when she jumps at a soft touch on her arm. Heart hammering, she turns to find the vicar at her shoulder.

"I didn't mean to startle you." He quickly removes his hand. "Are you Eleanor?"

She nods, frowning.

"Your aunt asked me to find you. Would you mind coming with me for a moment?"

Eleanor glances apologetically at Will, whose jaw is still slack with surprise. "Wait here for me," she says, and then follows the vicar back through the silent church. It is so different now all the pews are empty, and yet there remains a heightened energy to the air. At the front, Arabella stares out of her portrait into the empty, cavernous space, past the wilting flowers, beyond the vicar and Eleanor hurrying down the aisle, as though she can see nothing and everything at the same time.

Eleanor tries not to look at the photograph as the vicar guides her toward the cracked wood of the arched vestry door and opens it for her.

Susan paces the small area inside, hands repeatedly smoothing her clothes, her head jerking slightly with each rapid breath.

"Susan?" Eleanor begins tentatively.

As soon as Susan sees Eleanor, she rushes across and grabs Eleanor's hand, pushing a bunch of house keys into her palm. "I want you to go and get the girls from school as fast as you can," she says. Her voice is steady, but her eyes are wide. "Take them straight home, and do not talk to anyone until you've heard from me. Do you understand?"

There will be no refusal, Eleanor realizes that. Susan is not asking a question, she is giving a command. "Yes," she replies.

"I'm going to get a taxi to the police station and meet my lawyer there," Susan continues, pulling her bag off her shoulder and fumbling inside it. She opens her wallet, and Eleanor watches her fingers tremble as she pulls out a fifty-pound note. "Here," Susan pushes the money toward her. "This is probably too much but just take it—I'll collect the change later. I've already called a taxi for you, and the school knows you're coming. Remember, don't let the girls talk to anyone, okay? And *don't* tell them anything except we are both caught up with work. I know Naeve won't believe you, but it doesn't matter for now. I'll talk to her later."

"Okay." Eleanor can feel the flush in her face as she takes the money. The responsibility of getting this right is daunting. She turns to go, keen to leave this unraveling vision of her aunt behind.

"They're making a huge mistake," Susan snaps to her back. Eleanor turns around and Susan's stare is fierce, unwavering. "I'll be back as soon as I can, and Ian will be with me. I can promise you that. I don't care if Nathan is out for blood, there's no way we're taking the fall for this. If you remember anything, Eleanor—*anything* about that night that you have yet to tell anyone—I suggest you tell me right now."

As Eleanor tries to hold her aunt's gaze, she can feel herself trembling. Is Susan threatening her? Is Susan telling her, while they stand facing each other in this centuries-old place of worship, that she doesn't believe Eleanor's story? Will she throw her niece to the hounds if it means saving her own skin?

Or is Susan just upset, and Eleanor paranoid?

"I don't, Susan, I promise," she replies.

Susan just stares at her. They have forgotten the vicar is there, until he speaks. Perhaps he senses the charged atmosphere and steps in to break it. "There is a back way out of the church," he says to Susan. "Would you like to use that?"

"Yes please," Susan answers. "You go out the front, Eleanor. The taxi will be here at any moment. You can give those journalists something to gawk at."

Eleanor takes her leave, hurrying back along the dim, empty aisle of the church, ever aware of Arabella's photo, refusing to turn to look at it, as though she might find Arabella's eyes were no longer gazing into the distance but fixed directly on her. She can feel them anyway, boring into her back, asking, *What did you do, Eleanor? What did you do?*

33

the cubby

April–May 2005

During autumn, the air takes a sharp turn toward coldness. Over the school vacation, Eleanor has set herself a project: to restore the cubby, so that she has somewhere to go. Somewhere she doesn't have to listen to the sounds of house construction and her mother and father snapping at one another. Somewhere the air isn't stippled with tension.

Aiden is disappearing more and more with his new friends. He probably feels the same, but she hasn't asked him. He seems to enjoy winding her up when she tries to talk to him nowadays—rolling his eyes, shaking his head, sticking his tongue into the bulge of his chin. She's given up for now, just hopes he gets over himself sooner rather than later.

Nevertheless, she's hollow and wistful when she heads down to the site of the original cubby on her first free day. Was it really only a few months ago that she and Aiden had built it together? She doesn't want a remake of the original, but to create a new structure close to that first site, under the shelter of a large paperbark tree, which will hopefully afford it some protection from the wind and rain.

It takes five times as long to build it as it had done with Aiden, and it is smaller and not so impressive, but every time she heads down to the bottom of the block and sees it waiting, she is proud of her solo efforts. For the first few days she lies inside, her chin propped on her elbows, staring out of the entrance, looking up at a few white clouds scudding innocently across a blue sky, watching insects scurry through the patchy grass. She has managed to snag a piece of laminate flooring that was just lying around—she didn't bother asking, just took it when no one was looking. She doubts anyone will head this way any time soon. Yet even with the laminate, she often finds herself plucking at the small burrs that have hitched a ride on her clothes. She steals snacks too, and surreptitiously opens a cardboard box full of cushions to snag a few for the den, so she can read in relative comfort. It's not perfect, but it will do.

She brings *Harry Potter* and *Artemis Fowl* with her, as well as her sketchbook, but finds herself taking long, daydreamy breaks from her reading and drawing just to stare at the landscape that stretches away from her to another row of trees in the distance. On the left is the fence line that marks the boundary between their land and Solomon's. She hasn't dared to go over the fence again since that first time.

When she'd told her mother about the cubby, Gillian had seemed pleased. "Just tell me if you go anywhere else, won't you. I need to know where you are." But there had been no mention of a visit to see what Eleanor has been doing, which leaves Eleanor feeling half sad and half glad.

The month drifts on, and the cubby provides some respite from the tedium of the aimless weekends. During the week there is school and homework, but on Saturday and Sunday there is just Eleanor and her parents. Aiden goes out at sunup and stays out till bedtime. Eleanor watches her mother's gaze follow him everywhere on the rare occasions he's in the shed; the way her mouth opens and her tongue flits over her bottom lip, as though she's always on the verge of saying something but never quite able to go through with it.

Aiden's repeated rejection of their mother is difficult for Eleanor to watch, in part because it makes her feel guilty too. She knows she is doing similar things—answering in monosyllabic sentences, ignoring attempts to engage her—determined that her mother should know at all times just how hard this life is.

Sometimes, during the long, dry days, she falls asleep in the cubby. One unseasonably warm day in May she wakes from such a nap to find a bee buzzing around her, and she stays still, irritated, hoping it will go away.

And then something else brushes against her leg and past her hand. Something cold and smooth.

A clap of panic makes her dizzy. It has to be a snake—a snake is gliding along the left side of her body, staying close. *No, it can't be*, she thinks, trying to rationalize her fear. Haven't snakes hibernated by now? Yes, it must be something else.

She lifts her head a fraction to look down her left side and sees a long brown reptile inching toward her, nestled into her body.

It's a snake.

Every part of her cries *move*, and yet she is pinned to the ground in terror. She has no idea what kind of snake this is—only knows that plenty are dangerous; that an eleven-year-old girl was on the news last summer because she almost died after being bitten. And that girl's parents had raced to help as soon as it happened, saving her. If Eleanor gets bitten, no one will know. No one will check on her for hours. It will take her a few minutes to get back to the house, and that's if she jogs—a few minutes with poison circulating in her body.

She might not make it back.

She cannot help herself. She begins to cry, snuffling as quietly as she can, aware all the time of the snake resting just a fraction away from her left hand, expecting to feel its strike at any moment. She tries to console herself with the thought that the snake seems far more relaxed than she is.

And then she hears barking, alarmingly close by.

The snake is aware of it too; it is moving along her left side again. *Go away, go away*, she prays, hoping it will glide out of the entrance, but of course the snake is far more sensible than that, and moves farther inside, retreating from this new threat, sliding right past Eleanor's head into the darkest recess of the cubby.

As its tail moves past her eyes, she makes a split-second decision. There's no way can she lie in here with the snake behind her, unsure what it is doing, how close it is, whether it is asleep or watching her. It might touch her again at any moment; it might slither right over her body. She goes to jump up, but desperation turns all her movements to slow motion. It seems to take half an hour from the time she raises her head until her hands hit the floor and help push her up on to her trembling legs. Every moment she expects to feel sharp fangs stab her skin. As soon as she is on her feet she charges forward, away from the cubby, panting as she runs, vaguely aware of a figure in the distance, and heading straight for it, for safety.

Solomon catches her arms as she bangs heavily into him. Charlie races toward the cubby but Solomon's "No, Charlie, stop!" echoes loud and sharp. Charlie seems to understand the danger, because he halts to paw at the ground instead, whimpering, looking desperate to go farther but not moving an inch or taking his eye off the cubby's entrance.

Eleanor begins to sob as she leans against Solomon's chest. She lets him comfort her, his hand patting her back slowly, saying nothing for a while, until her cries subside.

"Is it a snake?" he asks then.

She nods, still unable to speak.

"Loads of folks think they sleep for the winter, you know, but they don't always. They just slow down, so you gotta be careful. A nice warm day like this one will bring them back out for a while. That fellow was just looking for somewhere cozy and he found you. You must have had a scare there." He lets go of her, and her awkwardness returns as she nods at his words.

"What are you doing here?" she asks.

"Did you hear Charlie barking? He'd run ahead and was going ballistic, so I knew there was trouble. I climbed the fence after he jumped over it—haven't done that in a while, let me tell you." He puts his hands behind his back and manages a stiff-looking stretch. "Come on then, Charlie." He whistles and the dog responds immediately, racing past him without needing to be told where they are going, shimmying under a gap in the fence.

Solomon turns to follow the dog, and then stops. "Actually, would you like to come up to the house with me?" he asks. "There's something I'd like to show you."

Still wiping her eyes, Eleanor is caught off guard by the question. She wants to run back to her mom and dad, until she pictures the scene—trying to tell them how scared she had felt while their heads are stuck inside cupboards or their hands twitch impatiently, poised with hammers or drills.

Solomon is waiting for an answer, and she feels a surge of defiance.

"Okay," she says, and as he turns around and begins to walk away from the cubby, she sets off alongside him.

34

the school run

*F*reya Jackson, headmistress of St Josephine's, is brooding on the Mortimer family as she heads to the Year Eight classroom to collect Naeve. First they forget Savannah's carol concert, and now they're taking the girls out of school like this. Is it any wonder Naeve's drawings have been causing talk in the staff room recently? Ms. Jackson hopes they'll have sorted themselves out by the new year. She is used to dealing with recalcitrant parents, but she's not sure she's a match for Susan Mortimer. The woman scares the hell out of her.

When Eleanor gets to the front entrance of the church, to her relief Will is still waiting for her. "What's going on?" he asks as soon as he sees her.

"Susan wants me to go and get the girls." She looks across to where the journalists were standing, and realizes that quite a lot of them have gone. She's not sure why she'd assumed they would still be waiting, since all the main players in this drama are no longer visible.

"Can I do anything to help?" Will asks as he follows her gaze.

"Susan has called me a taxi." As she surveys the scene, she can see the top part of a black cab sitting outside the gate. "Could you check if that's it, and could you help me get past the press if needs be?"

"Of course."

"Thank you."

He runs down to the gate and disappears for a moment. When he reappears he gestures for her to come.

Eleanor's legs feel unsteady as she walks down the path. She flicks a glance across at the remaining journalists, and sees Aisha standing among them, watching her go. She tenses, waiting to hear her name called, but none of them move, even though their eyes follow her.

Will opens the taxi door for her.

"Do you want to come with me?" she asks desperately.

He shakes his head. "I'd better not, Susan might not like it. I'll call you later." And he pushes the door closed.

Eleanor sits on her hands, biting her lip. She is lost for a moment until a voice from the front says, "Where to, love?"

"St Josephine's school in Notting Hill. Do you know it? I'm not sure of the street name."

"It's okay, I know it," he assures her, and the taxi moves quickly away from the church. As she looks out of the small rear window, she sees Will walking away from the churchyard, his arms tight to his sides as though he's feeling the cold, his hands clamped in his pockets and his head down.

As she settles in her seat, her thoughts move to the girls. She's dreading their questions already. How is she going to look them in the eye and lie to them? They're bound to know something's up when they're being taken from school in the middle of the day. She hates that Susan has asked this of her; she can't stand the idea of setting herself on the side of the adults by keeping things from her cousins. She recalls the shock on her uncle's face as he'd hit the ground, and his slumped shoulders as the police led him away. Did they really need to do that so publicly? It made him look so guilty. Was that the intention?

Then she remembers Susan's words in the vestry. Her aunt will do anything to make sure the blame falls elsewhere.

She shivers. Wherever she turns she feels suspicious eyes upon her, as though everyone is trying to crack her apart, to pry out what is hidden. It's as though they sense her shame, her fear that there is something dangerous inside her, some power she can unwittingly turn outward to cast tragedy on all those who come too close.

She thinks of Arabella's portrait, staring down the main aisle of the church. *What did you do, Eleanor? What did you do?*

Keep calm, she tells herself. But she can barely sit still. How she wishes she wasn't on her way to get the girls. She doesn't want to be responsible for anyone else right now when she can hardly hold it together herself.

But they are here already, the driver is pulling up outside those imposing school gates. Eleanor is always surprised at how quickly you can get across London in daylight—she's so used to going below ground to the Tube.

"Can you wait for me?" she asks as she climbs out. "I won't be long."

"As long as you know the meter's still running," the driver replies gruffly.

She glances at the meter. Twenty-five pounds down. She should have enough if this doesn't take too long. She buzzes the speaker at the gate and tells them why she's here. There's a click and the gate begins to move, allowing her entrance. The security takes her aback. It's so different to her childhood, it's more like visiting a prison than a school.

The office is right by the main entrance, and through the glass door she sees Naeve and Savannah waiting on rigid seats. Savvie swings her legs back and forth as she reads a book, while Naeve stares into the distance. When they see Eleanor, they jump up and Savannah hugs her. "We get to leave school early," she tells her pointlessly as they head outside.

"What's going on now?" Naeve grumbles behind her, struggling to carry her oversized bag.

Eleanor doesn't answer the question, just says, "Come on, the taxi's waiting." As they climb inside, she is surprised to see another ten pounds has gone onto the meter—surely they weren't gone for that long.

"Harborne Grove, please," she calls out, and watches the meter nervously as they set off for home.

Savvie begins chattering on in her usual way about Christmas parties and Christmas food and Christmas movies, and Eleanor is bolstered by the girls' presence. It's only a couple of days until they finish school for the holidays. Perhaps things will seem better when they are at home every day, with Naeve drifting around and Savvie bringing lightness and laughter into the stultifying atmosphere. She hopes they will carry everyone through the festivities; she hopes they will be too excited to notice the forced gaiety around them.

She tries to picture them all opening presents together in less than two weeks, but the scene is like watching something on screen. She cannot imagine being part of it. She is not just counting the days but the hours until that moment, as though if they can get to Christmas they will survive this whole storm cloud that has come upon them, because it feels as if something terrible is lurking in the shadows, biding its time. She keeps thinking back to Ian's confession of his affair and to his scuffle in the churchyard. His vagueness has bothered her lately, but that is nothing compared to Nathan's blatant aggression. What would have happened if Ian hadn't been there to rescue her from Nathan's clutches a few days ago? How long would Susan have stood by and watched?

She tries to imagine what her uncle is doing right now, as he speaks to the police. They had all been caught up so quickly in this toxic situation, but was that only by chance? She has so many questions, but the biggest one of all hovers ever present at her shoulder.

Will Ian tell the police about the ring?

"Eleanor, Eleanor," Naeve is nudging her fiercely. "What's going on?"

It takes Eleanor a moment to reorient and work out what Naeve means, but when she does she has a renewed flash of fear. They are almost at the house, but a small crowd awaits them, gathered outside with cameras in hands or on tripods.

"Will you be okay, miss?" the driver asks, sounding less gruff now.

"We will be once we get inside," she replies with more conviction than she feels.

As he draws up to the curb, the journalists turn and start to converge on the cab. "Hang on a minute," the driver tells them. He gets out and opens the door, shouting at the crowd, "Let these young girls through to their house, please!" He has a burly bouncer's presence and the journalists automatically recede a step or two, but the cameras still click and whir as the cabbie shepherds the three of them to the door. Eleanor fumbles in her bag for the key, aware of all those eyes watching them just feet away beyond the garden wall. When she finally opens the door the cabbie ushers them inside, and she hurriedly closes the door on everyone with a bang.

Immediately, there's a sharp knock, and a voice beyond the door shouts, "You forgot to pay me, miss!"

Eleanor finds the fifty-pound note in her bag and pushes it through the letterbox, where it is snatched from the other side. "Thank you," comes his gravelly voice, and the letterbox falls closed again.

Once she has double-checked the door is locked, she turns to see both girls sitting on the expansive staircase, their backpacks at their feet, their gazes firmly on her, waiting. Savvie's bottom lip quivers; Naeve's expression is stony.

"Has something bad happened to Mummy and Daddy now?" Savvie asks, and a few large, fat tears break free and skim her cheeks.

"I keep telling her you would have told us that already, but she won't believe me," Naeve says crossly, putting her arm around her younger sister.

"Savvie." Eleanor goes and kneels in front of her. "I promise you, you don't need to be scared. Your mum and dad are caught up with work, and those horrible journalists out there are insisting on harassing everyone they can find because they want to know what happened to Arabella. Listen." She looks at each of the girls. "Let's go into the kitchen and find something really delicious to eat, something you're not normally allowed. There must be a stash of chocolate or biscuits somewhere."

Savvie nods enthusiastically, but Naeve shakes her head. "I'm not hungry, I think I'll just go to my room," she says, and sets off up the stairs before Eleanor can reply.

Eleanor's mind stays with Naeve as she and Savvie hunt through the kitchen for tasty treats. The best they can do is a box of Harrods assorted biscuits, but Savvie seems happy enough with that, and they take the whole tin through to the family room, where, luckily, Savvie knows how to switch the enormous TV on. Eleanor closes all the curtains. Even though the two small windows only lead to the back garden, she wouldn't be surprised to find that one of those parasites had jumped the fence so they could peer in.

"I'll be back in a minute," she tells Savvie. "I'm just going to check on your sister."

"Okay," Savvie replies, spitting crumbs, eyes fixed on the television, her worries forgotten for now.

Eleanor heads quickly up the stairs to Naeve's room, half expecting to find the door closed. However, it's wide open, and Naeve is sitting on the bed, her sketchbook in front of her. She carries on drawing a small flock of birds as Eleanor comes closer. Eleanor marvels at the way Naeve can add the smallest details to their body to lend them life and movement in flight.

"What do you want?" Naeve asks abruptly.

"I came to check on you."

Naeve shrugs and continues sketching. "You don't have to babysit me."

"I'm not. Anyway, I'm sure your parents won't be too long," Eleanor assures her, hoping she sounds convincing.

"I know they're not at work." As she speaks, Naeve's pencil scratches out bird after bird.

Eleanor has no idea what to say. After an eternity of silence, she changes tack. "I love watching you draw, you're so talented."

Naeve looks up and meets her eye. "I'm not the only one. I've seen your sketches too, you know."

Eleanor suddenly becomes still. "What do you mean?"

Behind her glasses, Naeve's eyes narrow. "Do Mum and Dad know you have a habit of drawing people with their heads in nooses?"

Eleanor's heart begins to drum loudly in her ears. She allows the wave of fury to wash over her, steadying herself so she doesn't say something she might regret about snooping and privacy.

Naeve waits, chin tilted high, challenge written in every inch of her posture. Then her whole body sags abruptly. "I'm sorry, I didn't mean to say that. It's none of my business."

Eleanor's anger softens as her heart goes out to her cousin. She sits on the bed.

"How much have your mum and dad told you about what happened to my family?"

Naeve frowns. "Hardly anything. We barely knew about you until you came to stay."

Eleanor feels a stab of pain at this. "Well, it's a long story," she says to Naeve. "And I will try to tell it to you, but now is not the time, because your mum and dad could be back at any moment." She doesn't yet know how she'll summon the words.

Naeve's eyes fill with tears. "Is every family so full of secrets and all this shit?" she asks, her gaze imploring Eleanor for answers. "At the moment I feel like I don't know Mum or Dad at all. I'm so scared that something really bad is about to happen to us all."

Eleanor pulls her cousin into an embrace, feeling Naeve's shoulders heave. How she wishes she could tell Naeve that it is going to be all right. But she will not add to her cousin's distress with those awful adult platitudes, when everything is so clearly wrong. And yet she also wants to say, *I know what you're going through; I know how it feels to lose faith in your own parents.* But she doesn't say it, because as Naeve begins to recover, she stiffens in Eleanor's arms. "I'm okay," she mutters, pushing Eleanor away, and Eleanor can almost see the shutters going down in front of her, one by one.

Nevertheless, her fury is building toward her aunt and uncle. Why are they behaving like this, causing their eldest child such distress? Can't they see what's happening around them, or are they too blinkered to think about anyone but themselves?

As she gets up to leave Naeve in peace, Eleanor glances at the drawing Naeve has been working on. Earlier, Naeve had shielded a portion of it with her hands, but she's forgotten about that now. The birds she has sketched are not just flying, they are attacking. They are diving and smothering and pecking the body of a woman in water. Obliterating the woman's face.

35

the farmhouse

May 2005

At the door to the farmhouse, Solomon doesn't use a key, just opens the front door, and Charlie bounds in ahead of them. "Used to be an outside dog," Solomon mutters, "lives in the lap of luxury now, since Lily died."

As they had trekked through the field of abandoned farm equipment, Eleanor had begun to have second thoughts about this idea. Solomon had said little on the way except to tell her of his previous encounters with snakes around the house—once even in their kitchen—talking as he threw a few sticks for Charlie. Meanwhile, Eleanor's feet had grown increasingly reluctant to step forward, urging her to turn around, but she couldn't because that wouldn't be polite, especially after Solomon had saved her back there. So now she waits behind Solomon while he slowly removes his shoes and puts on a pair of slippers.

There's no sign of the cat today, and inside the place isn't quite what she had expected. Once past the small porch they are straight into the front lounge, which contains two brown sofas covered with colorful crocheted rugs, and a television that looks like it should belong in a museum. There are numerous pieces of old-fashioned furniture and every available space is covered with an assortment of knickknacks: china animals, small vases, unidentifiable objects made of brass, trophies, glass jars, a few picture frames with cross stitch or dried flowers in them, and others with photos that she longs to look at more closely.

"Would you like a drink of water or a cup of tea?" Solomon asks as he heads through another door. She ambles behind, trying to take it all in. She's never seen a house like this before, so crammed full of stuff. Her nose wrinkles at the lingering scent of stale tobacco.

Shyness engulfs her. What is she doing here? She should never have come without telling her mom and dad.

"Just water, please."

Solomon runs the tap and fills her glass, and when he hands it to her he catches her eye. He looks even more unkempt than she remembers. White whiskers sprout over his chin and neckline, and he's wearing a pair of sweatpants. Perhaps he only makes an effort when he goes out.

It's uncomfortable standing so close together, and she casts around self-consciously with the drink clamped to her lips, desperately thinking of something to say or do that will make her feel less awkward.

"My wife did all this," he says, following her gaze. "My Lily. She's been gone nearly five years now, but I haven't moved a single thing. Still doesn't feel right." He stops and glances toward the window as though he might see someone familiar out there. Then he shakes his head and gestures toward the lounge. "Well, sit down, sit down," he says, ushering her back into his cramped living room, and she almost trips on a solid iron doorstop shaped like a large gecko. He carefully puts a coaster on the little coffee table in front of them, but Eleanor keeps her water clutched in her hands, unable to relax.

"When you've finished your drink, I'll show you why I brought you here," he says.

She nods. "Okay."

"I won't try to explain. Better you see for yourself."

He doesn't say anything more, so Eleanor downs her drink as quickly as she can, unsure whether she's keeping him waiting. When she puts down the empty glass he says, "Right then," and pats his knees then folds himself over to get up, going very slowly, as stiff as old dough. "Follow me."

They head back through the kitchen and turn another corner, into a darker recess of the house. Eleanor has a moment of acute fear, wondering if she should run while she can, but again her manners win out, because Solomon is saying something about his wife, about how she loved to sit in this room and paint, and then he says, "And here it is."

He throws open the door, and both the darkness and musty air are banished instantly as they enter a small glass conservatory, beautifully lit by the meek autumn sunshine. The view beyond the windows looks right across fields toward the sparsely wooded hills in the distance. There's a huge, old wicker chair in one corner, a little cabinet with over a dozen drawers on another side, and in the center, an old, paint-spattered easel.

"Lily would spend hours in here," he says, "working on these." And he gestures to a pile of canvases stacked up against one wall.

Entranced, Eleanor goes over and squats down in front of the first one. It's a painting of a blue wren—a watercolor, exquisite in its detail—as it perches on the end of a birdhouse, surrounded by flowers.

"Take a look through," Solomon says, and gingerly Eleanor reaches out and pulls the first canvas forward so she can see the next one. It's the profile of a magnificent brown horse, standing alone in a field, staring off into the distance at something beyond the frame. She keeps on rifling through the stack of paintings. There's a sunset field spattered with the silhouettes of kangaroos. The stare of a tawny frogmouth owl, its feathers fading into the background of black night. And right at the back, a portrait of Solomon, as he must have been twenty years ago, his face wizened but still full of life, not the disheveled ghost of a man who stands next to her, waiting.

"She painted our lives, and she painted the animals and land we loved. She exhibited locally, often won awards at the shows, but she rarely sold one. They meant too much to her. We ran out of space to put them up, so she just stacked them here when they were done. The joy of it was never about the finished product, not for Lily. It was the act of making them that she loved."

"They are incredible," Eleanor says when she looks up.

"I thought you would like them. Your picture of Charlie reminded me of some of Lily's sketches. And so, I have something for you." He holds out a small silver key. "This is for that door over there. You can use it whenever you like. I never come in now. There's too much of her in here. It's hard for me to be without her anywhere in the house, but it's the hardest in this room. I think she would like the thought of you coming in here to read or draw or whatever you want to do. I think she would much prefer that to you lying in a cubby with the snakes! It's not too much farther for you, is it?"

Eleanor gives him a brief smile as she takes the key, turning it over in her hand, unsure what to say. Could she really come down here and use this place? The idea of it is strange and thrilling. Her very own hideaway.

"Just make sure your parents don't mind," Solomon adds, watching her.

"Okay," she replies, thinking about how much her parents have interfered with her life of late. She decides there and then that she wants this place for herself, and that there's no way she's going to let them stop her from coming.

36

confession

*L*eyton Sims enjoys his job for the most part, but skulking around the posh front yards of Notting Hill in the rain, trying to keep his camera dry, isn't his idea of fun. Yet they are on to something here, he can feel it. That fracas in the churchyard had been brilliant. But the house is dark and all locked up—the only thing he can do for now is try to get some kind of picture through a chink in the curtains.

He has been careful enough to put his cell phone on silent, but he still feels it buzz in his pocket. He checks the message.

> Come back to the office. We've been called off.

He types quickly in reply.

> I hope you mean paid off.

When he sees the figure pop up on his screen he can't help but grin. *Thank you, Mr. Lane,* he says to himself as he climbs out of the garden, beginning to pack his camera away.

Eleanor texts her aunt, telling her that she and the girls are home safely, but there is no response. It seems there is nothing to do but wait. After a while, Naeve comes down and curls up in front of the television with Savvie, and Eleanor tries to join them but can't lose herself in the false gaiety of the Christmas movie they're watching. She's glad when her phone rings and she has an excuse to leave.

"Hi Will," she says, hurrying away from the lounge out of earshot.

"How's it all going?"

"I don't really know; we're just waiting for Susan and Ian to come back. There were quite a few journalists here already by the time we got home." She goes into the kitchen as she speaks, moving the curtain slightly. "I think some of them are still outside," she whispers, as though they might be able to hear her. Although it's dark, she can see shadows and the small lights of mobile phones bobbing around behind the wall.

"Bloody hell, Eleanor, this is crazy!"

"I know." She grimaces. "I just want it to be over."

"I'm just back from Arabella's wake, and believe me your uncle and Nathan were all anyone talked about."

"There was a wake? I didn't realize."

"Not an official one. Just a group of people from work getting together to talk and raise a glass. Everyone seems to think Nathan did something to her. And it turns out Arabella wasn't the only one having an affair. The rumor going around is that Caroline Cressman has given Nathan an alibi—although it's a pretty poor one."

"What?" Eleanor almost chokes on the word. "What do you mean?"

"Yeah, apparently they spent the night together last Thursday."

"He was sleeping with someone else while his wife died? That's terrible."

"Yep, I told you he was nasty, didn't I? Although now it appears that their marriage was pretty toxic from both sides. I'm still having trouble getting my head around your uncle with Arabella. That's pretty terrible too."

He sounds so affronted that Eleanor automatically says, "Yes." And yet she finds she wants to defend Ian and Arabella. It feels wrong to put them in the same category as Nathan after she's witnessed so much of his aggression.

Will is still talking. "Last Thursday a few people saw Nathan go looking for Arabella after she slapped him. And no one saw him come back to the party. So there's a convenient gap, but it wouldn't surprise anyone if he managed to wriggle his way out of it. Especially after today's performance. Do you think the police seriously suspect your uncle?"

"I really don't know."

"I can't stand this feeling of being under suspicion but having no idea of what's going on. Or whether the police have uncovered anything."

"I know, it's the same here. Sometimes I think this house is going to implode from the tension."

"I can only imagine. Susan must be mortified that all this is being aired in public."

"Yes," Eleanor agrees, thinking back to Susan's demeanor at the church. At the time it had seemed like she was holding up well, but now all Eleanor remembers is the twitchy way that Susan had moved around the room, and the tremor in her voice.

Will breaks into Eleanor's reverie. "Priscilla sent a message around this afternoon, telling us we don't have to go into work until after Christmas. A lot of people were taking the next week off anyway, to get a decent vacation. She's told everyone the office will be closed and locked for a week from tomorrow night, and everyone will be paid."

Eleanor wonders if she is likely to be paid, or if she's already off the books. Perhaps she's selfish for even thinking of it in the circumstances, but her funds are going to run alarmingly low over Christmas without any foreseeable income.

"I think it's all part of the damage control," Will continues. "After today they want time for the ruckus to die down. Can you imagine the place tomorrow—no one would do anything anyway; everyone would just be gossiping or on the internet doing last-minute gift shopping. Give it enough time and people will find other things to think about. It's a smart move. We've been told not to answer the phones either, and to refer all questions about Arabella's death to Susan's office. I'm sure Priscilla is loving it; she secretly thinks she runs the company anyway."

"So are you going into the office tomorrow?" Eleanor asks.

"Well, I'll have to pop in to collect some of my things," Will replies, "but I'll just tidy my desk and get out of there."

A thought occurs to Eleanor. "Could you get my stuff too? I left so abruptly that I didn't pick up everything. There's a couple of books and a sketchpad still there. I can meet you somewhere to collect them, if you have time?"

"Why don't you just come into the office?"

Eleanor hesitates. "I'm not sure. Susan told me to stay away."

"Well, whatever you want to do. I can meet you if you'd prefer. I doubt many people will go in, and if they do, they won't stay long. They'll want to make the most of the day off. I'm planning to get in and out as fast as I can in the morning."

"I could come and wait for you somewhere nearby," Eleanor suggests. "Would late morning suit you? Half past ten? Eleven?"

"Eleven would be good," Will agrees. "I'll see you then."

When Eleanor ends the call, she turns around to go back to the family room and finds Savvie standing behind her.

"Who was that?"

"A friend."

"Where's Mum and Dad?"

"I told you, they're caught up with work. I'm sure they'll be back soon."

"I'm hungry."

Eleanor nods. "Right, then, I'll see what I can find."

Savvie turns and hurries back toward the television. Eleanor goes into the kitchen and finds a tin of beans and some bread. A short time later she is taking trays of beans on toast to the girls. Savvie grabs hers gleefully, while Naeve offers a quiet "Thanks."

Eleanor sits and waits for them to finish, not feeling the least bit hungry.

Eventually, Savvie puts her knife and fork down with a clatter. "That was great," she says, her eyes still on the screen. Then she turns to Eleanor. "Mum and Dad *never* let us eat in the family room."

Eleanor snorts with laughter. "Now you tell me! Don't let on then, okay? Our secret!"

When she looks across, she sees that Naeve is also smiling to herself. It isn't much, but it buoys Eleanor through the next hour of cajoling them to switch the TV off and get into their pajamas.

The girls are both in bed by the time Eleanor hears the front door open. Savvie is spread-eagled on top of her covers, cheek pressed against the pillow, snoring softly. Naeve's door is closed but Eleanor doubts she is asleep.

Eleanor has been lying on her bed, browsing the web on her phone. She tenses as she hears the door, already forgetting the contents of a salacious gossip article about Johnny Depp. She jumps up and heads down from the upper floor, seeing Naeve already in front of her. They both hesitate at the top of the stairs.

By the front door, Susan and Ian are slowly taking off coats and scarves and boots. No words pass between them, not even a look. The clock on the wall is the only perceptible noise, until Naeve breaks the silence. "What's going on?"

As Susan glances up at her daughter, Eleanor sees that her eyes are puffy and red. "Come on," Susan says, heading up the stairs and reaching out to Naeve. "I'll tuck you in and we can have a talk." She doesn't even glance at Eleanor, just moves right past her as though she weren't there.

Naeve frowns at Eleanor before she turns to follow her mother, but goes as bid. Which leaves Eleanor alone with her uncle.

"Come into the front room," Ian says, beckoning her downstairs.

She takes the stairs slowly, then follows him through the large double doors.

"I need a drink," he mutters, walking over to a large cabinet set against the far wall. He takes out a bottle of amber liquid and turns to wave it at Eleanor. "You?"

"All right," she agrees, and he grabs two tumblers and pours them both a few inches. He sets them on the large coffee table and Eleanor picks hers up and has a sip, then realizes that the last time she felt this acrid burn down her esophagus she was in the midst of getting drunk on the *Atlantic*. She recoils and sets her glass down quickly, not wanting to touch it again.

"Susan and I have both made statements to the police about my whereabouts on the night Arabella died," Ian begins, tipping his drink down his throat in one smooth movement and going to the cabinet to pour himself another. "Although, since Susan was at the party and then went to the office for a while, we might need to get Naeve to make a statement too."

Poor Naeve, Eleanor thinks. "Did you tell them about the ring?" she asks quietly.

She watches her uncle's jaw and fist clench as he lifts up the bottle again. "I thought that would be your first question. I haven't mentioned it. We don't know how you came by it, so how can we begin to explain that to the police? Susan mustn't find out about it either, she's close enough to the edge as it is. After the memorial she now has to face Nathan and Ernie, and I'm not sure what will happen. They have friends in high places, I know that much. I'll deal with the ring, Eleanor, and I'll make sure Naeve keeps quiet. For all of our sakes, you mustn't say anything, okay?"

In the low light his glare is so fierce, so intense, that Eleanor finds herself complying. "Okay," she agrees, but this is just to buy herself some time. What will Ian say if she confesses to confiding in Will? The thought of it makes her squirm. Can she really expect Will to keep quiet for them all, forever?

Her uncle is watching her closely, as though he is near to reading her thoughts. She needs to divert his attention to something else. "Can you tell me again what happened when you found me on the doorstep?"

Ian grimaces. "I picked you up and you cried out, 'Stop! Stop!' but your eyes were glazed, I don't think you knew it was me. My entrance into the house was awkward, I struggled to hold you and banged about a bit, then Naeve appeared. I was sharp with Naeve because I didn't want her to witness the state you were in. I told her to go back to bed."

"And what about Susan?"

"She wasn't happy either when she saw the state of you." He pauses. "I managed to get you upstairs and took your dress off and covered you up as best as I could. I half expected we'd be calling a doctor in the morning. I couldn't believe it when you got up and went into work."

Eleanor flinches at the image of him putting her to bed, undressing her as she lay there, comatose. She doesn't know how to respond.

"Eleanor, please," her uncle says, "keep quiet, otherwise that ring might land one of us in great trouble."

Eleanor's sympathy is dwindling, and anger is rushing in. She had believed her uncle when he said he was desperate to protect his family, his daughters, but now—is this closer to the truth? Is he much more concerned about saving his own skin than what might happen to Naeve and Savvie, or to Eleanor? Or about what might have happened to Arabella, for that matter?

She jumps up as a wave of fury crashes over her. "Do you know you have a thirteen-year-old daughter upstairs who thinks her mum and dad are hiding things from her? What do you think it's doing to her, being told not to talk about this or that, without any explanation? Would you rather she was frightened of you than found out about your affair? Do you really imagine you are protecting her from anything? Do you think she senses nothing from the horrid atmosphere in this place? There were journalists outside the house all afternoon; we had to run the gauntlet just to get in the door."

Ian stands up too. He looks shocked rather than angry, but when he speaks his voice has deepened. "Eleanor, I thank you for all you did for the girls today. Please remember, though, that while we have welcomed you into our house, and you are part of our family, you do not need to tell me how to parent my daughter. We are doing our best. You are still so young—you think that if you tell the truth about everything, then all will be well. Real life doesn't work like that, Eleanor. The truth can blow people apart."

"And I promise you," Eleanor says, standing her ground, "that the lies will do that too. It might just take a little longer. Which would you rather: slow torture or quick relief?"

Her uncle moves closer. At once the room seems darker, with only the lamp in the corner casting an insipid yellow glow, as though it hardly dares to shine too brightly.

"All we need to do," he growls, "is to hold our nerve. Would you really wreck everything for just a few more days of waiting? The *truth* is that somehow you ended up with that ring. The *truth* is that neither Susan nor I were involved in whatever terrible thing happened to Arabella that night. We have invited you into our home, we have given you the benefit of the doubt, we have agreed that you were not involved in what happened—even though you were obviously plastered on some sort of drug high. If you wanted to confess you had the ring, then you should have done it right at the start, before the rest of us were dragged into it. Now, if you care for our daughters, if you care anything for us, Eleanor, I implore you to keep quiet and not destroy our family."

They stand facing one another, chests rising and falling as though they have just run a marathon. Something in Eleanor is building. She is afraid she might explode from being dragged back into things she had hoped she would never have to relive.

She glares at her uncle, eyes flashing, and snaps, "You sound just like my dad."

37

trespassing

May 2005

"Y ou didn't get bitten, did you?"

After his snapped remark, Eleanor's father begins to descend from his ladder as she tells her mother about the snake. As he walks over, at first Eleanor thinks he is coming to comfort her, but then he is there with his hands on his hips, watching her, his voice tired and annoyed. And the way he says it—his tone suggesting that it would be highly inconvenient if she had done something so stupid—makes her bristle. Her mother sighs and adds, "You probably shouldn't be down there on your own, just in case," shrinking Eleanor's world in a sentence. It's all of this that makes Eleanor begin to yell.

"You don't even care!" she shrieks. "Just leave me alone!"

She runs away from that hateful house and back toward the waiting, protective bulk of the shed, charging in and throwing herself on her bunk bed, half hoping and half dreading that her mother will appear.

For a moment she had almost forgotten the incident that set all this off but now she recalls that soft, cool form slithering next to her and she jumps from her bed and begins heaving the covers back in a fit, checking all around the mattress and doing the same on the upper bunk. When she is sure it is all clear, she tries to lie down again, but there is no chance she can relax now. This is all her parents' fault. They have deserted her. Aiden has deserted her. She hates them. *Hates* them.

She stiffens as she hears footsteps approach the shed. The door swings open, and both her parents come in. Her mother smiles at her, but it is her father who comes over, pulls her up to sit, and wraps his arms around her. "I don't mean to be so grumpy and distracted," he murmurs into her neck. "I'm sorry you had a scare."

Her mother sits down next to her and rubs her leg gently. "Are you okay now?"

"Listen," her father moves away from her but keeps hold of her shoulders, and she sees a new fervor in his face. "We wanted to keep this as a surprise, but we've got something that will really cheer you up."

Eleanor can feel herself lifting, as though her insides are filling with helium. He seems so excited, surely this will be good.

"We're going to move our mattresses today. We can finally sleep in our new house tonight!"

He looks so exhilarated that she hopes he doesn't notice that her glance flickers to her mother, who raises her eyebrows and nods, her shoulders lifting, clearly hoping that Eleanor will say the right thing.

"That's great, Dad," Eleanor replies, and hugs him again so he can't see her face, because she doesn't feel it's that great at all. She can't understand why, when she has been longing to get out of this shed for months.

"We'll have a picnic tonight," he continues. "Why don't you and your mum head out for some supplies now and have a bit of girl time together." He looks from one to the other as though he is bestowing an almighty gift, and they both smile back as required.

"Can Solomon come tonight too?" Eleanor finds herself asking.

Her mother looks surprised, her dad bemused.

"I don't think so, love," he says. "Why on earth do you want that old man at our family celebration? You're a funny thing, fancy asking that."

Eleanor smarts as though stung. She remembers Solomon's wistful face as he'd talked about his family. She imagines him now, alone, stroking Charlie while he sits in his old armchair and watches his ancient TV.

"Why, don't you like him?" she persists. She grips the key in her pocket.

What would they say if she told them about Lily's art room? Would her dad make fun of that too? Would they take the key from her immediately, without any hope of discussion?

"Martin . . ." Eleanor's mom says, her tone a warning.

"Solomon's fine," her dad answers, "but this is a special night just for our family."

Eleanor knows better than to say more.

"Come on, then." Her mom gets up and winks at her. "Let's take our chance while we've got it, eh?"

It seems a long time since she's been in a car with her mother. The school bus still picks her up and drops her off, and there's nowhere else to go. They don't say a lot as they travel to and from the service station, stashing three precooked pizzas on the back seat. Eleanor keeps touching the key in her pocket, remembering that little room, thinking through the possibilities of her own private kingdom. To her surprise, it seems so much more exciting than their brand new house.

They get back to find that Eleanor's father has moved the mattresses into each of the bedrooms, where they wait incongruously, each one a raft in its own sea of space. He has also found candles and lit up the empty floor of their lounge area. The empty white walls seem to peer disdainfully at the little feast on the tiles. They sit in a circle on lumpy cushions, trying to wait for Aiden, but when the pizzas begin to cool and harden, they have one piece each, and then another.

All the food is gone when Aiden finally appears after nine. Eleanor's father's disappointment makes him growl at his son about curfews. In reply, Aiden takes one look at the mattress waiting in his room and announces that he'd rather sleep in the shed. He storms out of the front door and doesn't reappear. No one goes to find him.

Eleanor spends a long time trying to get to sleep in the silent stillness of her new bedroom, with its strong smell of paint. Nearby, her bag hangs on the door, the silver key inside its pocket, waiting for Eleanor to decide what to do about it.

38

caroline

"*I need you to go into the office for me this morning . . ."*

Caroline sighs as she listens to the message. She has avoided Nathan's calls as much as possible this week, terrified of what she's found herself caught up in. But he is so persistent that it's almost impossible. She'll just put the papers in his letterbox, she doesn't have to see him. Then she hears the final sentence. "And when you come over, wear the red I like."

She goes to her lingerie drawer, all the while asking herself just how far she's prepared to go to keep her job.

As Eleanor wakes up the next morning she can hear knocking. She jumps up and opens the door to her room before realizing that the noise is coming from a little farther away. She heads down the stairs to the next level, to see Savvie standing at her mother's closed bedroom door.

"Mum?" Savvie presses her mouth against the wood as she speaks, then pauses and turns to Eleanor with a frown. "It's locked. I'm sure she's in there but she won't come out."

Savvie's worried little face brings to mind Naeve's scared expression last night. Eleanor searches for words of reassurance.

"Yesterday was a long day," she suggests. "She's probably exhausted. Why don't you try again in a little while?"

Savvie shrugs and wanders back into her room. Eleanor heads downstairs to find her uncle sitting alone at the kitchen bench, his head bent over a newspaper. He looks up when he sees her come in, and she holds her ground, watching as he folds the newspaper in half and leans back in his chair.

"I've arranged for the girls to go to a friend's house after school finishes," he says. "Kat will keep them there for as long as we need, overnight if necessary. She knows enough of what's been going on to understand our need for some space today."

Eleanor doesn't know what to say. She heads across to the fridge and helps herself to orange juice, taking her time in an effort to avoid his penetrating stare.

"What are your plans this morning?"

"I'm heading out for a while," she answers.

"Good. I was hoping you could make yourself scarce." Ian jumps up and walks out of the room, taking the paper with him.

Keen to get away from the brooding atmosphere, Eleanor grabs some bread and makes a hasty sandwich, then hurries upstairs to get dressed. These strange, short English winter days means she's walking away from Harborne Grove as soon as it's light, grateful she has planned somewhere to go today—and equally relieved to have made it through another night with no sleepwalking. As she goes she texts her mother early, hoping to forestall her volley of concern.

When she's close to Parker & Lane she stops in a small café. It's more than an hour until she's due to meet Will, so she orders herself a coffee and scans the morning papers. On page five of the *Daily Mail* she finds the banner "Broken Hearts," and beneath it is a picture of Arabella's memorial: June Blythe and her two surviving daughters, their arms around each other, while Dickon stares off into the distance, his mouth a grim line. To her surprise, the paper doesn't mention the skirmish in the churchyard.

There had been a whole bank of journalists there, it cannot have been missed. The only mention of Nathan is as Arabella's grieving husband, although there is no photo of him, presumably because he's less famous than the Blythes.

As she sips the scalding cup of coffee, a succession of snapshot memories besiege Eleanor. First, there's Nathan's enraged face as he tries to choke her. Then, Nathan's snarl as he speaks to her uncle at the funeral. Naeve's anxious expression and Savvie's worried one come next, and she remembers Will's words too: "... *he has friends in high places—I could easily become the fall guy.*"

She hadn't taken Will seriously at the time, but what if that is exactly what's going to happen? What if Nathan is going to sit back and watch as Ian and Susan's family is ripped apart? What if he's going to pin anything he can on Will, or on Eleanor? On anyone but himself?

A long time ago, when she was a child, she had felt the same way as Naeve. She'd known that a crisis was coming, and she had done nothing, because she'd had no idea what to do.

Not this time.

She jumps up and makes her way quickly to Parker & Lane, pulling her cell phone from her bag. "Will, I've decided to come in—I'm sure Susan won't mind. I'm just arriving at the office now," she says. "Are you here? Is the coast clear?"

"Yep, I'm here. There's hardly anyone around," he replies. "A few people have been and gone, and I think Malcolm O'Halloran might be in his office, but I suspect he sleeps here."

"In that case, I'm coming up. I'll grab my stuff, then I'll come to see you."

"All right then, see you soon."

She heads inside and doesn't bother to sign in, taking the stairs to the first floor. In the main office she quickly walks to her little pod, and pulls open the desk drawer, retrieving two Paulo Coelho books, a packet of pencils, an empty sketchpad, and a Mars bar. She thinks of all the movies she's seen in which people bring in cardboard boxes to empty their desks. She has barely had time to make her presence felt here, so she doesn't even need an extra bag for these items, just slips them all into her handbag and she's done.

However, she isn't quite ready to leave yet. She sits at the computer and brings up the work email account that Nathan shares with his assistants. It doesn't take her long to find his home address. She checks on Google Maps and sees he resides only a few blocks away from Harborne Grove. She had no idea the Lanes lived so close to the Mortimers—it must have made it easy for Ian and Arabella to meet.

It also means that Nathan has never been far away from them all.

She taps the details into her phone and logs off again. She gets up to leave, then stops.

Nathan's office door is right next to her, open and inviting. She hesitates for only a moment, then moves cautiously inside and surveys the scene. Everything is stacked neatly in piles or in trays on the desk. She knows from three weeks of working with Nathan that he can't abide disorder. She goes over to his desk and skims through the files and papers, and then looks around. She's not sure why she's here, or what she's hoping to find; all she knows is that she will never get another chance like this.

Then she hears a pair of heels tapping quickly along the corridor, getting closer. Eleanor looks around desperately and sprints over to the leather couch, throwing herself behind it.

The person is talking on the phone in a whisper as they shut the office door. "Okay, okay," a woman's voice says, and Eleanor hears the grating of metal on metal as a filing cabinet drawer is pulled open. "Yes, got it."

The office door opens again, and Eleanor dares to look over the back of the sofa as she hears the footsteps move away. She sees Caroline Cressman's smart-suited form moving briskly down the corridor.

An indignant rage overtakes her. She thinks of Susan, without even the energy to come out of her room, and Ian's tired, wan face. Her family is breaking down and Caroline is swanning around here like nothing is wrong, when she was probably the reason Arabella had slapped Nathan and run away in the first place. Caroline was as culpable as any of them. *In fact,* Eleanor thinks, pushing herself up quickly and charging after Caroline, *she is probably taking away evidence right now, to help Nathan conceal his crimes.*

"Hey!" she shouts to Caroline, who turns around and stares at Eleanor in surprise.

"Eleanor? I thought you'd been fi—I didn't think you worked here anymore. What are you doing here?"

"Just collecting my things." Eleanor fixes on the envelope in Caroline's hand. "What have you got there?"

Caroline looks down at the envelope and back up in surprise. "I'm collecting some things for Nathan—and it's actually none of your business," she adds. She frowns as she walks forward. "Can I have your key card, please? You shouldn't have it anymore."

Eleanor walks toward her, but instead of passing over the key card, she snatches the envelope out of Caroline's hand. She pulls out the contents, eagerly scanning them, sure she will find something incriminating. But her hopes begin to fall as she sees page after page of figures and the titles of the *Super Kid* books written across the top of each one.

Eleanor looks up wordlessly, to see Caroline's mouth has dropped open in surprise. Her face darkens as she snatches the sheaf of papers back. "I don't know what the hell you're playing at," Caroline says, "but you are never to come back here again, do you understand?"

"Caroline? Eleanor?"

Eleanor turns around to see Will standing behind them, looking from one to the other in confusion. She reddens, but she cannot stop herself now.

"How the hell can you be Nathan's alibi?" Eleanor hisses at Caroline. "You know what he's like. Do you really want to end up like Arabella?"

"Eleanor!" Will cautions.

"Just what are you implying?" Caroline cries out, and steps back as though Eleanor might be about to hurt her.

"She didn't mean it like that," Will says, coming to stand closer to them. "Everyone is aware of Nathan's temper, that's all she's saying."

Caroline's eyes narrow. "What are you playing at, Will?" Then she glowers at Eleanor. "Nathan thinks *you* know something," she snaps. "And he's not a man to stop until he has answers. I'd be very careful, if I were you."

She turns on her heel and storms away.

"What the hell do you think you're doing, Eleanor?" Will blurts as soon as she's gone.

"Looking out for my family," she retorts, annoyed at his tone. "I have to go. I'll call you later." And she hurries down the corridor. Caroline has disappeared, and Eleanor doesn't try to find her. Instead she pockets her key card and heads out of the building, past the security gates, not looking back. At the road, she waits impatiently for a free taxi, and when she hails it and climbs inside she double checks the address she'd written down at the computer. She tells the driver where to go, and then settles back in her seat.

39

clandestine visits

June 2005

Solomon's key has been hidden in a zip pocket of Eleanor's wash bag for weeks. There has been no sign of him here, and no opportunity to head down to his house to see him again, thanks to rainy days and too much homework. The time she spent inside Lily's art room seems unreal now—and yet her thoughts repeatedly flit to that beautiful space full of light, and those paintings in the corner. She desperately wants to see them again. But now she has left that little house, the suggestion of wandering down there, alone, makes her feel shy and nervous. She really wants to go back to study those paintings more, but can she? Should she?

These questions become an ongoing internal refrain. She debates telling her mother about Solomon's offer, but every time she starts to, she stalls at the last moment. If her mother decides that it isn't a good idea, then it's game over. Solomon doesn't come to see them anymore—she remembers her father sighing the last time he'd seen the old man arrive. Perhaps Solomon's help isn't appreciated as much now her mother has the use of her arm again. Perhaps her parents don't like him, even after all he's tried to do for them. It doesn't seem very generous of them, but then she is so unsure of her parents nowadays.

In late June the flooring arrives, an expensive, treated pine that needs to be laid by hand, and everyone is called on to help. Aiden does a couple of days grudgingly, before beginning to disappear even before breakfast. As a result, dinners are tense and stilted affairs, resentments burning as steadily as the eucalyptus candles in the center of the table.

Eleanor tries to help too, but the beams are heavy, and it doesn't take long before she drops one on her toes. The next day, still hobbling, she gets a painful splinter in the palm of her hand. "You have your schoolwork and your drawing to keep you busy, don't you?" her mom suggests apologetically as she uses the tweezers to remove it, wiping her brow with the dirty sleeve of her arm. She is dressed in combat pants that seem far too big for her, and one of Eleanor's dad's baggy old shirts.

Eleanor nods of course, because that is what is expected of her, and because she really doesn't want to say anything that might make her have to lay more flooring.

"Perhaps I'll go for a walk with my sketchpad, see if I can find something to draw," she ventures, half expecting her mother to say no. But her mother isn't really listening, and the snake incident is all but forgotten now.

"Sounds good," her mom agrees, as she replaces the tweezers in her medical kit and begins to wash her hands.

Eleanor knows this is her chance.

She doesn't tell her parents where she's going. Although, she has a suspicion that if she announced there were wild elephants walking down the track next to the house, they wouldn't bat an eye. They'd just say, "that's nice" and "be safe" and "drink lots of water" and "watch out for snakes." All they are interested in is getting as much done as they can in case the weather turns and the rain comes in earnest.

Besides, her life seems to be so much in their pockets that it is nice to keep something to herself.

As she trudges across the grass clutching her bag, she looks over to where her parents are trying to carry one of the recently varnished internal doors into the new house. Her mother is struggling to lift it by one heavy edge, trying to blow her bangs out of her eyes as she concentrates, hunched and red-faced. Her father yells instructions from the other side. Eleanor turns away and quickens her step.

As she heads down to the bottom of the meadow, not far away she sees the neglected cubby. A pile of leaves has built up over the laminate, and she wonders if the snake is still there. Perhaps it has made the cubby its permanent home now. It crosses her mind to tell Aiden about it, but then, Aiden never comes down here anymore—he's too busy doing "god knows what," as her mother always says, with his new unfriendly friends.

Eleanor has been around these boys a few times now. She's watched them greet each other with high fives and back slaps, and has been largely ignored, except sometimes Timmo looks her up and down in a way that makes her feel like an exhibit at the museum—his big, lolling gaze traveling over places that leave her feeling exposed and uncomfortable. Originally, she wanted to join in with their games, but she soon realized that she would never be invited along, and it is probably a good thing. She cannot understand what Aiden sees in them. Perhaps he is just trying to fit in the best he can in this strange new life they are all living.

At the property boundary she climbs over the fence onto Solomon's side with ease, jumping down and heading past all the old farming detritus scattered over his land, until she's on the crest of the hill and can see the little cottage again, not far off.

As soon as she begins to head down, Charlie starts to bark. She has a moment of nerves, and takes a quick, longing look back the way she has just come, but it is too late for that, because Solomon is standing on his doorstep now, watching her approach. The little tabby cat mills around his legs, leaning in to rub its neck against his pants.

She makes her way across to them, self-conscious and shy. "Hello," she says.

"Good to see you, Miss Eleanor," Solomon replies. "Charlie here has been hoping you would come by again. Still got yer key?"

"Yes."

He gestures toward the back of the house. "Well, like I said, you're welcome to use it—don't let old Charlie's barking put you off. You know the way."

He ambles behind Eleanor, and she pauses at the outer door. "Go on, then," he says gruffly, gesturing to the key in her hand. He stays to watch her unlock the door and enter the little sunlit room. Then he murmurs, "I'll leave you in peace then," and closes the door behind her.

Once alone, Eleanor looks around. At first she is disappointed. It's not quite how she remembered it because the intervening weeks have built up its glory in her mind, so the colors seem muted, and the area is smaller than she'd thought. But when she kneels before the stack of canvases, everything else is forgotten.

She sets the first one on her knee and examines it: the sweeping brush strokes, the different shades of blues and browns and greens. Then she puts it down and steps backward, watching the way each mark of color merges with its neighbor, coalescing into a pastoral scene, the silhouettes of horses in distant fields across a long valley. She glances out of the window and sees a similar view, minus the horses and the sunshine.

Looking back at the painting, she longs to try to replicate this. She heads over to a table where paints are laid out—a mishmash row of half-used bottles that won't have been opened for years. She unscrews a lid and finds that although the rim is flaky and dry, there is still usable blue paint inside. But the easel is empty and there are no blank canvases here, so she looks around, and her gaze falls on a sketchbook that sits on a table in the corner. She goes across, somewhat furtively, and picks it up, tentatively opening the first page and beginning to flick through.

There are landscapes here as well, but mostly people. All in pencil, simple black and white, and yet all the more stunning for that. She recognizes Solomon as a younger man, and there's a girl of about Eleanor's age, who turns slowly to a woman as the book progresses. Their faces are constructed in series of lines and shading, in such richly textured detail that they seem to come out of the page as though in 3D. The ones drawn with their eyes trained toward the artist seem to study Eleanor as carefully as she studies them. A thrill runs through her as she holds this book. There's so much here she can work with; so much she can learn from one pad.

She props the book on the easel and moves the table closer to it. She pulls her own sketchpad out and begins to copy one of the pictures of the young girl sitting on a tree stump, her face drawn in side profile. Eleanor works slowly and carefully, noticing the discrepancies between the two and checking where her careful pencil strokes may have gone awry.

She is so lost in what she's doing that the knock on the door makes her jump. Solomon pokes his head in. "Want some tea and biscuits?" he asks. "You must be getting hungry, you've been in here for hours."

Eleanor comes back to her surroundings in an instant. "No, that's fine," she says, jumping up and quickly gathering her things. "I'd better get back."

"I'm not shooing you out, you know."

"I know."

He comes forward and notices the drawing she has been copying. "Ah, that's our Philippa," he says. "Lives way up north now with her fella. Only see her at Christmas, and that's if I'm lucky."

Eleanor doesn't know what to say. She looks back at the portrait of the little girl, notices the wistful expression in her profile, and tries to imagine growing up here on your own all that time ago. Had she been as lonely as Eleanor felt now, she wonders. Had Philippa's parents understood her, or had she felt as disconnected from them as Eleanor does from hers?

"Well, go out the way you came and lock the door behind you," Solomon says, interrupting her thoughts, "then you'll get used to how it works."

She nods as she grabs her bag and looks longingly at the book on the table. It's school tomorrow; she can't do this again for at least six days. But there's nothing to be done about that. She heads to the door and, once outside, is glad the key turns easily in the lock. Then she runs back over the fields until she sees her own half-finished house waiting for her in the distance. She is disoriented, as though she can't tell whether she is entering a dream or leaving one.

40

the town house

Jenni Madaki sees the "Broken Hearts" headline online while taking a break from calling real-estate clients. The inset picture of Arabella Lane gives her a jolt. She googles the name and has her hand clapped over her mouth by the time her colleague comes into the office. "I think I saw this woman," she says, shaking her finger repeatedly at the screen. "You remember that crazy girl I told you about, the one who tried to jump off the Hungerford footbridge? It took half a dozen of us to pull her back, and I'm sure this woman was one of them." She turns around wonderingly to stare at her colleague. "It's so bloody sad, isn't it? You know what that means, yeah? On the night she died, Arabella Lane helped save a life."

The taxi takes Eleanor a familiar route, heading toward Harborne Grove, only diverting away at the last moment. *What are you doing?* demands a looping, worried voice in her head. The memory of Will's stunned expression as she confronted Caroline keeps recurring. *Ignore it*, she insists to herself. *You are taking control. You are not unraveling.*

A few moments later they turn into a quiet street, and the driver pulls up outside a row of tall town houses. Number fifty-three is written clearly on a whitewashed pole, but the windows are lined with thick curtains, which are all closed. Eleanor rummages in her bag for money. In her haste to get here she hadn't considered the cost of this trip, but it leaves her with less than ten dollars in her pocket. Good job she's close to Harborne Grove, because she'll be walking back.

As the taxi pulls away, she looks up and down the road. The whole street is much the same as Harborne Grove, a few trees spaced evenly along the pavement, but there's nowhere she might hide at short notice without trespassing onto someone's property. Initially, she had been so fired up she would have just knocked on Nathan's door, but now that she's here in this eerily quiet part of suburban London, her nerve begins to falter.

She swallows hard and grips the phone in her pocket. In the taxi she had practiced starting the recording device on it, while keeping it hidden. She will set it going as soon as he answers the door. Then she just has to get him angry enough to tell her the truth.

The phone buzzes in her hand and she quickly pulls it out, walking away from the house in case she is overheard.

"Hey," says Will when she answers in a whisper. "You ran out on me there. I didn't mean to come across as judgmental, I was just a bit shocked, that's all. By the time I'd grabbed my stuff you'd gone. Where are you—do you want me to meet you?"

"I'm fine," she says, "but . . . but if I don't call you back within the hour, then maybe call the police and tell them my last known address was fifty-three Whitworth Avenue." As she says it, she's relieved to have some kind of surety. Although Nathan won't dare hurt her, will he, if he's trying so hard to avoid arrest?

Unless his temper really does get the better of him, that insistent little voice in her head chimes in, remembering how hard his fingers had squeezed her windpipe. But she doesn't have time to think about that, because Will is shouting down the phone.

"Hang on, that's . . . that's Arabella's address. *Eleanor!* What the hell are you doing? You're not trying to confront Nathan, are you? Don't be insane."

She glances around as though this whole hushed street might be able to hear their exchange. Nothing and no one moves.

"I can't talk about it now," she trills, and hangs up on Will before he can try to talk her out of it. However, his words sting, and her skin prickles with anger. *I am not insane.* Bolstered by adrenaline, she marches back up the street and knocks on Nathan's door before she can second-guess herself any more.

There's no answer. She raps again, not quite as forcefully this time, and begins to look up and down the street, as though he might come up unexpectedly behind her. She's slightly distracted, therefore, when the door finally opens.

"What the hell are *you* doing here?" says a woman's irritated voice.

Eleanor finds herself face to face with Aisha. "It's you! What are *you* doing here?" She straightens. "I'm looking for Nathan, is he in?"

Aisha looks annoyed. "Oh, Eleanor, this is not a good idea at all," she says patronizingly, folding her arms. "He won't want to talk to you."

"Is he here?" Eleanor ignores Aisha, peering past her.

"No, actually, and you should be glad about that, because I don't think he'd like the fact that you are standing on his doorstep."

Eleanor bristles. "So who are you, Aisha? What the hell did you think you were playing at, coming into our house the other day?" Her voice is much louder than she intends, and out of the corner of her eye she sees the curtain flicker in a nearby bay window.

"You invited me in, if you remember correctly," Aisha replies smoothly. "I'd leave it at that, if I were you."

"So, what are you to Nathan? Are you just spying for him, or are you sleeping with him too?" Eleanor persists.

Aisha laughs. "You cheeky cow. Think what you like," she says. "I really don't care." And she begins to close the door, but Eleanor wedges her boot in before it shuts fully, wincing with pain as the door traps the delicate bones of her foot.

Aisha sighs, and eases the door back. She comes closer to Eleanor.

"Don't play this game," she says. Her eyes bore into Eleanor's. "He will win. He's employed me to find out all of Arabella's dirty little secrets, and to investigate anyone close to her. I saw his reaction when I told him about your uncle. You don't want him anywhere near you when he's angry."

Eleanor seizes on this. "And what if he's guilty? Why do you want to work for someone so awful?"

"I don't have to talk to you, Eleanor." Aisha steps back, as Eleanor pushes the door open farther, trying to keep the conversation going. "That was just a friendly warning."

Eleanor lets go, and the door finally slams shut.

As Eleanor turns around, she sees a small face pressed against the window to her left, a little girl curiously watching the action. Unbidden, her memories skitter backward to her own face pressed against a window in the back seat of their old Toyota, her father grabbing her mother's arms in a grubby motel parking lot, her mother shaking him off, covering her face with her hands, getting into the car, sobbing, leaning back to Eleanor, stroking her hair briefly as she slams the door closed. Her father banging on the window, making Eleanor jump. Her mother saying, *Don't look back, Eleanor, don't look back,* as the growl of the engine roars into life and the car jolts away. Her father disappearing in the dust behind them.

The memory makes her stagger on the steps and she almost misses her footing. The little girl still watches from the window. She can't meet the child's eye, looks back instead to Arabella's house, but there is no sign of anyone now. She tries to imagine Arabella on this doorstep every day: in casual wear collecting the post; in jeans going shopping; dressed up and heading into town. Had the little girl heard arguments from the house before? Or violence? What had really gone on behind those closed doors? Was it enough for a husband to hate his wife so much he might kill her?

Perhaps Nathan is really in there, hiding from everyone.

She walks quickly down the street, trying to get her bearings, thinking back to the man on the bridge on Saturday. She'd thought she was being paranoid, but if Aisha is some kind of an investigator, then perhaps Nathan has had other people watching her too. Hadn't Ian said he thought he was being watched as well? She swings around, but the street behind her is quiet. This is becoming too much; she needs to retreat and gather her strength before her paranoia gets the better of her.

And she needs to tell her uncle what has just happened, because if Nathan is looking for a scapegoat, as seems ever more likely, then Ian is an irresistible target.

She looks to her phone for directions back to Harborne Grove, but the internet won't connect. There are no Tube stations nearby and no buses evident. Eventually she meets a passerby who points her in the right direction. She has forgotten her words to Will until her phone buzzes with a message.

Call me.

She doesn't want to hear his disbelieving voice again, suggesting she's unhinged, so she texts him back.

I'm fine. Nearly back home now. No emergency call necessary :)

He doesn't reply. Perhaps he's had enough of her.

When she reaches Harborne Grove her adrenaline evaporates, and her footsteps are tired and heavy. The promise of a much-needed nap urges her on, but as she turns onto the road she stops, and a new wave of fear rushes through her.

Lilian, the housekeeper, is standing outside on the steps to Ian and Susan's house. She's gabbling on her phone, walking frantically back and forth, looking up at the house and gesturing with her hands. It only takes her a moment to spot Eleanor, and as soon as she does, she sets off toward her at a run.

41

aiden

June–July 2005

Everything feels askew once they are living in the new house. Sometimes Eleanor creeps in to her parents' room and watches them sleep, longing to crawl in with them but not daring, knowing how exhausted they both are and how mad they would be at being woken up. Her mother seems so tired now—she doesn't check up on Eleanor as often as she used to, she's barely interested in what's happening around her, and she often goes to bed before her children.

The house is still a husk: no pictures on the walls, no furniture unpacked beyond the basics. Yet Eleanor has to concede a few things have improved. They have plumbing; the porta-potty has been towed away, and she doesn't miss it at all. It is total luxury to be able to go to the bathroom without having to worry about darkness and spiders. However, she does find herself looking out of the kitchen window across to the shed.

To her surprise, after all the times she'd told herself she hated it, she misses it. It had made a difference when they'd been forced into physical proximity with one another. There had been no TV and only so much her father could do in the dark, so sometimes they would play card games in the evening. In the shed, if Eleanor couldn't get to sleep, the bouncing light of her mother's head torch was a comfort in the darkness. In her new bedroom, the only light shining through her bare window is the faint glow of stars or the faraway moon. And now that they are able to scatter in this huge house, they invariably choose to do so. Her father always tinkers with things in one of the spare bedrooms, keeping out of the way. He's painting or wiring until the moment he heads for bed. When her mother is up, she stays in the kitchen with the television on permanently, as though gorging herself on the outside world after being starved of it for so long.

Aiden had slept in the shed on his own for a fortnight, before the damp weather and lack of heating made him relent and move into the new house. The door to his room is permanently closed. Eleanor misses him too. It's an ache that has lodged permanently in her nowadays, one that won't disperse. She's getting used to it.

Eleanor had thought that the house might make a difference to her life, but it has only compounded the loneliness. And, disturbingly, it feels more permanent here. The shed had always been highlighted as a temporary lodging; she had almost forgotten that their plan was to stay here indefinitely.

She still doesn't have any friends at school. The highlight of her weeks is the time she spends in Lily's art room. She has filled her sketchbook with her own pen and ink copies of Lily's work, observing with satisfaction how she has improved from her first attempts. As she heads down to the little room again, early in July, she tries to ignore the fact that her parents still don't know she comes here. They are unlikely to find out, since Solomon never visits the house nowadays. It's like the neighbors have forgotten each other's existence.

She works for a couple of hours, practicing her sketches of one of the horses, before giving up for a while and reading. Eventually she gets tired and realizes she is thirsty. Although Solomon is as good as his word, and never comes in the little room while she's there, occasionally she goes to ask him for a glass of water. She knocks gently at the door that connects the room to the rest of the house, waits for a while, but there is no response. Eventually she goes outside and heads around to the front of the house, knocking again. Only then does she realize how quiet the place is today. No Solomon. No Charlie.

As she tentatively pushes the door open, she can hear the television chattering away. She creeps toward the sound and as she enters the little lounge she can make out Solomon's bulk in the armchair.

A dizzying wave of heat rushes through her. He's so still. What if he's dead? She edges closer to try to see his face. As she peers around the side of his chair, to her relief she can see his chest rising and falling. Embarrassed now at intruding like this, she begins to back out of the room, but she forgets about the stupid iron gecko that holds the door open, and her foot wobbles on it, upsetting her balance and sending her banging into the door.

By the time she rights herself, Solomon is on his feet, staring at her.

"I'm so sorry," she says, her face aflame. "There was no answer to my knocks, I just wanted to check you were okay."

"Must'a fell asleep there," Solomon replies hoarsely, then breaks into a series of coughs. Eleanor goes quickly to the tap in the kitchen and fetches him some water.

"Thank you, Eleanor," he says, after a few sips have restored his voice. "Was this what you were after too?"

She nods.

"Then help yourself. I'd best go and see where that Charlie boy has got to."

After she has finished her water, she heads back to the little sunroom and carries on reading until, a short time later, she becomes aware of a strange noise in the distance, an unearthly wail, getting louder. She jumps up and goes to the door that leads outside, her nerves on full alert again. She can't see anything here, but the noise is getting louder still. Cautiously, she goes around to the front of the house, toward the sound, and sees Solomon stumbling across the grass, his arms full of a writhing mass of fur, his face set in a grim line of concentration, his mouth moving. Although she is too far away to make out the words, her body lurches with fear.

"Go home!" Solomon shouts as he gets closer. In his arms, Charlie continues to writhe, making that piteous noise. "Now!" he roars at Eleanor, who sets off at a run up the field, petrified, her belongings forgotten. It takes her just a few minutes to get through all the farmyard detritus, and as she scales the fence, she hears one sharp, ringing sound. A few galahs in the trees nearby take off squawking. She sits astride the fence, crying, and only once she has jumped down and wiped her eyes does she realize that in the lee of the ruined cubby sit three boys, all smoking, all watching her.

It takes a moment for her to recognize that the one with the red-rimmed eyes and sallow face is her brother.

42

susan

"Is that Detective Inspector Prashad?"

"Yes."

"Sergeant Marlow here. We've had an address come up that's been flagged as under your investigation. Asking for assistance. There's a car on the way, but I thought you'd want to know. It's Harborne Grove, number eight. There's a man inside with a head injury, the woman who called thinks he's been assaulted."

Prashad is already waving madly at Kirby across the room. "Cancel the car," she says, "we'll take this one, thanks." She grabs her jacket and races for the door.

"Eleanor! Eleanor!" As Lilian reaches her, she grabs Eleanor's arms. "Come quickly, Eleanor, it's your uncle."

There is no time to protest because Lilian is dragging her forward to the house, and up the steps. At the door, she stops and waves Eleanor inside. "He's in the front lounge," she says. "Please, Eleanor, help him. I will stay out here and wait for the police."

Eleanor recoils from the wild look in Lilian's eyes. "What's happened?"

"Susan has been destroying her beautiful house. Smashing things. It is a big mess."

As Eleanor looks past the front door toward the entrance of the formal lounge, a couple of thoughts strike her almost simultaneously.

I don't want to go in there.

I have to go in there.

She glances back at Lilian, who has her arms wrapped around herself as she watches Eleanor nervously. Then she steps into the house and walks slowly over to the front lounge.

The scene inside is one of devastation. Pictures have fallen off the walls. There is glass everywhere. The entire contents of the liquor cabinet have drizzled onto the floor, pooling liquid between a thousand shards of glass, and it smells like a distillery. And sitting on the sofa in the midst of it all, holding his head, is Ian.

Eleanor rushes over to him and kneels, careful to avoid the glass, unable to miss the gaping gash across his forehead. "Oh my god, what on earth happened?"

"She went mad," he mutters, his voice odd and shrill as he clutches his head. At first he won't look up to meet her gaze, but as she waits, not knowing what to say, eventually he tilts his head so their eyes lock. His expression is wild; he looks like a cornered animal.

"I've never seen her like that before."

"Who?" she asks, because she needs to hear it, even though she knows the answer already.

"Susan."

Eleanor glances around the chaotic living room. If this is the aftermath of a fit of rage, she's relieved she didn't witness it. She turns back to Ian.

"Where is she now? Are the girls still out?"

"Yes, the girls are still with Kat, thank god. Susan's gone. About an hour ago, I think. I have no idea if she took anything with her. And I've no idea if she's coming back. She went at me with a golf club, Eleanor. A golf club! Look." He points to the silver club lying on the floor. "She almost knocked me out. My ears are ringing."

"That cut is nasty," Eleanor says. "You might need a stitch in it."

"Oh god." Ian covers his eyes and his body heaves in what looks like sobs. "What am I going to do, Eleanor?" His voice trembles. "No, don't answer that, you're twenty-one years old, for god's sake, you don't need to answer that. You shouldn't be witnessing any of this. What a fucking mess. Literally." He erupts into a bout of bitter laughter, then grows somber again.

Eleanor begins to pick up some of the biggest pieces of glass. "I think Susan might need some professional help," she says.

"No, no, no." Ian jumps up, wincing and touching his head again. Eleanor gets to her feet, but before she can back away, he comes so close to her that their faces almost touch. "You have to understand, Eleanor," he says, his tone fierce, but desperate, "it's not her fault, it's mine. I did this to her. She never wanted children, she's always been so driven in her work and so independent, but when we got married, I pressured her into having a family. I promised her that I would be the primary caregiver. She was so worried that she would lose everything she'd worked so hard for, and she was sure she would go mad if she had to stay in the house with a baby all day. But I reassured her over and over again, and finally she agreed."

Eleanor lays the glass carefully on a side table as she listens, uneasy about hearing these private details. Nevertheless, her heart goes out to her little cousins, trapped in this war zone. She has a fleeting memory of the lengthening silences between her own parents, and wonders if this would almost have been better—with cards on the table, rather than the bitter battle of attrition her mother and father began to wage as the house building became protracted and stressful, the way to victory blocked by a broken pipe or tile, a carpet a few centimeters short of the wall. Until even the victories no longer felt like victories. Her nine-year-old self had trusted her parents not to quarrel about unimportant issues, but if she could go back now she would stand up in the middle of one of their stand-offs and point out just how stupid and inconsequential their worries were.

Ian is still babbling. Eleanor's not even sure he's entirely aware of her presence. "Only after Naeve was born did we both realize we had no idea of what we'd taken on. Susan went back to work, of course, because she was right—she would have gone under if she'd stayed home—but those early years nearly killed me. And yet, neither of us had known what it was like to fall in love with a child. Or thought of what a child might need. Neither of us knew the heartbreak Susan would endure when she left every day and her daughter screamed for her mother. Or when Naeve stopped screaming and refused to go to her instead, always clinging to me and rejecting Susan. But, of course, I still talked her into Savannah: a companion for Naeve, a way of evening things out, a fix-it baby, a complete family—every reason I could think of that worked for every-one but Susan. I made her go through it all over again. I saw the agony it caused her, and Savannah was a difficult pregnancy too. I witnessed the pull she had toward another tiny baby, there was another round of couriered breastmilk, which says it all, doesn't it? And since then I have watched Susan slowly build up walls around herself in order to be able to keep going with this life. *I* pushed her into all this, *I* made her feel like an outsider in her own home. And then my head was turned, and now I may have played a major role in tearing down the rest of her achievements as well. Believe me, Eleanor, one whack to the forehead is probably letting me off lightly, all things considered."

Eleanor isn't sure how to respond. In truth, she wants to ask if he knows when Susan discovered his affair. Because if Susan has been aware of it for a while, and if her rage has been building, might she have had a good motive to go after Arabella too?

She stares at her uncle, wondering how to broach this subject, then realizes that over his shoulder, beyond the window, she can see strobing red and blue lights.

"The police are here," she tells him.

"What?" Ian turns to follow her gaze. "Oh fuck, *fuck*," he barks, keep-ing his voice low. "What the hell are they doing here?"

229

"It's Lilian, she's waiting outside. She said she'd called them."

"Fuck," Ian snaps again. "I totally forgot we'd asked her to come today, to get the house ready for the holidays. I was in a daze after Susan left. When Lilian came in and said she was going to get help, I didn't realize . . ." Ian wobbles a little, and Eleanor puts a hand on his arm.

"Are you okay?"

He grimaces. "Fierce headache, but I'll live. Let's get this over with."

Finally, Eleanor remembers what she had to tell her uncle about Nathan, but there is barely any time. There are voices heading closer to them as they both move slowly toward the door.

"I need to talk to you about Nathan," she says, clutching her uncle's arm so that he turns to her with a frown. "I think he might be trying to set you up, because of you and Arabella. What if that's why I have the ring? What if it's some kind of message, or meant to get one of us in trouble?"

But as she says it, she realizes it doesn't make sense. When would Nathan have had the opportunity to plant the ring on her after Arabella had died? And even if, somehow, he had, he wouldn't be able to simply accuse her of having his wife's ring. That would be far too convenient, and it would cast suspicion back on him. There must be something else, something she hasn't thought of. She just has to figure out his plan.

Ian's eyes are wide, but there is no time for further discussion, because there are people in the doorway, and Eleanor finds herself face to face again with Kirby and Prashad.

"What on earth happened here?" Priya Prashad says, glancing around in amazement.

Eleanor looks at Ian, who grimaces. "Domestic problems, I'm afraid. The stress of Arabella's death is getting to us all."

"That's a nasty cut," Steve Kirby interjects, his gaze fixed on Ian's forehead.

"I know." Ian grimaces.

"If someone did that to you, no matter who it is, that's assault." Kirby continues, "You do know you could press charges against that person."

Ian gives a bitter laugh. "I won't be pressing charges. It hasn't happened before and I'm sure it won't happen again. I may well have deserved it. All I want is to get this room sorted and go and lie down."

"Are your children here?" Prashad asks.

Ian's jaw tightens. "No, they have been at school and now they are with a friend. This will all be gone by the time they get home, I can assure you."

Prashad nods. She takes a few moments to look around the place and then asks, "And where is your wife at the moment, Mr. Mortimer?"

"I don't know," Ian replies quietly. "Cooling off somewhere, I should imagine."

"I hope so," Prashad says, fixing him with that knowing stare of hers. "Could you give us a call when she comes home, please, just so we know she's safe?"

Ian opens his mouth but no words come out. Eleanor watches him struggle with himself. For a moment she thinks he is going to get angry, but the shadow across his face is gone almost as quickly as it comes. "I can do that," he replies with a resolute nod.

As they talk there's a knock on the door. Lilian opens it to find an EMT outside. "Head injury here?" he asks.

"Bloody hell, this is completely unnecessary," Ian sighs.

The EMT comes in anyway, sizing Ian up. "Looks like a nasty cut, sir. Why don't I just check it out while I'm here?"

Ian sits on the stairs and lets the paramedic get to work. "Now," Prashad turns to Eleanor, making Eleanor wish she were still a bystander in this situation, "we have had some new evidence come in within the last few hours, Eleanor, and we'd really like to talk to you again at the station, if we could? Would you be able to come with us now?"

Eleanor glances at her uncle, but he won't meet her eye. There is nothing to do except turn back to the detective and say, "Yes, of course I can."

"Let's go then," Prashad says, and Eleanor moves off with them, but not before casting another desperate look toward her uncle. Is she imagining it or is he refusing to look at her? Instead he motions to Lilian, who is still waiting nervously by the door, and Eleanor hears him say quietly, "Could you help me fix this, please?" He points toward the front room. "I'll pay you double to stay as long as you need to."

When Lilian nods and hurries inside the room, Ian leans back against the stairs, allowing the paramedic to continue to dress the gash on his head. Before she knows it, Eleanor is on the steps again with Kirby and Prashad, caught up in an unwanted déjà vu as they lead her to their car.

43

completion

July 2005

Eleanor pushes her pasta around her plate, her stomach contracting painfully. She has hardly eaten all day, and the few bites she has managed so far have felt sticky and dry in her mouth.

"What's the matter, Eleanor?" her mother asks, finally discerning her lack of interest in the food.

Eleanor shrugs. "Not hungry." How can she be, when her ears are ringing with that piteous whining noise Charlie was making; an echo stuck on replay. She has never heard anything like it before. It wasn't the noise of a dog in pain. It was something worse.

She swallows another urge to retch. Fights the desire to run back to Solomon's house, because she has to know what's happened. In truth, she thinks she wouldn't make it anyway. Her fear would stall her before she reached the bottom fence. She's better off not knowing.

But, she thinks desperately, she left her books behind. And if she wants to visit Lily's room again, she will have to find out sometime.

"Eleanor?" Her mother is still watching her.

"Sorry. What?"

"I was just asking what you got up to today."

"Yes, Eleanor," Aiden says with a smirk, "what did you get up to today?"

"Shut up!" she yells at him, jumping to her feet. Her reaction has both her parents laying down their cutlery, seemingly lost for words at their mild-mannered daughter losing her temper.

"Only asking," Aiden singsongs back, continuing to shovel his food rapidly into his mouth. A few moments later he pushes his plate away and rocks back on his chair, continuing to give Eleanor that infuriating grin.

"What's going on?" Eleanor's father asks, looking between them.

Eleanor is having a hard time standing still. She wants to go over to her brother and pound that smirk off his face, but even more infuriating is the knowledge that he's stronger than she is, and she would lose. When had Aiden become such an idiot?

However, there is other weaponry at her disposal, and she doesn't hesitate to aim and fire. "Aiden was smoking with his friends in the cubby today," she announces.

Aiden's eyes widen and his mouth drops open. Then he snarls, "You little sneak."

"Hey now," their father says, but then Aiden adds, "Meanwhile, Elly the Elephant here was climbing over Solomon's fence post. And it's not the first time I've seen her either. Ask her why she's spending her spare time with a grubby old man. Go on, ask her."

"Both of you, stop it. Stop it now." There are tears in Eleanor's mother's eyes. "I feel like I don't know either of you. What the hell is happening here?"

"Eleanor?" her father presses.

Three pairs of eyes watch her, waiting for more.

"What about Aiden's smoking?" she bites back.

"We'll deal with Aiden's smoking too," her dad says in a low voice. "Now tell us why you were on Solomon's property."

"He's—he's been letting me use his wife's art room, to sit in or draw and paint," she blurts out.

No one says anything, so she begins to find her stride. "It's such a beautiful room. And Lily's paintings are amazing. I've copied a lot of them into my sketchbook. Here, I'll show you."

She runs to her room, grabs her tattered sketchbook, sprints back, and throws it into her mother's lap.

Her mother opens the book and flicks through the pages slowly. Eleanor watches, wondering why she isn't saying anything. Eventually, her mother exhales, leans back in her chair, and closes her eyes. Her dad rubs his hands over his face. Eleanor stares at them in puzzlement. *Why are they acting like this? What's wrong now?*

"Were you ever going to tell us about this?" her father asks eventually.

Eleanor tries to ignore Aiden, who is smirking again.

"I thought you'd be pleased that I've been doing something useful with my time," she replies. "It's better than smoking with a bunch of losers in a field."

"You're right about that," her mother cuts in, snapping to attention and leaning forward. "Aiden, can you not think of anything better to do?"

"Maybe I would, if you hadn't brought me to the middle of bloody nowhere," Aiden replies. Eleanor gets up, collects her plate, and takes it to the kitchen while the others begin a familiar argument. She sneaks off to her room as their voices get louder, until Aiden screams, "Just leave me alone!" The front door bangs, and she knows he is gone.

When her mom knocks on the door a short time later, she is still flicking through the sketchbook. She comes in and sits next to Eleanor on the bed, holding the book out to her. "These are great, Eleanor—amazing— when did you get so good?"

The question makes Eleanor want to cry and smile at the same time. Instead, she shrugs.

"So, you've been spending time at Solomon's house, have you?" Gillian begins carefully.

"Yes."

"And what does Solomon do while you're drawing?"

"Watches TV, I think."

"You think?"

"He lets me use Lily's room, but he never comes in. He says he misses her too much to go in there. But he seems to like me being there. I think he's a bit lonely, Mum."

Her mom doesn't say anything, but a new kind of quiet falls over the room. In the uncertain space between them, Eleanor thinks about Charlie again. Tears come to her eyes. "Oh Mum, something horrible happened today. Solomon was carrying Charlie, and Charlie was yowling. Something seemed horribly wrong. Then Solomon shouted at me and told me to go home. And now I can't stop thinking about it."

"He shouted at you?"

"Yes. And I left so fast that I've left my bag and my reading books there. Now I don't know what to do. And I'm scared. The noise that Charlie was making, it was awful."

"Has Solomon ever shouted at you before?"

Eleanor frowns. Isn't she listening? This is about Charlie, not Solomon. "No," she says grumpily, "he hasn't."

Her mom puts an arm around Eleanor's shoulders. "Would you like it if we went down there together tomorrow to get your things and check everything is okay?"

It's such a relief to have her mother's support that Eleanor begins to cry harder. "Yes, please," she nods through gulped breaths.

Her mom holds her close. "What's the matter, honey, tell me?"

"I don't think everything is okay," she says into her mother's chest, and at first she is thinking of Charlie, but then Aiden's twisted face comes to mind, and her lack of friends at school, and her dad's disinterest in her, and then she is crying harder than ever, because she can't remember how long it has been since her mother gave her a proper hug, a real hug like this one.

It is strange heading to Solomon's house with her mother the next afternoon, climbing the fence together, watching her mother glance uncertainly around at the decaying farm sheds and equipment, leading her over the crest of the hill until they can both see the farmhouse a short distance away.

They stop at the top of the incline, but her mother rallies first. "Come on then, let's go and see how he is." They head down together toward the little house and Gillian knocks smartly on the door.

Eleanor waits, saying nothing, but since they left the ridge of the hill, the pit of fear inside her has deepened, because not once has she heard the sound she's been hoping for. There is no barking from Charlie today.

They have to knock again before they hear a shuffling from inside, and then the door opens and Solomon peers out at them. His craggy face looks grayer than usual, the loose skin hangs in jowls beneath his chin, and his whiskers are scraggy and unkempt.

"Hello, Solomon," Gillian says, "we've just come to see how you're going. Eleanor has been telling me how worried she's been about you and Charlie."

To Eleanor's horror, as soon as her mother says these words, two great tears well up inside Solomon's red-rimmed eyes and fall unabashed down his cheeks.

"Charlie isn't with us anymore," Solomon announces, his hand trembling as he keeps tight hold of the door handle, as though he might fall over if he lets go. "He took a bait. You know, the poison meant for the foxes and cats. The bloody birds must have brought one into our field. Poor bugger was in agony." He waves a hand toward the garden. "I buried him out there last night, I put him in the sunshine, in his favorite spot."

"Oh no, Solomon, that's terrible," her mother says gently, patting Solomon's shoulder. Eleanor turns to look toward where Solomon is gesturing, and to her horror she sees a fresh mound of churned-up earth. She doesn't want to picture Charlie's lifeless body beneath it, but she can't help it—his lolling tongue in that black hole, even the smell of him, it comes to her already packaged and makes her lean against her mother for support.

"We got that dog as a pup, me and my Lily," he says, staring out into the garden. "When she was ill, he sat on her bed all day, wouldn't hardly leave her in the weeks before she died. Oh, I am sorry." He pulls out a tissue and blows his nose, then pushes it back into his pocket. "I'm not myself at all right now. Would you both like to come in?"

"We don't want to intrude on your grief, Solomon," Gillian says, so tenderly that Eleanor is grateful for her mother's presence. She can't imagine what words she might have found for Solomon if she had come here on her own.

"You're not intruding, as long as you don't mind seeing an old man blubber. Would you like to show your mother Lily's little room?" he says to Eleanor. "I thought you might have come down here for an inspection, I'm surprised it's taken you so long."

Gillian flicks a glance at Eleanor, who prays her mother won't let on that she's only just found out about her visits. "This way," she says quickly, and leads her mother around the side of the house. As she opens the door to the little sunroom, her mother steps inside. "Oh, Eleanor, I can see why you like it in here. It's so lovely and light, and what a view!"

They look down over the fields toward the woods in the distance.

"And here are Lily's paintings." Eleanor goes over to the pile in the corner.

Her mother kneels before them and looks through. "Oh wow, these are great. I can see why you're inspired, Eleanor. It's a pity . . ." She stops herself.

"What?"

"Oh, I was just thinking it's a pity we didn't put a room like this in our house." She tries to smile but it doesn't reach her eyes. "Maybe one day," she says, rubbing Eleanor's shoulder.

"Maybe," Eleanor agrees, wondering why they do this—pretend about things they know are never going to happen.

Solomon hasn't followed them. Once Eleanor has collected her bag, they walk back around the side of the house and pause at the open front door. Gillian pushes it back and calls, "Hello!"

"Come in," replies a gravelly voice. As they walk through to the lounge, with Gillian glancing all around her, they find Solomon back in his armchair, the little tabby cat on his lap. "Thank you for letting Eleanor use Lily's room," Gillian says. "It's a beautiful space." Eleanor is just relaxing into this visit, when her mother adds, "But perhaps it might be better if she had a break for now, you know, to let you have some peace while you're grieving for Charlie."

Solomon doesn't turn around, but he waves a hand at them. "She can come whenever she likes," he says. "Charlie enjoyed having her here and so do I."

Eleanor turns to her mother, who bites her lip and doesn't say anything.

Then she realizes that her mother's gaze has traveled past her. She follows it to see it is trained on the television. On the screen there are pictures of the fluorescent stripes of ambulances, vehicles parked haphazardly across roads, and people wandering dazed along the streets.

"What's going on?" Gillian asks.

"Bombs have gone off in London," Solomon says. "My old home-town. Still feel the pull when stuff like this happens, even though I haven't visited in over forty years."

Eleanor's mother inhales sharply. "My brother lives in London. He has a baby girl."

At her words, Solomon shuffles slowly around in his chair so that he can look up at her. The cat jumps down from his lap and disappears. "There are a lot of people in London. Chances are he'll be fine."

Gillian swallows hard. "I know, thank you, Solomon, but we'd better get back and call them. Come on, Eleanor." She turns to leave then glances back. "Solomon, is there anything we can do for you?"

"It's kind of you to offer, Gillian, but I'll be fine. Life goes on, doesn't it. I'm doing much better than I look." He lets out another croaky laugh that quickly becomes a cough.

"You stay there and rest, we'll let ourselves out," Gillian says, and beckons Eleanor to follow her. When they are out in the garden Gillian says quietly, "Eleanor, are you sure you have everything with you?"

Eleanor looks through the things she's collected. "I think so."

They move quickly back up the hill past all the scattered farm equipment, and her mother says nothing until they have climbed over the fence.

"Are you worried about Uncle Ian?" Eleanor asks, hurrying to keep up.

"Yes. I'll try to call them when we get back. I'll drive out toward town and see if I can get a signal on the mobile."

They hurry on. "Can I come with you?" Eleanor asks as they get back into the yard.

"I'll just be a moment," her mother says, running into the house.

Eleanor waits on the dusty gravel until she gets back, thinking how different Solomon seemed today. So lifeless, so uninterested, as if he were just tolerating them until they left.

As they get into the car, Eleanor says tentatively, "Lily's room is beautiful, isn't it?"

Her mother turns to her as she starts the engine.

"It is," she agrees. "But Eleanor, sweetheart, I can't let you go back there on your own."

"Why?" Eleanor asks softly, bending her head as a tear slips down her cheek.

"Oh Eleanor, I like Solomon too," her mom says in reply, putting the car into gear and swinging it around in a wide circle to head toward the road. Eleanor waits for the next words, the ones she had long imagined her mother saying as soon as she found out about Lily's room. "I can understand why you've fallen in love with that beautiful room. But we don't know Solomon all that well, do we? It's just not right to keep letting you go down there on your own."

44

suspicion

"Will you be okay if I have a lie down?" Ian says, coming into the front room once the paramedic has gone.

"Sure." Lilian smiles until he has left the room and then purses her lips. This room is a nightmare. She'll do it for the extra Christmas money, but she's going to have to sort something out in the New Year. She'll miss seeing those girls, but she's no longer comfortable around the Mortimers. In fact, in the past couple of weeks she's felt more and more nervous around them.

For the second time in a week, Eleanor is in the police station. Emptying her pockets. Receiving instructions from Howard Greene, the criminal defense lawyer. Waiting for the detectives, *again*. Wanting to vomit, *again*.

When Prashad and Kirby come into the room, she tries to read their body language, their facial expressions, but they give nothing away. Kirby pulls out a seat courteously for Prashad, who sits and puts a manila folder down in front of her.

"First of all, thank you for coming in to speak with us again," Prashad begins. "As with last time, you do not have to say anything, but it may harm your defense if you do not mention when questioned, something which you later rely on in court. Anything you do say may be given in evidence."

"I understand," Eleanor nods, feeling like a bit part in a TV movie.

"We have received a new witness statement," Kirby begins. "A couple think they saw Arabella talking to a man on the night she died. According to this person, they were having a rather animated discussion, and Arabella looked upset."

He stops, and the silence lingers.

"Okay," Eleanor says uncertainly.

The detectives both watch her carefully.

"They also recalled a girl holding her shoes, who seemed to be hiding nearby. The description of this woman—tall with long, straight dark hair—would appear to closely match yours. They noticed this woman because she was standing a short distance from Arabella and the other man who were arguing, and she seemed to be watching them intently."

Eleanor tries to absorb this information as they wait for her to speak. "I'm sorry," she says eventually, "but as I told you last time, I don't remember much."

"Much, or anything?" Prashad cuts in quickly.

"Anything," Eleanor says hastily, reddening.

Howard Greene leans forward. "I need a moment to speak to my client, please."

The detectives nod and get up. When they have gone from the room, Howard turns to Eleanor. "You don't need to volunteer information, Eleanor. See how easy it is to talk yourself into a hole? Just answer their questions."

Eleanor squirms. "I'm only trying to be honest."

Howard sighs as he gets up to open the door again. "Just answer their questions, Eleanor. Nothing more."

The detectives troop back in.

"Are you ready to continue, Eleanor?" Prashad asks.

Eleanor nods.

"All right, then. As I was saying, we have witnesses who saw Arabella talking to this man. Unfortunately they didn't see his face, they just recall that he had dark hair and was wearing dark clothes. You don't recall witnessing this conversation at all?"

Eleanor is thinking hard. This must have been Will, mustn't it? He told her he'd chased after Arabella and their chat might have looked like an argument. But she doesn't recall following them, and Howard Greene's caution is still ringing in her ears.

"No, I don't."

"Okay, then. Well, as you would imagine, we have been checking CCTV footage all over the place, and we recently received this."

Prashad lays a series of photographs in front of Eleanor. The picture is grainy, and looks west along the street, a very distant Big Ben just visible in the upper right-hand corner of the photo, and the Hungerford Bridge and footbridges just in the frame on the left. The pavements are quiet, and the few people visible are mostly hidden by umbrellas. "This footage was taken just after twelve thirty on Friday morning," Prashad says. "We believe this is Arabella." She points to a figure heading along the roadside path of Victoria Embankment, leaving the bridge behind her. Arabella is the only person in a thin party dress, with no protection from the rain. To the right of her is a low wall, and beyond that everything is black. Eleanor knows what is there, though—the merciless, freezing water of the Thames.

"Do you know this area well?" Prashad asks, drawing a circle around the picture with her finger.

"Not really," Eleanor replies. "I've not been in the country for long."

"Well, there's a monument just out of shot, called Cleopatra's Needle." Prashad opens the file in front of her and leafs through the contents, pulling out another photo. "This is it," she says, setting it in front of Eleanor and pointing to the obelisk monument in the middle of the photo. "There's an entrance to it at this point here—see the gap in the wall, between the sphinxes?—and a few steps lead up to it. We believe Arabella may have gone into the water close to that location. Now . . ." She returns the photo to the folder and grabs her iPad. "I'd like to show you some moving footage from the same CCTV." She tinkers with the device for a few moments before turning it around so Eleanor can see it as it lies flat on the table. Eleanor watches Arabella walk briskly along the path, until she is out of shot at the bottom of the picture.

"This is the last footage we have of Arabella so far," Prashad says as they watch. "And this is what happens next."

They continue watching the street from the same angle, and in the top corner another figure moves into shot. It's too far away for Eleanor to make out details, but she knows she's looking at herself—a pair of shoes dangle from one hand as she follows Arabella. However, before she disappears from view, she stops and leans over the wall, looking to her left.

It's as though the scene in the room has been frozen. No one moves as Eleanor wills her brain to form these memories, to recall what she had witnessed. But there is nothing. She might as well be watching a stranger.

She looks up, stricken. "I don't remember this." She begins to cry. "I didn't do anything to her, I'm sure of it," she stammers, even though she can't trust her own words, because how does she really know that for sure when she can't remember anything?

"Eleanor?" Kirby's voice brings her back to the room. "We are not accusing you of killing Arabella."

Disorientated, Eleanor turns her tear-streaked face toward him. "You're not?"

"No," he says, "we just want to encourage you to remember what happened. There's still more to show you."

Prashad doesn't take her eyes off the screen. "Keep watching, Eleanor. On this footage you appear to be looking in the direction of Cleopatra's Needle."

The next few minutes seem to last an eternity. Eleanor is standing there, her gaze still to the left, her movements so small as to be indiscernible from this distance. Eleanor grows more and more uncomfortable. What are they waiting for?

"Here it comes," Prashad says.

And suddenly her figure on the screen turns and takes off at a sprint back in the direction she had come, vanishing in seconds.

"What made you run like that, Eleanor? What did you see?"

Eleanor stares from Prashad to Kirby, confused. "I have no idea."

Prashad sighs. "We were afraid you would say that. You have no idea what you saw?"

Eleanor shakes her head. "No."

"Okay." Prashad grabs the iPad again and makes a few adjustments. "Watch this."

This time the cameras are facing the road, with a park on the left-hand side. As they watch, a dark figure holding an umbrella hurries out from under the trees and jogs across the road.

"This person is unidentified and is heading toward the last location Arabella was seen," Prashad explains. "He is hurrying toward Cleopatra's Needle. We believe he may have seen or been involved in Arabella's death. He is coming from the opposite direction, so you would not have crossed paths. But we believe you saw what happened. What's more, we think you may know this person."

Eleanor squints at the image put in front of her and shakes her head.

"I know," Prashad says. "He's a dark shape under an umbrella. We're pretty sure it's a man from the way he moves, but other than that it's hard to tell much. As yet, this is the best footage we have. He's only there for a few minutes then he runs back across and disappears under the trees next to the Embankment Gardens. We have tried to follow a CCTV trail, but so far we haven't been able to track him, partly because everyone is holding umbrellas in the rain.

"Eleanor, we don't have to keep reminding you that if you can recall anything at all you haven't told us, then it could be vital to the investigation. You are our only key witness so far, unfortunately."

Eleanor nods. Prashad sighs.

"Before we finish," Kirby takes over, "we just want to show you one more thing." He grabs the file from Prashad and finds another photograph, turning it around so Eleanor can see. "We believe this to be you, near Embankment station."

Thanks to the station lights, this image is much clearer. Eleanor's face is visible, and her features are crumpled in distress. Her arm is raised high as though she is trying to flag down an approaching taxi. She looks so haunted that Eleanor can't help but glance over the rest of the picture, half expecting to see a shadowy apparition following her.

She closes her eyes, trying to dispel the terrible image, unnerved at witnessing her own terror. She feels herself beginning to hyperventilate and tries desperately to get a grip before the world begins to swirl and she passes out. She clutches the table. "I'm so, so sorry, I wish I knew what had happened."

Prashad leans forward. "We understand that you can't remember, Eleanor, but we wouldn't be doing our job if we didn't check that those hours are really lost to you, and you haven't just suppressed them because something—or someone—might have frightened you into silence."

45

intruders

September 2005

"I'm taking your mother out tonight," Eleanor's dad announces at breakfast.

The statement is so unexpected that Eleanor is instantly intrigued. She has been pushing her cereal around the bowl, wondering what her mother might have planned to keep her occupied today, hoping it isn't cleaning. It has been almost eight weeks since Eleanor's last visit to Solomon's house, because nowadays her mother won't let her out of her sight. But tonight, maybe . . .

No. She can't go in the dark. And who knows whether Solomon will even want her there anymore? As the days turned to weeks, and the weeks have blossomed and faded, those cherished hours in the sunroom have grown distant and dreamlike. She imagines the place now: dull, cold, and empty, the paintings stacked in the corner, no one to admire them. Has Solomon missed her at all? How is he coping without Charlie?

She tunes into the conversation again as Aiden is saying something. "Can we come with you?"

"Not tonight, kid. I want you to take care of your sister."

"Seriously?" both Aiden and Eleanor reply at the same time.

Their father laughs. "Aiden, you'll be sixteen in a few weeks. You've done almost nothing to help construct this house. The roof is on, the floors are done, we're down to fittings and fixtures, and it's time me and your mum had a treat. So tonight you can pitch in. Teach Eleanor how to play cards or something; watch whatever you can find on the television. We'll be leaving at six and we'll be back between nine and ten. You are both old enough to manage for that long."

That evening, Eleanor watches her mother get ready for their meal, silently selecting a nice blouse and skirt and jacket and her heeled boots, taking time over her makeup, each action done steadily but without any noticeable enthusiasm. Eleanor wants to ask if she can go with them, but how can she begin to explain the gripe in her belly whenever she's around Aiden nowadays?

Once their parents have gone, Aiden doesn't say anything at all. Eleanor sits next to him in front of the television watching *Neighbours*, but quickly gets bored. Since their extended time with no TV she's lost track of who is who. Eventually she goes to her room, collects her sketchpad, brings it back to the lounge, and begins to flick through it.

Finally, Aiden looks across. "What you doing?"

"Just drawing."

As she says it there's a knock on the door. Aiden jumps up and answers it, and to Eleanor's dismay she hears the guffaws and snorts and back slaps of Aiden's awful friends.

As they walk in and see Eleanor, Timmo's eyes light up. "Hello there," he says. "You gonna party with us tonight, eh?"

"Leave her out of it," Aiden replies tiredly, but Eleanor sees her brother cast a wary glance toward Timmo. Her nerves begin to skitter, struggling to resettle.

Coby is already rooting through the cupboards in the kitchen. "One won't hurt her," he calls out. "We all gotta start somewhere."

Eleanor frowns at Aiden as he sits down again. Timmo is by his side, singing the *Neighbours* theme in a horribly whiny voice and laughing at himself as though he's hilarious. Having not spent much time with her brother and his friends before, she hasn't had the chance to notice Aiden's demeanor, but now she realizes it doesn't look like he's enjoying himself at all.

"Here we go." Coby comes across holding three glass tumblers. He puts them down on the coffee table, and then produces a bottle and three cans from inside his jacket. "Right then," he says, pouring a splash of clear liquid from the larger bottle. "Chasers first, eh?" He roots in his pocket and pulls out a packet of cigarettes, grabs one, and puts it in his mouth.

"You can't smoke in here," Aiden says, snatching the cigarette, which makes Coby cry out a gruff, "Hey."

"There's bloody smoke alarms everywhere," Aiden snaps, gesturing toward the ceiling.

"All right, all right, I'll go outside in a minute." Coby puts the packet back in his pocket, catches Eleanor's eye, and gives her a crazy grin that makes Eleanor shudder.

"It's good your folks are out tonight," Timmo says as he takes a slug of his drink. "Makes a change from sitting in the car in the bloody bush." He nudges one of the glasses toward Eleanor. "Go on then, have a try."

The liquid in her glass smells like acid and tastes worse. The first mouthful sets her throat on fire, and try as she might, she cannot stop herself from coughing.

The boys all laugh at her as she looks up with watery eyes, but Aiden doesn't find it quite as funny as the other two. "You don't have to drink that, Els," he says when she's finally stopped coughing.

"You'll be right, won't you, Elly Belly," Timmo chuckles, pouring her another generous splash of liquid. "Go on, down in one."

The tension in the room is palpable. Eleanor looks across to her brother, who appears to be frozen. She raises her drink to her lips and tips it back just like they are doing, letting it wash down her throat, coughing and spluttering again at the fire running through her.

Aiden's friends cheer and Timmo goes to pour her a third glass.

"Stop!" Aiden shouts. "Eleanor, go to your room. Now."

As Eleanor stands up, her head becomes light and strange. She hears Timmo cackle behind her as she heads to her room, and Aiden snap, "Leave her out of it, Timmo."

"Or what?" Coby asks.

Eleanor shivers. She doesn't hear Aiden's reply, but she does make it to her room. By the time she shuts the door she feels a bit queasy and her head is already beginning to spin. The clock says seven thirty, still about two hours until her parents come back. She picks up a book but can't focus on the words. She tries to draw but her eyes don't seem to be working properly.

She falls onto her bed and drifts into a doze.

The next time she comes to, every single thing in the world seems to have changed.

46

running

Preston Harlen puts down the paper with a sigh. Every time he sees the Atlantic mentioned in conjunction with Arabella Lane's death, he can't help but squirm with embarrassment. He has already had the cops around asking him about drugs in the restaurant. The whole thing is terrible, but he's worked for years on this menu, this business plan, his clientele, and he doesn't want his dream crashing because of the friggin' notoriety of some politician's daughter.

"You understand where I'm coming from, don't you?" he says as he explains all this to his wife.

Mia smiles vaguely, choosing to tactfully ignore him, since Arabella had masterminded her book campaign.

Eleanor is squashed into a corner seat on the first deck of one of London's red-top buses, watching the city go by. The world outside looks the same as yesterday, but things are changing for Eleanor. She can no longer resist the avalanche of memories. Her experience of time is not the steady ticking of clock hands anymore, nor the solemn click of a turning number. She is unaware of the drizzle on the windows. As the bus shudders along, she puts her fingers to the pulse on her wrist, counts the beats of her heart, trying to reset herself against that steady rhythm. But despite the crush of bodies all around her, she is far away, back in the darkened recess of Solomon's house, on the night she woke up there in her nightdress, shivering.

No.

She shifts in her seat, fighting the memories. She is only twenty-one years old and already she has witnessed two terrible deaths. Why is it that the one she needs to remember is a gaping blank, while the one she wants to forget is imprinted above all else in her mind?

When the police let her go, she had read sympathy in the faces of Kirby and Prashad. It seemed as though they believed her. That should have been a relief, but it hasn't made their questions or their revelations any easier to bear.

She had turned down a ride to Harborne Grove. She was dreading going back there. Once outside, she had called the only friend she could think of. "I realize I've been acting a bit crazy today," she had said when Will answered. "Do you have time to meet me? I need . . . I need a friend."

"Of course," said Will, the kindness in his voice making her cry. He had given her step-by-step directions to a pub in the city. His local, he'd said. He'd be there as fast as he could.

She focuses beyond the steamed-up bus window. Solomon had once said he was from London. Had he strolled down Bond Street years ago, young and carefree, no inkling of the future, of how things would end for him half a world away? *Don't think too hard,* she wills herself, *or you will summon his ghost.* She shifts her focus again. Outside, she can see men in anoraks and women in beautiful woolen coats. Men in smart overcoats and women in Puffa jackets. Kids are bouncing rainbows of color. Most of the shops and houses are festooned with tinsel. There are lights everywhere. Soft fairy lights frame the edges of windows, or wind around Christmas trees, indoor and out. Decorations glint on lampposts, or dazzle where they are propped in the middle of roundabouts. Smears of color bounce from car lights, phone lights, and buildings. They make streaks of brightness that flare for a moment like fleeting thoughts, and then disappear as quickly as they come. Some people move in groups, huddling close, talking and laughing. Those alone travel purposefully, heads down, keen to reach the places they belong.

And where was the last place Eleanor had truly belonged? Could it really have been in a dead woman's art room eleven years ago?

Perhaps. It's certainly not on the top floor of a town house, choking each night as the questions rise like hot air to overwhelm her. Nor had it been in the sheds and houses of the outback. And even though she and her mother had lived in their modest town house for nearly a decade, Eleanor had never felt she belonged there either. When is she going to find a place she can feel fully herself?

The swaying bodies in the bus are cramped together, sharing oxygen in the damp air, shoulders hunched over handheld devices, only one or two people talking. A week ago Eleanor would have found it all fascinating. Now it is overwhelming. She's giddy, wants to call out to everyone and everything to cease moving until her head has stopped spinning. She would close her eyes, but she is afraid of drifting off and missing her stop. However, while she remains conscious, she is terrified of the ghostly faces crowding in on her. They are whispering things she doesn't want to hear.

As the bus progresses slowly with the heavy traffic down Tottenham Court Road, Eleanor longs to curl up and sleep. She doesn't know how she'll find the energy to even get up out of her seat. Finally, the bus reaches her stop, and she drags herself to her feet and heads down the stairs, squeezing past the people who are packed into the aisles. The cold air rushes to greet her as she jumps off the final step onto the road, and she pulls her scarf over her nose and mouth, then heads down one of the side streets, away from the main road, until she sees the Mighty Oak pub on the corner.

As she approaches the pub a blast of nerves makes her pause. How is she going to explain everything to Will? Why does she want to, when he was a virtual stranger a week ago? But he's the only person reaching out to her, he's the only person who seems to care about what she might be going through, and she's desperate for someone to talk to. Suddenly, she thinks of her mother, and realizes that Gillian hasn't been in touch at all today. Now she thinks about it, her mother hadn't contacted her yesterday either, had she? She frowns, forgetting everything else for a moment. That can't be right—Gillian never leaves her alone for this long. A new pang of fear strikes her. *Please don't let there be something wrong back home too.*

Her hands begin to tingle. *It's the cold*, she tells herself—but it's also an unwanted reminder of the anxiety that kept her trapped in her room as a teenager, refusing to go out for weeks or sometimes months. Until she was taking the medication again. She reaches the door and steps inside quickly, before she can dwell on this neurosis, unwinding her scarf and pulling off her gloves.

She spots Will straightaway, but he doesn't notice her for a moment. He's staring into his pint, looking solemn. She pictures herself going across and putting a hand on his, or an arm over his shoulder. She imagines leaning forward and feeling his warm breath close to her cold lips. She remembers what he said on the phone—*I want to take you ice skating again after all this is over, so I can hold your hand*—and the way he comforted her and held her hand as they headed to the memorial. These small things suggest something more between them, and yet the lure is making her nervous. He's attractive, certainly, but is that what draws her to him, or is it that he's the only one offering her support?

She hesitates, but then, as though he can feel her eyes on him, he looks up and sees her. She waits for him to smile as he waves her over, but he doesn't. His face is serious, and full of questions.

Her legs grow less steady as she makes her way past the early-evening drinkers, toward him. As she reaches the table, Will jumps up and puts a hand on her elbow as she slumps into her seat.

"Eleanor? What's happened?"

His voice is full of fear. She glances up at him, can feel her chest rising and falling as she says, "I saw Arabella, Will. I was there. I may have witnessed what happened."

The color drains from Will's face. "Have you remembered something?"

"No. The police, they showed me—they have CCTV. I ran away, Will. They think she waited for someone at a monument on the Embankment, they called it Cleopatra's Needle. There's some footage of a man going toward it, but he's holding an umbrella, you can't make out who it is. What if I stood and watched when I could have helped her? How come I can't remember it?"

She leans over, puts her head in her hands, breathing hard, trying not to break down.

"There was a man there?" Will repeats, as though he can't quite believe what he's hearing. "They've seen it on the CCTV?"

"Yes. What if Nathan waited for her after the party? What if he followed her when everyone else had gone? They'll have to question him more now, won't they? I'm scared of what he might be planning for me if he wants to cover this up."

She is trembling now, and Will jumps up and comes around to her. "Come on," he says, his tone a mix of concern and urgency, "we can't stay here while you're like this. Let's go back to my place. We'll order some food and try to figure out what next. Don't worry, Eleanor, it'll be okay."

She gets up and lets him lead her out of the warm pub. Once in the frosty evening air her mind begins to quiet, even though she's still trembling. They don't talk much as they travel through a few quiet lanes, until eventually, they arrive at a tall brick building. "As you're about to see, my place is pretty cozy," Will says, opening the main door with a passkey. "Come on in."

She follows him up a flight of stairs and a short way down a long, featureless corridor. At one of the doors Will stops and rummages for his keys. "Here you go." He opens the door and holds it so she can go in first. Once they are in, he locks and deadbolts the door behind them.

The apartment is not as small as she'd expected. There's a lounge area, with plush furnishings, a large flat-screen TV and evenly spaced speaker system. A small dining area adjacent to a gleaming white kitchenette. Next to that, a door leads to what she suspects will be the bedroom and bathroom.

"Sit down," Will says, "and I'll get you something to drink. Do you want a hot drink or something stronger?"

"Tea, please," she replies.

"See, you're picking up our English habits already," Will calls as he walks over to the kitchen.

She settles back onto the comfortable sofa, staring at the blank screen of the TV while Will makes the drinks. This all seems so normal. For these few moments, she could almost forget that the rest of her life is a nightmare.

Eventually Will comes across with two mugs of tea, sets them down, and says, "Okay, fill me in, from the beginning."

The beginning.

It sounds so simple. She tries to picture her life as a storybook, its chapters laid down one after the other, like stepping stones through a stream. Instead she sees torn pages strewn across parched grass as the ground begins to burn. She watches them smolder, shriveling at the edges, going up in smoke before she can find the one she wants.

"Eleanor?" Will touches her arm. "Are you okay?"

"You really want to know?"

"Of course I do."

"Then I need to start at *my* beginning," she murmurs, turning to him. "I need to tell you why this doesn't feel like the beginning of a nightmare to me, but the end of one."

Will frowns as her thoughts tumble backward, flailing until she begins to speak. She describes the move to the country when she was nine. She outlines the cracks that slowly appeared in the family, ". . . until one night, when the house was almost finished, my mum and dad decided to go out." She takes a long, slow breath, readying herself to say the next words.

"And when I woke up, I wasn't in my own bed."

September 2005

When Solomon brings her around, she screams at the shock of being so far from home. She is rattling the door to Lily's room, trying to unlock it again even though she has no key. Solomon is in his pajamas, gently shaking her.

"Eleanor? Eleanor?" She looks down in the dim moonlight to see that her feet are bare, her toes caked with mud.

"What's happened, Eleanor?" Solomon asks urgently. "What are you doing here?"

But before she has time to answer, the world behind them explodes.

47

protection

September 2005

Solomon and Eleanor freeze as flames shoot high into the air, beyond the ridge of the hill. The fireball rises and falls, gone so fast that Eleanor might question if she had seen it at all, if not for the flickering glow that remains in the distance.

Solomon recovers first and staggers away from Eleanor toward the hill. As he stumbles up in his pajamas, Eleanor watches, unable to move. When he reaches the crest of the hill he doesn't hesitate, turning on his heel, running back down toward her, shouting, "Get in the truck, Eleanor! In the truck now!" When she still doesn't move, he comes across and grabs her roughly by the arm. "We need to go."

He half helps and half drags her away from the house, toward the waiting vehicle. His grip is surprisingly strong. Eleanor is trembling as he pulls her with him.

"Where are we going?" she asks once they are inside and Solomon has gunned the engine. Her body is still shaking violently; she can't seem to stop it.

"Is your family in the house?"

Eleanor tries to focus. Her head still feels strange, both heavy and fuzzy. "My brother is, I think. My mum and dad have gone out, but they might be back by now." She gathers enough composure to look at the clock on the dashboard—nine thirty—and tries to remember what they said. "I'm not sure if they'll be there."

"Let's hope they are; let's hope to god they saw that."

Eleanor shakes her head to try to dispel the grogginess, but this whole scene is so disorientating, she cannot clear it. "What was that?"

"My shed going up in flames. My side's clear, but there's a lot of fuel on your land. I told your dad he needed to work on his firebreaks—why didn't he listen to me? Bloody city cowboys think they know everything."

"Should we call the fire brigade?"

"I don't have a phone." Solomon's rough voice wobbles as they travel fast down the bumpy corrugated driveway that leads away from his property.

"I thought everyone had a phone."

"Not everybody needs one!" he shouts.

She doesn't dare say anything.

"Let's go and get your family, get *your* phone."

"He didn't have a phone?" Will cuts in, incredulous.

Eleanor shrugs. "He was an old man, with no family, no visitors. Perhaps he couldn't afford it. I wonder, from a few things my parents said, if he was actually really poor. When I think back to that winter we lived there, his house was cold, he was wearing so many layers of clothing . . . I just didn't connect the dots at the time."

She stops. She can tell some of this story, but not all of it. Not yet.

Will seems to sense how distressed she is. He strokes her back and passes her the cup of tea, and she tries to steady herself by taking a few long, slow sips. Even so, she is not really in this small room anymore, but still rattling along in the dark in Solomon's car, hanging on as he drives erratically over the unsealed road.

September 2005

A truck races by in the opposite direction, heading away from the house way too fast. Eleanor turns to watch it go and remembers Aiden's friends.

"Running away, no doubt," Solomon mutters darkly as he drives. "I knew those boys were up to no good, messing around down there with all my stuff. I shoulda stopped it long ago, before this could happen. But I didn't, you know, because I thought they might turn nasty. And now look what's happened."

Eleanor's not sure what he's talking about, but to her horror, as they draw closer to the house, the car begins to be softly pelted with debris, some black, some still glowing orange. Their new house, the house her father has built by hand, is an ominous silhouette, framed by a background of flickering orange light.

"Where are they all?" Solomon grunts, pulling up but leaving the engine running. The smoke and the darkness make it hard to see anything, but Eleanor feels an inexorable pull toward the house. She goes to open the door of the car, but Solomon stops her. "No, Eleanor, it's too dangerous. Wait, let me think."

She watches more of the embers float toward the ground. Ahead of them, a few patches of grass begin to smoulder.

Solomon winds down his window. "Aiden!" he calls. "AIDEN! GILLIAN! MARTIN!" But there is no answer. Even from the passenger seat Eleanor can feel the wind, uncomfortably warm.

The embers come faster and stronger. Outside it is raining fire.

"What do we do?" Eleanor begs. "Where are they?"

And then there's a new flare of fire, bursting into life right on top of the roof. Eleanor screams. The roof of their house is burning. What's happening inside? Where is Aiden?

Solomon climbs out of the car. "Stay here," he says firmly, and he stumbles into the smoky gloom.

Alone and terrified, Eleanor waits. Time ceases to exist. She thinks she can see flames inside the house now. But the smoke is stronger; she can hardly see the house at all. The embers are raining down on the car, glowing orange spots skitter across the hood. What if one of them sets the car on fire? It will blow up! It will blow up with her inside!

Suddenly, her parents' car pulls up next to her in a fierce spray of gravel. As she opens the passenger door her father jumps out, so close she could almost touch him, but he's completely unaware of her presence. He is screaming, "Oh no, no, no, no, no!" as he races toward the house. Her mother sprints from the other side calling, "Eleanor! Aiden!" To Eleanor's horror they both disappear from view, and Eleanor can wait here alone no longer. She jumps down from the vehicle in her nightdress, wailing in the searing heat, her arms over her face to protect herself from the ash and embers that rain down on her, stinging her skin. She runs blindly toward the house, as a group of people reemerge in a huddle, and when her mother spots her she screams, "Eleanor!" and comes at a run with her arms wide open, and Eleanor is lifted as she hasn't been since she was a toddler, wrapping her legs around her mother's waist as her mother dashes away with her to their car, and pushes her into the back seat.

She's aware of the door opening on the other side, and Aiden climbs in. Eleanor only sees his face in glimpses, his wide eyes, the tears on his cheeks, and then the car begins to move and something is wrong and they are both screaming for their father, who isn't with them. And their mother is yelling at them to be quiet, and a fire truck is racing past the car, and finally the air seems cooler and so much easier to breathe and their mother has pulled up on the side of the road and her head is on the steering wheel and she is sobbing.

For a moment, Eleanor is too distraught to carry on. She only registers Will's shocked face as she stops speaking.

"Eleanor, I'm so sorry, what a horrific thing to go through."

"That was just the start of it," she tells him, exhausted, as though her body has undergone that panicked flight from the burning house again. "It seems so ironic," she murmurs, "that I can remember that night eleven years ago in minute detail, and yet I don't have a clue about what happened right in front of me last week." As Will opens his mouth, she cuts in, "I know, I know, it was the drugs. I get it, but I still hate it, Will. It's brought all these nightmares flooding back. I've done everything I can think of to try to put them behind me, but it's impossible. The memories never leave me—they spin around and around in my mind, tormenting me. I don't know if I can bear another weight like that on my conscience."

"But you didn't start the fire." Will frowns, clearly confused. "Why is it on *your* conscience?"

Eleanor shakes her head. "It wasn't that, it was what came afterward." The body on the rope moves into her mind's eye. She feels dizzy and drained. "I can't talk about it anymore tonight."

"You don't have to," Will says, still holding her. "It must have been terrible."

Eleanor is slowly readjusting to the present, remembering why she's here. "It was, and I can't change any of it, but I still feel like I could change what's happening now, if only I could remember what I saw. Otherwise Nathan's going to get away with it, Will, I know it."

Will sits back, watching her. "Why are you so sure that Nathan's responsible?"

Eleanor hesitates. "He has the motive. Arabella had just slapped him in front of everyone, and he obviously has a violent temper. And . . . and what if he already knew she was sleeping with someone else? He might not have realized it was my uncle until recently, but what if she taunted him? I doubt it would take much to provoke him. Or what if he just wanted to get rid of her so he could carry on with Caroline?" She pauses. "He has so many reasons, not just one. And I'm missing something that will help convict him, I know it. It'll come to me, if I keep looking for long enough. Why did I end up with her ring? There must be a reason. Perhaps Nathan had a plan to divert suspicion toward me."

"You know what," Will says quietly, "Nathan has always had this strange power over women. They seem to interpret his arrogance as confidence, and he dazzles them with fake charm. I've never known anything like it, but I thought Arabella would eventually prove a match for him, perhaps expose him or ruin him. From the way she slapped him, it looked like she was ready to take him on. What better motive than that for killing her?"

"Yes, but how do we prove it?" Eleanor asks.

"Well, that's the million dollar question, isn't it?" As he speaks, Will takes Eleanor's empty cup from her and goes across to the kitchen.

Eleanor watches him, and then glances around. "Your place is very nice," she says. "You made out it was a box!"

"Small but homely, I guess," Will answers as he rinses the cups.

"Is this your family?" she asks, spotting a frame next to the television and leaning across to pick it up. In the photo, Will sits in the middle of a happy group of five.

Will comes back across as he dries his hands on a tea towel. "Sure is. Mum and Dad, and my two little sisters, who both have my parents wrapped firmly around their little fingers."

"You guys all look so happy," she says, noticing the little Yorkshire terrier at their mother's feet. "It's like one of those photos that comes with the frame when you buy it."

"Oh, we have our fair share of skeletons," Will replies. She glances at him, half expecting to see him smiling, but he looks deadly serious. "My younger sister has had problems with drugs and the wrong kind of guy. I've had to help my dad in a few difficult situations, extracting her from messes."

"I can easily see you as the protective big brother. It's kind of what you've been doing with me."

Will sits down next to her, putting a hand on her knee. "Believe me, Eleanor," he says quietly, "I wouldn't describe my feelings for you as brotherly."

It takes Eleanor a moment to absorb his words, but when she does, she leaps up. "I have to go."

Will jumps up too, as his face falls. "No, you don't. I'm sorry, it wasn't the right time to say that. It was completely inappropriate. Forget I said it."

Eleanor tries to smile reassuringly, but at the same time she's shrugging on her coat. "It's okay, but my uncle will be worried if I don't come home tonight, and I need to check he's all right." A modicum of loyalty to her aunt stills her tongue about the events earlier on.

"Let me call you a taxi," Will says, standing close by, his disappointment palpable as she winds her scarf around her neck.

"No, I'll get the train," she demurs, aware her funds are too low for taxis now she's out of a job.

"Well, I'll walk you to the station, then," he says, grabbing his coat. As he holds the door open for her she feels a surge of relief, which is quickly replaced by confusion. Will is kind and warm and good looking, so why is she so resistant to his charms? When he's so obviously reaching out to her, why does she keep running away?

48

the surprise

Aisha slides down in her car seat, noting the time. She's getting fed up with these stakeouts. She's not sure why Nathan is so paranoid about Eleanor; to Aisha she seems more irritating than anything. But then again, if they can find something on her, she might be the perfect person to take the fall. Aisha has done a thorough background check, both in the UK and overseas, and it seems that Eleanor Brennan definitely has enough history of mental disturbance to be capable of pushing someone into the Thames.

Will and Eleanor hardly speak as he guides her to the station. As he leaves, he looks so dejected that she almost apologizes, but he gives her a brief peck on the cheek and disappears fast. It is nearly ten o'clock by the time she boards her train. A large portion of her fellow passengers are dressed up, probably having attended one of the many Christmas parties still going on around the city. Others are in casual clothes, giving less away about where they've come from, or where they might be headed. Eleanor wishes she had her sketchbook with her, but instead she finds herself picking a few people close to her and trying to imagine their lives. As they sit squashed side by side, their stories, their secrets are all hidden. She stares at the woman with the shopping bags, the man listening to his iPod, the couple in formal wear who can't keep their hands off one another. She starts to invent a narrative for them, but it is all so reductive, based on shallow observations of clothes and expressions. There's no way of knowing what's held deep inside them. As she watches them, the woman catches her eye and quickly looks away. What do they make of her, Eleanor wonders, in this close space they share? For how long will they remember Eleanor's face, or will it have vanished by the time the Tube doors close, discarded by their minds as unnecessary?

Was it the same for Eleanor? Had she disregarded some piece of information as trivial, when it might be the clue that will unlock everything for her? She has never thought to ask herself how much she knows about her own life. She has assumed, as most do, that she knows everything. Until recently she hadn't considered all that has gone, through the losses and lapses of memory. She hasn't questioned whether there are things she blames herself for that are not at all as they seemed. She hasn't asked whether she's guilty of anything more than she's aware of.

As soon as she gets off the Tube, she gets that horrible sense of being followed again. She scurries faster and faster down the lamplit streets toward her uncle's house, telling herself she's paranoid, and if she doesn't sleep tonight she'll soon be delusional too. As she finally sees the house she is overwhelmed by the exhaustion she's been holding at bay. Nevertheless, she's apprehensive as she approaches the door and steps over the ghost of herself the week before, refusing to dwell on that bedraggled, drugged woman at her feet.

This day has been so long and eventful that she can't imagine there is more to come in the last couple of hours, until she opens the front door and sees Savannah grinning wildly in the hallway.

"What are you doing up so late?" Eleanor asks as she comes inside.

"We've been waiting for you!" Savannah trills. "Haven't you checked your phone—Dad's been leaving message after message."

Eleanor pulls her phone out of her pocket. "Oh dear, dead battery," she says. "Not in trouble, am I?" she asks, although from the look on Savannah's face it doesn't seem like it.

Surreptitiously Eleanor glances toward the closed door of the front room, but eagle-eyed Savannah sees her do it.

"Oh, you can't go in there," she says cheerfully. "It's dangerous."

"Dangerous? Why?"

"Daddy saw a mouse earlier. He whacked his head trying to catch it and smashed into his drinks cabinet, and now he's set traps in there. We're not to open the door under any circumstances in case the little bugger runs out."

As Savannah finishes talking, Ian comes down the corridor. One side of his head has swollen nicely, forming a deep purple wound surrounded by redness.

"Nasty knock," Eleanor says deadpan.

"Yes," Ian replies. "We're so glad you're back, Eleanor, I was beginning to get worried. Come through."

He walks off down the corridor and Savannah grabs her hand and pulls her with them, leaving Eleanor no choice but to follow.

As they open the door to the family room, Savannah yells, "Surprise!"

Eleanor looks inside and gasps as she sees the three people there. Naeve is curled up under a blanket, watching Eleanor. Susan is seated in one corner, holding a cup of tea. And opposite her, face turned toward Eleanor and lips trembling with emotion, is Eleanor's mother.

Gillian jumps to her feet and comes across to her daughter, enfolding her into a hug. Eleanor puts her arms around her mom and sags against her, but she doesn't have the energy to return the tightness of her mother's squeeze.

Her mother steps back but keeps hold of Eleanor's shoulders. "I hope you don't mind," she says. "I wanted to surprise you for Christmas."

"Of course not," Eleanor says, but there is a tumult of emotions coursing through her. Has Gillian planned this all along, or does she have other motives for being here? Will her mother's presence help her gain some perspective on the week's events, or will it just remind her of everything she has struggled with for so long?

Over her mother's shoulder, she sees Susan watching them. It's almost as much of a surprise to find Susan here tonight. "How are you, Susan?" she asks cautiously.

"Much better, thank you," Susan replies.

The atmosphere in the room turns uneasy, and Savannah seems the only one oblivious. "Auntie Gillian is going to take us to see the Christmas lights tomorrow!"

Eleanor can't help but smile at her enthusiasm. "That sounds great." But she can't maintain the facade. Her body is crying out for rest, her knees are about to give way. She looks between them all. "I hope you don't mind but it's been a really long day and I'm very tired. I think I'll go to bed."

Susan and Ian nod, and her mother looks concerned. "I'll come up with you. I told Ian and Susan not to waste time making up another room, and I think I've stayed up long enough to have a chance of beating the jet lag. Good night, everyone."

They head up both flights of stairs silently. Inside the little loft room, Gillian's suitcase sits on the bed.

"I hope you don't mind sharing," Gillian begins as soon as they shut the door. "I just didn't want to be any trouble, and when Ian met me at the airport, he told me that he's sometimes in their spare room. Apparently, he and Susan aren't getting on all that well. Have you noticed anything?"

Eleanor almost laughs at the question. "It's impossible not to notice, Mum, when you live here. What else did Ian tell you? Did he say that Susan whacked him on the head with a golf club and gave him that shiner?"

Gillian looks shocked. "Good god, no. What on earth has been happening here?"

Eleanor flops down on the bed next to her mother, and closes her eyes. "I may have witnessed Arabella Lane's death last week—and it might have been a murder."

Even though they are barely touching, she still feels her mother stiffen. "What do you mean, you *may have*?" Gillian asks softly into the ensuing silence.

"I was drugged," Eleanor confesses. "Something was slipped into my drink, and I don't remember all of the night. But the police are investigating—they've got CCTV—they've shown me that I was there."

At this moment she is too tired for emotion, and of course her cold, rational voice is entirely wrong for this announcement, which she knows as soon as her mother practically jumps off the bed and begins to pace.

"Oh my god, I've been worried you might be in some sort of trouble, yes, but I never imagined *this*."

Through her exhaustion, Eleanor realizes this conversation is going the wrong way and she has to change it fast, before they both say things they will regret.

"We're all in trouble, Mum. Your brother was having an affair with Arabella. The dead woman. Yep, he's been interviewed by the police too. And Susan is some kind of ice-maiden whacko. This morning she took a golf club to her husband, and tonight they're sitting there like it's the perfect family gathering. There's so much crap going on in this house, I can't tell what's real anymore."

Gillian sits down heavily and rubs her eyes. "Okay, this is too much. Can you start again and tell me exactly what's going on?"

Eleanor lies back down. "You know what, I'm exhausted. I haven't slept well at all lately. Tomorrow, I'll tell you everything you want to know."

Her mother doesn't say anything, just goes to the bathroom and stays in there for a long time. When she comes out and switches off the bedside light, Eleanor is drifting off, but Gillian's voice brings her back to the room.

"Don't be too hard on your aunt and uncle for pretending things are okay when they're not," she says. "Because sometimes pretending is the only way to find the strength to carry on." There's a pause. "Eleanor, I know that coming here is all about stretching your wings and being independent," Gillian says softly into the darkness, "but please don't start hiding things from me. I always want to help and support you—you know that, don't you?"

"Yes, Mum," Eleanor says softly, hiding her face under the covers, unable to prevent the tears from welling. Thinking to herself: *I haven't started hiding things from you, Mum. I've been hiding things from you for years.*

49

persuasion

September 2005

Aiden is hospitalized for smoke inhalation. His hands are burned. He had been so quiet in the car that neither Eleanor nor her mother had realized the extent of his injuries at first, but as soon as they had, her mother had driven at breakneck speed to the nearest emergency department.

Eleanor sits alone in a small room in the hospital for much of the night, checked on at intervals by her mother and the nurses, wondering where her dad is, desperate to know how her brother is doing. She wonders if there's anything left of the house and makes a mental list of all her possessions, distraught at the thought of her sketchbooks burning.

She doesn't see her father until the dawn has broken outside and the ringneck parrots are gossiping in the trees beyond the hospital window. As soon as she looks into his yellowed, smoke-ravaged eyes, she knows he is not the same man as yesterday. He grips her hand tightly and she studies the grime on the hills and ravines of his blanched knuckles. As she does so she has the first inkling, although she cannot name it, that a cage has fallen over her family, a trap like the one she sometimes used for the spiders and tiny insects that strayed into her territory in the shed. Something bigger than all of them now holds them in its gaze, and when it is ready, the world is going to change, one way or another.

When Eleanor wakes up in the little room in Harborne Grove there's an empty space beside her. She could almost dismiss her mother's arrival last night as another crazy dream, were it not for the open suitcase in the corner, and the smell of lemongrass permeating the room.

Once she has given her eyes time to adjust, she checks the clock; to her surprise it is almost eleven. She has slept soundly, uninterrupted, for nearly twelve hours.

She takes her time getting dressed, unsure of what awaits her downstairs. Despite her mother's presence, Susan is still an unknown quantity, and Eleanor is sure her uncle will be keen to quiz her on events at the police station yesterday.

That CCTV image still unnerves her, and the only way to deal with it is to keep moving. She heads downstairs and finds everyone in the kitchen. Susan is reading a newspaper while Ian shows her mother how to use the coffee machine. Eleanor is thankful, as always, to see Naeve and Savannah there; she feels so much safer with them around. Their presence lessens the chance of any ugly confrontations.

"No school?" she says to the girls, helping herself to the pot of fresh coffee.

"Last day was yesterday, silly," Savannah says, giving her a hug. "I told you, Auntie Gillian is spending all day with us. We're going to see the Christmas lights later too."

"That's great," Eleanor replies. As she looks around she might—almost—be able to pretend that nothing is wrong, if it weren't for the strained silence of her uncle and aunt. Then Susan's phone rings and she offers a polite "excuse me" as she walks out of the room to answer it.

Eleanor realizes there is something to be thankful for in her mother's visit, because Gillian's presence will most likely mean that Susan will remain polite and guarded for the duration of the holiday. Eleanor might be intrigued by the thought of her unhinged aunt brandishing a golf club, but she's not keen to witness it.

She studies her uncle as she leans against the counter sipping her coffee. Ian's head is down as he calmly reads the newspaper. She remembers her mother's words last night. Perhaps everyone has to pretend to some degree. Yet it has reminded her of how multifaceted people are, constantly choosing which of their many sides to turn to the light. Perhaps it's not something to be so wary of; perhaps it's just a way of getting through life. Is self-protection really such a bad thing?

But as soon as she asks this question of herself, she is nine years old again, back in a hospital room with her parents, waiting for her brother to come around from his sedation.

September 2005

"Look," she says, glancing out the window and pointing toward the parking lot, "there's Solomon."

She watches as Solomon climbs slowly and stiffly out of his pickup, as though every single one of his bones is aching.

Her dad marches across and peers over her shoulder, then heads for the door.

"Martin," her mother calls after him, a warning in her voice. But he has already gone.

Eleanor sees the expression on her mother's face. "What's the matter?"

"Nothing," Gillian snaps. "Come away from the window, Eleanor."

But she doesn't. She watches Solomon look up as though he can see her beyond the glass. She presses her hand against the windowpane, wanting to reach him, to thank him for being so kind last night, and then she sees her father dash down the front steps and his arms are waving, and it looks as though he is shouting at Solomon, even though they can't hear a word.

Her mother is next to her, trying to drag her away, but she won't come. Solomon looks surprised and steps backward, and as he does so, he holds his hands up as though trying to placate Eleanor's father and calm him down, but Martin gestures angrily at the pickup and then storms back inside. Solomon stares after him, then shakes his head sadly. He still hasn't moved by the time Martin reenters the room, his face red.

"What did you just say to him?" Gillian demands.

Eleanor has never seen her mother so angry. She has gone a deep puce color, and her whole body is shaking.

"I told him to stay away from us for good."

"Martin! What the hell . . ." Gillian stomps toward the door. "I'm going after him. He helped us last night, can't you see that? Why are you taking it out on him?"

As soon as Gillian has left, Martin marches over to stand close to Eleanor. "What do you think it looks like, that you were at his house in your nightie?" he growls, spitting the words into her face, his eyes ablaze with fury.

"I was sleepwalking," she stammers. "I'm sure it's just because I was missing Lily's room."

"Do you know how much trouble that man has caused us?" her father continues in a menacing voice. "He's cost us everything—everything."

Eleanor flinches. How can this be Solomon's fault? He had tried to help them, hadn't he?

"You," Martin shakes a finger in Eleanor's face, "are never to visit him again, ever, do you understand?"

Eleanor nods hastily, just wanting her father to move away from her.

"Dad," comes a weak voice from the bed. They both jump and turn to see that Aiden is awake, watching them, his face stricken. "You shouldn't be mad with Eleanor. You should be mad with me."

"Eleanor? Eleanor?"

She is standing in the Harborne Grove kitchen, and her uncle is staring at her.

"Where are the others?" she asks, confused. How can they have all gone without her noticing?

"Savannah has dragged your mother away to her room," Ian says. "I need to talk to you. Come, quickly, please."

She follows him through the house, to his office. Naeve waits for them inside, and Eleanor balks at the door, remembering her secret incursion in here, sure that Naeve has finally confided in her dad, and that she's now in trouble. But when she turns around her uncle is right behind her, already shutting the door.

"I told you things would begin to come to light if we just hung on for a few days," Ian begins, his eyes shining feverishly. "Susan has just had a phone call from Ernie. Nathan has been arrested. He gave some sort of false alibi, apparently, and the person he was with has retracted it."

Caroline? Eleanor thinks immediately. Had their conversation yesterday actually made a difference? Had Eleanor pricked her conscience?

"So can we tell them about the ring now?" Naeve asks quietly.

"No," Ian growls, making both girls jump. "Do *not* say anything until we find out what happens to Nathan. Not a word to either of your mothers," he continues, pointing to Naeve and then Eleanor. "I've already paid Lilian a sizable sum to ensure she doesn't mention it. It's only going to get messier if it all comes out, and god knows what Susan would say or do." He gingerly touches his fingers to the purple-black lump on his forehead.

"You bribed Lilian?" Eleanor gasps.

"Bribed is the wrong word, Eleanor. I am just protecting our family until the truth comes out. What we have to do now is get on with our lives and act like a normal family preparing for Christmas, okay?"

Eleanor opens her mouth to reply, but before she can say anything else there's a small knock at the door. "Dad? Naeve? What are you all doing in there?"

Ian opens it and they all stare at Savvie's flushed, excited face. Ian picks her up and smiles at her. "Christmas secrets, Sav," he says, tapping his nose. She giggles.

Eleanor can't stand being part of this. She's sick of all the games. She turns away and as she does so, she catches Naeve's eye. From the astute look on her cousin's face, she suspects she has an ally.

50

the lies

"**W**hat have you got to make this stick?" Superintendent Louise Thornton asks Detective Inspector Priya Prashad. "It's Nathan bloody Lane. You're going to have to be on top of your game."

"We've got evidence of domestic abuse. The fact he was having her followed. The texts to her sisters, where she sounds terrified of him. Plus the witnesses who says he went after her when she slapped him. We might have the CCTV too."

"It's not enough," Louise says, shaking her head.

No, it's probably not, Priya thinks, but she's too darn stubborn to say it, because she's sure Nathan Lane is a wife beater, and, one way or another, she's determined to see him held accountable.

Eleanor thinks about her uncle's words. What we have to do now is get on with our lives and act like a normal family.

He's right, she thinks. Nathan is under arrest, and isn't that what she's wanted all along?

So why doesn't she feel pleased?

Act normal.

For most of the afternoon, it's as though she is caught inside a bubble. Susan and Ian are nowhere to be seen. Instead she's forced to watch the spectacle of Gillian getting to know her nieces. Savannah insists on them dancing to Christmas music, eating mince pies, and watching crap Christmas TV. Naeve gives Eleanor regular pleading looks—it's clear that acting normal is as uncomfortable for her as it is for Eleanor, but Eleanor can't figure out how to rescue them. Finally, as dusk draws near, Gillian agrees to take Savannah to the local park to see the Christmas lights, and the house falls quiet again.

In the lull, Eleanor heads up to her room and sits on the floor, next to her mother's suitcase. She picks up a wrapped Christmas gift and tries to guess what it is. For a moment she is in their very first home again, eight years old, and her mother is laughing as she snatches a package from Eleanor's prying paws, chiding her, "No cheating!" It was the last Christmas she remembers when the laughter wasn't forced. One of the last they had all been together. The next year they'd been sheltering in the shed, that ill-fated toy dalmatian the highlight of her day.

And then the year after that . . .

No, she tells herself, *don't go there.* But she can't stop herself.

The next year there had been no Christmas. Just Eleanor and her mother stumbling through the days, trying to come to terms with all they had lost.

September 2005

In the hospital room, Eleanor watches her father march over to her brother.

"Do not say another word," Martin says, leaning over Aiden. "Not a word. You are not to blame, do you understand?"

"But, Dad . . ." Aiden is crying. Eleanor is scared. She edges over to the window and can see her mother talking to Solomon on the front steps of the small country hospital, her hand placed comfortingly on Solomon's arm. *Come back up here*, she wills her mother. *Come back fast.*

"No buts, Aiden," Martin draws his chair close to Aiden's bed, and beckons Eleanor over. "Listen to me, both of you. The house is gone. All that's left is the bits and pieces we've got in the shed. We need the insurance money, okay? The fire began on Solomon's property, Aiden. That's not your fault."

"But, Dad, I . . ."

"No, Aiden, you were asleep in bed when the fire began, weren't you? Weren't you? No one needs to know anything else. Not even your mother."

Aiden stares at his dad for a long moment, then nods.

Eleanor comes back to the present, her thoughts interrupted by her cell phone ringing. When she sees it's Will, she squirms as she recalls the awkwardness between them last night. She lets it ring out, and a moment later there's a short trill telling her she has a new voicemail. She dials and listens.

"Eleanor, I'm really sorry if I freaked you out last night. I know it's been a horrible time, and I didn't mean to make you uncomfortable. Look, I'm going home to my family for Christmas tomorrow, and I wondered if you wanted to meet me tonight. Just as friends. There's this beautiful ice rink at Somerset House, and it's forecast to snow later. I think you would love it. No pressure, just let me know."

He sounds so friendly; she feels bad for being reticent. She calls him back straightaway.

"Nathan's been arrested," she says as soon as he answers. "Ernie rang Susan this morning to tell her."

Will gives a long exhale. "Thank god. Finally! I was beginning to think it would never happen. Why now?"

"It sounds like Caroline retracted her alibi. It all seems too easy, doesn't it? Or am I just getting skeptical and suspicious about everything now?"

Will gives a short laugh. "Maybe. I guess we'll have to wait and see. How are you today, Eleanor? I've been thinking a lot about everything you told me last night. You didn't finish your story, did you? There's more."

She hesitates. "Yes, there's more." But she doesn't want to talk about it. *Act normal.* "Do you still want to take me ice-skating?"

"Of course."

"Then how about I meet you there in an hour and a half? Would six o'clock be okay?"

"Great," he replies. As they finish the call, there's a knock on her door. Eleanor jumps up to answer it and finds Naeve looking anxious on the other side.

"Can I come in?"

"Sure." Eleanor steps back for her to enter. Naeve comes inside then turns and pushes the door closed behind her. She hovers close to it, saying nothing, and Eleanor realizes how nervous she looks.

"What is it, Naeve? Has something happened?"

Naeve sits on the bed. "I want to ask you something."

"Okay." Eleanor sits next to her, a fresh round of nerves beginning to flutter.

"You don't agree with Dad, do you? You think we should tell the truth?"

Eleanor isn't sure what to say. "What do you think?"

Naeve doesn't speak, but she slowly opens her clenched right hand. Nestled on Naeve's palm is Arabella's ring.

"Naeve!" Eleanor jumps up and puts a hand on her cousin's arm, to steady herself as much as Naeve. "What are you doing with that? Where did you get it?"

"Dad asked me to hide it."

Eleanor blinks rapidly, repeating the words in her head, trying to take in what she just heard. "Did you just say your dad asked you to *hide* it?" she manages to stutter eventually.

Naeve nods. "He asked me to put it in my school locker, so it was out of the house. He said he couldn't take it himself, in case he was being watched. It was end of term yesterday, so I brought it home, and now he wants me to get rid of it. He told me to put it in the trash when I went out with Auntie Gillian, but I didn't go . . . because . . . because I thought you might want it back." She opens Eleanor's hand and puts the ring into it. "I think you should decide what to do with it. I know it shouldn't go in the garbage. You had it first. And you've been looking for it too, haven't you?"

Eleanor recalls her cousin's face when Naeve had caught her leaving Ian's office. "Yes," she says, "I have." She stares at the ring—so much smaller than she remembers, so innocuous in her hand. As she curls her fingers over it, the sharp little diamond edges jut into her palm. Her uncle's words play in her mind. *Not a word about the ring to anyone.* But the voice she hears is her father's.

Not a word.

Fury is building inside her. She jumps up. "Where is your dad right now?" she asks in a strange, even voice, not wanting to frighten Naeve.

"He had to go out. He'll be back after dinner, he said."

"Right, then." She opens her hand and stares at the ring. Then she turns back to the awkward thirteen-year-old in front of her. This girl who shares Eleanor's flesh and blood is making a brave, bold choice. She is trusting Eleanor to do the right thing.

"Leave this with me, Naeve," she says.

Naeve nods and turns to go.

"Naeve," Eleanor calls after her.

Her cousin looks back.

"Your dad should never have asked you to do that. You know that, don't you?"

Naeve nods. "I know," she says softly.

Once Naeve has gone, Eleanor slips the ring carefully into the zip pocket of her jacket. She wants to confront Ian, but then what? How can she trust him? It would be safer to take the ring straight to the police and let them deal with it.

She checks her watch. Only an hour until she has to meet Will, but she can't leave Naeve in the house on her own. While she's waiting for her mother and Savvie to come back, she selects the map on her phone, and looks up Somerset House. As she locates the nearest Tube station, she glances over the screen and sees landmarks she recognizes not too far south: Hungerford Bridge, Embankment Station, and a small symbol of a monument, tagged as Cleopatra's Needle.

She shudders. Does Will know how close they will be to the scene of last week's crime?

Not that close, she tells herself. *Get off the Tube at Temple and you won't even go past there. Stop being paranoid.*

She grabs her coat and bag and runs down the stairs. On the first landing she hears voices in the kitchen. Her mother and Savvie are home. Before she goes down, she knocks on Naeve's door.

When Naeve opens the door, her eyes are red and blotchy. Eleanor can't stand the thought of her crying alone, but Naeve looks so sullen that she instinctively knows not to mention it. "Where is your mum?" she asks breathlessly.

"I don't know. She texted me and said she'll be back for dinner."

"Listen," Eleanor leans close to her cousin, "I have to go out for a while. When your mum gets in, tell her everything. Tell her about the ring, and tell her what your dad asked you to do. You shouldn't have to keep these secrets."

Naeve begins to shake her head rapidly, and Eleanor grabs her hand to stop her. "It will be okay. Talk to her straightaway, and I will back you up."

"Where are you going?" Naeve frowns.

"I promised a friend I would meet them at Somerset House. I'll only be a couple of hours."

"Okay," Naeve says, nodding and biting her lip, looking close to tears again.

Eleanor reaches out and squeezes Naeve's shoulder, then runs down the next flight of stairs. In the kitchen she sees her mom and Savvie setting out mince pies. "I'm going out to meet a friend for a little while. Naeve is upstairs, Mum. Keep an eye on her."

"I will." Gillian looks concerned, but Eleanor keeps going. As she opens the door, a blast of cold air almost takes her breath away. She hurries down the road toward the Tube, checking and rechecking the ring in her pocket. Things are turning full circle, she can feel it—the ground is unsteady, as though the world is about to shift again. Something is coming. She needs to be vigilant. She needs to be ready.

51

the fall

Naeve lies on her bed, head hidden under the covers, her heart racing as she listens to the voices downstairs. It's only a matter of time until she has to admit what she's done.

Sure enough, the knock on her door comes minutes later. "Come in," she says, and braces herself, preparing to face down her dad.

Eleanor and Will step onto the rink in the frosty night air, surrounded by a throng of happy, glowing faces, everyone wrapped up warmly. The skaters glide clockwise together on the glittering white ice, circling one another in an intricate, elegant dance, the majestic backdrop of Somerset House behind them. The pillared balcony that runs the length of the two-story building is lit up with columns of warm yellow light, and in front of that, on the right side of the rink, an enormous Christmas tree sparkles and shimmers with a thousand golden fairy lights of its own.

As soon as she arrived, Eleanor knew it had been a mistake to come. She is watching the scene from a distance, her thoughts preoccupied with

Naeve. However, as Will takes her hand and leads her onto the ice, it has already begun to snow. *Finally!* Eleanor reaches out to catch some of the soft flakes as they float onto her gloves. *Just for a few moments*, she pleads silently, *let me belong in this fairy tale.* The scene around her is picture perfect—if only there wasn't a small ring in her pocket, its circle of diamonds like a dozen shards of ice.

She wants to confide in Will, but every time she tries to mention it, she cannot get the words out. She remembers the last time she had produced the ring in front of him, the shock and fear on his face. She can't do that again. She's going to have to figure this out on her own.

Unaware of her reluctance, Will leads her among the crowds. "This place is amazing, isn't it," he shouts over the music and the voices, turning in front of her so that he's going backward while pulling her forward with him. Eleanor smiles, holding on tight, trying not to wobble as they travel in circles around and around the rink. The spinning, the blur of people, it's making her nauseous. She tries to steady herself, but she can't focus on anything because nothing will stay still. The snow has died away, but the world is a kaleidoscope, reshaping her thoughts into memories, entirely against her will. She is shivering, not from the cold but from the fear that her life is about to crash down around her again.

October 2005

It is the first time she has been back to the charred wreck of the house. The place still reeks of smoke. Her father wanders aimlessly around the perimeter, as though searching for salvage. Gillian has stayed behind in town to talk to the bank, because she doesn't trust Martin to handle anything without losing his temper. The past few days in the local motel have been filled with contemptuous silences or angry discussions in low voices.

Eleanor loiters close to the car with Aiden, who is refusing to get out. She can hardly bear to look at the burned ground, the broken windows, the blackened boughs of trees. Instead, she focuses her attention on the shed, which has, incredibly, survived intact.

They all turn as they hear a car race down the driveway toward them, sending stones spinning from beneath its tires. Solomon's truck skids to a halt and a stout woman gets out and slams the door, marching across to Martin.

"Are you Martin Brennan?" she demands, charging right up to him.

Martin looks flabbergasted at being accosted like this. "Yes."

"My dad is in the hospital because of your bloody family," she says. "How dare you accuse him of starting this fire. He hasn't moved that stuff in his shed for years, and there has never been a problem until your lad and his troublemaker friends started hanging out close to his house. He knows they were down there the other night. I wouldn't be surprised if they killed his bloody dog an' all."

This must be Philippa, Eleanor realizes, aghast. She is unrecognizable from the girl in the paintings. She is in her late fifties, her hair a gray cropped into a dome and her face a ruddy red.

"You have no proof of any of this," Martin stutters.

"Not yet, maybe, but you bloody well wait," Philippa retorts.

As she swings around, she notices Eleanor for the first time. Eleanor moves in front of Aiden, trying to shield him so that Philippa doesn't see him.

Philippa's face softens as she walks toward Eleanor. "Dad liked you very much, and I'm sad it's come to this," she says. Then she spots Aiden behind Eleanor and her frown turns to a glare. "But you, boy, I hope you're bloody well ashamed of yourself," she spits. "Do you know my dad's had a heart attack because of all this—hooked up on wires and all sorts. If he comes through it, he'll never be the same. He's been a proud, independent man for as long as I can remember, he's fought in a war for god's sake, survived all that, and now you've reduced him to being spoon-fed like a baby. I hope you can live with what you've done."

She storms back to her vehicle without a backward glance, and moments later the truck roars away.

No one moves or speaks at first. Then Eleanor thinks of Solomon in hospital, of Aiden cowering in the car, and before she knows what she's doing, she is charging at her father in undiluted rage. She manages to propel her small body with such force that she knocks Martin off balance, winding him as he staggers back. She slams her fists into his chest, crying out, "I hate you! I hate you!" Aiden is behind her, pulling her away, and her father storms off quickly to the blackened tree line, toward the place the cubby used to be. Aiden still has his arms around Eleanor as they hear their father release one long howl—whether of rage or distress or self-pity, she will never be sure.

When Eleanor comes back to her surroundings, she is falling. Her knees hit the unforgiving ice hard. Disorientated, she puts her hand inside her pocket and clutches the ring.

Will hauls her up. "Are you okay?" He is smiling to begin with, but his face drops as he sees the tears in her eyes. "Oh, I didn't realize . . . Shall we have a break and get a drink?"

At her nod, he helps her over to the side. They say little as they remove their boots and collect their shoes. "I'll get you something," Will says as they walk across to the bar. "How about mulled wine?"

"That sounds nice," Eleanor agrees.

"You go and find a seat," he tells her, heading away.

As she waits for Will, her phone rings in her pocket. She pulls it out and sees it's Susan calling. Her heart plummets. Naeve must have told Susan everything—how angry will she be?

While she's thinking this, the ringing stops, the call times out but then it immediately starts again.

Clearly, Susan really wants to get hold of her. Eleanor's nerves begin to buzz as she takes the call.

"Where are you?" Susan asks immediately, her tone urgent. She doesn't sound angry at all, Eleanor realizes with a start. She sounds frightened.

"I'm—I'm at Somerset House."

"What are you doing there?"

"Will asked me to come."

"Will? You don't mean Will Clayton?"

"Yes."

"Why on earth are you spending time with Will Clayton, Eleanor?" Susan's voice is unnervingly shrill. "Don't you know he was one of the last people to see Arabella? He's still under suspicion. The whole company knows he's been in love with her for years. Don't let him latch on to you— once he does, he doesn't let go."

"What?" Eleanor jumps up from her seat. "Really? What do you mean he's still under suspicion? I thought Nathan had been arrested?"

"Nathan has been released, and he's already called me, looking for you. He says you've been trying to set him up, telling Caroline lies, and turning up on his doorstep. Is any of that true?"

The heat drains from Eleanor's face. "Have you spoken to Naeve?" she asks. "She needs to talk to you."

"I've only just left work," Susan answers. "I've been trying to calm Nathan down, but I'm worried about you, Eleanor. I'll come and get you, I'm not far away."

"Okay, I'll wait on the river side of the Embankment," Eleanor stammers, grabbing her bag and jumping off her bar stool. But when she turns around, phone in hand, Will is standing in front of her with two steaming glasses of burgundy wine.

"Going somewhere?"

Eleanor thinks fast. "I really should get home. My mother is here. She turned up last night, to spend Christmas with us."

Will stares at her. "What, now? Surely you've got time to try this?" He raises one of the glasses. Then his eyes narrow. "You look like you've seen a ghost, Eleanor. What is it?"

Eleanor takes in his expression. If he's acting a part, he is doing an incredible job. She glances around them, at the people laughing and joking and sipping their drinks.

"That was my aunt. Nathan is out and on the warpath again." She looks at the phone, realizing Susan has hung up. Thank god she is on her way.

Will's face clouds. "I knew it was too good to be true," he mutters. "Nathan will always wriggle his way out of a situation."

Eleanor doesn't pause for breath. "Susan also said you've been in love with Arabella for years. Is that true?"

Will stiffens. He sets the glasses down on the table without looking at her, and then says, "Please, can you sit down for a moment?"

Eleanor glances around then moves slowly back onto her seat.

"We were friends, first and foremost," he says, staring at his drink rather than meeting her eye, drawing slow circles in the condensation on the glass. "But yes, I have always had a thing for her. I knew she wasn't happy with Nathan, and I thought that if I hung in there long enough . . ." He laughs bitterly. "Well, she might have had plenty of affairs, but they weren't with *me*."

Eleanor leans forward, stares hard at him. "What else haven't you told me, Will? Were you there when she died?"

"No!" Will answers sharply. "I asked her to come with me. I wanted her to let me help, I swore I'd look after her, but she laughed at me and told me to go away, before she walked off. She humiliated me, once again, so I left. Eleanor, I promise, everything I've told you about that night has been the truth. I didn't tell you how I felt about Arabella because . . . well, because I like you." He studies her expression and reaches for her hand. His touch is clammy. "Please, you have to believe me."

She snatches her arm away and jumps up. "I have no idea what to believe, and I'd better go." She gestures toward the scene around them. "Has this all been an act? Are you just looking for information, trying to save your own skin?"

"No!" Will cries, but she watches him redden. His eyes shift past her as though searching for something, and then alight on her again. "I didn't go to the police about the ring, did I? That could have saved me, but I chose you."

I chose you.

Eleanor pauses, suppressing a shiver.

Don't let him latch on to you, she hears her aunt warn her.

She summons her courage and meets his eye. "I have to go, Will."

"No. Wait." Will leans across the table and grabs her arm to stop her, then seems to think better of it and lets go. "At least let me walk you to the station," he pleads. He sounds desperate, but his stare has steel in it, and the defiant way he holds her gaze is unnerving.

"No thanks, I'll be fine on my own. Have a good Christmas, Will," she says, collecting her bag and heading quickly away, determined not to look back.

She's thankful to be away from him, but as soon as she's outside, she gets that disconcerting, familiar feeling of being watched. There are plenty of people around this early in the evening, but they are all strangers whose intentions she can't read, who don't know her enough to care. As she crosses the road to wait for Susan, she begins to doubt her next move. *Are you ready to go back to Harborne Grove?* she asks herself. *To meet Susan? To face Ian?*

Stop, she commands her thoughts, shifting from foot to foot as the cold night creeps beneath her clothes, chilling her skin. Everything around her seems to be in motion: the people, the cars, the lights and shadows. Even the leaves on the trees are rustling. It's making her unsteady.

She cannot stop fidgeting. *How long will Susan be?* She turns longingly in the direction of Temple station. Perhaps she should keep going and meet Susan at home. She'd feel better if she could keep walking. However, as she stares down the road, she sees Will on the opposite side, waiting to cross. He's looking the other way toward the oncoming traffic, but any moment now, he is going to turn toward her. Perhaps he has seen her already. Is that why he's here?

She becomes intensely aware of the river behind her, the same dark body of water that had filled Arabella's lungs a week ago and stolen her life. Will knows that Eleanor was there that night, bearing witness. How could she have trusted him? What had made her so sure that Nathan was a killer?

It was Will, she thinks frantically as she watches a break in the traffic. *Will made sure I thought the worst of Nathan.* And now he is beginning to cross the road, getting closer every step, his head turning toward her.

Panic seizes her, jolting her into flight. She runs in the opposite direction, away from Will, from Temple station, from her agreed meeting point with Susan. She sprints close to the low wall of the Embankment, beneath Waterloo Bridge, past a long row of parked bicycles. Her nerves are on fire; at any second she's sure she'll feel a hand on her shoulder, a voice next to her ear. Each breath burns, but she doesn't slow down until she finds herself next to a dark statue of a lion, in front of the towering obelisk of Cleopatra's Needle.

Fate has brought her full circle. She swings around, expecting to see Will, bracing herself for confrontation. He isn't there. She waits a while on wobbly legs, steadying herself with one hand on the wall, but still he doesn't appear. Slowly, her breathing becomes calmer. *What now?*

She puts her hand in her pocket, feeling for the ring, rubbing her fingers along the little cluster of stones. If she's ever to remember anything, it will be here, she realizes. She keeps one finger hooked through the ring, as though this single solid link to Arabella might forge the hazier path to her memories. Then she walks slowly past the monument and back again, stopping at intervals to peer over the wall.

Nothing.

Eventually, she walks up the steps to the paving stones set around the monument. Ahead of her, a low wall forms a barricade to the river. To either side of her, stone staircases lead away, disappearing into the water. She goes down a few steps on the right-hand side, and sits with her back against the wall, hidden from the road. As she watches the dirty brown water milling a dozen steps below her, she implores her memories to find her.

It is quieter here. Snow has begun to fall lightly again, but it's wispy and insubstantial, disappearing as soon as it touches the ground. The walls block the view of everything beyond, muting the sound of people and traffic. Ahead of her, tourist boats are moored against jetties. The *Atlantic* will be among them, just past Hungerford Bridge. Even though it's only eight o'clock, the darkness is concealing. Is that how Arabella had slipped into the water here, unnoticed?

But someone did notice, didn't they? comes that taunting voice in her mind.

"Stop," she begs out loud. She feels so tired. Her eyes blur as she watches the dark water lapping softly at the steps, inviting her closer.

She looks up along the wall that stretches away down Victoria

Embankment. If Arabella's life had ended right here, had Eleanor watched from just up there? She cannot fathom it; it's unbearable. "I'm sorry," she whispers, pulling the ring out of her pocket and squeezing it tightly, praying it will help her recover those hidden hours. But there is nothing.

What if she'd stayed to help instead of running? Could she have made the difference between Arabella living and dying? What if she could have emerged from the fog of those drugs enough to tell someone what had happened?

What if?

What if?

Does she really have to live with such terrible doubts all over again?

"I'm sorry," she whispers again, but this time she's not only thinking of Arabella. She's thinking for the millionth time that if she'd talked to her mother about Aiden's guilt, his friends, Philippa's words to him on that fateful morning, rather than let her Dad coerce her into silence, then she might have saved her brother.

October 2005

The next time they decide to go back to the charred remains of the house, Aiden refuses to go. He has rarely gotten out of bed for the past few days unless he's needed the toilet. Gillian has been trying to cajole him into a shower for the past forty-eight hours, but every time she suggests it, he just grunts and doesn't move.

Meanwhile, Martin's mood swings have turned into an impassioned fervor to get back to building. "It's a miracle the shed wasn't touched," he keeps saying. "It was fun living like that, wasn't it? We'll be fine in there while we come to grips with the extent of the damage." He has reordered the portable toilet to be delivered on Friday. Once that's in, he tells them, they need to get out of this motel—they're being robbed blind for this room—it's time to move on.

Gillian has said little since Martin shot down the idea of moving back to their old suburb close to the city. "We can't go back, Gill, not after all this. We've got to see it through." When Martin heads to the car on Thursday, determined to restore the shed to its former glory, Gillian initially refuses to go, until Aiden begs her to leave him be.

"I've left food in the fridge for you," she says to him sadly. "Please eat something."

Eleanor climbs onto the bed next to her brother. "I don't want you to be sad," she says.

He rolls away from her. "Leave me alone, Shrimp. There's nothing you can do."

Eleanor leans against the cold wall of the monument steps, tears streaming down her face as she remembers. She pictures herself chasing Arabella, having just seen her slap Nathan. She remembers the CCTV footage, of Arabella holding up her hands, saying something to Eleanor as she backs away.

"Leave me alone," she imagines Arabella cry. "There's nothing you can do."

Words similar to those would have been enough. They would have called up Eleanor's ghost, and lured her toward the dark water of the river.

Because the next time she sees her brother his head is hoisted up to the beam and twisted at an unnatural angle, a chair kicked back behind him. His body is slack and swinging on a rope, his feet almost touching the ground, but not quite.

The scene is seared into her mind, imprinted in a flash of devastation. *She stumbles blindly toward him, her foot catching on the bed they have been sharing, sending her sprawling onto the covers. Her hand hits something spiky and she jumps back again, seeing scattered scraps of paper littering the bed. No, they are not scraps. They are paper cranes.*

And then she is up again, lunging at her brother and screaming. And the next instant her mother is behind her, beginning a horrendous keening noise that can never be unheard. Then there is shouting and more wailing, while she stares transfixed by her brother's lifeless body, his gray face twisting slowly around toward them as her father lunges at his knees to give his son some support, even though he is obviously far, far too late. When strong hands drag Eleanor backward, she goes roughly like a snake shedding its skin, leaving a part of herself forever in that damned room.

Eleven years have gone by since then. And no matter what Eleanor has tried—the counseling, the interventions, the medications—that feeling of terror has never completely gone away. It is a curse she has to come to terms with, because she will live with it forever.

The snow turns to icy rain as she sits on the cold steps in the dark, squeezing the ring repeatedly, willing herself to recall something, anything to stop the unknowns of this new tragedy embedding themselves in her soul. But the ring has no magical powers of restoration. Her mind is still the blank, dark space it has always been.

She lets her hand slacken, almost dropping the ring into the water, but in the quiet, with her eyes closed, she hears footsteps behind her.

And then comes a soft, familiar voice.

"I've been looking for you, Eleanor. I should have known I would find you here."

52

the truth

etective Inspector Priya Prashad listens to the voice on the other end of the phone, and realizes she's got it all wrong. But there's no time to think about that now. "This is it," she says, snatching up her keys and beginning to run. "I think we've got the bastard!" she calls over her shoulder as Steve leaps up to follow her. "But we're going to have to move bloody fast. Let's go."

Eleanor recognizes the voice. She knows exactly who is behind her. The rain falls even and persistent now, so cold it stings her skin and drips into her eyes. As she turns, her blurred, soaked vision distorts his face. She sees black shadows where his eyes should be, and a sullen down-turned mouth. She waits, realizing that this is the moment. There is no escape.

He comes to stand over her on the step above, his body close enough to make her recoil. "Why are you here?" he hisses, his voice low and dangerous. "Why can't you leave this alone?"

Eleanor glances beyond him. Could she make it if she runs? He has the upper hand, the higher ground, he could easily grab her, but it might be her only shot. She tries to will energy into her legs, but she is so tired of running, so tired of being hounded. She glances back toward the river; imagines herself hitting that freezing water. Is that the fate she deserves? Is that why she has escaped nothing by coming halfway around the world?

"I still don't remember anything," Eleanor says shakily, getting to her feet. "And I don't want to believe that it's you."

His hand grips her arm hard through her wet jacket. "Look at me. *Look at me.*" He pulls her roughly around and she flinches at his face so near to hers, aware of their bodies so close together next to this murderous maw of water. She has a flash of her father's face leaning ominously toward hers before her vision clears and it's her uncle again, spitting words at her in the downpour.

"Before you judge me, let me tell you a few things, because you have no idea what Arabella could be like, Eleanor." His eyes are wide, his tone fierce. "In the beginning, I thought she was incredible. I didn't know anything of the manipulative, game-playing side of her. When I slowly discovered what she was like, and I ended it, she wouldn't believe it was over. She looked for any opportunity to dig at me, sometimes she wanted me back, at other times she wanted to rant at me. What she wanted most of all was attention. Good or bad, it didn't matter. She was just a petulant child. She would ring me in the middle of the night to taunt me, threatening to tell Susan, high on whatever drugs she'd taken. It was so hard to stay calm, time after time—and pointless, really, because the more level-headed I was, the more agitated she became. But she was shrewd too, she saw everything. Even though I wouldn't leave Susan, Arabella knew how attracted I was to her, she reveled in the power she had over me. And she could tell I didn't love Susan the way a husband is supposed to love his wife. She didn't hold back on her opinions about *that.*"

As he speaks, every word is kindling, slowly and steadily building a fire in Eleanor. Each new lick of flame is turning her fear to anger, her indecision to resolve. All her senses have sharpened. She is acutely aware of every part of her body, the feel of different fabrics against her skin, the tension of each muscle, the hard circle of the ring in her hand. "Are you telling me that Arabella deserved what happened to her?" she demands, steadying herself, standing her ground.

Ian frowns. "I came here to calm her down, that was all, until she said she'd already called Susan and told her everything. Susan had gone back to work late after the party, and Arabella had phoned her and announced we were leaving together. She meant to put me in an impossible position, to force my hand. I was horrified, and angry too, yes. We fought, it got physical, and she fell into the water."

"Really?" Eleanor throws up her arms disbelievingly. "She just fell in?"

"Yes."

Ian doesn't flinch, but Eleanor knows now just how good a liar he is.

"If it was an accident, then why all the lies?"

Ian's eyes are bulging, as though he can't quite believe he's still having to defend himself. Water drips from his brows. "Don't you understand, Eleanor? I've been forced into the lies, can't you see that? To protect my family. Including you, Eleanor. You love Naeve and Savvie, don't you? Well, Arabella didn't care at all. She would have destroyed them too if it meant she got what she wanted. She played with you as well, didn't she, drugging you, giving you the ring?"

Perhaps Eleanor would have been unsettled if he hadn't mentioned Naeve and Savvie. Those names are a payload of fuel, and the small fire in Eleanor catches and explodes. "You know what," she cries, "I believe you. I absolutely believe that's what you tell yourself. How else could you cover up a woman's death so shamelessly? How else could you have the gall to make your thirteen-year-old daughter hide evidence in a murder investigation?"

Ian's mouth opens and closes again, but no words come out. She senses him flounder, but only for a moment, before his face hardens. "Why did you take the ring from Naeve, Eleanor?" he asks in a low voice. "What are you planning to do with it?"

Eleanor stiffens. "How do you know I have the ring?"

"Because I got home early to find Naeve hiding in her room. And Savvie told me her sister hadn't gone out with them this afternoon. As soon as I laid eyes on Naeve I knew there was trouble. She's good at keeping secrets, but not so much at outright lies. She confessed she'd given it to you and told me you'd gone to Somerset House. I watched you talking to your friend in there, then when you left and stepped outside and began to run, I knew you were heading here."

As he speaks, he maneuvers Eleanor down a step closer to the water. Her anger is subdued by an icy dread. She shivers, thinking of him watching her from the shadows. She tries not to show her fear, to hold herself together. "All along, I tried so hard not to doubt you," she shouts through the rain, hoping desperately that someone is within earshot, "but when Naeve told me what you'd asked her to do, I couldn't excuse you any longer. I knew just what you were capable of. So what now? Are you going to kill me too?"

Ian casts frantically about as she speaks but no one is nearby. In an instant, he is shoving her so hard that her back is forced painfully against the stone wall, directly beneath the road. The only way someone would see them now is if they walked right onto the monument, and even then, his body hides hers from view as he leans over her. She is all too aware of the water just a few feet below them, but she is no longer afraid.

She is livid.

As she had spoken of Naeve, understanding had flooded through her. She and Naeve had both been caught up in their fathers' delusions and excuses. And yet, since Aiden's death, Eleanor has spent most of her life stuck in the wrong fight. She has been attempting the impossible, trying to escape the voices and actions of others, but instead they have transmuted into all her doubts and fears. That was what had led her to the pills and the despair as a teenager. That was what had caused her to end up drugged and desperate on a bridge just last week, ready to jump into the Thames.

But Naeve is only thirteen years old. She shouldn't be the victim of her family's catastrophic choices. And neither should Eleanor.

She screams and tries to push Ian away, but he is too strong. Water drips down her neck and inside her collar, a few cold trickles running between her shoulder blades.

Ian's grip on her tightens. His lips are close to her ear. "I want us both to walk away from this, Eleanor," he insists. "You just have to work with me. There *will* be a way out of this. Just give me the ring and we can figure out the rest."

Eleanor shakes her head. The pressure on her back is excruciating, there are shooting pains down her legs. "Why is the ring so important? Tell me the truth."

"It's a message." Ian spits each word into her face. "It's a *fuck you* to Nathan. And a noose around my neck."

Eleanor flinches. Her stomach heaves. Does he know what that image does to her? She tries to focus on her surroundings. "What do you mean? How can you be so certain?"

"Because it's not the first time Arabella's done it. She told me all about it one night when she'd had too much to drink. She ran away a couple of years back, with one of Parker & Lane's illustrators, and left the ring on Nathan's desk. Only she came back a week later because she hadn't realized her lover lived in a hovel. Nathan went after him. Cut off all his contacts in the industry. Six months later he was addicted to god knows what. Twelve months after that he was dead."

Eleanor is trying to digest all this information. "But Nathan knows about you and Arabella now."

"Yes, and I have no doubt he's plotting revenge. But the ring has to disappear. I had no idea about it until you confided in me, but I'm certain Arabella meant for you to give it to Nathan. She knew you were his new assistant, didn't she? If he ever finds out about the ring, it will tip him over the edge. He'll use that as evidence one way or another, lawfully or unlawfully, to destroy me. To destroy all of us."

"So you're happy to let the police accuse him of killing her instead?"

"Seriously, Eleanor? He tried to choke you. Have you not learned enough about him yet? Do you still have sympathy for him? Nathan deserves everything he gets. Do you know how many times Arabella had strange bruises on her body during the time I was with her?"

"I can't tell when you talk whether you loved her or hated her."

"You know what, neither can I sometimes." Ian's voice cracks. "Those emotions are closer together than you think. She drove me crazy but . . . haven't you ever hated someone you loved?"

As she hears the slip in his speech, Eleanor takes her chance and pulls against him, trying to break free. However, he tenses fast; there's no way she can beat him on strength.

Ian senses the moment too. "Where is it?" He pushes his hands into her pockets, frantically searching. "Please, Eleanor, we can drop it into the water right now, and no one will ever know—"

"Let her go, Ian."

Ian stops dead.

Eleanor's eyes meet her aunt's over Ian's shoulder, seeing a mixture of desperation and fear. Susan stands two steps above them, her hands in the pockets of a thick, black dress coat, her hair loose and flattened in the rain. She looks so much older than a week ago, paler, more vulnerable.

"Why didn't you wait for me?" Susan hisses at Eleanor. "Thank god I spotted Will at Somerset House, and he'd seen you running this way."

"What are you doing here?" Ian growls, hostility writ large on his face.

Susan's stare turns stony as it falls on her husband. "I've been speaking to the police," she says, her chin high, her gaze steady. Her left hand clutches her phone. "I just called them again, they're on their way. Naeve phoned me as soon as you left the house, told me everything. This has gone far enough. It's over, Ian. We can't do this anymore."

At her words Ian lets go of Eleanor and crumples, hunched over, his breaths heavy and rapid. "Why the hell would you do that? You'll be arrested too. You gave me an alibi."

"What are you talking about?" Eleanor asks, looking from one to the other. "What alibi?"

Susan turns to her. "After Arabella called me and told me she was leaving with Ian, I stayed at the office for most of the night. I never saw you lying on the doorstep. Ian told me what had happened and persuaded me to lie to avoid awkward questions. He said he didn't want the family to suffer for his mistake. I thought he meant the affair."

"Don't play the innocent," Ian sneers. "You would have thrown me to the lions if you could; you were just trying to save your job."

"Maybe," Susan declares, "but I also believed your lies. I didn't realize you were capable of killing someone. You only told me you spoke to

Arabella on the phone. You mentioned nothing about coming here to meet her."

Ian's eyes flicker uncertainly between them. "You've no proof of that."

"Actually, you're forgetting there's a witness. Naeve saw you, Ian. I might not have been there, but she was. She heard you leave, and come back, and watched you find Eleanor and carry her inside while you were fully dressed, at two in the morning. She won't be lying for you any longer. And Eleanor has Arabella's ring. It's not like it's the first time Arabella had taken that ring off and run away. I think you're in trouble, one way or another."

Ian lunges at his wife. "You bitch!" he roars, grabbing her by the throat. "After everything I've done for you!"

Susan screams and Eleanor watches in horror as they struggle on the edge of the steps. As they begin to stumble, Ian loses his balance, flails, and lets go of Susan. Eleanor catches her aunt's arm before she falls. But Ian is momentarily airborne over the stairway, landing with a sickening thud.

The women cling together in silence, staring at Ian spread-eagled below them. Most of his body is under water, the gentle tide lapping at his face as though it would love to suck him under. His eyes are glazed with shock.

"What now?" Eleanor whispers to Susan.

Her aunt stiffens but doesn't reply.

Eleanor lets go of Susan and steps back, sagging against the wall, imbibing the crisp night air. Her gaze moves slowly beyond the black void of the Thames to the city lights that bejewel the skyline.

In the distance there are sirens.

53

into the night

Christmas Eve

Susan had never realized there could be more than one type of silence. Yet as she ascends the stairs to her bedroom in Harborne Grove, she understands the finality of the quietness tonight. It is not the temporary sojourn between her family sleeping and waking; this is the soundless, immovable space of absence and loss.

She is not allowed to leave the city. She may well be charged with an offense. Her career, her reputation, her family—they have all gone. What does that leave her with? Who am I, she wonders, behind all of that?

Perhaps she'll find out in the morning, she thinks, exhaustion setting in as she finally reaches her bed. As she picks up the hard little bottle of pills on the bedside table, she is ambushed by her loneliness, and all these questions begin to crystallize into the overwhelming desire for rest.

In less than twelve hours it will be Christmas morning. Eleanor imagines that most children in the country will be busy putting the finishing touches to their stockings and leaving out treats for Santa. But not Naeve and Savannah. They are both fast asleep in the back of the car, their coats over them as blankets, while their aunt drives fast through the night, the lights of the M25 now replaced by smaller, darker roads. Behind them is London, where their father has been taken into custody and made front-page news, while their mother is still busy talking to her lawyers, and quite possibly on the verge of a breakdown.

In the trunk of the car are two sacks full of presents. When Susan had asked Gillian and Eleanor to do this, having already booked a small Hampshire cottage, they agreed it was something, at least, that might lessen the unbearable gloom. For the past few days, they have all moved like wraiths: silently and stealthily, saying little, lost in their own thoughts. Naeve had refused to open her door for almost a day, until Susan unscrewed the entire locking mechanism and sat on the floor for much of the night, cradling her devastated child. Savvie has been quiet and confused, not heartbroken yet, but still sensing that life has gone terribly, irrevocably wrong.

"I'm glad they're both sleeping," Gillian says into the darkness. "They need it."

"We all need it," Eleanor replies, considering her mother. Gillian had been shocked and devastated at her brother's arrest, apologizing repeatedly to Eleanor for suggesting she stayed at Harborne Grove. It had reminded Eleanor of how easy it was to take on a mountain of unwarranted guilt.

Eleanor's phone buzzes in her bag. It's Will again.

> Can we talk?

It's the seventh text he's sent today. She sighs and deletes it. Tomorrow she'll figure out how to block his number.

She looks around at the two girls again. "How are we going to look after them, Mum? How are we even going to try to celebrate Christmas?"

"We'll do it because they need us to," Gillian replies. "They need us to try to be positive, and to carry on with everyday things, so that when they are ready, when the grief of all this lessens even a little bit, they will have hope that there's still a decent life for them out there in the world."

"I don't know if Naeve will ever be ready," Eleanor whispers. "She's been manipulated so much; she's pushed her feelings so deep down. How can we begin to help her recover?"

Gillian sighs. "I don't have all the answers, Eleanor. You realize that, don't you? Otherwise I would have waved my magic wand and taken your pain away. But I never could, and I still can't. I can only be here, and tell you I love you, and talk it all through as much as you need, or just be silent and hold your hand while you try to make sense of it all. Naeve will need to lean heavily on those around her, of course she will, but ultimately she'll also need to believe in herself to get through."

"Do you think that's where I went wrong?"

Gillian glances sharply at her before turning back to the road. "Everyone goes wrong, Eleanor. It's what happens next that matters. You've always been strong enough to pull yourself back from the edge. And now you have a cousin who looks to you for guidance. You gave her the courage to confess her part in all this. Without you she might still be creeping around that house, eavesdropping and terrified."

Eleanor is silent for such a long time that eventually her mother asks, "What are you thinking about?"

"I just don't think I'll ever feel proud of myself after what happened with Aiden—" She stops talking as the familiar pressure starts to build in her chest. "Mum . . ." she begins, trying not to think about how important this moment is, "Aiden started the fire that burned down our house. He confessed to Dad. I didn't tell you because Dad made us promise, and then, after he died . . . I don't know . . . I felt it was wrong to tarnish his memory. I was trying to protect you."

There is a long silence. "Oh, Eleanor." Her mother's voice breaks. "What did Martin do to us? To you? Of course I knew! There were so many rumors, even though your father would never speak of it. I didn't tell you about it for exactly the same reason. I would never have wanted you to carry that burden alone." She lets out a moan of frustration, and then takes a long, deep breath before she speaks again. "Well, now it's time you stopped blaming yourself for the decisions other people made when you were only a child. I understand because I blame myself too, all the time, and the only way I can get past it is by vowing to be better for you.

That's why we walked away from your father—because all that was keeping me alive back then was the need to keep you safe and well, and your dad was still lost in his own insane ideas. You do know it wasn't the drink that took his life eventually, don't you? It was the guilt."

Eleanor doesn't want to think of the last few times she saw him, the disheveled man who shuffled around his half-built, two-bedroom house, wasting away from addiction. "I wish I could remember him more in the early years," Eleanor says. "I have vague wisps of memory, of times he made me laugh, but so much of it has gone."

"Yes, well, memory's a bit short of kindness at times, isn't it? If you're not careful, it can discard the good stuff and make the bad bits a little too important."

"That's true," Eleanor murmurs. But she's still thinking of her father, and of something Ian said to her. *Haven't you ever hated someone you loved?* She had hated her father so much for so long that until just now, she had forgotten how much she loved him. She'd always thought it was the hatred that was making her suffer, a dark root in her that she couldn't excise. But could love have been part of the problem, all this time? Because how could she ever reconcile her deep, abiding love for him with everything else that had happened?

She turns once more to look at Naeve, who is still fast asleep, then settles back in her seat. *Maybe I'll never understand it all,* she thinks, beginning to feel sleepy, thankful for her mother's presence beside her. But perhaps she doesn't have to. Perhaps she only has to take enough from the past to try to build a stronger day tomorrow.

afterword

Everything would change if you were gone.

This novel touches on themes of abject loneliness and despair. Out in the world there are a million remedies for this, but we know from all we see around us that these feelings continue to thrive. "Talk to someone" is the oft-quoted advice, but what if you can't? Once upon a time, I couldn't. Back then, I was saved by books.

My favorite writers could read my mind before I could find my voice. They could answer my questions without me having to ask them. They pulled me through then, and they still do now. I believe there is at least one book out there that will do this for everyone. Probably many. If you ever need them, I urge you to search them out and bring yourself back to the world. Seek out *your* books, not the ones you are told to read. Find *your* truth. Do *your* soul work. And while you do, keep the faith in a brighter day tomorrow.

acknowledgments

Writing might be a solitary occupation, but books don't get published without a whole lot of support. My deepest thanks go to my agent Tara Wynne and the entire team at Blackstone. It's been a pleasure and a privilege to work with you all.

To all my family and friends, thank you for your support and encouragement, and for understanding why I'm so scatterbrained and unsociable at times, and work such long, strange hours.

Natasha Lester, thank you for all your excellent advice; I've loved supporting one another on our parallel journeys.

Fiona Thorp, thank you for all the advice about bodies in the Thames! Louise, Paul, Laura and Amy Clarke, thank you for your practical support. And James Foster—you're always so generous with your time. I won't forget the video and soundtrack that saved me from losing the plot, in more ways than one!

Mum and Ray, thanks for understanding the considerable challenges I've faced in getting this book done, and for helping me through them.

Matt: you know I couldn't do it without you. These books are in many ways yours as much as mine. When I get stuck you always have the best ideas.

Finally, to my girls, Hannah and Isabelle: thank you for your patience as I work, and for your wholehearted excitement when you see my books in print. If I make you even a tiny bit as proud of me as I am of you two, then I'm doing all right.

Sara Foster